KALAYLA

KALAYLA

Cover Design by Greg Martin
Typesetting by FormattingExperts.com

ISBN 978-0-578-49075-5

FROM THE AUTHOR

ACKNOWLEGEMENTS

I am most grateful to my husband, Ed Martin, and to Venerable Dhyani Ywahoo, my mentor, for their continuing support of my creative efforts.

Additionally, I am indebted to all those who read *Kalayla* at various stages and shared thoughts and reactions, or special knowledge: Dot Valhouli, Sharon O'Brien, Sally Kirouac, Pamela Lordi, Bonnie Hershey, Frank Challant, Roberta Wilson, Gabrielle Bryne and Lisa Loosigian.

Special thanks to Greg Martin whose cover design evokes the potential of an opening heart, and to the staff of Formatting Experts for professional guidance.

JEANNIE NICHOLAS

KALAYLA

Joanne,
May you find joy
in the growth of all
the characters here —
Life takes us strange
places.
Dec 2020
Jeannie

SUMMER 1999

LENA MANERO BARZETTI

THAT GIRL

Never let it be said that I'm one of those old biddies who spend their time watching other folks instead of minding their own business. But there are some people it is impossible to ignore, in spite of good intentions, and that girl Kalayla was one of them.

The first time I got a look at her was mid-June last year when I was walking back from Mickey's Market a couple blocks from where I live. You know, one of those perfect sunny days when you actually might believe you could live happily ever after. *The National Scoop* headline went right along with that by announcing "Princess Diana's Death Revealed as Hoax."

Kalayla was ahead of me, half swaggering, half strutting in a way that was so familiar I felt like I must know her. I puzzled over it, and finally it came to me: the girl walked the same way my twins did when they were showing off. Which was pretty much from the minute they got up 'til the minute they went to bed.

How many times had those two boys been in front of me swaggering, strutting, taunting each other? Mikie daring Jimmy, "Bet it takes you more than 20 seconds to shimmy up that streetlight." And Jimmy giving it back, "Bet you can't get five bucks panhandling between here and home."

And off they'd be, running and laughing, shoving and punching. Their laughter echoed back through the years, making me grateful for some good memories.

A horn blast jolted me out of my daydreaming, stopping me short or I'd have bumped right into the girl. She was staring into the window of Hanson's Book Store. Her huge green eyes glanced my way. I pegged her for one of those Cambridge street kids scraping her way from one meal to the next, an old hand at trash picking and layering up with everything she found, at least three layers on top with a mess of colors and designs. She must have dressed in the dark and not bothered to look in a mirror. That is, if she had a mirror, or a place to sleep inside.

She was maybe an inch or two shorter than my own 5'3". I couldn't tell how old she was, but most girls in their teens are interested in showing off to their best advantage, which she definitely was not. So she must be younger, maybe around 10 or 11.

Her baggy pants might have been shorts on the right sized person. If somebody cared to tug on the rope holding them up, I expect we would have been treated to a show of skinny brown butt and legs. Her kinky orange-brown curls were squashed down with a beat-up blue-and-red baseball cap, brim turned backward.

Her hair, light chocolate skin, and saucer-size green eyes were bright, shiny, and clearly her own.

After that, it seemed like everywhere I went, the girl was someplace nearby. She was always by herself and I got to wondering why, and I have to say it bothered me. The only way my four boys were ever alone was if they were going to or coming from someplace where other kids were hanging out. Even my boy Mark, who was always getting in fights, had plenty of friends. If I was that girl's mama, her being alone so much would sure have made me worry.

On Saturday morning about two weeks later, I was coming back from buying milk, eggs, and my favorite raisin bread when I saw the girl across the street in front of Eddie's Eatery. Eddie's was right across from my apartment building, so I stopped by sometimes in the afternoon for a coffee or snack. The girl was talking to Maureen, the red-headed woman who'd been waiting tables there for the past year or so. Maureen was always friendly and seemed cheerful, even though she didn't fall all over herself blabbing personal stuff the way some folks do. Eddie was the one who told me she was a widow with a daughter.

Maureen kissed the girl on the forehead and then went into Eddie's. That explained it. She had to be the daughter with the same huge green eyes and fine sculptured features. But her skin tone was darker, and her hair a mass of unruly curls. That got me to wondering what her daddy looked like.

As I stood there watching, the girl crossed the street and went into my building. You can believe I hurried up to see where she was going, but by the time I got there, she had disappeared.

Now, I had lived in that building a long time, and the fact was I didn't just live there. I owned the place, and I knew all the tenants. Off-hand I couldn't think of a single person the girl might be visiting. The apartment house and the building across the street where Eddie's was located were the first properties my husband Joey and I bought when we got married, and our families solidified their business partnership by forming Manzetti Properties.

Joey didn't turn out to be much of a husband, but his family knew all the angles when it came to rehab and construction, and my family knew all the angles of shrewd buying and marketing of real estate.

My job was to search for vacant buildings or ones where the owner might be interested in offloading the property fast. I kept my eye out for small local contractors, too. It was good public relations to involve local folks in any small tear down or rehab and leave the big jobs to Joey's crews. My office was at our corporate headquarters, and I still worked one or two days a week.

I knew there was only one vacant apartment in the building, and that was across the hall from me. So far as I knew, nobody had moved in.

My brother Dominic was the financial wizard that handled all accounting and expenses. That man would likely work until the day he dropped dead. He'd supposedly been training his son and daughter to take over for about the last three years. Although Dom said that he was shifting the oversight of building maintenance and occupancy to them, the truth was he'd just added that on to his workload.

When I asked him if he knew anything about the girl and her mother he laughed, and said, "Have you been walking around with your eyes closed, Lena? Those two moved in across the hall from you."

Well, I never! I must have been volunteering at Helping Hands Shelter for Women, or having supper at Dom's or maybe one of my sisters, or out with my best friend Carlotta when they moved in. That girl didn't come across like she was trying to keep a low profile, but voles hunkered down underground would have gotten my attention faster than those two did living right across the hall.

A few days later, I saw the girl on our landing, staring out the window like a lost soul, and I tell you, it wrenched my heart. I thought of all the times I looked out the window wishing I'd see Jimmy or Mikie strutting down the street. But no amount of wishing could bring them back from the dead.

And no amount of wishing changed the fact that girl reminded me of them. When we finally did speak, it was no surprise the first thing out of her mouth was a smart-assed comment just like one of those boys would have made.

Back when my boys were growing up, Carlotta was always telling me I should wash the twins' mouths out with soap. 'Course Lotta never raised kids or she would have known you can't go sticking a bar of soap into a child's mouth, no matter how tempted you might be.

KALAYLA LEEROYCE

THE OLD LADY

That Crabby Old Lady would swear I never paid attention to a word she said, but she'd be wrong. Her name was Lena Barzetti, but I called her Crabby Old Lady because that's what she was just about 100% of the time. Crabby and for sure the oldest person I ever met. I mean she was SEVENTY-TWO YEARS OLD and boy, did she look it. That summer, I was hanging out around the new neighborhood, or I probably never would've gotten to know her.

The best thing about summer was it stayed light for a long time, so I could be out on my own without flipping Mama out. Mass. Ave. had sidewalks, so I'd walk one side going and the other side coming back. I explored going toward Arlington, past Porter Square 'til I got bored and headed toward Harvard and Central Square. Our building was on the corner with a light, maybe halfway between.

Sometimes I walked around just so I could meet people out with their dogs. Pets weren't allowed in our building, and when I told Mama it'd be real easy to sneak in a dog or cat, she freaked and started yelling about me not doing anything to get us kicked out.

There was plenty of good stuff within three or four blocks of our apartment like Second Time Clothes, White's Fruits and Vegetables, or Carlson's Beer and Wine. Mickey's Market had just about everything. You could get your nails or toes done at Tammy's Tips or your hair fixed at Creative Creations.

I tried hanging out at Shape Up, but they were too cheap to give me free workout tips. I told them I didn't want to be around with a bunch of fat women anyway. The owners of Magneson's Flower Shop were nice, but my favorite place was Clean Duds Laundromat.

Regulars knew better than to go on an errand and leave their laundry with nobody watching it, so I got a good business going. I could earn an easy buck or two for making sure nothing was stolen while they went for an errand. I'd sit with my feet propped up on the windowsill looking like I owned the place.

Even if I was reading a good book, I could keep a lookout for anybody giving the place the shifty eye. Like, say they came in with an empty basket or bag and stood around acting like they were lost while they checked the place out. I'd give them a big smile and say something like, "You need help? That's why I'm here." That cleared out the stealing types pretty quick.

Anyway, one day I was standing on the landing between the third and fourth floor of the apartment building staring out the window, planning my afternoon. I heard these slow footsteps coming up behind me. Wouldn't you know, it was that Old Lady who dressed in black. I mean totally, completely in black, her dress, socks, shoes, all black. Like she worked at a funeral home.

She was half dragging a couple duffle bags. She was really dumb living on the fourth floor of a building with no elevator. She was probably gonna collapse any minute, and I'd be stuck dialing 911.

She stopped when she got to the landing, and I could see the bags were stuffed with black clothes. She must've come from Clean Duds, which proved she was dumber than dumb. Nobody smart that lived in a fourth-floor walk-up would wash everything they owned in one huge load.

If I felt like starting a conversation—which I didn't—I might've pointed that out.

Anyway, she stood there staring at me, and finally she said, "Little girl, if you don't have anything to do, I can give you some work."

Dumber than dumb, right?

"First thing is I'm not a little girl. I'm eleven years old. Second thing is, if it looks to you like I'm hanging here waiting for a job, you need glasses."

She stared at me long and hard, like she was thinking about saying something and then changed her mind.

Then she said, "Well, maybe you want to be an architect, and you're staring at those buildings to get ideas. Good view from up here."

I gotta say that was worth a laugh. "Nah," I said, "I'm just hanging out."

"Then how about helping me carry this laundry?"

"My mama told me not to talk to strangers or carry laundry for them. Never can tell what might happen to a good lookin' girl like me."

She stared at me again, even longer and harder this time. Anybody could see I wasn't gonna get crowned queen of the apartment building even competing against people like her, but maybe her eyes really had gone bad.

"Well," she said, "I'm interested in your muscles, not your looks, and for sure not your mouth. I'll give you a Coke for pay."

"I don't like Coke. I'll take a root beer."

"All kids like Coke, and I don't have root beer. I have lemons and water and sugar to make lemonade. And I can throw in a few cookies. Will that satisfy you?"

"What kind of cookies?"

She rolled her eyes like she couldn't believe I'd ask that, but I wasn't gonna lug laundry for plain old sugar cookies.

"Peanut butter—fresh made."

"Fine!" I said, heaving one bag over each shoulder.

Her apartment was pretty much the same as ours, but had a whole lot less stuff. I mean, like it was practically empty. The walls were white and there was nothing, not one thing on them. The shades on her windows were white, and so was the rug in front of the sofa.

And get this: the living room sofa and big chair were both white! Mama says the problem with white is that you have to wash it or get it cleaned about every other day, so even I knew NOBODY but a rich person would buy a white sofa. The old lady sure didn't act rich, so she must just be a real whacko.

"Put the bags in the closet in the spare room."

At home that'd be my bedroom, but I couldn't tell what it was for her. There were more white walls and white shades, a white rug in the middle of the room, plus a small wood table and a straight back chair near the window. Maybe she lived somewhere else and just came here so she could do her laundry at Clean Duds.

I dumped the bags on the floor in the closet, but it felt like I'd messed things up.

She was in the kitchen mixing up the lemonade, and I decided to ask her straight out. "So, do you live in a monastery and you know, like just keep this place to store stuff?"

I don't think she appreciated that 'cause she gave me a big-time stare and said, "That smart mouth must get you in a lot of trouble in school. What do you know about a monastery?"

"A lot. I read this book that said they have white walls, and you get a chair and a bed and an extra robe and pair of shoes plus a box to store them."

"Is that a fact? So, you read books?"

"Yeah. What of it? You never met a kid who reads books?"

Crazy old lady—why wasn't she asking me the usual stupid adult questions like how I was doing in school and how many brothers and sisters I had?

"That would be an example of the mouth I was talking about. I've got a lot of books you could look at if you wanted to."

She was crazy if she thought I'd want to borrow her crummy old books. It was my turn to do the staring thing, but I don't think she even noticed. I was thinking about leaving until she brought out the peanut butter cookies to go with the lemonade. I tasted one and decided I'd stay long enough to have a few.

"You can call me Lena," she said. "And I suppose you have a name."

Did she think my parents named me Girl the way some jerks name their dog, Dog?

"Sure I got a name. It's Kalayla."

"Ka lay la," she repeated slowly. "That's unusual. And pretty, too. Is that some kind of family name?"

"Naah. My mama thought it up. She's smart about some things."

Sometimes that old lady annoyed me so much I wanted to spit, but she made good lemonade, and I drank a lot of it that summer 'cause she was asking me for help about every five minutes.

I didn't really mind. Mama was working about 100 hours a week, and I didn't see much of her. After we got a car last year she started cleaning houses before her shift at Eddie's. If I stood on the landing between the third and fourth floor, I could see Mama serving customers or clearing tables. She worked the four-nine shift, and when I felt like it, I'd go over and hang out and talk to whoever was there.

Anyway, I was used to Mama being busy all the time. When Daddy was alive, she was always working on some kind of art project like painting or a collage or whatever. I learned to make out okay on my own and not bother her during one of her 'creative inspirations.' The only difference was now she was too busy working to spend time on art. Anyway, we didn't have enough room for her to have a studio.

When summer came, she must've felt guilty being away so much 'cause she decided we should have Sunday Morning Talks. That was supposed to be our special time together when we'd sit at the kitchen table while she drank coffee, and I'd fix whatever I felt like eating.

Mostly she asked me questions and I tried not to lie too much when I answered. Like this morning she said, "Are you going to the library today?"

I never bothered telling her that the library was closed on Sundays during summer. She'd have got all nerved up about what I was gonna be doing all day and where I was gonna be going.

"Haven't made plans yet, Mama. Why? Is there something you want me to do?"

"Well, no, but if you're going out, maybe you could put on something more … something less …"

Cow turds! Like anybody cared what I wore 'cept her. Even the old lady didn't bug me about how I dressed, and she bugged me about plenty of stuff. Sometime I might try going naked and see if Mama liked that better!

Just to keep her quiet, I went into my bedroom and dug into the pile of clothes in the closet 'til I found a blouse and shorts the Easter Bunny gave me. Yeah! As if I EVER believed in any stupid old Easter Bunny!

Sometimes in our Sunday talks, Mama would get going on how important family was. Which was kind of dumb because there wasn't any family on her side. They all died in a gas explosion about the time Mama and Daddy got married. And then after Daddy died, Mama was always thinking up ways to avoid seeing his family. I decided she liked talking about family more than she liked being with it.

The only one Mama couldn't avoid was Daddy's asshole brother Clarence. After Daddy died Uncle Clarence thought he'd be doing us a big favor by "checking" on us. As if we needed him! Anyway, Mama started doing cleaning jobs because Clarence offered to find a car for us, 'cause one thing he knew about was what he called "locating" cars.

The Sunday morning Mama was telling me about his offer, she kept moving her coffee cup from one hand to the other the way she always did when she was nerved up. And she was always nerved up when it came to Clarence. Daddy used to call him, "My brother the Flim-Flam Man." I just called him a jerk.

When she asked what I thought about the idea, I said, "Yeah, his usual big talk. He'll get us a car about the same time he gets a job."

"Layla, I really do wish you wouldn't say things like that about him."

"It's the truth, so why shouldn't I say it?"

"Because he's your uncle. You should be respectful."

"I am respectful. I never called him an asshole to his face, did I?"

Mama sighed one of those big sighs like she always did when she wished I'd shut my mouth, but she knew I wouldn't.

Anyway, that time Clarence did what he said. He went over to Quality Cars and picked out a blue Ford with eighty thousand miles and not too many scrapes and dents. He was never gonna stop bragging about it, either. He went on and on about it having a fine American engine and how he detailed it himself.

That really pissed me off, so I said, "Yeah? That must have been the first time you ever did any work!"

I knew he'd wanna slap my face for that, so I took off before he could.

My grandparents lived in another part of Cambridge over near Inman Square, and after Daddy died, Grandma said we had to stay with them because, "your daddy's passing has exhausted your mama and she needs rest."

Yeah, right! Mama wasn't exhausted. She went whacko and had a nervous breakdown, and Grandma knew it. And I knew it, and everybody else did, too.

I hated it at their house, mostly because they were always dragging me to church. I could've told Grandma she oughta be taking Uncle Clarence instead of me, but she would've said I was being rude and put it on her list of complaints about my behavior to take up with Mama after she got better.

When Mama finally got back to normal, we moved back home and she started working. She said we needed to move to a smaller apartment, and that meant she'd have to give up her art studio.

"It's okay, Layla. I don't have time for art now, and once we move, I'll get to decorate the new apartment and that'll be my project," was what she told me. I knew it wasn't really okay 'cause she loved doing art, and fixing up an apartment was no way the same thing.

It was kinda funny, but once we moved to the new apartment, the person I saw the most was the Old Lady. It turned out she liked Clean Duds, too. Just about every day she'd drop by carrying an iced coffee from Eddie's. I guess life was pretty boring for anybody that old, and she must've been looking for something to do. Like take up all my valuable time with her talking.

She'd pull up a chair next to mine and say something like: "Too hot to be out."

Now that was about the dumbest thing I ever heard 'cause it was just as hot inside as it was out. Clean Duds had a couple of those big standing fans chained to the wall, but they didn't do much 'cept blow hot air around and make a lot of noise.

"So, why are you wearing black?" I asked her on one of those broiling days. By then I knew black was the ONLY color she ever wore.

She gave me her usual stare and said, "I wear what I wear because I choose to, and why I wear it would be NO concern of yours!"

Fine, let her fry! It would serve her right.

When the old lady wanted help carrying her stuff or had other chores for me, she'd always ask if I wanted to earn a Coke. That got to be a joke, and I'd say something like, "I'll have a vanilla Coke float with chocolate ice cream today, thanks."

I got used to the whiteness in her apartment. In a way, I kind of liked it. It was like a blank page you could decorate any way you wanted. A small bookcase in the corner had a bunch of books and a few photos, most of them some boys. Mama had photos of her and me and Daddy everywhere in the apartment, but the Old Lady's place wasn't normal like ours, and her photos kind of freaked me out.

One of 'em was of a woman standing barefoot at the beach with waves coming a little above her ankles. Her hair was real dark and sort of flowing around her shoulders. The wind was blowing her dress up so you could see her legs. She was real pretty. Two little boys that looked alike were making a sand fort or maybe a sand castle at the edge of the water in front of her.

The next time I was over there, I pointed at the photo and said, "So who's that, a friend of yours?"

"A friend? That's me you're looking at, Kalayla. In my younger days."

Right! I covered my mouth quick to keep from snorting. I almost said, "Yeah! Like a couple hundred years ago?" But I didn't because she would've gone into her Being Polite Lecture and I had that memorized.

A few other photos showed the same woman with four boys. In one, she was holding the two little boys so they couldn't squirm away. Two older boys were standing straight as statues on the other side of her.

"Those your kids? How come I never see them here?"

She didn't say anything for so long I didn't think she was gonna answer me, but finally she said, "I had four sons and those pictures were taken a long, long time ago. You better be getting home, Kalayla. Your mama will be waiting."

LENA MANERO BARZETTI

THE MAMA

That girl was sticking her nose in places she shouldn't, and no good was going to come of it. Like asking me about my boys. What good would come of me telling her about them? Two of them were dead. One—I hoped—was living, but who knew where, doing who knew what. The other was a big shot businessman who thought I was about as desirable a mother as a field of poison ivy would have been.

I decided it was about time I got to know that mother of Kalayla's better. The fact I'd done a bad job raising my boys meant I could give her plenty of good advice on what not to do.

I loaded up with a batch of Carlotta's cookies and took myself over to Maureen's the next Sunday afternoon when I knew Kalayla would be off somewhere.

Maureen answered my knock and her smile was genuine, "Lena! I'm so glad it's you! Please come in. I hope you'll like what I've done to the apartment. I'm an artist, you know, well, not a real artist … I mean, I've never earned any money with my art, but … Oh, do come in!"

I walked into their apartment and stood there, blinking. Sweet Jesus, what a sight it was! There was color everywhere—wonderful, vibrant colors, and it made me think of photos of those tropical fish with all their brilliant colors.

Dom told me Maureen asked if she could choose wall colors and do the painting herself, and he'd said yes. Of course, he would say that. It didn't matter that the business was thriving and had been for years and years. Dom was still pinching every penny, nickel, dime, and quarter, his knee-jerk reaction from the old days when we were starting out, and he had to scrounge funds for maintenance any place he could. The joke on him was that he didn't know how much Maureen loved color! The whole apartment would have to be repainted when she moved out and he'd be on his high horse about that!

So … the kitchen was alternating walls of yellow and orange. I never would have dreamed of doing any such thing, but I sure did appreciate the result.

And the decorations—my goodness! All I could think was Maureen must have been playing around with designs in stripes and polka dots and geometric shapes just to see how they'd look. The chair cushions, curtains and wall decorations were a mixture of shapes in yellow, orange, green, and white.

The result, well, I have to say the result was … beautiful … and surprising. She used different colors in every room—some with the walls all one color, some with two—but each room was like a unique world of its own. My, oh my!

"Maureen, this is … well now, I have to say I don't know what to say except that what you've done is so full of life that it's just plain wonderful!"

"Oh! I'm so relieved you like it. I mean, when Layla told me your apartment was all white, I was afraid you might ask us to paint everything over in white or, you know, at least tone it down and make it less, ahh, less ahhh …"

"Don't you be taking the fact I got my place all white to mean I don't like colors. My big old house used to be full of color—not that the colors were anything like yours here, but they were full of life too. You ought to be thinking about getting a job as a home decorator instead of waiting on tables and cleaning houses."

"Oh, I would love that, I really would, but I need to work, and I don't have time to go to school anymore—for training, you know. Anybody who hires you wants to know your experience, and I don't have any, and I don't have a degree. I mean, I started on one, but …"

If Maureen had gone on talking instead of stopping mid-way, I would have found out right then about how life happened to her and how she had to adjust. Same way we all have to adjust to things we didn't plan on and couldn't change.

Once we finished touring the apartment, we settled in the living room with coffee mugs and Lotta's cookies. When Maureen told me Kalayla was at the library on a Sunday afternoon in July, I knew I'd come just in time. She had no idea that girl was lying to her. I decided it'd be smarter if I got to know her some before getting into the fact her daughter was prone to altering the truth if it suited her. Anyway, I didn't need to say anything about it right then because Maureen started in talking again.

"I'm so glad you came over, Lena. I've been hoping we could talk, and even though you come into Eddie's all the time, I can't really chat when I'm working. I wouldn't want Eddie to think I was wasting time."

"Don't you worry about Eddie. He's a good guy. He'd cut you some slack. Is this your first job?"

"Oh dear, is it really that obvious? I never had to work when Jamal was alive because, you know, he was working, and I was so busy with my art. I was enrolled at Rhode Island School of Design, well, sort of enrolled but not as a full-time student because it's over an hour's drive from here and I couldn't take the required classes like a regular student because I'd be spending so much time on the road. And then I got pregnant, and it was such fun painting all kinds of animals to decorate her nursery.

"So, I was taking one or two classes at a time and of course it was taking forever, but at least I was doing what I love. Our apartment was big enough that I had a studio, and I could take Kalayla's crib there and then later her pack 'n play. It was a little bit of a problem when she started crawling because I'd lose track of her. She can be so quiet when she wants to. One day I went looking for her, and there she was in the kitchen with everything from the bottom cupboards strewn all around her on the floor. Luckily, Jamal found some baby-proof cupboard locks and we put gates across the doorways, and they worked fine until she figured out how to climb over them.

"Then Jamal died, and I had to get a job and I didn't have any real skills. So that's why I'm waiting tables and cleaning houses. I like Eddie's especially now that we live right across the street. Everyone there has been really nice to us."

I took a sip of coffee, waiting for her to go on, but she'd evidently run out of steam. She fiddled with the handle of her mug until I said, "Your family must have been a big help when your husband died."

Stricken. That's the only way to describe her expression, and I knew right then I'd stumbled onto a right big sore spot.

"My family? Oh, no, not my family. They wouldn't … they couldn't help. But Jamal's family did. His brother Clarence found the car for me. And Lucinda—that's my mother-in-law—she said her family would help when we moved, but I didn't know if that would cause problems for Kalayla and me. So, I called B. U.—that's where Jamal and I used to hang around—and hired two students to help."

I didn't bother asking why Maureen thought having Jamal's family help with the move might cause problems for her and Kalayla because I knew the answer. We might be living in 1999, but the idea of whites marrying blacks still rubbed a lot of folks raw. Kalayla was fine-looking like her Mama, but her skin was brown and anybody could tell her parents were a mixed-race couple.

It wouldn't have caused any problems with me if her husband's family moved her in, but it was hard to tell about other folks. You never could tell what might be under the surface waiting to spew out when you didn't expect it.

I was guessing that black guy I'd seen coming into the apartment house and leaving about ten minutes later was the Uncle Clarence. Some uncle he was! I'd only seen him a couple of times in the past two months. Any uncle in my family would have been over there all the time, doing everything he could to make things easier for the widow and her daughter.

Families were different, but when it came to helping, you'd think the uncle would do more than a drive-by on the way to somewhere else.

Before I got a chance to say anything, Maureen said, "Kalayla told me she sees you over at Clean Duds. So, I'm glad I have the chance to ask you. You haven't seen her getting into any trouble, have you? I mean, like hanging out with the wrong kids?"

Huh! Here I'd been thinking the girl needed friends and her mama was afraid she'd find the wrong ones!

"Far as I can tell, she doesn't hang out with any kids at all. She's always alone."

"Oh, that's good. I mean, it's good she's minding her own business the way I told her. So, Kalayla told me you have four boys. They must have been such a handful growing up! I'm having a hard time with one girl. I can't even imagine what it would be like with four boys! You must be so glad they're all grown. How are they doing now?"

I admit that stopped me.

Most everybody around knew about my family, and there was no need for explaining why or when or how things happened to my boys or my husband.

If I had a mind to, I could have told Maureen the reason my twins joined the Marines right in the middle of all the anti-war protests. I could have told her my second son disappeared from the face of the earth about fifteen years ago, and I didn't know if he was still alive, or I could have told her I worried that JJ, my oldest, had turned into a clone of his dad which was maybe the worst thing he could have done.

And I sure wasn't going to tell her anything about my husband Joey. The best thing I could have done for any of my boys was to leave Joey when I found out what kind of man was hiding underneath all his good looks and charm. But I couldn't leave him, and my boys paid the price. Same as I did.

"My boys," I said finally. "My oldest, JJ, runs the construction side of our family business. Joey planned for JJ to take over someday and was training him for that. After Joey died in 1969, my brother and I kept on with that until JJ showed he was ready. My second boy, Mark, moved someplace out West, and I'm not sure where he is now or what he's doing. And my youngest were the twins, Jimmy and Mikie. They were killed in Vietnam less than a year after their dad died."

The color drained from Maureen's face.

"Oh," she said. "Oh, how awful for you! But now it makes sense … I mean, that you only wear black. That seemed so strange, and I'm so glad I understand why … Oh dear, I didn't mean it that way. I meant … I just meant … I'm so sorry."

Yeah, everybody was sorry, especially me.

LATER IN THE DAY

Talking to Maureen got me to thinking about my husband Joey and how he loved high living, how he loved being "The Man," how he bragged that his boys were just like him. And how I hoped they weren't.

Joey told me we had to expect acting out from our boys because they needed to prove themselves. He pointed out that they all had plenty of friends, and it did seem like the trouble they got into was good, harmless fun. That's what I thought until I realized that not all the fun was harmless.

I was sure my second born, Mark, was doing fine in school until I started getting calls. I remember the first time the school called about him.

"Mrs. Barzetti? This is John DiSilva, the principal at Mark's school. I'm calling about an incident we had at lunch today. Mark stole another boy's lunch and then took the pie out of the lunch bag and smashed it in the boy's face."

Now, I knew Mark had a temper, but I'd never seen it get out of hand. At least I'd never seen him turn on anyone except his brothers. Joey told me all boys fight with their brothers, and I should ignore it. So I did. But picking a fight outside the family was different and gave me cause for worry.

"My Mark?" I said. "That doesn't make any sense. I sent him to school with a good lunch, a chicken sandwich, chips and an apple. Why would he smash pie in the other boy's face? Mr. DiSilva, I think you must have my Mark mixed up with some other boy."

"I don't think so, Mrs. Barzetti, but you can ask him yourself. He's sitting right here in my office."

Well, I couldn't deny the truth when it hit me right in the face, and there was no doubt it was Mark's voice saying:

"Yeah, Ma, I know you made me lunch. I ate it. It was good. But that asshole does stuff that aggravates me. Like, he's always giving me looks. And he's always bragging. Today he was bragging about how he had a steak sandwich and cherry pie. I got sick of it. You should have seen him with cherry pie all over his face, red dripping down onto his shirt. I hope he gets a beating for ruining his shirt when he gets home."

"Mark! Shame on you! That's not ..."

"Ma, okay, okay, don't start yellin'. Anyway, you know Dad wouldn't have put up with it either."

"Don't you be telling me about what your dad would do. This is about what YOU did!"

"Ma, ... I know, really, I know. I promise I won't do it again. Here's Mr. D. He wants to talk to you."

Mark said he wouldn't do it again, but he made a lot of promises like that he never kept. And nothing was ever his fault. Fighting over aggravations became the story of his life.

"I'm trying, Ma," he'd tell me, "but that fag said ... or did ..."

In his own way, maybe he did try. And he never had anybody watching his back the way the twins did for each other.

Joey made it worse. From the time JJ was four and Mark was three, Joey told JJ his job as the oldest was to toughen up his younger brother, which JJ did by using Mark as his personal punching bag.

At first, Mark came running to me for protection, but that stopped when Joey started calling him "Mama's boy." That was far worse than anything JJ did to him.

Later on, Joey nicknamed Mark 'The Shrimp' because he was only 5'9" while JJ was 6'2", the same as Joey. It didn't help that the twins grew faster than the weeds in my garden and were 6'1" by the time they turned fourteen. That gave Joey more reason to rub it in, and what Joey did, the boys did.

I never got calls about the twins getting into fights, so I assumed they were behaving like I taught them to.

Their first day in kindergarten, I found out there were a lot of other ways boys could get into trouble.

The principal suspended them from the school bus for three days because they were teaching the other boys to play poker, which the school considered a form of gambling. I told Joey we should make them walk to school as a punishment.

He laughed, "Why should they walk? Chips off the old block, that's what they are. Don't you worry, Lena. I'll talk to them. And the next time they do it, they'll be smart enough to hide the damn cards and not admit to anything. And I don't want to hear any talk about them walking. If you want to keep that car I bought you, you'll drive them to school."

So I did.

It didn't matter how much I talked about good behavior. Those two were always huddled together whispering, planning, getting "smarter" about what they did just like Joey taught them.

The day Mikie came home with a brand-new backpack, I said, "Where'd you get that? You didn't steal it, did you?"

Both of them laughed like mad, and Mikie said, "Ma, come on, we'd be lousy thieves, but we're the best at working angles. Look it—it has all kinds of cool pockets. It's a lot better than my old one."

I wasn't sure what the twins meant by "working the angles," and the truth was I didn't really try to find out. I wasn't getting calls from the school or from parents, so I let it go.

The twins learned to hide behind a flow of fast talk and explanations, Joey style. By the time they got to 7th grade, I gave up telling them to return things they "worked angles" to get, things like a leather jacket, a signed baseball, a camera.

And of course, Joey didn't care. All he said was, "If they're smart enough to get it, they can keep it. It's good for them to learn there are a lot of ways to skate on thin ice without falling in."

Joey taught them every way he knew, and they learned more on their own.

They were eight when I grounded Jimmy for forgetting a chore, and they informed me they now had a 'Punishment Sharing Policy'. I told them I'd never heard of such a thing, and Mikie said, "Oh, yeah, Ma, we know that. We just invented it."

"Your turn," Jimmy would say, and Mikie would take the punishment for something his brother had done. It nearly drove me crazy.

When I tried punishing both for something one of them had done, they cocked their heads, gave me their lopsided grins, and said together, "AHH, Ma, come on. That's not fair!"

Those two shared everything, and not even Joey could drive a wedge between them. When Mikie wrecked his bicycle, he and Jimmy made do with one bike, taking turns riding on the handlebars, giving me heartburn. Joey would have bought Mikie any bike he wanted, but Mikie was happy sharing with his brother instead.

When the twins turned 16, Joey told them he'd buy each of them a car. Mikie and Jimmy huddled together discussing his offer, and then told Joey one car would be enough. They went to every car showroom within biking distance, and spent hours studying brochures, debating the pros and cons of every model.

When Joey offered them his advice, they said, "We got it covered, Dad, thanks anyway."

They finally agreed on a Shelby Mustang GT 500, and naturally Joey got a good deal with extras thrown in. Mikie won the buck up over color, choosing dark moss green—and Jimmy picked the black leather upholstery.

They named the car Miss Clementine, and one or both of them was always out polishing her. When Joey said Clementine was a ridiculous name for a car, they turned away from him, walked out the door, calling, "Hey Ma, we're taking sweet Miss Clementine for a ride."

They were smart enough never to push Joey too far and they got around me with smiles, sweet talk and what I believed were good intentions. They'd give me a dozen roses for my birthday or a purple silk scarf for Christmas or a three-pound box of candy for Mother's Day.

When I asked where they got the money, they said, "We do a lot of stuff to help people out, Ma. Like errands and raking leaves and shoveling snow. You oughta be proud of how helpful we are!"

All I could do was hope they were telling the truth. I believed they were trying to be good, but I also knew they always explained their behavior with the most positive interpretation.

And then there was our firstborn. Of course, we named him Joseph John Barzetti, Jr. after Joey. Everybody called him JJ. He never made any trouble in school. JJ worshipped his dad, and he spent his free time following Joey around and listening to everything his father told him.

I was certain Kalayla's mama was not intending for her to run wild any more than I had intended that for my boys. I never was a young widow working two jobs and trying to keep track of an 11-year old daughter, but let me tell you, I sure did know keeping track of kids was like chasing marbles going downhill. They kept on rolling, and you kept on running.

Somebody had to do something to help Maureen, and I sure didn't see anybody volunteering. I guess that left it up to me.

KALAYLA

HELPING THE OLD LADY

The Old Lady always had a reason for doing stuff, and most of the time, what she did was stick her nose in my business.

Like the time she came into Clean Duds with a paperback book and said, "I dug this out of the boxes of books in my storage unit."

The book had a black girl on the cover.

"So? Why'd you bring it to me?"

"You said you like to read. My boys read this in school. If you said you liked to play marbles, I might have searched around for an aggie. I probably have a few buried under the books."

"I don't play dumb games like marbles and I got plenty of books to read."

She let out one of her big sighs and stuffed the book back in that old black canvas bag she was always carrying. I could tell she was working her way up to saying something I didn't want to hear. So I beat her to it.

"I gotta go," I told her and ducked out the door before she could get going on whatever was next on her list of lectures for improving my behavior.

Did she think she was doing me a big favor by bringing me a book about a black girl 'cause my daddy was black? Tomorrow she'd probably be bringing me a book about a white girl 'cause my mama was white.

What made me really mad was that it made me think of something that jerk Uncle Clarence said when Mama and I had to stay with Grandma and Grandpa LeeRoyce after Daddy died.

Naturally it only took Grandma about 15 seconds to get me enrolled in a school near them. My second day there, I was standing in the hall near my classroom when some fat-assed girl bumped into me.

She said, "Hey, new kid. I heard your grandma told you to pass for black so you could get into a fancy private school next year. That right?"

I could've slammed my fist into her big fat face, but I didn't. I could've told her I bet she ate cow turds for breakfast. But I didn't. The bell rang, and I ducked into class without saying anything. I knew better than to make trouble at school. Anyway, I was used to asshole comments from asshole kids.

When Uncle Clarence asked me about how I liked the school, I made the big mistake of telling him what the kid said.

He cracked up laughing and said, "If you ever decide to pass, Kalayla, you pass for white and find yourself a sugar daddy. You're going to be a looker like your mama. There's a passel full of dudes who'd pay plenty to get their hands on her creamy white skin. Your skin ain't white like hers, but it sure is a sweet chocolate!"

I heard him laughing all the way out the front door. I never liked him, but after that I hated him.

Before Daddy died, when I said something he didn't like, he'd tell me to watch my mouth. One time I told him Uncle Clarence's mouth was way worse than mine. Daddy didn't like that at all.

He said, "Listen here, Kalayla, you be nice to Clarence no matter what he says. He's the only uncle you've got."

I didn't tell him having no uncle would have been better 'cause he probably would've made me sit in the corner facing the wall, which was his and Mama's favorite punishment when I pissed them off. Most of the time I hated that more than I hated shutting my mouth.

And that Old Lady was another one. I wouldn't've bothered putting up with her 'cept it turned out she was a good cook, and she started inviting me for dinner. The first time was after I did some shopping for her.

When I brought her the groceries she said, "You better get yourself over here to eat. You get any skinnier, you might disappear altogether."

I didn't mind 'cause Mama was working an extra shift. After that I started going there all the time. I never bothered telling The Old Lady I learned how to cook when I was a kid, or I would've starved a long time ago.

When Mama was going to art school and working on a project, she never thought about fixing dinner. Her brain was good at shutting up her stomach and so was Daddy's, but nothing shut mine up. By the time Mama did think about food and finally started cooking, I was practically dead from hunger. She didn't care how late we ate, or if we ate the same thing four nights in a row, or if we ate at all.

When I complained to Daddy, he just laughed. "That's why we have a refrigerator and stove, skinny girl. Knock yourself out and make something for me while you're at it."

Right! Anything Mama did was fine with him. So what if I starved!

The Old Lady must've enjoyed having me run all over the place for her 'cause she was always asking me to do stuff, like take some papers over to her brother Dominic or go to Mickey's and buy her milk and a few Snickers bars.

I started thinking maybe I should be getting more than food out of the deal, so one day when we were sitting at Clean Duds I said, "How come you never pay me for all the stuff I do for you? Don't you have any money?"

"Paying you? Sweet Jesus, girl, haven't you heard of doing a good deed just for the sake of helping another person?"

"Sure, I was thinking this morning how good helping you makes me feel. I was thinking I probably earned my way into heaven already. Since it might be a while 'fore I get up there and collect my reward, I was hoping for a little cash to use while I'm still here on earth."

That time I knew I got her 'cause she tried to hide her smile by looking out the window, and I knew she was gonna say okay.

"Well then," she grumbled, "I guess I better put you on retainer."

"Retainer? What does that mean?"

"It means I pay you a certain amount now, and IF you keep working for me, and IF your work is satisfactory, you get more later."

I knew there must be a trick in there somewhere. "What do I get now?"

"Twenty-five bucks."

She dug around in her purse and handed over the money right then, so I wasn't gonna argue. And I wasn't gonna bother to tell her I'd have done it for ten bucks retainer.

Anyway, I kind of liked going to her place. I'd sneak a look at that photo of her on the beach and try to figure out what was so different. Sure, she was old now, and back then she was young. But that wasn't all.

For some weird reason she made me think of the silverware Mama had me polishing back when she and Daddy gave parties. It came from Daddy's family, and Mama took real good care of it and stored it away in soft cloth bags, one for spoons, another for forks, about eight bags altogether. She said the bags protected it, but the silver turned dull and dark anyway.

That's how the Old Lady looked—dull and dark, 'cept nobody stuffed her in a bag and put her on some shelf in a closet. And no matter how much anybody polished her, she was never gonna look that young and happy again.

LENA

CAMBRIDGE RESOURCES

Cambridge always was a city where you could get anything you wanted any way you wanted it. Back when I was a kid, we all lived in Watertown and hung around with kids from the Lake, the Italian section of Newton. Lotta and I would beg my mother to make Dom and his friends take us along when they went to Cambridge. Sometimes she would, no matter how much they complained.

Lotta and I would hang around Harvard Square and maybe get a Bartley's burger, or ice cream at Bailey's. The boys would cruise around looking for trouble. Back then, that meant finding somebody who'd buy them a six-pack or three.

Nowadays, it wasn't just the boys who did the cruising. You'd see girls, too, headstrong ones like Kalayla, doing whatever they pleased. I'd been wracking my brain to come up with something that would keep her from wandering the streets or hanging out at that damn Clean Duds. You never could tell who might drop in there and decide that girl was easy pickings.

The city did a lot to keep kids occupied in the summer. Classes at the library were free, but Kalayla was way too old for Story Time and too young for Films or Book Discussion groups, but there was an active summer crafts and sports program.

I made a few phone calls and found out most city clubs and sports had a fee. I was pretty sure Maureen didn't have extra money, but that didn't worry me. I could take care of the money IF Kalayla was willing to do something besides guard laundry.

The next morning started out sunny and 73 degrees, going steadily up from there. I got my coffee and was at Clean Duds before 10 a.m. Kalayla was reading a book with her feet propped up as usual.

She looked up when I came and said, "Hey Lena, you been hiding under a big rock? I didn't see you yesterday."

"I've been minding my own business, which is something you'd benefit from doing. You're turning into a couch potato with no couch. Most kids are playing sports during summer. Giving their muscles and their brains a good workout instead of lounging in a hot old place like this."

She gave me a dirty look. "Sports? You mean like be on some team with a bunch of jerks? In your dreams, Lena, in your dreams!"

Well, wouldn't you know, she was pigheaded enough to rule out team sports before I even got a chance to give her my team sports pitch. No matter. Her stubbornness wasn't going to derail my train now that I got it going. My boy JJ played tennis for a while, and I knew Cambridge still had a fine tennis program.

"You could play tennis," I told her. "If you were good enough, you could play singles. Singles, that means by yourself against one other person."

"I know what singles means! Why'd I waste my time chasing a stupid little ball around so I could hit it with a stupid racquet? If you asked me about doing something useful, I might be interested. Like say, if you had a gun hidden away in one of those white rooms, and you offered to teach me how to shoot it, maybe I'd say yes."

Sweet Jesus! I took a deep breath, trying to stay calm. That girl had no idea how much she sounded like one of my twins. And wouldn't you know it, she picked the one thing I could have taught her, if I had a mind to. Which I sure as hell did not.

Joey owned a lot of guns, and the twins were always begging to see them. A week didn't go by without Joey unlocking that footlocker. He'd lift out one of his precious collection, caressing it like a lover.

He introduced each of the boys to shooting the day they turned eight. That was the age limit for the Highland Gun Club. They started with pistols, just like I did. Next came bench rest rifles and then when they were strong enough, shotguns. I never cared for the heavier ones and stuck with the pistol.

"You could beat the ass off anybody on the women's side," Joey said, pushing me to compete. "Husband and wife both champions—now that'd be something to brag about!"

I gave in, and we won both titles four years in a row. That didn't matter to me. The only one I ever wanted to beat was Joey—and I never did.

Well, two things were clear. Cambridge's summer programs were not the answer for Kalayla, and there was NO way I was teaching her to shoot. I'd have to come up with some other idea. I turned and walked toward the door of Clean Duds. No point wasting time.

"Hey," she yelled after me, "Too hot in here for you today?"

The very next day, I saw her across the street talking to one of the local lowlife types, Ray Ray Bingha, a numbers runner, bouncer, and God only knew what else. The guy was about 6'5", maybe 250 pounds of muscle, and a mouth loaded with gold that sparkled when he laughed. His dark brown hair was pulled into a ponytail that trailed about four inches down his back. I was certain NOBODY ever teased him about having a girly hairdo.

Ray Ray enjoyed terrorizing folks with Thor, his enormous bullmastiff. You never saw Ray Ray without that dog. He loved bragging about all the special training Thor had. Special training or not, you didn't need a 'Beware of Dog' sign to warn you Thor would rip out your throat if Ray Ray gave the word.

You can bet I beat it across that street as fast as my legs could carry me.

"Ray Ray!" I called, stepping from the street to the sidewalk and giving myself a chance to catch my breath. Ray Ray's hands looked big enough to handle two footballs without any trouble, and I could see he was holding Thor's leash with one finger. One that he might let go, if Kalayla bugged him too much. Ray Ray's temper was well known, and I doubt he'd have much tolerance for a smart-mouthed girl.

"Well, Mrs. Barzetti," he grinned. "I ain't seen you in quite some time. Thought maybe you dropped dead and was buried."

He hadn't seen me in quite some time because I rarely had any need of the freelance muscle types that did occasional work for JJ on the construction side of Manzetti Properties.

"Well, I'm not in the habit of trolling the streets like you, Ray Ray. I came over to warn you this girl here has allergic fits when she gets close to dogs. You keep that Thor away from her."

Of course Kalayla had to butt in all indignant, shifting her mouth into high gear without thinking, as usual. "Where'd you get such a dumb idea, Lena. I love dogs!"

"Whatever," Ray Ray said laughing, showing the gold. "I was just explaining to this little girl that my dog Thor don't like her."

"I'm not a little girl, and I'm so likeable he'd probably drool all over me!"

Sweet Jesus! I swear I could have slapped that girl's face. Somebody needed to teach her to zip that mouth of hers!

She looked like she was about to reach out and pat Thor's head when a soft, "Don't!" from Ray Ray froze her hand in mid-air.

"Only way Thor'd find you likable be if he could eat you as an appetizer for his dinner! Don't you worry, Miss Lena. Thor won't be bothering this funny little thing. She ain't got enough meat on those bones to make it worthwhile for him."

And with that, he and Thor went strolling on down Mass. Ave.

Kalayla put her hands on her hips and of all things, stamped her foot. "Why'd you come running over here, Lena? Lucky you didn't have a heart attack. And why'd you tell that guy I'm allergic to dogs when you know I'm not?"

"I must have dreamed you were," I said, taking her arm like I needed something to lean on. "Come on home with me. I need help sorting some of the books in my storage bin."

All the way home, I kept on taking deep breaths, willing myself not to reach out and shake Kalayla until her teeth fell out. Ray Ray was the kind who likely had more than one gun tucked away. And if she happened to run into him again and somehow the subject came up, I bet giving her a gun and teaching her how to shoot would give him a good laugh.

I had to do some quick thinking because that girl had no more sense than a bug. For sure I needed to consult with my friend Carlotta. Some of her ideas might be off the wall, but she'd think of things I never would. And I needed all the ideas I could get! Before going to see her, I needed to do a little research.

Cambridge might be a big city, but it was like a woman's handbag with a whole lot of different size compartments, and I was sure information about Kalayla's family was tucked away in one of them.

I knew exactly how to find out which one.

The best place to get information was from the Ladies Knitting Club, which was mostly made up of old Townie women who took great pride in sharing their hoard of knowledge. Not all the members were born in Cambridge, but we all grew up living close enough that if you had a mind to—and they did—you could find out more than a person needed to know about any family, including all the rivalries, tragedies, and trivia with information based on a combination of fact and gossip.

I never was a knitter and didn't plan on becoming one, but this was the best place for undercover snooping. They were always open to new members, which was something of a joke because it was one of those ladies' groups where you had to know somebody who knew somebody to get in.

I wasn't worried about being welcomed. I had an ace in the hole. I could drop a few snippets about this and that in the Manero-Barzetti clan—most of which would be fabrication.

Skill at telling good tales was highly prized in my family, and I learned early on never to pass on anything to anyone outside. Nana and Mama taught us every trick they knew about what they called "playing one note and making it sound like the whole orchestra."

Anyway, while the ladies were digging in knitting bags and pulling out their latest projects, I went around admiring their fine work. By the time I moseyed my way to remarking that a girl named Kalayla and her mama Maureen moved in across the hall from me, the ladies were ready to fall all over themselves telling me everything they knew.

Maureen's husband, Jamal, came from an old established black family that kept a low profile in a mixed-race neighborhood in Cambridge. They were solid churchgoers and community-minded, especially Jamal's mother Lucinda. She'd been running a soup kitchen for their church for years and occasionally took in stray kids. She was active in the community when it came to rights for blacks. Back in the days of forced busing, she argued that it was a lose-lose situation, and if that Judge Garrity had come visiting Roxbury and South Boston, he would have understood that.

The ladies admitted they didn't know the whole story about Jamal and Clarence. They thought the younger boy, Clarence, had mental problems when he was young and now he sometimes took a job as an auto mechanic. The older one, Jamal, was good in sports and school and went to UMass Boston on scholarship. He'd been killed racing cars with his brother a couple of years ago. It was out of season at a track in New Hampshire and they'd sneaked into the place. Or so the ladies presumed.

Which confirmed to me that the slick-looking black guy who came visiting definitely was the uncle. I hope I didn't snort too loud when the ladies said they thought Clarence was straightening himself out because he'd been looking after his sister-in-law and his niece.

I naturally assumed Maureen's family had stepped up when her husband died, but when I said that, the ladies jumped all over each other to set me straight. What they told me about Maureen's family was close to unbelievable, and I needed time to let it sink in before I went over to Lotta's.

One thing that took no sinking in time was the fact that Kalayla could get herself buried underneath a mountain of trouble unless I did something pretty darn quick.

LENA
BEST FRIENDS

Carlotta Eccli had been my best friend forever, and I knew any idea coming out of Lotta's head was bound to be different from anything I thought up. To her, life was simple and straightforward with no gray areas.

Lotta was of the opinion that I enjoyed wallowing in murky gray. To prove her point, she periodically pointed to examples, such as:

The fact that I had stayed married to a vicious bastard;

The fact that I never bothered to dye my hair, which she considered an insult to a stylish woman like herself;

The fact that I insisted on wearing black, which, according to her, made me look like a corpse in search of a coffin;

The fact that I lived in a fourth-floor walk-up apartment, even though I could afford to buy a penthouse at the Ritz.

Whatever.

I knew I could count on Lotta no matter what, and she knew the same. Anyway, she was a fabulous cook, and even if she came up with some off the wall idea, I'd get a good meal.

Walking is good for a person of any age, and half a mile wouldn't likely kill me. Lotta might consider me dumpy-looking, but she had to admit I hadn't loaded on fat like so many of our high school classmates. And I planned on keeping it that way.

Lotta's house was nestled in a Cambridge neighborhood that boasted yards with trees, shrubs, and lawns. A five-foot-high chain-link fence surrounded the back of her yard, which in an otherwise "fenceless" area, had not pleased her neighbors.

"Well," she told them, "would you rather have dogs running free and shitting all over your lawn?" According to her, that put an end to objections about the fence.

Lotta loved to redecorate on the spur of the moment, but this time, when I walked in the front door, I wasn't surprised by a new look. Her kitchen was still black and white, the living room and dining room pale aqua, each with an accent wall in a slightly darker shade of aqua. The furniture was all modern Scandinavian design like they sold at Form in Teak.

As usual, her table was exquisite: yellow Damask tablecloth, napkins in silver filigreed napkin rings, and a centerpiece of yellow and white roses. We were finishing the main course of Coq au Vin and buttery noodles when I decided it was time to mention Kalayla.

"So, Lotta, did I tell you I attended the last meeting of the Ladies Knitting Circle?"

Lotta clanked her fork down on her plate.

"Well, isn't that just like you, Lena! Making an outrageous announcement as if it's the most normal thing a person could say. You know good and well you do not knit, have never knitted, and will never knit. Besides, you and I both know those old gossips spend more time talking than they do knitting."

I broke off a piece of baguette to mop up the last of my Coq au Vin. "That's exactly why I went. I'm trying to help a poor fatherless child and her hard-working, widowed mama. I needed to find out a few things. So, what's for dessert?"

Carlotta shook her head and rolled her eyes. "Mocha squares with almond topping and a dollop of whipped cream. And what exactly was it that you were so hot to find out?"

"Well, something in the story the mama told me smelled like dead fish, and I had to find out why. Her eleven-year-old daughter Kalayla has been wandering around this city like it's her personal playground. You know how dangerous that can be."

"Mother, daughter, dead fish. Lena! Say whatever you've got to say in plain English."

"Oh, for goodness sake! I'm talking about Maureen, the mother, and her daughter Kalayla, and the family on the mother's side. When I asked Maureen if her family helped when her husband died, she said her family wouldn't or couldn't help and then she fell all over herself changing the subject. Naturally that made me curious, so I asked the girl about her mama's family.

"She told me they had all lived over in Brighton and every single one of the family had been killed in an explosion at a family party about

13 years ago. A big Irish family all killed in an explosion—now, do you remember any such thing? Because I sure don't."

"Back around '86? No, I definitely do not remember anything like that. A whole family wiped out? The story would have been plastered all over the news and in the *Globe* and *Herald* and all the rags. No way we would have missed something like that."

"We didn't. It was all a lie!" I ate a bite of mocha square. "This is yummy, Lotta."

"That makes absolutely no sense, Lena. Why would anybody make up anything that outrageous? Are you sure you've got the story right?"

"Of course I'm sure! Now wait until you hear the rest of it. You remember that bitchy Carol Simmons, the one who was all hot to date my Joey? Well, she knew the most, and she fell all over herself hushing the others up so she could tell the story.

"The deal was this: Kalayla's mother Maureen was the pride of the O'Rourke family. I don't think you've seen her, but she is one gorgeous woman, with green eyes, red hair, movie star figure. I guess she was as smart as could be, taking advanced placement in most of her high school classes. Her mama had it all planned. Maureen was going to college, and then she was going to marry a boy named Timothy O'Brien, whose father owned a family law business."

"HA! We all know how well those plans work out. So, did Maureen suck it up and go along, the way YOU did?"

I gave her a dirty look. "As a matter of fact, she didn't. She fell in love with a black boy and ran off and married him!"

"OH, MY GOD!"

I had to laugh. Lotta's mouth dropped open, she pushed herself half way to standing, leaned over the table and repeated, "Oh my God!"

"So, they kicked Maureen out of the family! I mean, really kicked her out! Maureen's mother disowned her and has never met her own granddaughter! Can you believe that?"

Carlotta flopped down in her chair. I knew she was struggling to wrap her head around that idea the same way I had.

She and I came from big Italian families with the philosophy no matter what you did, you could always come home. Lotta was divorced twice, didn't want children and had casual relationships with men, but none of that caused her parents to turn their backs on her. Of course, Lotta could do what she wanted because she was never the critical pawn in the family's business the way I was.

"What a vicious woman! And the family went along with her? Oh, my God. What a vicious family! But why in hell would Maureen lie to her daughter about what happened? The kid will find out, and then her mother will have hell to pay! Maureen sounds like a real loony tune, Lena. Do not open the door if she comes knocking, and do not give her or the girl another thought!"

"Well, funny that I can't think of one single time you turned your back on an abused dog or cat because getting involved with the owner might cause you problems."

I took a sip of coffee and set my cup down carefully. I KNEW that would get her. From the time we were kids, Lotta had driven her parents crazy, bringing home all manner of stray or hurt animals. Which is exactly why she was the perfect person to be owner/operator of an animal shelter. The most respected and best run shelter in Cambridge and the surrounding towns, I might add.

Carlotta turned toward me and sighed. "It is not the same. Animals can't help themselves. People can. People make the most stupid … oh hell! I can see you've got a burr in your side over this, and nothing I say will change your mind. Instead of wasting time, why don't you just spit it out. What ridiculous plan do you have in mind?"

"Well, unfortunately I've run out of what you call ridiculous plans. I did talk to Eddie. One of his regular girls quit, so he can put Maureen on the day shift and give her more hours. And I talked to him about giving her a raise. That should help. But Kalayla is a disaster waiting to happen. I have no idea how to get her involved in constructive activities. That's why I'm asking you."

Carlotta didn't say a word while we cleared the table and loaded the dishwasher, so I knew she had switched into problem-solving mode.

Finally, she said, "All right. I'll make fresh coffee and we'll think it through. First you better tell me what you tried that didn't work."

Relief flooded me. "I looked into all the city programs, but she refuses to play sports, and she turned up her nose at crafts. She spends all her time hanging out at Clean Duds, or roaming around by herself."

"Hummm. Well, I do agree, that is not good. Not good at all."

I settled into a chair in the living room while Lotta continued puttering.

I knew she wouldn't join me until she'd thought through the options and considered the consequences.

My best friend always made sure she covered every possibility. That included when she got married. Back in the late "40s", girls were definitely not thinking about leaving the back door open in case they needed an exit from their marriage. But dear Lotta was, and that's what she did. When she caved to family pressure and married Stan Loprete, she convinced Stan a civil ceremony at City Hall would be just fine.

Except that for any good Italian Catholic girl, that was the opposite of just fine with her family. Joey and I had the kind of wedding the families expected. We said sacred vows during a wedding mass, and celebrated the union with 176 guests at a dinner/dance reception with church and family approval and blessings.

Lotta's parents were furious because a marriage at City Hall wasn't recognized by the Catholic Church. They were hell-bent on convincing her and Stan to have a proper wedding, but Lotta was already maneuvering her way toward the exit.

It turned out Stan's idea of a good time was slapping her around, and Lotta wasn't about to put up with that. She went to her younger brother for help. He always backed her up, and he had a heavyweight influence in the family even back then. He apparently convinced Stan that leaving Lotta and moving out of town would be his best option.

Two years later, Lotta married Jeff Procopio, once again in a civil ceremony at City Hall. This time her parents resorted to mumbling and shaking their heads while assuring everyone their daughter would eventually do the right thing.

No need for them to worry. Lotta decided the right thing was getting rid of Jeff. She couldn't stand his endless romantic gifts, sappy notes, and need to be her constant companion. Her brother Mattwo stepped in again and Jeff agreed that under the circumstances, divorce would be his very best choice.

That was the end of Lotta and marriage, and all of us heaved a sigh of relief.

I heard dish noises coming from the kitchen and then the soft hum of the dishwasher. Lotta came out of the kitchen, handed me a coffee mug, and flopped down on the sofa. She curled her legs under her the way she had so many times over the years.

"Well," she said, "maybe we'll get lucky and find out the girl has as much sense as a cat or a dog."

I laughed, "OK, so what do you think?"

Lotta stared at me for a full minute before she said, "You probably won't like the idea, BUT … I think Matty's Way is worth a try. It worked for your twins, and you might recall they weren't what any sane person would call easy."

I came close to spilling my coffee.

What was I thinking? Of course Lotta would suggest Matty's Way.

Her father had started Matty's Way as a dojo offering judo and karate in the 1920's. Her brother Mattwo taught there and then took over management when their dad retired. He had expanded and turned it into an exercise gym. His son, Lotta's nephew Rico, was next in line to run the gym.

My twins loved the challenge and competition of karate, both earning black belts. Lotta was right. Matty's Way got them off the streets, and maybe it could do the same for Kalayla.

The problem was, I never planned to go there again. Mikie and Jimmy's ghosts haunted me enough without me going back to their favorite place.

But the twins weren't the only thing holding me back. If I went there, I'd likely see Lotta's brother Mattwo. He'd been in love with me when we were in high school and all the kids knew it, but I'd said no to him and married Joey.

Joey never liked that I was close to Carlotta and he couldn't stand Mattwo. Lotta's dad wanted to pass on his name, so they named her brother Matthew Eccli II which morphed into Mattwo. Joey took any opportunity to put Mattwo down, like making fun of Mattwo's name. "Yeah," Joey told everybody, "Matt Two—get it?—number two because the only thing that comes out of him is shit and more shit."

Ridiculous as it might sound, I was still feeling shy around Mattwo, even though I'd seen him at Eccli family parties over the years. I didn't need Carlotta to tell me how off the wall that was. It wasn't as if he'd spent his life waiting around for me. He married Angi Santano, who was a few years younger than Lotta and me, and they'd raised a family. Lotta told me Angi thought Mattwo's name sounded French and was very sexy. Angi died four years ago.

None of that stopped me from wondering how different my life would have been if I'd said yes to him instead of Joey. And Lotta was no help.

Every chance she got, she told me I was a fool for not chasing after him the day Angi died.

And now she was suggesting that getting in touch with him would be the most logical thing in the world, even though she knew damn well for me it wouldn't be.

Once I decided to call him, I spent the rest of the day and almost all of a sleepless night deciding what to say.

48 HOURS LATER

The walk to Matty's Way was shorter when I was younger. The closer we got, the slower my feet moved, but that had nothing to do with distance.

We were almost there when Kalayla said, "Why are you walking so slow? Your feet hurt? Why aren't we taking one of those taxis you love so much? If you weren't so cheap, you'd buy a car, and I could drive you around."

Sweet Jesus! Just what I needed—an eleven-year-old chauffeur!

"Oh, quit complaining—it's about time you did something to earn that retainer I paid you. Anyway, Matty's Way is on the next block."

I wasn't about to explain the reason I didn't own a car.

After Joey died and the twins came home in body bags, Carlotta found me passed out in a bar for the second time. She confiscated the keys and donated the car to the local veteran's association.

"Kill yourself if you want," she told me, "but I'm not letting you kill anyone else!"

I gave up the bottle but kept a permanent arrangement with Safe Ride Taxi. If I didn't use them, I took a bus or walked. And Kalayla could, too!

Anyway, it wasn't my feet that hurt. It was my heart, and she didn't need to know that either. Memories of the twins came gliding around me, a kaleidoscope of shifting images of them showing off in their bright white uniforms, arguing about which of them would graduate to the next belt fastest, and always showing off combinations of moves to Joey.

The closer we got, the more I felt like Matty's Way was sucking me into an emotional quicksand, but that wasn't because I was nervous about seeing Mattwo. On the phone, he said his son Rico would meet with Kalayla and me to decide which classes might be best for her. Which made it pretty clear I was about a half-century too late if I was thinking about romance with him.

Seeing the sign over the door of Matty's Way gave me a shock, but not one of recognition. It was dark grey with bright gold lettering, shiny enough that it might have been hung earlier that morning. Everything looked brighter and newer. The building had undergone a facelift with a second story addition, and the exterior was painted light grey instead of dull brown.

I looked up and down the block and across the street and realized the whole neighborhood had turned into a yuppie haven. Colors, designs, even signs were similar, smart looking and up-scale, a fine example of the city's neighborhood renewal program.

Sweet Jesus! Where was my brain? Manzetti Properties had done the rehab for this whole section of the city, and JJ supervised the project. That must have been about five years ago and things still looked good.

The funny thing was I felt less off balance. Nothing had changed in my memories, but what I saw in front of me had no relationship to that past life.

Kalayla bumped into me as I stopped to stare.

"Cripes, Lena, what's the matter with you? Is this place freaking you out? Don't worry. I'll protect you." She darted ahead, held open one of the glass doors, bowed and waited for me to walk through.

My, oh, my! The lobby area was an expanse of creamy white with spring green woodwork—open, clean, and inviting. Nothing like the beige walls and dark wood of years ago. I wanted to nose around and inspect all the changes, but Rico was standing in front of the check-in counter, obviously waiting for us. The minute he saw me, he came over, held out his hand and said, "Hi Miss Lena. Good to see you again."

I had to admit, my heart did a tiny skip. Rico looked exactly like his dad had so long ago, six feet of muscular build, curly dark brown hair, friendly brown eyes, and an open face.

"I've brought Kalayla," I said, wishing away the awkwardness.

"Kalayla, this is …"

The girl had been right next to me, but before I could get the words out, she turned and walked away. And then, I couldn't believe my eyes.

She started strutting around like a blown-up peacock showing off for a mate, acting like she could do anything she pleased. Such as grabbing a bunch of brochures off a stand and scattering them across the check-in counter before walking around the back of the counter to stick her head in the offices.

Rico was staring at her same as I was, probably wondering if she was an alien from Mars that landed in the wrong place. I didn't blame him one bit. I realized my jaw had dropped open, and I clamped my mouth shut. What had gotten into that girl?

Rico finally turned to me and said, "Miss Lena, this can't be the kid my dad told me about. Dad said the girl was lonely and needed friends, and the mom was stretched thin. This one is oozing attitude and spoiling for a fight."

"Well, there's only one Kalayla, and you're looking at her. I sure don't know what's going on. This is way beyond her normal smart-ass routine."

The truth was I was used to Kalayla, but this was the first time he'd met her. Between the way she was dressed and the way she was acting, it was easy to understand why he thought I'd brought the wrong kid.

Naturally, she was wearing the baseball cap visor backward, her second skin. To that she added the red plaid high top Keds without laces, a pair of long baggy blue shorts with yellow butterflies and a navy-blue drapery cord holding them up. On top she was wearing a pink cami under the loudest Hawaiian flowered shirt on this planet.

She had moved from prancing around the offices over to the trophy cases, where she was pressing her nose against the glass, leaving finger and nose prints just like a two-year-old child.

She finally turned around, looked at me and then at Rico. "Now I get why the Old Lady dragged me here. You're gonna teach me how to kick the shit out of the asshole kids at school. About time somebody taught me something useful."

Sweet Jesus! Talk about making an impression! Rico probably thought I was off my rocker trying to help her.

Whatever he might have been thinking, what he did was to walk over to her. Although I didn't think he was planning on slapping her face, I have to say that sure was what I felt like doing.

Rico looked directly at her, and I could see him take a deep breath before saying, "The only thing anybody needs to teach you is some good old-fashioned manners. I assume your parents tried to do that, but they obviously weren't successful. Miss Lena didn't drag you over here. She brought you here out of the goodness of her heart. And this is how you thank her? Shame on you!"

I sucked in my breath. There was no way in hell this could end well.

And it didn't. Kalayla did something just like my boy Mark would have, with no thought of consequences or stopping until somebody made him stop.

Kalayla put her head down and charged. Rico held her off with one arm, dodging her fists, moving away smoothly like I'd seen the twins do. She kept on charging, and he kept on dodging.

Until—finally—she wore herself out. Slumped over and panting she said, "You take it back, you asshole. Take it back!"

I didn't have a clue what she was asking him to take back. It couldn't be that she needed to learn manners. I'd told her that more than once and she never flipped into a rage. But she'd never met him before—maybe she thought he was criticizing the way her mama and daddy had raised her.

Rico stood watching, and it seemed like he was trying to decide what to do. Then he said, "Listen, Kalayla, the fact you lost control is no reason for me to take back anything. You repaid Miss Lena's kindness by acting like a jerk. And I doubt very much your parents would be applauding the routine you just pulled. Seems to me you're the one who needs to take something back."

Without giving a person time to blink, that girl stuck out her tongue at him, gave him the finger, and stomped out the door.

I had to move my old legs faster than I had in a long time to catch up with her. She was halfway down the block before I yelled for her to wait up. I thought she was going to ignore me, but she didn't. She stood waiting for me with her hands clenched at her sides, and with a look on her face that would have scared off the neighborhood ghoul.

Neither of us said a word on the walk home. Street noise echoed around us, filling in the silence. All I could think was that my grand plan had backfired right in my old face, and I didn't know what to do about it. Which was nothing new.

I never knew what to do with my Mark when his temper exploded. He was always getting into fights over something as ridiculous as the way a kid looked at him. The year he went to high school he got into three serious fights before Christmas, and the school administrators were talking about expelling him. Joey went to talk with them. I didn't know what he said, but he convinced the principal and vice-principal everything would be fine if they moved Mark to a different school so he could get a new start.

I didn't dare point out to Joey that high school was supposed to be Mark's new start.

Whatever the reason, they agreed. Mark transferred to a new school and managed to graduate with his class. I hoped he had learned to control his temper, but while he was there, four kids from his school were attacked by an unknown "assailant." Each of them ended up in the hospital.

Not one of those boys ever accused Mark, but in my heart, I believed he was doing exactly what his father had drilled into him. He was taking his rage underground so he wouldn't have to face any consequences for what he did.

When I heard about the first kid, I asked Mark if he knew what happened. "Nothing to know, Ma. The kid was always running off at the mouth, and now his jaw's wired. Good joke, huh?"

I didn't bother asking him about the other kids. With all four of my boys, I reached the point where I felt like no matter how much I wanted to help them, there was nothing I could do. I guess that was when I gave up and let them be what they were: Joey's boys. The family expected me to play the cards I was dealt. I did the best I could, but mine was always the losing hand and Joey held all the aces. I couldn't quit and walk away, but I gave up believing I could do anything to help my boys. And finally, I just plain gave up trying.

Here I was again, trying to help a child and failing. So, what was I going to do? Give up and walk away like I did before? I could tell myself Kalayla didn't want my help. I could tell myself she wasn't my blood kin, and I had no business butting in. I could tell myself there was nothing left for me to do.

That might be true. But …

I could not let myself give up on her the way I gave up on my boys. No matter how bad my hand was, I had to stay in the game, even if I kept on losing. Because if I gave up, I wouldn't be able to live with myself.

Something made Kalayla explode. I didn't know what, but somehow it was connected to me. I thought taking her to Matty's Way was my last best hope for helping her. Maybe if I'd come right out and said that to her, she might have listened. But I was afraid she wouldn't, same way my boys didn't listen. So, I didn't tell her anything at all about where we were going or why.

However poorly she reacted, I guess she did have cause to be angry. What was I going to do about that? It took me 72 years, but I think I finally understood. I had to keep trying.

KALAYLA

SELLING COOKIES

I was teaching that Old Lady not to mess in my life. I hadn't talked to her in more than a week, and I didn't plan to anytime soon. When I saw her coming my way, I went in the opposite direction. If she came into Clean Duds, I kept reading my book and acted like nobody was there 'cept me.

Then one day she surprised me coming out of Mickey's Market, almost bumping into me when I was going in.

Before I could turn away, she said, "Don't you know it's unkind to ignore people just because you're mad at them?"

She was so dumb she didn't know she was the only "people" I was ignoring.

I would've punched her, but she would've fallen over and what was I gonna tell 911 when they showed up? If I said it was an accident, the old crab would've told 'em I was lying.

I squeezed my fists so hard they hurt and said, "Nobody decides who I talk to 'cept me."

"Well, nobody said you have to talk to me. I have something I need to say to you, and all you have to do is listen! I can see now that not telling you why we were going to Matty's Way was wrong, and I'm sorry about that. I thought about asking you. I truly did. But I was afraid you'd say no like you said no to everything else I suggested. I've been worried that if you keep roaming around this city on your own, you'll end up getting hurt. I was hoping Rico would convince you to take some classes and that would keep you busy. That's why I did what I did."

The Old Lady stopped talking, turned away from me, and walked down the street slower than usual. I could tell her hip was bothering her. Served her right for being such a know-it-all, for thinking she could go behind my back and tell that jerk stuff about me. She should've asked me first 'stead of acting like I was some kind of needy kid like the ones my Grandma took in 'cause their parents were whackos and couldn't take care of them. My mama was taking good care of me. At least she was trying her best.

Anyway, if the old crab would've asked me, I might've surprised her. I might've said yes.

I found out one thing by going to that gym. Those trophies with the Barzetti name on them—I bet they were her boys. So why didn't she brag about 'em, like any normal mother would? Something was wrong with her and I was gonna find out what it was. I decided I better hurry up and not give the old bag a chance to do something else dumb—like croak on me.

A WEEK LATER

The next Sunday morning Uncle Clarence stopped by. People were always giving him stuff, and this time it was a ton of cookies. I decided I'd sell them, and the Old Lady's was gonna be my first stop. I loaded up a few kinds and knocked on her door, smiling my best smile. She oughta be real impressed that I was willing to talk to her and give her a chance to buy some.

"Hey Miss Lena," I said as soon as she opened the door, "You know how a lot of folks around here support the Girl Scouts? I've got four kinds of cookies to sell, but the chocolate covered mints are the best. If you're not sure what you want, I'll give you a sample so you can decide."

"You better bring them in so I can take a good look. And since when did you become a Girl Scout? Here, let me see one of those! And since when did you start calling me Miss Lena?" she said, grabbing the box I was holding out to show her.

Crabby old bag! She probably thought I stole the cookies! Now I was gonna have to tell her what she'd know as soon as she read the label.

"Well," I said, "I'm not exactly a Girl Scout. And these aren't exactly Girl Scout cookies. But they could be, you know, because they taste so good."

"Oh, yeah, so how come I didn't hear you say a thing about similar to or almost like Girl Scout cookies? Are you trying to con people out of their hard-earned money? How'd you come by all these cookies, anyway?"

She was lucky I didn't throw a box of cookies at her. I stood there thinking about how I'd like to more than anything. Just throw a box or two and walk away and never see her again. I might do that but not 'til after she bought some.

"Somebody gave them to my Uncle Clarence. He passed them on to me. He says with my gift for words, I could turn a sale easy."

"Humph! I do imagine he knows a whole lot about selling things he got for free! And I also imagine what he really told you was that you'd be good at reeling in a sucker with your smart mouth. Let me try one of those samples."

I almost bit through my lip to keep from yelling at her. What she said about Uncle Clarence was true, but I wasn't gonna tell her that. I got out my samples and made my first sale.

If she didn't watch out I was gonna stop talking to her again, and then she'd be sorry!

MAUREEN O'ROURKE LEEROYCE

JAMAL

I stared into the bathroom mirror, turning my face first one way and then the other. I couldn't see any wrinkles or brown spots yet—thank God. But what would happen in October when I turned 30? I groaned. Would I have to spend the rest of my life searching for signs of decay and worrying about going downhill?

Turning 30. I couldn't help thinking about how different this birthday would be if Jamal were still alive. We would be planning a fabulous celebration, and he would have teased me out of feeling like I was free-falling into middle age.

I knew exactly what I would have chosen: romantic and intimate, candlelight and gardenias, an overnight getaway, just the two of us.

I never would have chosen anything as scary as he did.

"Come on with me, Sweet Babe of mine," he told me. "I want to see what it feels like to jump out of a plane and float through the clouds. What a rush! We'll hold hands all the way down."

He knew I couldn't resist his gorgeous brown eyes and gentle coaxing. Besides, jumping out of a plane wasn't nearly as terrifying as the way I felt the very first time we met at the beginning of my senior year in high school.

My best friend, Katie, was dating a high jumper, and the last Saturday in September we went to a five-town meet to watch her boyfriend compete.

Every year there was a ceremony to give special awards, and sometimes they'd induct a new member into the district-wide Athletic Hall of Fame. Jamal was that year's honoree. All four years at Cambridge High and Latin he won every event he entered, from sprints to long-distance runs.

Katie and I sat in the front row to watch the presentations. Jamal was on the platform near the podium, and every time I glanced his way, he was staring at me. I could feel my face getting hot, and I knew I was blushing. When he got up to accept the award, I couldn't help but notice the muscles in his brown arms and the easy way he moved with feline grace. If he'd been a white boy, I would have nudged Katie and whispered that he was really sexy.

When the program was over, he pushed through the crowd in his slow, easy way, until he was standing directly in front of me, not closer than was proper, but still close enough that I could feel my body urging me even closer.

"Hey," he said, his voice low, a magnet drawing me in, "What would a guy like me have to do if he wanted to get to know a girl like you?"

I caught my breath, and my heart leaped exactly the way I'd read it would when I met my true love.

I knew that was THE most stupid thought I'd ever had! What if I had accidentally blurted it out? He would have thought I was crazy. There was no possible way a black boy could be my true love.

I knew that was what he meant when he said "a guy like me" and "a girl like you." No girl in my neighborhood would be seen with a black boy. I wasn't even sure Mummie would allow me to have a black girlfriend.

All us kids knew how Mummie felt. When she saw something on TV about troubles blacks were having, she'd say, "Those blacks should stay where they belong, and we'll stay where we belong. If you ever have to work with any of them, you be polite, but don't you think about being anything else. Polite but distant. You remember that, all you kids, you remember that."

I didn't want any trouble, and making friends with a black boy would be the very worst kind of trouble. That's what I was going to tell him.

He waited patiently for my answer, half smiling, while his eyes, those incredible eyes watched me. He was standing so still and seemed so open and vulnerable …

I willed myself to tell him there was absolutely nothing he could do because there was absolutely no way he would ever get to know me.

But the words wouldn't come.

Katie had gone off to find Johnny, and really, I knew I couldn't keep standing there saying nothing like a complete dolt. What if he thought I wasn't answering him because I had a terrible speech defect and didn't want to talk? Oh dear! Another stupid thought! What was the matter with me?

All he said was, he'd like to get to know me.

He asked me a simple question. All I had to do was give him a simple answer. I knew the simple answer Mummie would give him. She'd say I absolutely never could be friends with him.

I never had any reason to think about whether I agreed with her. Until now.

And now that I did, I didn't see why I couldn't have a conversation with him. I mean, we'd just be talking, exchanging a few words. Nothing more.

I remembered all the things the priest and nuns told us when we were preparing for First Communion and Confirmation. The list of do's and don'ts:

We shouldn't be mean to our brothers or sisters. We shouldn't hurt other people, either. We shouldn't lie or steal or say mean things.

We should love each other and be good to each other and help each other.

Because Jesus loved everyone and gave everyone a chance, even people who were leading sinful lives.

I was very, very certain of one thing: Jesus would never tell me not to be friends with someone because his skin wasn't the color of mine.

The crowd was thinning, and someone from the stage crew was folding the chairs on the podium, but neither of us had moved.

I reached down deep inside and pulled out the words, "He'd have to ask."

His laugh was deep and full, and he slapped his hand on his thigh. "That's all? I wouldn't have to slay a dragon or find a treasure or fight off the thundering hoards to prove that I was worthy of you? I might do that, you know, if you asked me to, and especially if you gave me one of your smiles."

I knew for certain I was blushing then. I couldn't stop myself from giggling at his outrageous, charming boldness.

And then he said, "I'm Jamal LeeRoyce. How about having a coffee now? I know a place over near B.U. I went to UMass Boston, but a couple friends of mine went to B.U. so I got to know the area."

Oh! I imagined myself walking off the field with him, getting into his car, sitting at a table with him. All such natural things to do—if he was a white boy.

He was asking me to go to a place I'd never been before.

I knew this was a really, really important decision.

Treat other people the way you would like them to treat you. That's what I'd been taught and that's what I believed. All he was asking me to do was treat him the way I wanted to be treated. How could I say no to that? I hoped no one would ever say they wouldn't be my friend because I was an Irish Catholic white girl.

Jamal had been waiting, again, watching me, giving me time to think it through the way I needed to.

"It will be ok," he said. "I promise I won't take you anywhere you don't want to go." He didn't move closer or reach out and touch my arm the way I thought he might. He simply stood, breathing in and out slowly, waiting.

If I said no, I was certain he would say, "Okay, then," and walk away without looking back. I couldn't let that happen. If I did, I would be turning away ... from what I truly believed was right.

I took a deep breath and said, "I'm Maureen O'Rourke."

Jamal waited near the stands while I found Katie and told her I wouldn't need a ride home.

She and Johnny were joking around with a group of friends, and when I told her, she grabbed my arm and pulled me away from their group. She whispered, "How are you getting home?"

When I didn't answer, she sucked in her breath looking horrified and scared and she squeezed my arm so hard it hurt. "You're not getting in a car with that black boy, are you?"

I didn't answer.

"Oh shit, Maureen! You are, aren't you? Are you crazy? Your mother will KILL you!"

"Katie, please, I'm not doing anything wrong. I'm just going to talk to him. All you need to tell Mummie is that I got a ride home with somebody else."

Katie dropped my arm and said, "I can't believe you'll really do this. Call me and I'll come get you when you change your mind."

But I didn't change my mind.

We didn't say much on the ride to Coffee Grinds. I kept thinking how strange it felt to be riding in a car with a black boy, how different it felt from anything I'd ever done, or thought about doing.

We finally found a parking place and when we went inside, I gasped. The lighting wasn't great, but I could see artwork on every wall: oils, pastels, acrylics, and geometric mobiles hanging from the ceiling.

Everything else was what you'd expect at a coffee house: a few stools looking out the large picture windows onto Huntington Ave., tables for two or four, the coffee counter with a glass snack case, and a whole board of coffee choices on the wall behind it.

Jamal smiled at my surprise. "The arty types hang out here. Back there—on the far wall, you can hang a painting if the owner says OK. She's pretty picky, or so my friends tell me."

I laughed and told him how much I loved art and that I was going to apply to RISD even though Mummie planned for me to go to nursing school at BU.

No one was paying any attention to us. At another table, a black couple leaned toward each other deep in conversation, and a few of what my mother would call "those disheveled, unkempt art students" huddled at the back wall. I could feel myself relaxing.

We talked and talked, until Jamal cocked his head and said, "So, do you have a bewitching hour when I need to get you home?"

Without thinking I blurted out, "Oh my god, you can't take me home! I mean, my mother wouldn't … she would … Oh dear!"

I looked at my watch. "Oh my God, it's 8:00. I have to go now!" I stood up and grabbed my jacket. "Do you think there's a bus to Brighton from here?"

He thought for a minute.

"I doubt it. But how about this? I can drive you to Newton Corner, and you can probably catch a bus on Waverly or call someone to pick you up. Sooo, does this abrupt departure mean I won't see you again? I'd really like to, but if that's something you can't do—or would rather not do …"

I didn't answer him immediately. In fact, I didn't answer him that night. When he dropped me off, I told him I needed time to think, and I'd call him.

"I get that," he said. "But I really hope you'll call no matter what you decide—so I'm not wondering."

I knew I wanted to see him again. But I had to figure out how I could do that without causing a major family blow-up. I was sure Mummie would come around when I told her that he'd graduated from UMass and was working for a tech company that invented medical devices—not as impressive as being a doctor, but in a respectable, growing field. He was polite and clean-cut, and both his parents went to college.

I was going to be the first in my family to do that, and Mummie had been planning that for years. In fact, she had my whole life planned. First, I would graduate from college. Then I'd marry the O'Brien boy and become a lawyer's wife.

Yes, she had my whole life planned, but it was her plan, not mine.

Daddy always told us Mummie was "on the fragile side," and I was afraid of what might happen if I came right out and told her I was going to spend time with a black boy. I needed to prepare her, but I had no idea how to do that.

I decided not to tell her.

I'd meet Jamal for coffee at the Grinds or we'd go to a museum, things like that during the day. I kept telling myself maybe I'd never need to tell her because I wouldn't like him enough to keep seeing him.

Except that I did like him. I liked him more and more, and I wanted to spend more and more time with him.

Katie knew I was sneaking out to meet Jamal, and she told me I was stupid and naive to think Mummie would ever accept him. I wanted her and Johnny to meet him, but she said it would be too uncomfortable. I saw less of her and more of him.

Katie didn't tell Mummie. Mummie ran into her and Johnny at the mall when I'd told Mummie I was spending the day with Katie. It was Johnny who said, "Oh, Maureen's too good for us now that she's spending her time with a spook!"

That night when I got home, Mummie was beside herself—almost hysterical with rage.

She screamed at me. "If the O'Brien boy finds out what you're doing, he'll never consider you! None of the boys from good white families will ever consider you! And it won't just be you. They'll shun our whole family. I won't allow it! Do you hear me, Maureen! I won't allow you to drag us down and destroy everything I worked for."

I thought I could count on Daddy to listen to my side, but that time—the most important time—he didn't. "All you're thinking about is yourself, Maureen. I took your mother out of Southie, but she remembers what it was like to be called white trash like it happened this morning. She dreamed of a better life for the whole family, and that's a thing I love about her. You've got the right to go your own way, but you can't take the rest of the family with you. You'll have to face the consequences on your own. You need to think this through very, very carefully."

Mummie called Father McManus and he told me that I was throwing away such a bright future, and that I had no idea of the difficulties I would face if I keep 'doing what you're doing.'

Mummie never stopped. She said the same things over and over and over again, "I should have known you'd do something like this, Maureen. When you said you were going to be an artist, I should have known. All you think about is yourself. You don't care what a terrible position you put the family in. You bring a person that color into this house, how do you suppose the neighbors will react? I don't know you anymore, Maureen. You're not the daughter I raised."

Maybe she was right. Maybe I had been inching away from being the daughter she raised since way before Jamal came into my life. I didn't want to be a nurse. I didn't want to marry her O'Brien boy. I didn't believe the things she believed. I believed you should give people a chance.

I was going to keep seeing Jamal.

And that meant I wasn't going to be Mummie's shining star. It was like I was crossing a raging river on a narrow, shaky balance beam. I hadn't fallen off, but I wasn't sure if I would make it to the other side, and if I did get there, I had no idea what I would find.

Jamal opened his heart to me. He encouraged me to trust my instincts, to follow my heart. And my heart led me to him.

I knew that made him happy, but he was ever level-headed. "Everybody we know will have something to say about us being together. Friends will drop us—and not just your people. Some of my family and friends will call me a honky lover. And that's just the people we know."

"But they'll come around once they get to know me and once they get to know you. My parents will. I know they will. People aren't that … my family isn't that …"

"Oh sweet babe, you are so dear to me, and you are so naïve. If you and I go on together, you're going to find out how bigoted people can be, and how they will justify themselves any way they can, by twisting religion or history or whatever else. You have to decide if you're willing to be with me no matter what happens. With or without the approval of anyone else."

I respected him so much for saying that. I knew he didn't want me to be hurt. But everything he predicted came true.

The chasm between my parents and me grew deeper and wider, so deep and wide I had no idea how to bridge it. But I never gave up hope, even when my mother went from ranting rage to cold silence.

What should have been my glorious senior year turned into a roller coaster of joy with Jamal and despair at home. My parents weren't ready to build a bridge, and I went on without their blessing or support. I graduated first in my high school class and gave myself the only graduation present I wanted. I married Jamal.

Mummie cut me off the way you would cut off a gangrenous limb.

She wasn't the only one.

Katie didn't return my calls, and her mother told me to stop bothering her.

Jamal never said, "I told you so," but that must have been what he was thinking. He was all I had. It was like we lived on an island all by ourselves.

I took classes at RISD, did my art with Kalayla in her crib nearby, and sometimes we saw his family. I was too afraid to make new friends because I didn't know how they'd react when they found out my husband was black. Concentrating on an art project helped me forget that I felt lonely and isolated. But no matter what, Jamal was always there to encourage me, tease me, make me laugh, and most of all to love me. His strength and courage surrounded and protected me every single minute of every day.

Until it didn't.

It all happened because Clarence saw that ridiculous old movie, "Rebel Without A Cause" and said they HAD to try drag racing. He pushed and pushed and pushed until Jamal finally gave in.

When a tire on Jamal's car blew and he died in the crash, my whole world fell apart. I would never stop missing him. I would never be sorry I married him.

What made me sad and sorry and upset was that my family hadn't been able to see beyond the color of Jamal's skin. I could understand missing Jamal, but why would I miss my family, too? They turned their backs on me, but I couldn't give up the hope that someday that could change. The family gatherings were what I missed most, the times when we were all together.

Mummie would be planning a huge party for my 30th birthday, and deciding if she should bake one or two or three orange crunch cakes, the very best cake in the whole world.

We'd all fill Meme's and Papa's old house, and everyone would be laughing and telling family stories or jokes. Everyone would be interrupting everyone else with, 'No, listen, my story's better.' Like a wonderful jazz improvisation moving seamlessly from one person to the next with everyone included. Uncle Sean would play the Uilleann pipes, sad songs to make us cry, and joyful songs for us to dance …

I closed my eyes, and willed myself to let all those memories go, to let all those wishes go.

I forced myself to focus on today, instead of on what I'd lost or hoped might someday happen.

Kalayla. My baby girl. I would make sure she never felt abandoned the way I did. I would always love her and support her, no matter what choices she made. No matter who she wanted to marry.

I glanced at my watch. Time to go, first to fill in on the early shift at Eddie's and then to a cleaning job.

That was a big, fat joke on Mummie, really. She'd be absolutely horrified to know her precious daughter was cleaning houses, even though she was the one who taught me how to keep a spotless house. She'd put on white gloves when I told her I was done cleaning, and she'd wipe every surface. "This is the proper way to do it, Maureen. There can't be a trace of dust or dirt on the glove. Someday when you have a big house with household staff, you'll hold them to this standard."

Deep in my heart, I knew Daddy would laugh at the irony. But I couldn't, I really could not let myself think about Daddy.

Kalayla was the only one who mattered now.

LENA
MAUREEN'S STORY AND RICO'S CALL

Kalayla could bury the truth in a maze of lies when it suited her, but as far as I could tell, her reactions were as transparent as a newly washed window. When it came to anything about family, she could flare up like a defensive bonfire. Leastways, that's what it seemed like happened when she thought Rico was insulting her mama and daddy.

Maybe that first day on the landing, I should have walked up the stairs without saying boo to that girl. But I didn't. Now I was in the middle of an alphabet soup that was boiling over with letters I couldn't turn into words.

No matter. I was clear as could be about what Rico told me after the fiasco at the gym. I was sitting at the kitchen table with a piece of my friend Carlotta's chocolate raspberry cake and a cup of coffee when the phone rang.

"Miss Lena," Rico said, "I'm so sorry about what happened this morning. I don't know what to tell you. Except what you could see for yourself. Kalayla's got a real chip on her shoulder and I bumped into it at just the wrong angle."

"Well," I said, "you know she's had a hard time, what with losing her father and her mama working two jobs, and the girl has no friends as far as I can tell. What you said set her off, but I was just as shocked at her reaction as you were."

"The thing is, Miss Lena, any kid who comes in, if we're going to teach them a martial art, we've got to find out how they might react under stress. It's kind of like taking in a stray dog and finding out if it'll bite or run or lay down if you give it a shove.

"Sometimes when we push kids—and that could be either physically or emotionally—they turn to mush and blubber. Sometimes they strike back, maybe taunt you, maybe shove you back. BUT, it's rare to find a kid that gives you no warning and charges at you full throttle like Kalayla did. She's got acceleration, but no brakes. And that means somebody better be doing damage control. If you know what I mean."

Damage control. I had a whole lot of experience with that, and it was exactly what I was trying to avoid.

"But on the phone, your dad told me that you teach a lot more than fighting now. There must be something at the gym she'd like. She's said no to everything I suggested."

"Could be there is, but the thing is, Miss Lena, she said no to the gym, too. You can tell a lot by the way kids act. Kalayla was aiming to make a statement, and she didn't like the way I responded to it. A lot of kids storm out the way she did at the end. When they get calmed down, they come back. Some hang around out front, waiting for us to notice. Some come back with a friend. Some come back alone. I'm just saying nobody can force her. Matty's Way isn't the right place for her unless she decides it is."

"But maybe she will. Rico, you've been telling me a lot about 'the thing is this' and 'the thing is that.' The real thing is I've run out of ideas and I was hoping you'd give me some."

"I wish I could. All I know is somebody has to teach her to think before she reacts, or she'll find more trouble than she can handle. From what you're saying, there's nobody to do that."

Oh my, I really wished he hadn't gone and said that. I just really wished he hadn't. Because that's exactly what I was thinking. It was one of the thoughts that had me stuffing my face with a big fat piece of cake.

Good as that cake was, far as I knew, Carlotta hadn't baked any solutions into it. I'd tried a lot of things in my time, but eating my way out of being scared was something new. I shoved the cake away.

I was just an old neighbor woman acting like I knew a whole lot more than I really did. If I closed my door on her, who was going to be there when that girl needed help?

There had to be a way I could teach that girl what I wasn't able to teach my boys.

I had high hopes for all my boys, maybe most of all for my first-born, JJ. Back before he started working with Joey during the summers, he listened to me.

I'd gotten him a tennis racket when he was around seven. He'd go to the city courts and always find somebody who'd show him strokes and discuss strategy. He loved that sport like he'd never loved anything else, and I encouraged him as much as I could. But I never once heard him talking about tennis with his dad, and I never once saw his tennis racket laying around the way his baseball glove might be.

The year JJ went to high school, everything changed for him. That summer before school started, the tennis coach came over to the house one afternoon to talk with him.

"Ma," JJ said after the coach left, "Coach says I'll make varsity, and there's a chance I can play singles. He says if I keep at it, I'll have colleges after me. Is that cool, or what?"

He told Joey that night. His father was sitting at the kitchen table having a beer while I was getting dinner ready. JJ was glowing like a giant firefly lighting up the whole room, telling his dad the news.

Joey sat there, listening, without saying one word, and I could see the light from JJ's fire dim bit by bit, until every single spark died. He stood silent, waiting to hear what he knew his dad was going to say.

And what Joey said was, "I bet your mother got you into tennis, didn't she? Didn't you, Lena? Well, no boy of mine is going to turn into some sissy girl playing tennis. My son plays football, just like I did."

"But Dad," JJ said, "it's too late to join football. They already started practice."

I could hear the tears in my boy's voice, and all I could think was, "Please don't let him cry in front of his dad."

"Don't you worry about that," Joey told him. "I'll talk to Coach tomorrow."

I never knew what Joey said or did to make it happen, but JJ joined the team. And Joey bragged to his friends, "My boy is a natural athlete, just like me. No coach in his right mind would turn him down over something so stupid as starting practice late."

What Joey said was true. JJ was good at any sport. His junior and senior years, he was the star quarterback like his dad had been. JJ seemed happy enough scoring touchdowns, and bragging about the girls who made excuses to drop by the house or call their big football hero on the telephone.

It was more than a year after JJ joined the team that I got the cleaning bug in my head. I found a plastic bag shoved in the back of his bedroom closet, buried under shoes, boots, canvas bags, general junk. I stared at the destruction inside, and finally, it dawned on me. I was looking at the remains of JJ's tennis racket.

What would make a boy smash something he loved so much? If I were telling you about the JJ I tried to raise, I'd say he trashed his racquet along with his dream, and he didn't have the heart to throw it in the garbage. And I'd have cried. If I were telling you about the JJ that Joey raised, I'd say he was keeping it to remind himself never to act like a 'mama's boy' again. And I'd have cried.

I wasn't able to help my boys make good choices, but I might do a better job now without Joey around trashing every word coming out of my mouth. I wished I could ask Lotta for advice, but there was nothing about Kalayla she could tell me that I didn't already know.

The only two who knew more than I did was the girl herself—and she wasn't telling me anything—and her mama. At least Maureen was worth a try. I took myself over to Eddie's and set up a time for her and me to talk at my place.

It was a gloomy enough day already, mid-August steam heat making a person sweat. Rain was threatening, a thunderstorm possible. If I believed in weather as a genuine omen of what was to come, I might have thought more about what I was doing before I went ahead and did it.

When Maureen came over, she flopped right down on the sofa, and started talking non-stop like she was desperate for somebody who'd listen.

What got her started was that I said, "Well, I guess what I wanted to say is that I'm worried about Kalayla."

"Oh, Lena, I'm just so glad you want to talk. I know she spends a lot of time with you and all I do is worry about her, what she might be doing and I worry about taking care of her. I mean, you know, if I'll be able to take care of her. I don't have professional skills so I can get a better job. And after my breakdown, I just had to do something. Oh, I guess you didn't know, but I had a breakdown after Jamal died and we—Kalayla and I—had to live with my in-laws and it was awful because I just couldn't get hold of myself and …"

"Slow down, girl! Just slow yourself down. You're going too fast for this old brain."

Maureen paused for about five seconds, took a deep breath and charged on, "Oh, okay. So, I had this breakdown, you know, because Jamal was all

I had. I mean, except for Kalayla. And I couldn't cope, so Jamal's mother said we could live with them, and I wouldn't have to go to a hospital or a sanitarium or some other awful place, and Kalayla could go to school.

"She hated that school, well really, she hates every school, so it wasn't just that school. And Lucinda, that's Jamal's mother, really, she was very good to us, but she's a very scary person. I mean, if she ever came face to face with the devil, I think he'd turn and run."

I couldn't help but laugh even though she was being so serious, and after a minute, she laughed, too.

I guess there was so much bottled up in Maureen, when she popped the cork, it was all bound to spill out every which way. Best thing I could do was keep my mouth shut and listen.

"Well, it's true. Lucinda was the one who scared me into being normal again. She came into the bedroom one day—I was spending lots of time in bed. Really, I was spending most of the time there.

"Anyway, she came into the bedroom and she said, 'Maureen, I have been patient with you because I know this is a terrible shock. But you are not the only one who lost Jamal. I did, and so did your daughter. You've left that girl all on her own, and I'm beginning to wonder if you've forgotten about her. In fact, I'm beginning to wonder if maybe God means for me and Harmon to be the ones to raise her. If you can't get out of that bed and face your responsibility to her, I'm thinking she'll be living here with us permanently.'

"Can you imagine how I felt? My heart was pounding, and I got so hot I was sure I had a fever, but I didn't dare say a word. I knew Lucinda meant exactly what she said. She would take Kalayla away from me, and then what would I do?

"And then Lucinda just walked out of the bedroom and closed the door. And I was afraid that meant she might be closing the door on me for good.

"I had to do something, but I didn't even know where Kalayla was. I got out of that bed and got cleaned up and dressed as fast as I could.

"I couldn't let her take Kalayla. I couldn't let anyone take her. You're a mother, Lena. You know I couldn't do that. I lost my family and Jamal and I couldn't lose her, too. I went out into the living room, and there was Clarence, sprawled out on the sofa like he had nothing in the world to do.

"When I asked him where Kalayla was, he snorted and said, 'Since when do you care?' And I thought, oh, my God, they all think I'm a terrible mother. I told Clarence right then I was going to take Kalayla home where she belonged—where I belonged.

"He smirked and said, 'She's in school, where she's been every day since they brought you here. You haven't figured out how things work in this family yet, have you, Maureen? You don't get to take up space and not give back. In case you didn't realize it, I'm the only one that gets a pass on that and I don't have to pay for that privilege. But you, my lovely one, have used up your idleness credits, and your bill has come due.'"

I shook my head, but Maureen probably had no idea why. If that man was looking after Maureen and Kalayla, there had to be something in it for him. He sure wasn't trying to earn points toward an Uncle of the Year Award.

"I went right to the school," Maureen went on, "and I picked up Kalayla, and I took her home, back to our apartment.

"When I opened the door, I almost couldn't make myself go in. It felt so lonely and scary without Jamal, and really, I had to force myself to stay because Kalayla was so happy. She ran right to her room, and well, she was just so happy. And the truth was, there was no place else we could go."

I nodded. It sounded to me like she'd pegged that Lucinda just right, but I sure couldn't blame the grandmother for saying what she did.

"And that was when you got a job and moved?"

"I got the job right away, but we didn't move until this apartment came up. Eddie told me about it and everybody at work has been so nice—and you have, too. And since we got the car, I'm making more money and that really helps. And besides ..."

I could have been listening to her talk all day, but I told myself there was no point in all my listening if I let her ignore the elephant that was living in her apartment. Because if I did, at some point that elephant would be ambling across the hall and moving in with me.

I decided the only way to find out what I wanted to know was to come right out and ask. So I did, "What about your family?"

She pulled her knees up to her chest and hugged them, burying her face without saying a word.

Be that as it may, I was past the point of waiting and not about to give up. I asked again, "What about your family?"

Her voice was muffled, and my old ears strained to hear what she was saying. "My mother … my mother … disowned me when I married Jamal. Because he was black. But I didn't believe she really meant it to be forever. I was sure she was punishing me and she'd forgive me. When I found out I was pregnant, I was so certain she'd want to know, and I was so excited, I just had to tell her.

"Jamal warned me not to. He said, 'I'm afraid it won't work out the way you hope, Sweet Babe.'

"And he was right. I was too scared to go to the house, so I called. My mother answered, and I blurted out the news and she … she didn't say anything at first. And then she said … and then she said, 'I don't have a daughter named Maureen,' and she hung up. She hung up and for the first time, I realized maybe she really did mean forever."

Now I'd heard the story from those old lady knitters, but listening to them was a lot easier than listening to that child's heartbreak. I took a few deep breaths and let it sink in: Maureen was a child, too, older than Kalayla, but just as much in need of a mama.

I went over and sat down next to her and put my arm around her. She started in crying, and I had tears running down my own face. The two of us together must have been a real sight.

Her parents had done a terrible thing, but I couldn't see how that explained the ridiculous story that Kalayla told me about them being blown up.

So, I asked, "Why does Kalayla think your family is dead?"

She groaned, lifting her head, torture on her face. "Because that's what I told her. And I have to tell her the truth. I always knew I'd have to. And it was so hard on Jamal. But I didn't know what to say. How could I tell her my mother disowned me because I married Jamal? How could I tell her that her own grandmother didn't want to meet her, that her own grandmother refused to acknowledge that Kalayla was her granddaughter? I couldn't bear it.

"But I never intended to lie about it. When she was little we didn't need to tell her anything about my family. And then one day, it just happened. She was four years old, and we had just come home from Christmas breakfast at Jamal's parents. I'd unhooked her seat belt, and she squirmed out of the car, telling me she didn't need any help. She was so adorable in her bright red snowsuit and so proud of her new red and green plaid snow boots.

"I was collecting presents out of the car when she skipped back and looked up at me in that intense way she has sometimes. And she said, 'Do you have a mama and daddy?'

"I almost died right then. Jamal was half out of the driver's seat, but he slumped back down without saying anything, and I couldn't see his face. I knew he was waiting for me to answer, but all I could do was stare at her.

"Until she tugged on my arm and said, 'Mama!'

"Then I said, 'Well, of course I do, Layla. Everybody does.'

"Her huge green eyes wide open, trusting me as she said, 'Are we going to their house today? 'Cause I wanna build a snowman first.'

"Thank goodness her attention shifted and she began jumping up and down, kicking the snow with her new boots, laughing, impatient to be off.

"I was paralyzed, Lena. And then, all of a sudden, the words came out. I don't know how it happened. I didn't decide what to say. I just blurted out, 'We can't go to their house, Layla. We can't ever go to see them because my mommy and daddy are dead.'

"And once I got started, I kept going. It was like someone pressed PLAY on a recording, and I couldn't stop it or pause it.

"My parents were giving your daddy and me a huge wedding party, and everybody was there early except daddy and me. There was a huge explosion, and my whole family—every one of them—was killed. Of course, we'd go visit if they were alive. They'd love you so much and they'd give you lots of presents and …"

'Oh, okay,' Kalayla said, without waiting for the recording to end. 'I'm going to make my snowman.'

"And she stomped off, scattering snow with each step. Jamal got out of the car and, Lena, the way he looked, it was awful. He walked right past me into the house and I didn't know what to do. I wanted to run and hide, but I made myself follow him.

"He was in the living room, pacing back and forth. It scared me, Lena, really scared me to see him looking so—I can't really describe it. He just looked horrified and shocked and sad all at once, and I knew it was because of me. Because of what I said.

"He shook his head and the way his eyes looked at me—so accusing and I knew he was angry. 'Why would you tell our beautiful, precious daughter such an outrageous lie?'

"And I felt so guilty and stupid and I said, 'But Jamal, you saw what happened. I didn't have any time to think. I didn't plan it out. She probably didn't even believe it. She's building her snowman. She doesn't even care.'

"He stood there with his hand on his hips and total disbelief on his face. 'Damn it all, Maureen! You've had five years to think about this day. Kalayla is four years old! Of course, she believes it. She'd believe anything you told her. And what are you going to tell her—that you made it up on the spur of the moment? I get that you have a really hard time facing the fact that your parents are racists. And I get the fact that you are possessed by the idea that they can change, but at some point Kalayla is going to ask questions. And then you won't just have to explain what your parents did. You'll have to explain why you lied.'

"I, I'll just tell her the truth, that I was stupid and afraid and I didn't know what to say."

"'Stop. Please, stop, Maureen. I can't listen anymore.'"

"He turned away from me and he went out the front door and he didn't come back that night. I have no idea where he went. I didn't dare call his parents or Clarence, and there was no one else to call. I was frantic and terrified, and when Kalayla asked where Daddy was, I didn't know what to tell her, so I said he'd be home soon and she should go play in her room.

"He came home the next afternoon, and it was so awful because he looked haggard, and exhausted and beaten down. And he looked so, so sad. He didn't take my hand or call me his Sweet Babe or anything.

"He walked into the kitchen, and I followed him, and we sat there at the table. He leaned over the table, his head in his hands. 'I don't know how we can fix this, Maureen. I'm not sure that we can.' He closed his eyes. I knew he wasn't done talking and I was too afraid to say anything.

"Finally, he looked up at me. 'I love you, Sweet Babe. The first time I saw you, I fell in love with you. I knew it would be hard for us to be together and I never pushed you, because I knew you'd have to be sure. I thought that if our love was deep enough, we'd be able to deal with all the shit that would be thrown at us. I never thought we'd have to face anything like this. But somehow, we will have to.'

"He sighed and shook his head, 'I will not put our daughter in the middle by telling her that you lied. Things are going be hard enough for her. She didn't choose to have a black father and a white mother, but that's what she got. And that's what she'll have to deal with her whole life. Now your lie is added on, but you can fix that right now, today. You can make up a story about why you said what you did, and she'll believe you. You can fix it now.'"

Maureen got quiet then, her arms still wrapped around her legs. And then she said, "Jamal was right, but I was afraid I'd lose her no matter what I told her."

Her green eyes, the mirror image of Kalayla's, were pleading for understanding. What could I tell her? That I had created an unbelievable, incredible, horrible mess? How would that help? I finally said, "You show her every day the kind of person you are—and she obviously loves you. When the time comes, that should count for something."

"But Lena, that's probably what my mother thought, that she was showing me every day how to live the kind of life she wanted me to—and look how that worked out for her. What if Kalayla is like me? What if she turns out to be the opposite of what I hoped she'd be? What if she hates me and I lose her? I couldn't bear that."

I understood why she was afraid. I'd lost a husband, and I'd lost children, and for certain the loss of a child was worse. My boys were my flesh and blood, inside the womb and after they left it. Always and forever part of me. Losing them was losing part of myself.

And not one of my boys turned out the way I hoped. I truly had no answer for her. She was living with a long list of 'what if's,' and every single one meant the end of the safe haven she and Jamal hoped to build for each other and for Kalayla.

I remember when I was a girl and my family took us to the beach in the summer. Every time the tide came in and went out, the waves reshaped the sand. We'd build sand castles and forts, and then come back and find the angles smoothed out, the walls partly gone, or maybe nothing at all would be left. Those waves showed me nothing was forever.

Lotta used to ask me why I refused to see what kind of man Joey was. It wasn't that I couldn't see. I just couldn't believe what I was seeing was forever.

And Maureen, the woman-child curled up next to me, staked everything on the hope her parents could change, would change. She and I both thought if we held tight to our beliefs, everything would work out fine. Now I know we can't force people to change any more than we can force them to stay the same.

Here I was thinking that finding something to fill up Kalayla's time would keep her out of harm's way. Now I knew there was no way to keep her safe. Wandering on her own around Cambridge might hurt her, but what was coming at her from her own mama—that hurt could be a lot worse.

And there was no way I could stop it. When she found out the truth … well, Lotta said it straight out the way she always did: when Kalayla found out the truth, there would be hell to pay.

All I could do was be there when it happened. Be there for Kalayla. Be there for her mama. I'd do my best and pray it would be enough.

FALL 1999

LENA

WAITING AND THINKING

Sitting here, staring out the window and drinking coffee wasn't accomplishing much besides giving my plumbing exercise, and I was getting pretty tired of that. Even though darkness was squeezing out daylight on both ends now, the days felt a lot longer because I didn't have to guard Kalayla while she was guarding Clean Duds.

It wasn't like I had nothing to do. I still played an active role in the family business, but when I turned 70, I promised myself I'd cut my official work down to one day a week, plus Board meetings. I figured that would set a good example for Dominic, who was almost 73 at the time and still going in every day. In spite of the fact the younger generation was perfectly capable of taking over—we'd been training them for some time—neither of us was eager to close the door of Manzetti Properties behind us.

I could always fill the time by volunteering more hours at Helping Hands, but the bottom line was I was too busy worrying to fit in much of anything else.

Kalayla was back in school, and you'd think my worrying would have eased up since her time for cruising the streets was cut short. But facts are facts: you let a child into your life, and there was no end to worrying.

It was like fireworks on the 4th of July. You'd always read about batches of them being recalled because they might explode when you least expected it or when they weren't supposed to. You couldn't trust fireworks and you couldn't trust Kalayla. If she blew up, anybody around her might get hurt—including me.

Now, say for the sake of saying it, she did manage to keep herself together when she found out about her mama's family. That wouldn't be the end of my worrying.

No matter what kind of metal detector and guards the schools put in, there was no guarantee some kid wouldn't figure out a way to turn a safe place into a horror scene the way those two nut cases did in that Colorado school.

Her mama was cause for another kind of worry. What if Maureen decided to curl up and tunnel inside herself like she did when her husband died? She would be leaving Kalayla on her own again, and what was I going to do then?

My grand schemes for catastrophe prevention were a bust, but I wasn't about to take Lotta's advice and kick Kalayla and her mama out of the apartment.

Instead of that, I was imagining what might be coming and thinking about what was long over. The point being, I had way more time to think than I needed. Maybe I should go back to working full time. I had no trouble at all making business decisions. When it came to personal decisions, Lotta always said I spent too much time deciding and way too little doing. I was never able to treat my personal life like a business deal, and I always envied that Lotta could do that. If I'd been more like her, I might have gone to divorce court right off in spite of the Catholic Church and my family. But then I got pregnant, and any hope of leaving was gone forever.

It didn't take me long to find out what a fool I was to think that our marriage would be everything I dreamed. The illusion of him as the perfect husband crumbled almost immediately.

Joey was a lot of things, but stupid wasn't one of them. When we first got married, he explained my bruises and scrapes with a laugh and joked that marriage had turned me into a hopeless klutz. It wasn't long after our wedding that he decided he wanted to add some spice to his life. That spice was any number of other women. He was very good about hiding what he called his condiments from everybody except me. He wanted me to know what he was doing. One time when I was sick with the flu, he took one of them to a friend's party and introduced her as his cousin visiting from Milwaukee. He asked me if I wanted to meet her in case anyone asked me about his cousin. No one suspected, or at least they never mentioned it to me. Then again, why would they? Joey could do anything he wanted without paying a price.

I hated the bruises, and then the ugly, discolored skin. I'd always loved wearing shorts and halters, but that first summer I wore long sleeves and slacks, even when the temperature hit the 90's.

Lotta pointed out the absurdity when she saw me sweating in the sweltering heat. "What the hell, Lena. Is this your version of a cheap sauna?"

I shrugged it off. "My doc said the sun aggravates my skin and might be causing the bruises so I should cover up. Weird, huh?"

Lotta looked at me like I had three heads, and I knew I hadn't heard the end of it. At the time, she was dating a cop who told her a pattern of bruises and falls didn't happen by accident. He told her anybody who said they did was full of shit. She came charging over to my house with that little snippet of information. "So, Lena," she asked, "Does that mean you're full of shit, or what?"

I shrugged that off, too.

When I told Joey what Lotta said, he laughed. "Somebody needs to teach Lotta to mind her own business. But don't you worry. I know a way to make us both happy. You'll be able to wear shorts and I'll ... well, you'll see, won't you?" He slapped my butt and laughed again.

Joey meant he'd be able to hurt me without leaving tell-tale evidence like bruises. That night was my first experience with pressure points. His big joke was to call me his guinea wife. He laughed when he said, "Get the joke, Lena? You're like the guinea pigs they use in laboratories. And you're all mine!"

He took pleasure experimenting to find the spots that caused me the most pain. The first time I fainted scared him enough that after that he would ask me, "Not going to pass out on me, are you, Lena?" That was fifty years ago, but the memory still makes me shudder.

JJ was a year and a half and I was pregnant with Mark when I told my mother what Joey was doing to me. I'd tried everything I could think of, bought whatever Victoria's Secret was advertising, learned to cook Greek and French food, done everything he wanted in bed, but none of it had changed the way he treated me.

I didn't think I could stand it any longer, and I was sure my mother would help me get away from him.

What my mother did was wipe my tears and sit me down next to her. "Oh, Lena," she said, "my poor baby girl. I thought you understood what marrying Joey meant. I thought you understood your marriage cemented a business partnership with blood ties. I wish you could leave, sweetheart, but your dad and Joey's dad wouldn't stand for it. And you know that Joey would never let you.

"You have to make the best of it. I can't help you get out, but I can help you stay in. You come to me when you understand that's the way it has to be."

I had no idea what she was talking about. I left my mother's house, went home, and called Lotta. When she came over, I told her everything about how Joey hurt me. But I couldn't bring myself to tell her about UG's.

Lotta was sure we could run from him, sure we could take JJ and hide. Except that neither of us had a clue how to do that, and neither of us realized how easy it would be to trace two women with a toddler, one of them pregnant. We thought we'd be safe at a Holiday Inn near Greenfield.

It took Joey less than twelve hours to find us. He sent Lotta home with a warning, but he told me I just proved how much I needed a 'real' lesson in obedience. That was one of the worst times, and when it was over, he said, "Maybe I should introduce Lotta to UG's. You know, take her there with us. Once I get her in the right mood with booze and a pill or two, she'll love it. I could think of lots of things to do with her while you watch. And if she gives me any trouble, she can go to obedience school along with you."

UG's. I've tried to bury the memories of that place and time but even now, all these years later, I feel disgust and shame.

We'd been married a month when Joey said it was time he took me to his favorite hangout over in Somerville. It was mid-July, on an evening that smelled like rain, and I was still a blissful, ignorant bride. We parked on a street lined with ordinary brick office buildings, a couple of upscale restaurants, and a pizza joint. Nothing flashy or garish, nothing that gave any hint of what was to come.

Joey put his arm around my waist as we walked from the car, running his fingers over my hip, pulling me close. When he turned us into the building, I looked up. The streetlight lit up a discreet sign that said 'UG' in tasteful white letters on a black background.

"UG? That's a funny name. What does it stand for, Joey?"

Joey laughed and hugged me. "UG stands for Underground and that means private. We can do whatever we want anyway we want—same as we can at home, with some bonuses thrown in! You'll see!"

A tall, muscular doorman in jeans and a black polo shirt grinned and winked as he said, "Hey Joey."

The entrance foyer was dimly lit but nothing unusual compared to the eerie lighting that engulfed us as we passed through a second door and into a room where strobe lights slowly circled the otherwise dark space. Languid, sensual music paced the movements of undulating dancers on a runway in the center of the room, each hugging a pole.

"Joey," I gasped, "those girls are practically naked."

Joey laughed as he moved his hand from my hip to my breasts, "You're not a mama's girl anymore, Lena. You belong to me, and this is what I like."

He steered me to a horseshoe booth, its heavy velvet drapes partly open. We sank into deep velvet cushions, enclosed in a private, erotic world. A waitress in tight shorts and bra top brought us drinks, his in a short tumbler, mine in a taller one. "A margarita special for you," he smiled. "You'll love it."

Glued together, we watched the dancers and I could feel myself moving with them, the alcohol dissolving my resistance to … anything. Joey pulled me onto his lap, stretched my body out on the cushions so I was facing the dancers.

"No more holding back, Lena," he said, breathing into my ear, running his hand circling my pelvis as I moved with the music.

"But Joey, this is … people can see us … I don't want to …"

I could feel his hardness pressing into me as he slid his hand under my skirt, under my panties, breathing into my ear, whispering, "Oh yeah, Lena, come on. Let yourself turn inside out."

When I tried to squirm away, he yanked me around and breathed into my face. "Don't you fight me, Lena."

That night I did. And that was the first time I saw what Joey was like when he lost his temper. He slapped my face so hard my ears rang and then he dragged me out of UG's and when we got home, he beat me.

A few weeks later, Joey said I was ready for the "next phase." He said it didn't matter if I didn't like it. He said if I wouldn't give him what he wanted, I'd have to watch other women do it. It was humiliating and shameful, and there was no way I could stop him except to give in. And I refused to do that.

Joey had more in mind than his personal pleasure. We were on the way to UG's when he explained his plan. Even now I feel anger boiling up, and that night it was a miracle we didn't have an accident. I screamed and launched myself at him, fists flailing but it did no good. He invited his business associates one at a time, the privileged few, to a private room at UG's. The chosen guest got to sample the women along with Joey. While I watched.

Sometimes now when I'm sitting in my spare room looking out the window across to Eddie's, shame washes over me when I remember how helpless I felt in those days. I told Joey I didn't care if he went, but I didn't want to go, he laughed and said, "Tough shit, Lena. This is the 'obey' part of our marriage vows. And you're going to obey one way or another."

Being pregnant was what saved me. No matter how he might hurt me, he had no intention of hurting his potential heir once he could see the evidence from my growing stomach. After each birth, he made up for his restraint.

What a fool I was. Joey owned me, and every man he invited to join us. He'd hidden three cameras to record these secret pleasures. "Leverage in case I ever need it," he told me. Leverage. I knew all about that. He used to taunt me when I came home after Mama and I had gone to church on Sunday or whenever I went to confession. "Bet you didn't confess ALL your sins, Lena, dear. What do you think? Should I tell your mother about UG's?"

The week after Lotta and I had tried to run away, I managed to sneak out to see her while Joey was at work. The first thing she said when she saw me was, "We have to kill him, Lena. There's no other way. You'll never get away otherwise."

"I can't do that, Lotta. I could never kill him. He's the father of my children."

"Bullshit to that! Even if you are a fool, I'm not. I'll kill him myself."

"No, Lotta, please. Don't even talk like that." She had no idea what Joey would do to her and do to me if we tried and failed.

"Don't worry. If you won't help me, I won't have to do it alone. I'll get Mattwo to help us. He's always known what an ass Joey is. Besides, he was in love with you, Lena. You know that."

"Dear God, no, Lotta! If Mattwo went after Joey, one of them would end up dead. Maybe both of them. You know what that would do to the families. Please, please don't tell him."

Lotta closed her eyes and clenched her fists, knowing what I said was true and hating it. "What am I supposed to do? You think I can forget what he does to you?"

"If I can live with it, you can forget it. Just be my friend, Lotta. Please, that's all I need. You're the only one I have."

And she was, the only one I had besides my mother.

When I went to see my mother, I didn't have to tell her why I'd come. We went into her sitting room and when she closed the door, I knew we were going into forbidden territory. There were to be no closed doors in the family house. That was our father's rule, and his word was law. None of us kids cared when we were little, but privacy was important in our teen years. That didn't matter. We knew better than to argue.

If our father ever closed the door to his study, we knew something serious was happening that couldn't wait. Regular business was done at the two-story building in Allston that we called 'Home Base.' If you didn't blink, you might see the building as you whizzed by on the Mass. Pike. It would strike you as ordinary, an old brick office building with a small sign on the front door: Manzetti Properties. The offices and Board Room were modestly furnished, no flashy show of power or money. Anyone who did business with us understood that was camouflage.

Behind that closed door, my mother said, "I knew you'd come eventually," and then she laid out her plan for me clearly and simply. "You need to take an active part in the business, Lena. You need to make yourself indispensable. You're smart and charming, so they'll humor you at the beginning. And later, after you've built your power base, they'll respect you, but more importantly, they'll fear you.

"Insist on having an office in Home Base—next to Dom would be best because he'll help you. Continue searching out properties. Learn the business inside and out. Learn the markets. Get every scrap of information about clients. That will give you leverage."

I had to clench my fists. "Joey taught me about leverage."

My mother frowned. "Oh, not that crude kind of leverage! You'll find far more subtle ways once you set your mind to it. Don't let them tell you otherwise. Never, ever sell yourself short. And never ever lose sight of the fact that there is never a need to flaunt real power."

I did what she said. Quietly. Seamlessly. And if I do say so myself, shrewdly. With her advice when I needed it.

My success in the business didn't make Joey treat me any differently, but it showed me what I could do without his help—and often without his knowledge.

There were rare times when I was alone that I'd get sentimental and wonder how different my life would have been if I'd said yes to Carlotta's younger brother, Mattwo, back in high school. Joey and I were going steady before Mattwo got a chance to tell me how he felt.

Mattwo had never been under Joey's spell the way I was, the way everyone was. He tried to warn me what Joey was really like, but I wouldn't listen. It was obvious he cared about me, but I was a hotshot senior while he was a mere junior. But Joey, Joey was any girl's dream: star quarterback, president of the senior class, a modern version of Michelangelo's statue David. He was always bragging about us going steady, bragging that his girl had been the most beautiful May Queen ever and was going to be the most beautiful Homecoming Queen, too.

And I loved being in the center of his spotlight.

The fall of my senior year, Mattwo made varsity football as tight end. I was head cheerleader, so hanging around with him before or after games seemed natural enough. After all, I'd known him forever.

Maybe I was dropping by Lotta's more often than usual when I thought he'd be home. Not trying to lead him on … or maybe trying to do exactly that.

Things between Mattwo and Joey boiled over after the last game of the season when we won the city championship. The guys in the locker room said the two of them had an "all in" fight and had to be dragged apart.

All the kids thought the fight was over something that happened in the game. That made sense if you didn't know Mattwo.

It was fourth quarter with two minutes to go, and the game was tied 14-14. Mattwo got around every defender and was wide-open, waiting for the pass. Joey knew Mattwo could catch anything, and so did everybody else. Kids in the bleachers were jumping up and down screaming, sure that we'd win the game.

Instead of making the easy pass to Mattwo, Joey, as only he could, threw a near impossible pass, low and through blockers to Butch, who caught it as he was taken down two yards from the goal line. We scored on the next play, and won the championship for the third year in a row. Joey told everyone he was forced to make the harder pass because he hadn't seen Mattwo waiting in the open. Mattwo called him a liar, and that's what started the fight. The kids got down on Mattwo and said he started the fight because he was jealous that Joey was the hero of the game.

When Mattwo came over later in the weekend, I found out the truth.

The porch at my parents' house wrapped around from front to back. Two swings on either side of the front door were large enough for four. Mattwo and I sat on a smaller, more private one near the back of the house.

Sitting next to Mattwo made it easy to see the difference between him and Joey. Joey was the polished and smooth David, Mattwo was rough and earthy like Marlon Brando in *On the Waterfront.*

I pulled Joey's letter sweater close around me in the November chill. Or maybe it was Mattwo's words that brought the chill. He and Lotta were the same when it came to saying things straight out.

"The fight didn't have a damn thing to do with the game," Mattwo told me. "It was because Joey is an asshole. You oughta stop going with him, Lena. The way he talks about you . . . you shouldn't put up with his bullshit."

"Mattwo, come on. I know he brags about me all the time. Why should I mind that?"

"Yeah, well, you won't be so happy to find out what he was bragging after the game. He started in saying how excited you are to be Homecoming Queen, how beautiful you ..."

"He says that all the time, Mattwo. Why would that upset me?"

"Because that's not all he was saying. He told the guys you were even prettier without your clothes and twice as hot. He told the guys he could do anything he wanted to you. Even if that is true, even if you ... He should have kept his mouth shut about it. All he wanted to do was impress the guys. Fucking asshole!"

I felt sick to my stomach. I couldn't deny Joey had seen me in my panties and bra, but I couldn't admit it to Mattwo. And I knew saying anything to Joey would make things worse. He'd know Mattwo must have been the one to tell me because no one else would dare.

The swing moved a little as the wind picked up, a cardinal flew by and Bailey, the neighbor's dog, barked when a car door slammed. Clear and simple things.

The life that I imagined for myself was just as simple and clear. What Mattwo said turned everything complicated and murky. What could I tell him? He was waiting for me to say something. And I knew he was waiting because he wanted me to be his girl, not Joey's. For a split second I could feel myself lean toward him. If I slide my hand into his ...

Was it fear that yanked me back or the fact that I was caught up in the illusion of a perfect life with Joey? I hugged the side of the swing and squeezed my hands together. "We're getting engaged at Christmas," I told him. "The two businesses are merging. Mom and Dad worked out those details and Mom has already checked off half the bullets on her plan for the wedding. We'll get married after graduation in June."

Mattwo's face turned into a blank mask. He took a deep breath, and I could see him swallow before he said, "OK, then."

He got up, squared his shoulders, and walked to his car. He pulled out of the driveway slowly, and I sat there watching, until he was out of sight.

Too many memories, too much thinking, that's what I was doing. An old woman replaying a turning point that happened as fast as the flip of a coin at the beginning of a football game and determined the rest of my life. Shame on me for wasting time thinking about what was over and done and couldn't be fixed.

There's no way you can stop people from making mistakes no matter how much you want to. I couldn't stop myself. I don't know why I thought I could stop anybody else. I guess because I did learn one big thing. I learned that sometimes if you get help, you can help yourself.

Mattwo would have given me a way out, but there was not one thing he could do when I refused to take it. Thank God in the end I didn't say no to Dom and Lotta and my mother. When I turned into a drunk and tried out gutter life after the twins died in Vietnam, Dom was there, and my mother was there, and Lotta was there. All of them dragged me back from the abyss.

Lotta still took pleasure in reminding me how much I aggravated her back then.

Well, these days the one I was aggravating was myself. Staring out the window, drinking coffee, and reliving the past. Sweet Jesus, old woman, if you're going to do something, get on with it!

If the disaster I was predicting when Kalayla found out about Maureen's lie came to pass, I better start rigging up a shit shelter on the apartment house roof. Now.

KALAYLA

MY GREAT IDEA

Mama had a thing about her birthday. She acted like the world was coming to an end every time she had a birthday. When I told her that was stupid, she said, "Birthdays are for kids."

As if she knew anything about it! I was used to kids at school whispering about what they were doing for their birthday parties, like going to a gym and jumping on trampolines or going to some movie or going to a Patriots game. Dumb stuff like that. I never bothered to listen.

Every year Mama wanted to give me a birthday party and she'd ask me who I wanted to invite. Duh! Every year she got the same hurt look when I told her I hated birthday parties and I wasn't ever having one and wasn't ever going to one. I decided when March came around next year, I was gonna tell her to invite the Old Lady and Eddie for cake and ice cream just to shut her up about cow turds parties.

What got me going on birthdays was Mama's thirtieth was coming up. When Daddy turned 30, he and Mama acted like it was a BIG deal. He talked Mama into jumping out of an airplane. Clarence was always the one talking Daddy into stuff like that and making Mama half whacko, but jumping out of a plane was Daddy's own idea.

When I told the Old Lady what Mama said about her birthday, she started going on about how women shouldn't be pressured into feeling like they had to stay young forever. Ha! Now I knew why she kept that white mop on the top of her head, and didn't wear makeup, and always wore black! She didn't want to feel pressured. Sometimes she was as dumb as Mama.

Anyway, I knew Mama was sad 'cause she couldn't be spending time on her art and I decided throwing a big party for her over at Eddie's would cheer her up. There'd be lots of people and food, and I was thinking up ideas to make it real special for her.

After Daddy got himself killed, Mama told me I should ask him for help when I needed it 'cause he'd always be here in spirit. I wasn't gonna talk to any dead people even if they were my daddy, but I bet Mama probably asked him and her family for help all the time. So I decided her family would have to be part of the party—somehow. That was easy to do with Daddy 'cause I had plenty of photos of him and me and Mama to put up over at Eddie's, but I didn't have any of her family. I'd never seen a photo of anyone in her family.

Which really pissed me off. I bet most kids knew their grandparents and cousins and aunts and uncles and had seen pictures of them, too. So why hadn't I? All Mama ever told me was how much everybody in her family would've loved me. Yeah, well what good was that? They were all dead. Mama should've thought about what it was like for me not knowing anything about her family. She should've showed me photos and told me stuff about 'em.

When I was about five and we were over Grandma LeeRoyce's house, Grandma told Mama she was going to a funeral the next day and then gonna stop by to pay her respects at the grave. So on the way home, I asked Mama when we were gonna go to her family's graves to pay our respects.

She turned on her tear faucet, and I thought she was never gonna shut it off. Which is why I quit asking about them.

I did know that her whole family was Irish, and I started thinking about how I could fit that into the party. I looked up stuff about Ireland and found out the Irish flag was green and white and orange. I figured we could use green, white, and orange balloons and streamers to decorate Eddie's.

I was hoping the Old Lady would help with my next idea. I was sure not even a real whacko would toss family photos in the garbage. I bet anything Mama still had some, but what the heck did she do with 'em? The Old Lady had a way of getting information you didn't want to give, and she might be able to trick Mama into telling her. And then I'd get a bunch of 'em blown up and put them all around Eddie's. It'd be like having her family celebrate with us.

I went over to tell the Old Lady my ideas and to get some of her lemonade. I wouldn't mind having a few of the cookies I sold her. She told me she bought the six boxes "out of kindness," so I'd be less likely to get in trouble "for peddling fake and possibly stolen goods." At least she didn't make a fuss about paying cash. A couple people wanted to give me a check, but I wasn't gonna take a chance on that. Clarence explained all about how people would try and stiff me, so I needed to think two steps ahead and outsmart 'em.

The old lady was drinking her coffee and eating a cookie when I started explaining my idea about the photos.

I barely got a word out before she doubled over coughing like she was gonna throw up her guts. I jumped up, knocked over my lemonade, and the stupid stuff splashed all over my good sweatpants. It'd be just like her to go croak on me! I yelled, "Turds! I'm calling 911!"

The second she heard me say 911, she sat up and started waving her arms around and shaking her head 'no'.

She kept coughing like she must've got a cookie stuck in her throat, so I gave her a good whack on the back like Mama did when I was little and got chips stuck in my throat.

She shoved me away—hard. I mean real hard. That pissed me off because she was gasping and coughing, and anybody with half a brain could tell she needed a good whack!

"Leave ... me ... alone ... Give me ... a chance ... to catch ... my breath!"

I wasn't in the habit of doing what she told me to, but I figured she might get worse if I didn't. I stood next to her watching real close and waited about a year while her face went from bright red to the usual pasty old white and she finally quit coughing.

While I was sitting there being all patient and obedient and cooperative—which she always said I was not—I decided she might've looked like she was weak, but she sure wasn't.

I used to think she might take a fit and fall over flat if I talked back too much or gave her a dirty look the way I usually wanted to. Fat chance! She practically knocked me on my butt!

When she seemed about back to normal, I said, "You want me to get you anything?"

"I want you to sit there and keep that mouth shut. Give me time to get my brain in gear. And while you're waiting, clean up that mess you made."

Which made me wonder why I bothered trying to save her in the first place. By the time I got the table and floor cleaned up, she must've decided her brain was working again 'cause she started talking.

LENA

DEFLECTING PARTY IDEAS

Sweet Jesus! That girl could take the smallest whiff of a breeze and turn it into a tornado! Irish colors and family photos! What would she think of next? If this wasn't proof Maureen better get herself to tell that girl the truth pretty darn quick, I didn't know what was. Maybe this was Kalayla's way of opening that door her mama had barricaded shut.

Whatever it was, she dragged me smack dab into the middle of it all. If she'd given me a little warning, maybe mentioned the photo idea while she was thinking it through, I could have thought up a way of switching her train off the track it was barreling down. But she didn't give me any chance of doing that.

So now I was stuck putting out a fire before she started it. So I said, "It's good you want to do something for your mama's birthday. The thing is . . ."

Damn! Now I was sounding just like Rico did! Why is it when you don't know what to say you end up sounding so dumb! All I could do was hope my mumbling and fumbling would give me time to think up something that could cool her down. "Well, the thing is," I said AGAIN, "sometimes a real good idea can turn into a real bad one. For instance, if you don't think it all through beforehand."

Wouldn't you know this would be the one time since I'd known her that she kept that smart mouth shut! She sat across from me leaning forward, concentrating on every word I said. Her face squinted up like she was expecting me to tell her something important. Seeing her look so serious and hopeful made my heart sore.

"The thing is, Kalayla, you wouldn't want to make your mama sad on her birthday, now would you?"

She didn't say anything, but I could tell she was chewing on my words.

"What I mean is, those photos would start her thinking about the past, the way photos do. And they'd be reminding her of stuff that could make her real sad all over again."

It was a long time before she said, "I didn't think of that. I was only thinking that you don't throw away pictures of people you love, especially when you're never gonna see 'em again."

"Well," I said, "might be you're right. I keep a few photos out on the bookcase to remind me of happy times, but I've got others squirreled away."

"Why don't you put them out?"

"Because of what I was just telling you. They make me sad. And on your mama's birthday, you'd want to be reminding her of happy times. Wouldn't you?"

That seemed to satisfy her.

I gave out a big sigh of relief when she said, "Mama says next to marrying Daddy, the happiest thing ever happened to her was having me. She'll be real happy I thought of giving her a party, right?"

"Yes, I do believe that will make her very happy."

"Okay, so I won't try and find family pictures, but we can have lots of other stuff, right? Like she loves pretty flowers and bright colors and animals and dancing. She and my daddy used to dance around the living room, and he'd grab my hand, too, and we'd all be dancing and sometimes we'd be singing, too. Well, mostly Daddy did the singing. Mama said he had the best deep bass voice she ever heard. Daddy said Grandma LeeRoyce made him sing in the church choir 'cause of that."

"Well then," I said, "let's do something with flowers and dancing. But you know, girl, this party doesn't have to be a big splashy deal. You just want to show your mama you're thinking about her. That's what'll make her happy."

"But I want this birthday to be extra special the way Daddy's thirtieth was. We'll invite everybody that works at Eddie's. Do you think your brother Dominic might want to come?"

Now that I thought about it, I asked myself who in the world could Kalayla be inviting besides the people from Eddie's? She hadn't mentioned that dicey uncle or her LeeRoyce grandparents, so I was guessing she didn't plan on including them. And as far as I could tell, Maureen didn't have any friends she could invite.

Back in the days when I used to give parties, I'd invite family and friends and anybody else I felt like sticking in the pot. But Kalayla could get a case of brain strain trying to come up with anybody to invite besides the folks at Eddie's.

So I said, "Dominic loves parties and knowing him, he'll bring some family with him. Don't you be worrying. We'll do it up right for your mama. I'll help, and Eddie'll help, and my friend Carlotta acts like she earned a Ph.D. in throwing parties. Before I finish saying the word party, she'll be on her way over here."

Kalayla's eyes got big and I swear that girl looked astonished. And she obviously was, because she actually had the nerve to say, "You got a friend?"

As if me having a friend was the most unbelievable thing she ever in her life heard. Well! I gave her a look she won't be forgetting any time soon.

KALAYLA

BEFORE AND DURING THE PARTY

It turned out to be true. That Old Lady did have a friend. Her name was Carlotta. When I asked the Old Lady how she ended up hanging around with somebody so much younger, she gave me a vicious stare and said, "For your information, Miss Smart Mouth, Lotta and I were in the same high school class. AND we were cheerleaders together!"

Yeah, right, in her dreams maybe.

And when she said they'd help, what she meant was, they'd be taking over. And I do mean taking over. If I asked about food, they'd say, "Put it on the list." If I asked about inviting people, they'd say, "Put it on the list." I mean, like they could just order me around and I'd do what they wanted!

Anyway, I didn't know what they were talking about, so I finally said, "What list?"

"What do you mean, what list?" Carlotta said. "Your job is making the list. Our job is to do what's on it."

What a pisser!

Lena said they were best friends, but I didn't see how. They argued about everything until one of 'em gave in and said something like, "Fine, we'll do it your way. Otherwise you'll never shut up." The weird thing was, the next minute they'd be laughing and having a good time.

We used the Old Lady's kitchen table as our work station for making paper flowers for the streamers on the Maypole like we did in school a few years ago. It would've been dumb to call it the October Pole. I told 'em we should call it the dancing pole 'cause I knew if I asked them what they thought, they'd say, "Put it on the list."

Eddie was gonna attach the pole to the ceiling in the middle of the room so everybody could dance around it. Carlotta said she'd handle the music 'cause a friend of hers knew all about Irish music. The Old Lady snorted when Carlotta said "friend," and Carlotta gave her a dirty look.

We finally got all the decorations in boxes ready to take over to Eddie's, and Carlotta said my job was to get Mama out of the way for a few hours. When I told her Mama and I never did anything together 'cept sit in the kitchen and have our Sunday morning talks, she said, "Good God, child. Use your imagination!" She was a bossy know-it-all just like the Old Lady!

Like the afternoon of the party when we were putting up the decorations, she acted like she was the general, and we were all dumb ass privates that wouldn't know where to put a flower unless she told us.

I came close to telling her off when she informed me she was making the desserts for the party. I would've, too, 'cept the Old Lady went all bug-eyed and almost turned blue when I opened my mouth. So I just said, "OH. Goody!"

The closer the party got, the more nerved up I got 'cause Mama was getting that down low sad look. Clarence always told me I was lucky to have a poker face 'cause nobody could tell what I was feeling. Mama was the opposite.

Daddy said he watched her face to find out if she was doing okay. At the time, I wasn't sure what he meant, but since he was gone, I was stuck with the job of making sure she didn't go whacko again. I wasn't sure what would happen if she got too down, so whenever I was around her, I tried to be my usual jolly self as much as I could. I was counting the days 'til the party 'cause I knew that it was gonna make her real happy.

The night before the party, Eddie called and told Mama he had a family emergency and would be closed the next day. 'Course that meant Mama was off work, but the Old Lady said she was feeling sick and she needed Mama to fill in for her at the Women's Shelter. Mama got all worried, but she went. I gotta say those two old crabs were giving me a lot of ideas about how to fool people, adding on to what Clarence taught me.

We spent the time decorating like mad and when Mama got back, we were ready. I told her she had to get dressed up 'cause we were going someplace special. She put on her fancy green and orange dress and the necklace and dangling gold earrings that Daddy gave her one Christmas. I made her put on a blindfold and led her across to Eddie's.

'Course her favorite thing of the whole party was the dancing pole.

"Oh Layla, honey," she said, "it's just fabulous the way you're using what you learned at school."

Yeah right! She'd freak out if I told her some of the fabulous stuff I learned every time I went into the Girl's Room at school.

Eddie hung a huge "Closed for Private Party" sign on the door. When I told the Old Lady I wished I had more people to invite, she said, "Not to worry. We got that covered."

I found out what she meant when people started showing up. She and Carlotta invited everybody they knew, and I mean everybody.

Anyway, I was glad 'cause Mama was dancing around the pole and singing and laughing. She was happier than she'd been since before Daddy died. Everybody said she looked beautiful, and she did.

And everybody who came was all duded up. Carlotta and the Old Lady helped me make a black-eyed Susan costume to wear 'cause that was Mama's favorite flower. Carlotta had a couple yards of green material and we used that to cover my whole body for the stem. The Old Lady painted my nose dark chocolate for the button in the middle, and we made a hood of cool yellow petals. I went into the Ladies' Room while Mama was meeting the guests and I put it on. I looked pretty dumb, but when Mama saw me, she laughed, ran over, and nearly smothered me with a hug.

I almost flipped out when I saw the Old Lady come in the door. She had on a long funeral dress with puffy sleeves AND she was wearing a wide brim black hat. But, get this! There were GIGANTIC GREEN FLOWERS all around the brim! GREEN! Not black—GREEN! And that wasn't all! She had a green belt around her waist with a green flower on it, too!

It freaked me out. I figured something was really wrong with her, like maybe she'd gone color blind. Or—what a pisser—she was having one of those weird spells like she had when we were walking to that gym she dragged me to. Watching out for Mama was trouble enough, and if the Old Lady was gonna get added in, I'd be running a full-time whacko house.

When Mama got whacked out over a dream that had a bunch of monster numbers chasing her, Daddy would tell me, "Don't worry, Skinny Girl, she'll calm down. She just needs a hug."

I wasn't about to give the Old Lady a hug, but I got over to her as fast as I could. "Lena, you feeling okay? You think we oughta go to the hospital?"

She gave me a dirty look. “Now, just what makes you think I would leave this fine party and go to a hospital?”

“’Cause something’s wrong with you, even if you don’t know it.”

“Wrong with me? Nothing is wrong with me, girl! Where did you get such a ridiculous idea?”

“What’d you mean nothing’s wrong with you? You’re wearing green, that’s what’s wrong! You must be having some kind of mental attack. We better go to the hospital fast, before it gets worse.”

“I most certainly am NOT having a mental attack! I know perfectly well I am wearing green! I am wearing green because the guest of honor is IRISH. In case you forgot!”

Then she started laughing! Here I was all nerved up, and she was laughing!

“Sweet Jesus, Kalayla. I can understand you being surprised, and I do thank you for worrying about me. I did not mean to scare you. I wanted it to be a surprise, but I guess it was more of a shock.”

If feeling like you’ve been punched in the stomach was her idea of a good surprise, I was gonna try it on her sometime and see how she liked it!

“I wasn’t worrying about you! I was afraid you were gonna take a fit and ruin Mama’s party!”

I could tell from the way she looked at me the old crab was gonna reach over and grab me in a hug. I wasn’t gonna let her squash my petals! She might not be color blind, but there was something BIG wrong with her! She’d been wearing black for a hundred years and just when a person got used to that, she decided to wear green!

I turned around and shoved my way over to the food table and decided right off I was gonna stay there the rest of my life.

Carlotta had all these little signs in fancy writing telling you what the stuff was, like cheese & pesto stuffed shells or shrimp scampi linguini or Italian sausage & peppers, garlic roasted potatoes, spinach and feta ricotta pie. I gave up reading and started tasting.

There was more food than Grandma LeeRoyce had for her Thanksgiving and Christmas buffets combined, and I was gonna try out every dish no matter what it was.

For once, that Old Lady was right. I never tasted anything as good as Carlotta’s desserts. She made about ten different cookies, plus cannoli with chocolate and vanilla cream, and the birthday cake had about eight layers of chocolate cake with vanilla and raspberry cream in between.

I figure I might as well keep eating 'til my stomach exploded.

Everything was the best I ever ate, and when Carlotta came by, I asked her where I could buy some of that zucchini and sausage ravioli. Wouldn't you know she got all bent out of shape, like that was a BIG insult.

"Your mama should wash your mouth out with soap for suggesting such a thing!" she said. "This is an ITALIAN feast. EVERY bit of it is homemade by my family or Lena's. Everybody cooks in Italian families, the women AND the men!"

Well, pooh, pooh to her! I almost told her I bet she didn't make the butter or olive oil with hot pepper flakes for the bread, but I figured I better not after all she did to help. Besides, I didn't want to make her mad. I was planning to tell the Old Lady she oughta give herself a rest from cooking for me and Mama, and let Carlotta feed us once in a while.

Things were going great until I looked across the room and saw that turd from the gym. I ducked down quick, so he wouldn't notice me. I bet anything that Old Lady invited him just to piss me off!

I kept an eye on him 'til she came over to the food table. Then I grabbed her arm and the music was loud, so I had to shout in her ear. "What's that turd doing here?" I said, pointing at him. By then he'd worked his way over to Mama and was talking to her! What a pisser!

"I'm gonna go over and kick his butt out of my party. Right now!"

The Old Lady shoveled a hunk of cake on a plate and said, "What I think is, this is your Mama's party, not yours. What I think is, she's having a fine time talking to one of the guests whose name is Rico—if you recall. He happens to be Carlotta's nephew, so I imagine she invited him. AND, what I think is you should keep stuffing your mouth with food, instead of spoiling your Mama's good time."

She turned and went in Carlotta's direction. Before she got there, some old guy stopped her and started yakking in her ear. Probably asking where he could take a piss!

Mama was standing next to the dancing pole laughing and blushing like she used to when Daddy teased her. Except Daddy was dead, and that turd was the one making her laugh.

I felt like yelling and throwing cake in his face. I would've, but the Old Lady was right. Mama was having a good time, and I wasn't gonna wreck it, 'specially after all the work I did. I was thinking about going home, but not until I had more of Carlotta's cake.

MAUREEN

DURING THE PARTY

I feel pretty, Oh so pretty! I feel charming, and funny and sweet! I'm so happy I am me tonight! Just look at what my Kalayla has done! Balloons and streamers and people, so many people, all wishing me happy birthday, with hugs and kisses—so warm and friendly and funny.

Like all the wonderful parties I missed so terribly! And my baby girl, of all things, dressed up in a black-eyed Susan costume. And that wasn't even the most surprising thing! Lena was actually wearing green! I would never, ever have imagined anything so wonderful! Erin go bragh!

Of course, the food wasn't Irish, but every bit of it was SOOO good. And the Italian rum cake was absolutely divine!

And my beautiful girl! When I tried to grab her in a hug, she pushed me away, and said, "So what do you think of my dumb ass costume?"

Dumb assed wonderful, that's what I thought. My baby girl planned all of this! Really, I could just sit down and cry from joy! But I certainly was not going to do any such thing because Layla would think I was sad, and I wasn't. Not one bit. How could I look around this room and see everything everyone did and not be happy? What an absolutely wonderful thirtieth birthday party! It's like we crossed the ocean and were on the Emerald Isle instead of in the middle of Cambridge.

And I was so happy to meet Lena's friend Carlotta even though when Kalayla introduced her, she said, "This is the Old Lady's bossy friend." That was exactly what she said! Can you imagine saying such a thing? Carlotta must know what she's like because she just laughed.

In yoga class, they teach you to take deep breaths to get yourself grounded. I needed to do that because I was gliding five feet off the ground, looking at fabulous giant posters of Ireland—where I've so longed to go—and seeing so many Irish flags—where did they find them?

And the music! How could I possibly cry when I was standing next to a dancing pole and tapping time to Irish tunes from groups like The Frames and The Divine Comedy?

Someone put a hand on my shoulder, and when I turned around, this man took my hand and, of all things, said, "Green Greetings, my lady."

He was wearing a dark blue polo shirt and his arm was all muscle, and I could tell his chest was, too. Maybe he was a weight lifter or else his job required muscles. He definitely looked Italian, but that was no surprise because Lena and Carlotta invited their families. Which was so funny. It was like Italy invading Ireland.

"Hey," he said, "I'm Rico." His eyes darted to my left hand.

"I'm Maureen," I laughed, and suddenly I was feeling nervous. "I'm the birthday girl, well I guess I should say the birthday woman, now that I'm 30. It's such a big milestone, don't you think? I mean, you must have done something special for your thirtieth, didn't you? Oh dear, please don't be offended. Not that I meant to imply you look old or anything. Really, I didn't."

He laughed. "No need to apologize. Thirty-three is a lot older than thirty. But I hope I don't look too decrepit yet."

"No, no, you don't. You look … you look …" Oh dear, I was sure I was blushing. Why was I saying such foolish things? "What I meant was, really, you look fine. You know, healthy and strong and …"

Rico laughed, "This is some party. Carlotta is my aunt. She invited me, but she neglected to tell me the party was in honor of such a beautiful woman. All she said was, 'Show up!'"

"Oh, how funny! Does she always tell you what to do?"

"You wouldn't believe half of what she says or does! Once she told me it was about time I stopped beating my dog even though she knew damn well I didn't have a dog. And another time, I called her at the Animal Shelter and she said, 'Give me a minute, will you, Rico? I'm in the middle of humping my boyfriend.' Yeah, she actually said that! I think she does it to keep me off balance."

"She sounds like a real character! I had an uncle once who thought it was funny to moon the neighbors. My aunt swore the next time he did it, she was going to tie him to a lamp post and invite everybody in Brighton to see what he had to show."

Rico laughed, "Can you imagine if my uncle and your aunt ever got together? The families would run for the hills!"

Our families. Oh, how stupid of me telling him about Uncle Seamus. He might want to know more about my family, and I really can't tell him. I mean, what could I tell him? So what I did was to nod and change the subject.

"So, how'd you get the name Rico? I mean, that's not an Italian name, is it? Not that you need to have an Italian name, but ..." Oh dear, I was making it worse! He must think I'm a total airhead!

Rico rolled his eyes, smiled, and leaned a little closer. "That's a whole other story. My Grandpa was named Matthew and my dad—he should be here by the way, but I haven't seen him yet. My dad was Matthew Eccli, II and everyone called him Mattwo. So, when my parents named me Matthew Eccli, III, everyone started calling me Matthree. I absolutely hated that name, and so when I went into first grade, I told the teacher my name was Rico."

He was laughing as he went on, "I have to admit I was something of a prick. I went home that day, and at dinner I told the family I wouldn't talk to anybody who didn't call me Rico. And I didn't. My dad flipped out and gave me about a hundred lectures about carrying on the family name. It took two weeks, and my mom spent most of that time trying to calm him down. It drove everybody crazy but they finally gave in."

"What a hoot! So how did you happen to choose Rico? I mean, in first grade, how did you come up with that name?"

"I blamed it on my older sister. She was doing research for a school report and wrote the names Ricardo/Rico in her notebook with the meaning next to them. Evidently Ricardo meant great and powerful leader, and Rico was the nickname. I decided it would be cool to be a great and powerful leader, so that's why I'm Rico."

"Does that mean you are a great and powerful leader?"

"Not hardly! My dad thinks I'm a great and powerful pain in the ass. I've been taking over management of our gym, and every time I suggest a new idea—like offering yoga or Tai Chi—we get into a fight! The funny thing is I usually win!"

We laughed again—suddenly there was so much to laugh about!

"So, ah, Maureen, I don't see a wedding ring. Is there a boyfriend lurking around in this crowd?"

Oh! My stomach flip-flopped and I didn't know what to say and he could probably tell how flustered I was. I mean, I think maybe he was going to ask me for a date? Why else would he ask that? And I wasn't ready to date. I might never be ready. Never, ever.

"No, no husband, I mean not now. I'm not married now. But I was. I'm ... oh, I hate the word so much. I'm, I'm a widow. I don't have a boyfriend, but I do have a daughter. She's right over there at the food table, the one dressed as a flower. She doesn't usually dress as a flower, but ..."

Rico looked over at the table, squinted, and stared at Kalayla. He nodded and seemed to be thinking. I was so surprised when he said, "Well, actually, if the black-eyed Susan is your daughter, I have met her. Miss Lena brought her over to Matty's Way, the gym we own. But, ah, you couldn't say we exactly hit it off."

"Oh, how strange. Kalayla is very outgoing. I mean, she's always telling me about meeting people and, well, you seem outgoing too, so ..."

"Yeah, well, she was outgoing all right. But, ahhh, we had, ahhhh, you could call it a misunderstanding, and I haven't seen her since. If you want to have coffee sometime, I can fill you in on what happened. That's a more serious conversation and this is a time for dancing. If I'm not mistaken, that song is Neil Hannon's National Express. I heard The Divine Comedy in Ireland and got a bunch of their tunes."

"That's just who it is! And you really saw them!" I couldn't believe it. He'd seen my very favorite group AND been to Ireland. He was really into dancing, and if the other dancers hadn't made room for us, I think he could have lifted them up and moved them. Not that his muscles were huge and bulging, but he was ... beefy ... so different from Jamal's feline slenderness. Not that it mattered. All I was going to do was have coffee with him and find out what he meant about a misunderstanding with Kalayla.

And right then she was looking our way. I didn't think a black-eyed Susan could scowl, but that's what it looked like she was doing. Oh dear!

LENA

BEFORE AND DURING THE PARTY

Well, planning the birthday party showed me a whole new side of that girl! Except for Sunday morning, she spent most of her weekends over at my place.

"I have to be home then so Mama can talk at me," was her way of explaining it.

On school days, I could count on her pounding on my door right around 3:15, panting and ready to wolf down cookies and lemonade so we could keep going on decorations. I swear that girl would have kept us making flowers forever if I hadn't declared it ENOUGH when we reached 100.

I spent near a fortune on taxis chauffeuring us from one store to another in Cambridge or Boston. Every time she went off to the library, I knew I better be getting out my wallet and be ready soon as she got home.

"We gotta get a poster of Connemara ponies 'cause Mama likes horses. And the Cliffs of Moher 'cause they're pretty. Plus, those big stones leaning against each other, and castles, we gotta get lots of castles! Come on, Lena!"

Luckily the Coop had plenty of posters in stock, along with an inventory of others we could order with fast, pricey shipping, naturally! To her credit, Kalayla wasn't thinking I'd be the one footing the bill on all these transactions. The first day we went shopping she said, "I don't have enough money for all this stuff, but if it's okay with you, I'll work for free 'til I get it paid off."

"Well," I said, "that might mean I have your good service until you turn 21."

"I don't care. Working for you isn't the worst job I ever had."

Which wasn't saying much given that working for me was the only job she ever had! Regardless, there were times when I felt like giving that girl a hug!

She told me she was sneaking over to Eddie's every chance she got to "give him ideas on where stuff should go."

Eddie said she was driving him crazy. "Next thing you know, she'll want me to tear down walls. And when she does, I'm sending her right over to the owner of this fine establishment!"

The truth was, the more excited Kalayla got, the more we all pitched in to make sure things came out the way she hoped.

And talk about driving a person crazy, Carlotta did more than her share of that. She gave me and all of the cooks in her family and mine a list of what we had to make. Her list included where to purchase special ingredients—as if we didn't know—and a timeline for getting it done—as if we couldn't figure that out for ourselves. Now, really!

I finally had enough and said, "Lotta, you do remember this is not the first party I ever gave, don't you?"

To which she said, "Sure I remember, but that's such ancient history, I assumed you'd forgotten how. Now, I've been thinking I wouldn't make a strawberry cannoli filling—just chocolate and regular cream. What do you think?"

That was the way it went, until the very minute Lotta came over to change for the party. She was getting all dolled up in my spare room while I was in my bedroom doing the same thing and feeling more nervous every minute about what I was doing. When I went out into the living room, she was pacing back and forth.

"Well it's about ..." she stopped mid-sentence and stared at me, her eyes getting wider than I'd ever seen them. I knew what she was going to ask and I didn't have any answer to give her—or myself—that would make any sense. I just got up one morning maybe three weeks ago, and I knew something inside me was different. If you've been a certain way for so long you can't remember when it was any other way, you can tell when something is different.

That's all I could tell her or myself. I knew good and well that explanation wouldn't satisfy her, so instead I said, "Now don't you start, Lotta, don't you start!"

"And just why would I start? It wouldn't be because my best friend wore nothing but black for the last thirty years and now she's standing in front of me plastered in green flowers, would it?"

"I am not plastered in them! You don't know one thing about how many flowers should go on a hat, Lotta, and don't you dare say you do!"

She looked me up and down. "By God, Lena, I'm glad to see you finally decided to climb out of the grave! Now get yourself together and stop sputtering. We're going to a party!"

We were a little late getting over to Eddie's, and when we walked in the door, I sucked in my breath when I saw how everything had come together. Eddie had covered every window with alternating strips of orange, green and white tissue paper, and the whole place glowed! I've never been to Ireland, but I swear, that's where we were! And the music? I felt like kicking off my shoes and dancing a jig or whatever it is they do over there!

Seemed like everybody Carlotta and I knew was either there already or coming through the door after us. After I gave Kalayla a good talking to, she had finally invited her grandparents, but they were out of town at some church retreat. She wasn't the least bit sad about that. She refused to invite that uncle, and you can bet I didn't spend any time trying to persuade her.

And that girl—she looked cute as could be in her flower costume, which I swear was her own idea. Anybody seeing her might have thought she was a normal eleven-year-old—long as she kept that mouth shut, that is.

I guess I should have given her fair warning about my outfit, but I wasn't sure until I got dressed if I'd have the courage to show up wearing what I was wearing. I couldn't warn her Rico would be there because my dear best friend had forgotten to mention that fact. I had to keep Kalayla from making a scene about the fact that Rico was smart enough to make a beeline straight for her mama, but he wasn't the only one pushing in for a dance with that beauty. Lotta and I made it a point to ask all the younger family members and told them to bring along their friends.

Lotta smugly informed me she had invited her brother, and I wondered if Mattwo would show up. Well he did, and when I saw him pushing my way, I could feel myself getting tense, wondering what I was going to say to him. I sure didn't need to worry because he acted like me wearing green was as normal as being transported to Ireland.

"Lena," he said, "you're looking good. Added a little green for the celebration, eh? This is really something. You and Lotta do most of it?"

"Well, we did a lot getting it organized, but everybody helped out. Kalayla was the one supplying the grand ideas. Such as tearing down this building and putting up something bigger! Honestly though, most of her ideas were doable and she pestered us 'til she got what she wanted."

"Yeah, I heard from Rico she was ahhh, interesting to handle. If that's the way to describe it."

"You could say that. She didn't exactly cooperate with him at the gym, but I have to say he did his best."

"It wasn't his best if he left you thinking you had to go it alone, Lena. And I got the impression that's what he did. If you need any help ..."

I needed help all right, but it was with getting my seesawing emotions under control, and there was no way he could help with that.

"Mattwo, you did plenty enough setting it up, and Rico did as much as anybody could, given the way she was acting. I appreciate that, and well, I guess you ought to meet her, so you'll know for yourself what all the fuss was about. She's appointed herself guardian of the food table, and I'm not sure she'll let us get a thing to eat. She's likely planning to be the only one pigging out."

Now if I didn't sound like a babbling old dingbat!

He laughed. "Sounds like a typical kid to me."

HA! We worked our way through the crowd and found Kalayla with a plate and fork in hand, looking over the desserts.

"Kalayla," I said, "I want you to meet Mattwo."

She looked at Mattwo and frowned, obviously puzzled. Then she scanned the crowd, zeroed in on Rico before she turned back to Mattwo. His partially bald head and bit of roundness around his gut didn't fool her. No way to doubt they were father and son. Her eyes narrowed.

All I could think was Sweet Jesus, please don't let her cause a scene.

She bit her lip, which was a very good sign. I have to say I almost fell over when she stuck out her hand to shake his and said, "Pleased to meet you. Have some cake, but don't take too much 'cause there might not be enough."

I covered my mouth to smother a guffaw.

Mattwo smiled. "Carlotta's my sister, so I know all about her rum cake. I like her Tiramisu better, but maybe you already ate all of that. Have you tried the cookies? The Florentines are my all-time favorite."

Kalayla pointed at Mattwo's stomach, which in my opinion was not bad at all for a seventy-one-year-old. "If she was my sister, I'd be fat, too."

That girl!

Thank goodness Mattwo laughed and said, "Listen kid, I'm in damn good shape for a guy my age."

She shrugged, "So if you wanna stay that way, you better skip dessert. Get a hunk of that spinach feta pie. It's real healthy tasting."

Which probably meant she hated it, but at least she was polite. Well, as polite as she was likely to be.

Mattwo and I sampled the food and listened to the music. I saw Lotta looking over our way, not that there was a thing for her to see. Didn't matter. She'd add me talking to her brother to the green flowers, and I was never going to hear the end of it.

Not that it mattered. I was standing next to the man I probably should have married, talking to him like that was a perfectly normal everyday occurrence. I didn't know how the heck that happened, and I didn't have any idea what it might be meaning. The best thing I could do was eat the rum cake and ignore the dirty looks I was getting from the food guard.

DECEMBER 1999

MAUREEN
BEING A GOOD MOTHER

"I'm making all angels for Grandma," Kayala said, "so she'll give me a few extra fudge balls."

I laughed, "Layla, you know good and well Lucinda always gives you PLENTY of fudge balls! You don't have to bribe her!"

I heard Kalayla mutter, "That's what you think," under her breath, but I didn't have the energy to call her on it.

Our kitchen table was covered with cookie ingredients: flour, sugar, butter, cinnamon, ginger, eggs and sprinkles for decorating. This was our first attempt to make cookies, and I so hoped it would become a tradition. So far, she hadn't burned herself, ruined a pan, or set the kitchen on fire.

We really didn't have any family traditions. I know I should have created some long before now, but when Jamal was alive, I was so busy with my art and of course with him. But I really did want to spend time with her now, and it wasn't just because I felt guilty. She was old enough that we could do things together if I could just figure out what they were. And if she was willing. Finding anything Kalayla was either willing to do or could do was so much harder than I thought it would be.

I was much younger than Kalayla when Mummie introduced me to all the "feminine accomplishments." She practically devoted full time to my development, but she didn't have other interests the way I did. Besides, I was a willing, docile learner, and monogramming handkerchiefs, knitting scarves or embroidering dish towels were all easy for me.

My baby girl didn't take after me at all in that regard. Take sewing, for instance. I truly did my best to teach her, but it turned into a disaster. She stuck herself twice with the needle, then dripped blood on the white hankie which she threw on the floor and stomped on.

"This sucks blood," she yelled and ran out of the house.

I thought crocheting or knitting might be better. I mean, at least there wouldn't be any spilled blood, but according to Kalayla, the only thing the needles were good for was, "to stick up the butt hole of some kid I don't like."

I sighed. At least she liked cookies, so maybe that would work out better. Of course, we had to make tons of them as gifts, and I hoped she didn't get bored. I really wanted to thank everyone who helped her with my party—that fabulous party. They'd all been so kind.

"MAMA! Look how good this looks!"

Oh my! She was applying decorations in the most random way, but I didn't dare give her any more directions.

"You know what we should do, Mama? Let's talk Grandma and Carlotta into throwing a party for the whole city. It'd be fun as anything to see her and Grandma fight over who was the BIG boss. I bet Carlotta would win. She'd tell Grandma off and Grandma would lecture her about using bad language!" Kalayla giggled her way through cutting out several angels.

I had to admit that was a funny thought, but the fact was nothing about Lucinda was funny to me. I remember hoping I'd be a true part of Jamal's family. That was before I had realized how awkward and uncomfortable being around them would be for me.

I didn't think about meeting his family until we were serious about each other. And then of course I expected to. When I asked him if we should visit them, he shrugged off the idea.

"Trust me, Sweet Babe. It's better if you meet my mother after we're married. Don't get me wrong. She'll do her best to welcome you. But first she'll tell you to find a good white guy and not set yourself up for a lot of pain. All the type of stuff you and I have already talked about."

I didn't need to hear that from her or anyone else. Mummie already showed me how hard it would be. But I had always dreamed of having a big beautiful wedding. My mother used to point out brides in magazines and say I'd be a prettier bride than any of them. I thought maybe Jamal and I could have a small wedding and reception even though it would only be his friends and family. No one, not even Katie, would come from my side.

When I mentioned the idea to Jamal, he wasn't sure it would be worth the trouble and I finally agreed. We decided all we needed was each other. A justice-of-the-peace married us and we drove to NYC and spent three days there for our honeymoon.

He was truly a fine man and I was so happy we were married. I realized how strong he was and how much he'd been dealing with his whole life. I never knew people could be so incredibly cruel, but I was finding out they could be, and they were. I was finding out what Jamal already knew.

It never occurred to me we'd have a hard time finding a place to live. I told Jamal I'd look while he was working. We thought it would be fun to be in Boston, and I was so excited when I began the search. Twice I found nice apartments, but when Jamal went to look at them with me, the owners said the apartments had been rented. Even though both times when I talked to them earlier in the day, both had been available.

After that, we decided it would be better if the two of us went together, and we broadened our search to Cambridge. We finally found a big apartment on the first floor of a two-family house. The yard was along one side of the house so we weren't close to the next house, and the light was so wonderful, perfect for my studio.

I was so nervous when we told the landlady we'd take it and you can't imagine how relieved I was when she said, "If your money is green, it's good enough for me." The Asian couple on the second floor said she told them the same thing.

I didn't want to bring up meeting Jamal's family again, and I was so glad a couple weeks after we got married when he said, "Okay, Sweet Babe. Brace yourself. It's time for us to drop in on my parents."

I remember my heart gave a little leap of joy. "Oh, I'm so glad! I'll make your mom a little homemade gift, maybe some brownies …"

"Whatever. You've got to understand she wasn't thrilled with the news. She's probably the most realistic person you'll ever meet, so be prepared to hear a lecture about what we're up against."

His parents lived in a small, well-kept house with a nice yard across town from us in Inman Square. And I guess you could say that, in her own way, Lucinda did welcome me. "Well, daughter-in-law," she said, "now that my son has stopped hiding you, I trust we'll get to know you. I hope you're not as fragile as you appear, because what you've taken on will require a lot of strength."

Jamal's father Harmon was standing right next to her, but I guess she usually did the talking because all he did was nod.

Just then his brother Clarence came swaggering into the living room and saw me and said, "Hot damn! What a looker!"

He stared at me and his look was so intense I felt embarrassed and almost turned away. Jamal had told me Clarence had had a rough time and that he'd really come a long way. But I didn't see why he was looking at me like that, and what he said … well, it was more the way he said it, so exaggerated like he was an amateur actor trying out for a role.

I wasn't sure how to respond to him. I mean, how do you respond when you're not sure if the other person is putting on an act, or being their real self?

Then Clarence walked around me, whistled and said, "Whoa, Bro, those hips must be giving you some kind of ride."

Jamal reached out and grabbed Clarence's shirt and pulled him face-to-face, "Shut your damn mouth, Clarence, and keep it shut. She's my wife!"

I was so shocked because Jamal never, ever did anything like that. He was gentle and soft-spoken, and I couldn't imagine him hurting anyone. Clarence obviously didn't believe Jamal would hurt him because he just shrugged and smiled.

Seeing the two of them together was odd, too. They weren't that much different in size. Jamal was maybe two inches taller and maybe outweighed Clarence by ten pounds. But standing next to Jamal, Clarence seemed … small.

He gave Jamal a military salute and said, "Chill, Bro. It's cool you got such a prize. No disrespect meant."

But it felt like he really did mean disrespect. It all made me so nervous, I don't think I actually said hello to him.

I'd waited so long to meet Jamal's family, and I admit I built them up in my mind because I wanted a family so much, and I guess I thought they'd all be like Jamal. But Lucinda was intimidating and scary. I told myself she wasn't really a cold person, but she seemed so very far from warm. It was hard to imagine her giving anybody a hug. Ever. And I had no idea how to take Clarence. He might hug me, but if he did, I wouldn't be sure why he was doing it or what he meant by it.

I tried to talk with Jamal about how I felt because we always talked about everything.

"Look, Sweet Babe, I don't know what to tell you. Except welcome to the LeeRoyce family! Clarence … well, Clarence is Clarence. He's never gotten over what happened. And that was my fault, for using bad judgment. I never should have let him come with me. But he always followed me around, asking if he could do whatever I was doing. All I can do now is be there for him. That's the best I can do."

He shrugged his shoulders, as if he was trying to adjust the weight he was carrying. I didn't want to make it heavier, so I let it go. No matter how Jamal felt, I knew he wasn't the one responsible. The kids in the car were.

It happened in late August when Jamal was seven and Clarence was five. Jamal wanted to bike over to Fresh Pond and check out what was playing at the movie theatre. Clarence followed him everywhere, and that time Jamal knew he should say no because it was late afternoon and would be dark before they got home. But Clarence begged, and Jamal knew his brother would be lonely once he went back to school. And eventually he said yes.

It was a long ride, and they stopped a few times because Clarence was struggling to keep up. By the time they got there, it was almost dark. Jamal said ice cream at Friendly's would make him feel better. Afterwards they were walking their bikes to the theatre. That was when Jamal saw the car cruising around the parking lot.

White kids—high school or even older—were hanging out the windows and shouting at anyone they saw. Jamal hoped they were looking for girls and would ignore him and Clarence. But they didn't. They pulled over in front of Jamal and Clarence, and Jamal knew that meant trouble.

Five of them got out of the car. One of them said, "Hey, look what we got here. A couple of strays from a baby coon litter!"

Another one said, "Yeah, yeah, yeah, and look at that! The runt of the litter is gonna cry! I bet we're gonna see little black tears!"

They all laughed. One of them grabbed and held Jamal, but the one they really went after was Clarence. When he started bawling, two of the white boys danced around him, calling him a crybaby and a sissy.

One of them said, "Hey! Maybe he's crying because he's got a honey pot instead of a dick and he's scared we're gonna stick him!"

They pulled down Clarence's pants and jumped up and down around him while they pointed and hooted at how small he was.

One of them waved a knife and said, "Okay, let's have a vote. Should I cut off his little, tiny dick or cut out his big black tongue?"

"Hey, you jerk offs," the guy who was holding Jamal yelled at them, "He'll bleed like a pig and you're not getting in my car covered in coon blood. Here!" He tossed over what looked like a gun, "Stick this down his throat and pull the trigger."

When they tried to force Clarence's mouth open, he shit and peed all over himself. They jumped away from him and one of them yelled, "Fuck this! Let's get out of here before we catch cooties from coon shit!"

They all laughed, chanting, "Cooties from coon shit, cooties from coon shit," as they ran, piled into the car and burned rubber as they pulled away.

Clarence curled into a ball, and Jamal was afraid to leave him to get help. Finally, two white women who were going to the movies stopped to see what was wrong. One of them went into the movie theatre and called Lucinda and Harmon.

Jamal said Clarence wasn't the same after that. He wouldn't leave the house, and when Lucinda finally got him back to school, he starting shitting in the hallways and wiping it on the walls. The school put him in a special class, but that didn't help. Lucinda finally gave up her job teaching second graders and homeschooled him.

Of course, I knew it was awful and traumatic for Clarence. Really, I did. But it didn't make me feel any more comfortable around him while Jamal was alive, and now it was even worse.

Whenever Kalayla and I went to visit Jamal's family at holiday gatherings, I felt lonelier than I did when I was home by myself. It wasn't their fault, but I was out of place, a white dot in a black field.

Kalayla had no reason to feel that way. She was tied to them by blood and the minute we got there, she'd go down to the basement and play ping pong with the kids, and tell me afterward that she "beat the ass off them." Whether or not that was really true, she did enjoy going there. I would never cut that tie, because then she'd have no family at all. And having no family was a terrible, terrible thing.

"MAMA!"

Kalayla waved a hand in front of my face.

"I'm going to Mickey's for more sprinkles!"

Oh dear! While I'd been day-dreaming, she'd been decorating. Three empty packages of sprinkles were crumpled on the table, and she was halfway to the door.

"Layla, honey, wait. I'll go with you. We can pick up something for your lunches ..."

She rolled her eyes, "I got it covered, Mama ..." and then softly, "like always." She didn't slam the door, but I wouldn't have blamed her if she had. I was trying so hard to be a better mother, and I think she really did know that. How was it possible that I could be so smart in school, get A's on every assignment, test, or project and then be a complete klutz of a mother?

When I was having coffee with Rico, I told him how lucky I was that we lived next to Lena. I don't know what her grades were like in school, but she knew all about raising kids and I obviously didn't know a thing.

I told Rico the way Kalayla acted at the gym was probably my fault. He said I shouldn't be so hard on myself. He said being a parent was tough, and he should know because he made it tough for his parents. He really must have been a handful. I don't know what I would have done if Kalayla never paid attention to anything I said.

Really, it must have been so stressful for Rico's parents. I mean, raising a boy who did whatever he wanted, no matter what his dad said. Like working his way through college even though his dad wanted to pay, or like cycling around Europe for a year instead of going to work at the gym right after his graduation. Every time Rico came up with a new suggestion for the gym, his dad would say something like: "You get all these highfalutin ideas while you're riding around town on that damn bike? Why don't you get a car and act like a real businessman!"

Rico laughed, "He jabs at me all the time, but don't get the idea he doesn't support me. He does, in spades. Several years ago, before Mom passed away, I was living in an apartment a couple of blocks from them. Dad asked me over for dinner ahead of time, not the usual last-minute invite.

"When I got there, he and Papa were in the living room having a beer. They know I don't like beer and were used to me bringing my own wine. There was a wine glass set out and waiting.

"After the usual chitchat, Dad got straight to it, 'Your grandfather and I want you to move here. We left the third-floor apartment empty waiting for the right time. And this is it. You can go ahead and renovate any way you want.'

"I about gagged on my wine. Anybody else in the family would have considered that an honor not to be refused. But it would have been like living in a fishbowl with Dad and Mom on the second floor and Papa on the first.

"I stumbled through saying, 'Wow! That's—it's hard to take in, you know … the surprise and the honor … I don't know what to say.'

"Dad said, 'That's okay, kid'—he always calls me kid when he's happy with me—'You can decide how and when to tell the rest of the family. Your ma will probably want to make a party over it.'

"I avoided both of them for the next few days. I was looking for a way to say no without causing a major family upset. I finally set up a meeting with them, but when I walked into Dad's living room, Papa wasn't there.

"My dad said, 'It's better with just the two of us. All right, Kid. Tell me what you came here to say.'

"He knew. No shouting, no arguing. He knew, but he was waiting to hear it from me. So I told him. 'I thought a lot about moving in, Dad. I'm really honored that you wanted me to. But the truth is, I've got to have my own space. I need breathing room. I couldn't stand having everybody ask what I was doing or where I was going or who I was going with every five minutes. I love you and Mom and Papa, but I can't live in the same house with you.'

"He sat there without saying a word, looked up at the ceiling once, then sighed and said, 'Okay. If that's the way you feel, that's the way you feel.'

"And that was that. When I put a down payment on a house in a different section of Watertown, all Dad said was, 'You need any help with the move?' I never loved him or respected him more than I did at that moment."

When Rico finished telling me all that, I burst out in tears! It was so embarrassing, but I just couldn't stop myself. He was so lucky to have such a wonderful family.

And then I blurted out everything—everything about my mother and the lie I told Kalayla and that she still didn't know the whole awful story.

When I finally stopped talking, he said, "You're right. Kalayla will probably be furious. But you can't change that, and the longer you put it off, the worse it will be. All you can do is tell her how bad you feel about it and how sorry you are."

That's what Lena told me, too.

If Kalayla and I were more alike, I might know what to say. I mean, if she were like a blank canvas and I could paint anyway I wanted. But she wasn't. Raising kids was nothing at all like sculpting or doing a watercolor. Art work didn't have a mind of its own. It never talked back or left the room in a huff. I could take my time and experiment until the piece turned out the way I intended.

Kalayla never waited for me to figure out what to do with her. She roamed around doing whatever she wanted. She ate whatever she wanted, whenever she wanted. She dressed like ... like ... I didn't know how to describe the way she dressed and couldn't imagine how she decided what to wear. And what came out of her mouth …

Now that I thought about it, she sounded as strong-willed and self-reliant as Rico and I didn't have a clue how to deal with her. I never realized being a parent could make you feel so helpless.

I knew one thing for sure. I was good at making cookies, and that's what I needed to pay attention to when Kalayla got home with more supplies. I had just taken a batch out of the oven when she opened the door and said, "Wow, Mama! This smells like a bakery!" She dropped the grocery bag on the table. "I got M&M's and sprinkles and Red Hots. I'm putting horns and a tail on the cookie for dear Uncle Clarence and then sticking Red Hots all over it. I hope he burns his tongue!"

WINTER 2000

KALAYLA

USING THE INTERNET

Winter was a real pisser. All the dumb weathermen were jumping up and down 'cause we were breaking records. No more J-walking to Eddie's unless I climbed over a mountain of snow. Wind whipped my face and my fingers would've frozen 'cept the Old Lady gave me waterproof mittens with a down lining for Christmas.

I dressed like a mummy covered in layers top and bottom. I wound a scarf of Daddy's 'round my head and left slits for my eyes, like those vizor things the knights wore.

Nobody looked normal. Mama could've walked by me and she wouldn't've known who I was.

Streets got narrow and sidewalks were buried 'cept around schools. Guys with snowplows cheered, but everybody else got sick of slogging through snow or trying to find a way around it.

Clean Duds turned into a hot, smelly steam bath with dirty, wet floors. The cleanup crew showed up every night, but by the time I got there after school, it was a yucky mess. Weekends were the worst.

The Old Lady told me I could do homework or read at her place. That was okay when she was there 'cause she wasn't getting on my nerves as much since the birthday party. But I wasn't staying there when she was at work or at the Women's Shelter. I told her I wasn't some pet dog who was gonna wait around for her to come home.

I usually headed to the library 'cause it was on the corner of a main street where sidewalks got cleared. The new section was mostly windows and steel with big open spaces, but the old section had awesome little alcoves where you could hide out. The regular librarian liked me, so I thought she might let me put a 'Reserved' sign up on my favorite one, but she said that was against policy.

I didn't care. I fixed it so nobody else would wanna use it. Whenever I left, I moved the chair over to one of the tables. Everybody but me was too lazy to drag it back.

The social studies teacher gave us a research project, and we had to use old newspaper records and find stuff on the internet. I picked animal shelters and was planning to interview Carlotta about her shelter. Plus, I was thinking about telling her I knew a poor starving waif she could invite to dinner. I figured if I could get her to laugh, she might invite me.

The librarian showed me how to look up newspaper articles, and I found one about when Carlotta opened the shelter a few years ago.

That got me to thinking about Daddy's car crash. Grandma wouldn't let me read the newspaper stories or see the photos. She was afraid I'd go whacko like Mama, but I knew I wouldn't. Daddy always told me the two of us were made of steel, but Mama was more sensitive and fragile.

I asked the librarian to help me find articles about the crash, and she said okay after I told her Mama thought I was old enough to see them. Which wasn't exactly a lie. Mama probably would say it was okay—when I was about 25.

The photos of the car were pretty creepy, and that night I must've yelled in my sleep 'cause Mama came running in. I told her I was running away from a scary monster. Which was true. The monster was a smashed-up car breathing fire, but I wasn't gonna tell her that.

The articles said Daddy and Uncle Clarence were drag racing on a track that was closed for repairs. I bet anything going there was Uncle Clarence's idea, even though Grandma never said that. She was always making excuses for him.

The obituary said that Daddy was survived by Mama and me and his parents and brother. Which was a pretty dumb way of saying he was dead and we were alive.

Weekends dragged because I was stuck inside alone. Mama was filling in a lot at Eddie's 'cause she was the only one who could get to work. And 'stead of staying home the way she should've, Old Lady had that guy Ray Ray driving her anywhere she wanted in his big black truck with gigantic tires. He even brought along a step stool to help her get in! I wanted a ride in that truck, but she told me I was not to be associating with the likes of her driver, and anyway the dog had already claimed the back seat. That pissed me off. She was riding with him, so why couldn't I? She was just like Mama, making up dumb rules!

I got to thinking about Mama's family. She was worse than Grandma about not telling me stuff, and I was tired of waiting on her. I wasn't gonna cry like a baby reading about people I didn't even know. I wasn't like her.

Anyway, I didn't need them to tell me stuff. I had newspapers and the computer.

On Sunday afternoon I tried walking one of my usual routes down side streets near the apartment, but the wind and cold were pissers. I ended up at the library and decided to start my research on Mama's family. Nothing came up when I keyed in stuff like 'family killed in explosion,' or 'Brighton Gas explosion,' and I was getting pissed because I couldn't find anything.

I asked the librarian for help, but she couldn't find anything either, and she ran out of ideas, too. The worst thing was she didn't remember reading about it. She should've 'cause she read every newspaper every single day. I told her that didn't make sense. If a kid on a bike got hit by a car, it was a big deal. How could a whole family get killed without there being one single story?

She put on her serious librarian expression and said, "Kalayla, what makes you think there was an explosion?"

I almost told her. I could've, and I would've. But I didn't. I said, "I don't know. It doesn't matter anyway. I'll try researching something else. Thanks for the help." She looked kind of funny, but she didn't say anything.

After I left the library, her question kept buzzing at me like a wicked big mosquito circling my head. When I went into my bedroom, it followed me. When I went over to the Old Lady's, it beat me through her door. When I opened my locker at school, it smacked me in the face. Why did I think there was an explosion? I rolled myself up into a tight ball inside. Maybe if I got small enough, it wouldn't be able to find me.

But it did.

What was the point in asking Mama and getting her all freaked out? The Old Lady was always saying I should get my brain in gear before I opened my mouth. My gears were stuck, and pretty soon I wasn't saying much of anything to anybody.

'Course Mama didn't notice, but that sharp-eyed Old Lady did. Every time I saw her, she looked at me real hard and said, "Something wrong with you, girl?" Or, "What happened, girl? Something bothering you?"

I stopped going over to her place, but the question didn't go away.

It wasn't like I didn't have an answer.

I thought there was an explosion because Mama told me there was. Whenever I asked Daddy about it, he said, "Ask your Mama."

I woke up feeling worse every morning, so I stopped going to sleep. The mosquito kept biting, and I kept scratching 'til the blood came. 'Til I asked myself, 'What if there wasn't an explosion?' What if Mama was lying?

Was that why Daddy wouldn't tell me anything? 'Cause he knew she was lying? But if he knew, why didn't he say "Liar, liar pants on fire," the way he did when I told him I wasn't the one who decorated Uncle Clarence's hair with chewing gum while he was sleeping on our sofa?

Chicken Little had it easy compared to me. I was dodging millions of pieces falling out of the sky and coming up from the ground, and there was no place for me to hide.

On Saturday I went back to the library. I wasn't sure how to start, and I was just killing time, so I picked up The Chronicle and looked at a few of the articles. There was a sports headline that said, "O'Rourke Does It Again!" A kid named Sean O'Rourke who played basketball for Brighton High racked up 20 points in the last game against Cambridge.

I stopped reading. My grandpa's name was Kevin Sean O'Rourke.

My mama used to live in Brighton.

I could've put down the paper and walked away. But I'm no chicken. I asked the librarian if Brighton had a local paper. The sports page headline said, "O'Rourke Courted by Colleges." The photo showed him after one of the games. He was with his grandparents, Colleen and Kevin O'Rourke.

Colleen and Kevin O'Rourke. My dead grandma was Colleen O'Rourke. My dead Grandpa was Kevin O'Rourke.

I stared at the photo for a long time. You could tell they were related. I imagined Mama standing next to them. She would've fit right in.

I got that disgusting taste in my mouth like I was gonna throw up. I stood up and felt hot and dizzy. I went to the bathroom and splashed cold water on my face. I washed my hands three times.

I couldn't wash the thoughts out of my head. I had to find out if they were my dead family. I had to find out if Colleen and Kevin had children. I had to find out if Mama was their daughter.

I went back to the alcove, and this time I searched the net. I found out Colleen and Kevin O'Rourke had three children: Colin, Leah, and Kate.

Mama told me she had two sisters: Leah and Kate. She said she had one brother, Colin. They had to be Mama's family. Colin, Leah and Kate, but not Maureen. It didn't make any sense. Why wasn't her name with her sisters and her brother? Why did she think they got blown up?

I twisted and turned my brain trying to come up with reasons. I finally gave up because there wasn't any reason. Any dumb ass kid at school could've figured it out. Mama knew her family was alive. Daddy did, too. They should've been in the Guinness Book of World Records as the Worlds' Biggest Liars.

Mama was always saying how much she trusted me, but that was a big fat lie, too. She would've told me the truth if she did. Why'd they lie about something like that? There had to be a reason, and I was gonna figure out what it was. Maybe Mama and Daddy were in a witness protection program 'cause somebody bad wanted to hurt them. Maybe Mama's family were all gangsters and Mama and Daddy didn't want me associating with them.

I tried making up a lot of stuff, but not even a total turd brain would believe any of it. I felt like going home, hiding under the bed covers and never coming out.

The computer screen got blurry, but I didn't care. I sat there 'til the librarian came by and said, "We'll be closing in ten minutes, Kalayla. You better start getting your things together."

It was freezing outside and dark 'cept for the streetlights and headlights. The snowflakes pelted my face, and it was hard to see. Nothing looked familiar. I wasn't sure I could find my way back home.

LENA

A CHILD IN MY HOUSE AGAIN

The minute I heard that knock on my door, I got the feeling something bad had happened. The sound was so soft I wasn't sure I heard anything until it came a second time, just as soft. I opened the door, and Kalayla was standing there, her head down like she was concentrating on something on the floor.

I looked down, but there was nothing there I could see. When she didn't give me any of her usual smart talk, I got scared maybe she was hurt, maybe she mouthed off to the wrong person once too often.

I didn't see bruises or scratches or torn clothes, which I took as a good sign. I put my arm around her and led her through the door. Whatever it was, it was worse than bad. She never would have let me do such a thing otherwise.

"You come on in here, and tell old Lena what's going on," I said guiding her over to the sofa. She curled into a fetal position without saying a word.

I sat down next to her, and the only thing I could think to do was rub her back and shoulders.

I rubbed and worried and prayed that nothing had happened to her mama. I imagined Maureen had been poisoned or mugged or had heart failure or fallen and broken all her bones. My old brain knew too much about too much that could happen to people with no warning.

I waited and waited. All the times I told that girl to keep her mouth shut, and now I was wishing more than anything she'd open it.

It was past dinnertime and I thought for sure she must be hungry. If she got to eating, she might get to talking. I was about to go into the kitchen when she looked straight at me and said, "Lena, has anybody ever told you such a big lie you were sure it was true?"

Sweet Jesus! Something or somebody shined a spotlight on the elephant that was living with her and her mama. Even if I could have, there was no way I would have chased it back into the shadows. The time for facing it straight on was long past due.

I felt like crying for Kalayla and crying for Maureen.

"Not that I know of," I said. "But once, a very long time ago, I told a big lie and everybody believed it."

Her eyes opened wide like she was stretching to make room for a part of me she hadn't known was there. "You did? But why'd you do it? It's not right."

"Right doesn't always enter into it when you're trying to protect people you love. I told myself I was protecting my boys. Maybe your mama thought she was protecting you."

To my last breath, I will not forget how sad and hurt she looked.

"You knew," she said. "You knew, and you didn't tell me."

I sighed deep. Seemed like my whole life was filled with could haves and should haves, but there was nothing holding me back from telling the truth now. "Yes. I did know, but it wasn't because your mama told me. I found out on my own, and it wasn't my place to be telling you. Much as I thought you ought to know. That was up to your mama. I guess she finally felt ready."

Kalayla's eyes got fierce and she exploded. "No, she didn't! I found out by myself. On the computer. Mama should've told me, but she didn't. All she cares about is what she wants! She doesn't care about me! I hate her and I hate my daddy, too. He could've told me."

"AHHH, Kalayla, this has been a terrible shock, and I wish there was some way I could make it better. I know for sure your mama and daddy didn't hurt you on purpose. Your mama would never do that. Give her a chance to explain. And don't you be talking about hating. If you start with hating, you'll end with hating and the one you'll hate the most will be yourself."

I didn't know if she heard a word I was saying. She sat up ramrod straight, holding herself as tight as a coiled spring ready to let fly. Those big eyes came close to burning a hole straight through me.

"I don't care! Mama and Daddy didn't care about me. Now I don't care about them. I hate Mama and I'm gonna go tell her so right now!"

Before I could get myself moving, she bolted out my door and down the stairs. I saw her run across the street to Eddie's, where she just about knocked over two dinner customers who were trying to get out the door.

Later on, Maureen told me how Kalayla stood in the middle of the restaurant screaming with rage, "I hate you, Maureen LeeRoyce! You should've told me my family was alive. You should've told me the truth! You're a liar and I hate you."

Maureen dropped the tray of dishes she was carrying and went stumbling after Kalayla, but the girl barreled out of Eddie's and down the street.

By the time I got over there, Maureen was lying on the sidewalk crying, with Eddie doing his best to get her back inside out of the cold and snow. A few people gathered near her with some trying to help calm her down, and others snapping pictures with their damn phones. Probably sending them to the Chronicle, and some snoopy reporter would be breaking speed limits getting there.

Eddie and I half dragged, half carried her back to my place, with her sobbing all the way. She kept repeating, "I should have told her," over and over and over.

I wasn't about to say, "Yeah, you should have," but that's how I felt. Not that I didn't understand. Maureen likely hadn't realized that lie would shape their lives, and by the time she finally did, it had taken on a life of its own. She didn't need me telling her what she'd be telling herself for a long time to come. In the end, one way or another, she had to face the consequences of things she'd done. No point in pouring oil on the fire.

We barely got through my door before Maureen started in pacing around the living room, wringing her hands, switching between outright bawling and pitiful whimpering. Eddie had to get back to the Eatery, so I was left on my own dealing with her. I kept on telling her Kalayla would be stomping up the stairs any minute, but I wasn't convincing her any more than I was convincing myself. I got more and more worried as the time passed.

The clock kept on ticking and the temperature kept on falling. By 9:00, it was 28 degrees and going down. By 10:00, Maureen was slumped on the sofa, and I was the one pacing.

"Okay," I said, "I'm done waiting. It's time to go searching. I'll get people in the building organized. Eddie can roust folks he knows. You call the LeeRoyce clan and get them over here."

It took a minute for that to sink in, but once it did, Maureen's face turned ghostly white. "No! No! We can't call Jamal's family. I can't tell them anything. Oh please, Lena, please, we can't let them know she's gone."

"What are you talking about, Maureen? That's your girl out there in the cold. Her father's family will be over here in a flash, just like mine would be if it was me out there."

Maureen was sobbing all over again, and I had me a devil of a time making sense of her mumbled words. "But Lucinda … will take her … not a good mother … she said she'd … know she means it."

Sweet Jesus! I forgot all about the grandma saying she'd take Kalayla if she thought Maureen wasn't able to take care of her. That Lucinda didn't sound the type to give Maureen a pass. I suspect she'd faced plenty of stark facts herself and she was done with allowing her daughter-in-law to avoid them.

"All right, all right," I said, hoping she'd turn off the fountain. "We won't call the LeeRoyce family. You call Eddie and get him going. I'll get people from the apartment building and call my brother Dom and he'll turn out my family."

Half an hour later, we had around thirty people splitting up into teams taking off in different directions. The stores along the street were closed and traffic pretty much disappeared, which made street crossing a whole lot easier. Maureen and I took the area right near Eddie's. Once you got off Mass. Ave. you were in a family neighborhood, with a few apartment houses thrown in.

I kept on thinking about where a kid Kalayla's age and size could hide. I was lugging one of those big flashlights and shining it under cars, into a couple of treehouses, behind trash barrels, anyplace that might give a little shelter from the cold and wind.

You might think having Maureen glued to me would have been a help, but let me tell you, it was the opposite. The later it got, the more she carried on, and her wailing was getting on my nerves. Sometimes we had to walk in the street, and between guiding her and keeping myself upright, I was working overtime.

I felt sorry that she was having such a hard time, but when she flopped down on a curbstone and nearly pulled me over, I was done being patient. "You listen here, Maureen LeeRoyce, we're out here to find that daughter of yours, but that is not going to happen if I spend more time taking care of you than I do searching for her. Stop sniveling and start helping or GO ON HOME."

No doubt she thought I sounded like that Lucinda, but she shut up and we kept on going. One of the corner houses had a big yard and

I thought there might be a place Kalayla could be hiding. The minute we got in the yard, I heard a dog inside the house start barking like crazy.

Some guy opened the front door and yelled, "HEY! What the hell are you doing in my yard?"

I knew good and well we could get ourselves shot by prowling around private property in the dark. I sure hoped that guy wasn't a yahoo like Ray Ray. "We're searching for a runaway girl," I called.

The man yelled back, "Well, I don't see any girl here. If she's buried under one of those snow piles, I won't find her until the snow melts. If you want to come back then and collect the body, that's fine with me. Now get the hell off my property!"

I took hold of Maureen and dragged her back to the street. I knew some folks like that guy wouldn't offer help, but they weren't the ones worrying me. Some of the searchers were worried she'd freeze to death, but I wasn't one of them. I was afraid she'd find the wrong place to get warm. Being on the streets alone at night made her easy prey for perverts. That girl wouldn't smell danger even if it was stinking like a dead mouse.

It was almost midnight when I told Maureen it was time to call the police. She got that terrified look again, "Oh, Lena, please, not just yet. If the police come, it will be on the news and then Lucinda will find out. Can't we wait a bit longer?"

The only thing that kept me from dialing 911 that minute was I understood the kind of terror she was feeling. After Joey found Carlotta and JJ and me, I knew if I'd tried to leave him again, he'd have killed me, or crippled me, and then he might have done something a lot worse. He might have made sure I never saw my boys again.

I decided we could wait a couple more hours before getting the police, but we needed reinforcements. I could rely on Lotta's family to come and not ask a bunch of bothersome questions. Mattwo was the one who could marshal their family this late on a frigid winter night, so there I was, dialing his number for the second time on account of that girl.

It was just after midnight and he guessed what was wrong the minute I said, "Matty, I'm sorry to be calling at this time of night, but …"

"It's the girl, isn't it?" he said.

"Yeah. She's taken off and we're out searching."

"She picked a cold night to run. Where'll we meet you?"

Less than twenty minutes later, I watched him get out of his car. Seeing how strong and capable he looked gave my stomach a lurch. When he walked over without saying a word, reached out and pulled me into a hug, I could have stayed there forever.

I gave myself about thirty seconds to breathe in that safe feeling.

"We'll find her," he said. "I brought the cavalry." Lotta and Rico climbed out of his car just as three other cars filled with Eccli family pulled over to the curb.

I never was one for raving about cell phones, but that night I thanked whoever invented them from saving us from backtracking or duplicating our efforts. Mattwo and Rico went off together, and I sure hoped Rico wouldn't be the one to find the girl. Who knew what she'd do if she saw him before he saw her.

Maureen and I met up with them a couple times to check in. While Mattwo and I decided where to head next, Rico huddled with Maureen, talking quietly and getting her somewhat calmed down. Whatever his technique was, it was working better than the one I used.

Just after 3 a.m., when I was feeling like a puppy dog chasing its own tail, Rico called to say he found Kalayla wedged behind a dumpster about eight blocks from Eddie's. I could hear her screaming in the background, probably waking up everybody for blocks around. Maureen took off running, and I beat it after her fast as my legs could manage.

When I got there, Kalayla was still screaming and once she got Maureen on her radar, she included her along with Rico. Maybe all that screaming was keeping her warm. The variety of swears that girl knew was truly appalling and made me wonder where she learned them.

By that point Rico was about the same place on the patience scale that I was. He tried reaching in and grabbing her, the result being that she bit his hand and unloaded more swears. A snowball had better odds of surviving in hell than Rico or Maureen did of getting her to come out. That left it to me.

Once I saw she was safe, I wasn't in much of a mood for sweet-talking or cajoling. But I did give it a try. "Kalayla, you can't spend the rest of your life wedged behind a dumpster. You may as well come on out now."

"I'll stay here long as I want. Maybe for a year."

"You'll end up skin and bones and smelling like dead skunk way before that."

"Won't either! I'll come out during the day. Lots of people will give a homeless kid like me a meal and a shower."

Sweet Jesus! Homeless kid, my ass! I'd had more than enough of that girl and her mother for one night! "You listen to me, Kalayla! I spent this whole damn night looking for you. My bones are icicles. My fingers barely move. My back hurts, and I'm hungry. Seventy-two is way too old to put up with any more of your shit. Get your ass out here right now!"

She stared at me awhile, and then she said, "Well, since you asked so nicely." She crawled out at about the speed of an inchworm, making sure I knew she was coming out of her own free will, and not because I told her to. She stood up, brushed herself off, turned her back on Maureen, and stuck her tongue out at Rico.

Her teeth were chattering, and she was shivering. But when Rico offered his coat to her, she said, "I'd rather freeze than wear any turdy coat of yours!"

Mattwo took off his jacket and handed it to her. "Here," he said, "No turds on this one."

"Thanks," she said, pulling it tight. Five of her might have fit in it, but it was better than nothing on such a night.

The searchers straggled in, most of them yawning. The temperature felt like it was about fifteen degrees. Daylight was coming and these folks needed to climb into warm beds before it did. Which was exactly what I had in mind for myself.

Kalayla read my mind. She got that stubborn look and said, "I'm not going anywhere with HER. I don't care what you say, Old Lady. You can't make me!"

I was too damn cold to spend another minute listening to her, so I did the only thing I could. I took her home with me. I told myself that was probably best because Maureen was on the edge as it was. There was no point giving Kalayla a chance to shove her over.

Naturally the first thing she wanted was food. I sat her down at the kitchen table and fried up a three-egg omelet with cheese, onions, and frozen broccoli that I keep on hand for emergencies. She shoveled it in along with three pieces of toast slathered with butter and jam, washing it down with orange juice.

When she'd finished, I said, "You stink like you crawled inside that dumpster and rooted around looking for treasure. Get those clothes off and put in a pile along with Mattwo's jacket. We'll have to get that washed or cleaned or he'll never be able to wear it again."

"I know that!" she snapped. "I got money from my cookie sales, so don't start yelling about having to wash it or pay for cleaning because you don't!"

There was no point trying to talk with her then, so I said, "Get yourself into that shower while I get you some clean clothes. You used up your quota for dumb behavior for the next twenty-five years, so you stay put while I'm gone. You hear me, girl?"

She didn't like that anymore than she liked anything else I said, but I had long since gotten immune to her repertoire of nasty looks. Good thing I didn't try to drag her home. Rico opened the door. It probably wasn't a bad idea for him to be hanging around given that Maureen was dangling from such a thin thread. She mentioned having coffee with him after the birthday party but hadn't mentioned him since, so I assumed they hadn't hit it off. I might have been wrong.

I didn't get the chance to dwell on it because Maureen came rushing at me, "Is Kalayla okay? She's not hurt, is she? Did she eat? Is she coming home? Oh, Lena, I've made such a mess of things."

I couldn't stand listening to one second more of her mea culpa recording, but Rico seemed to be managing okay. I decided when I got the chance, I'd call Carlotta and see if she'd be willing to help take the load off me and keep an eye on Maureen. They'd hit it off at the birthday party, and Lotta would not get herself dragged into Maureen's emotional morass. When Maureen and I came out of the bedroom with Kalayla's clean clothes, Rico was rummaging in the fridge. I guess he offered to cook breakfast because he asked if she wanted bacon with the French toast.

By the time I got back, Kalayla was stretched out on the sofa wrapped in my fleece throw. She stared up at the ceiling and was as talkative as a speck of dirt. Sitting around watching her didn't suit me at all.

I tried making up stories about all the creatures I had to fight off with a flashlight while I was looking for her. She wasn't the least interested, but I was having a fine time amusing myself. After I ran out of make-believe creatures, I got to telling true stories, like about the time Carlotta asked Mikie and Jimmy to pass out flyers for one of her shelter fundraisers. The twins were doing a fine job making up anything they thought might encourage people to show up, such as saying Evel Knievel was going to be giving rides on his motorcycle.

Carlotta spit nails when she found out, but never in her life has she turned her back on a challenge. She convinced an ex-boyfriend who owned a Harley it would be fun to pass himself off as Evel's cousin. Mikie and

Jimmy drove the guy crazy begging for rides. Lucky for the two of them, Lotta calmed down once she saw the big turn-out for the fundraiser.

There I was talking about my twins, and Kalayla didn't raise an eyebrow, or crack a smile, or bombard me with questions. I doubt she heard one word, so I gave up on storytelling.

Once in a while I'd say something like: You look awful sad, girl; or, Parents do some awful dumb things; or All my talking must be pretty annoying. Didn't matter—that girl did not say one single word.

By then it was going on lunchtime. When I mentioned food, she actually grunted, and that empty pit she called a stomach led her to the table. How she managed to chow down two turkey sandwiches with tomato, onion, cheese, lettuce, pickle, and mustard would have been beyond imagining if I hadn't raised four boys who could do the same.

I ran out of turkey but was about to open a can of tuna fish when she decided she hadn't given up talking altogether. "If you wanted to be nice for a change, you could give me one of Carlotta's desserts." I cut her a big hunk of chocolate pie. She didn't say another word, and I figured it was time for me to shut up and let her be.

But not before I did one more thing. I went digging around in the back of the storage closet and pulled out a big old cardboard box tied with plain string. No fancy wrapping, no way anyone would know inside was the one thing I couldn't bring myself to give away, even after all these years.

Cody was wrapped in layers of tissue paper. I unwrapped a piece at a time, folded each one carefully and put them all back in the box. And there he was: a four-foot-high stuffed brown bear. His fur was rubbed off in a few spots, and one ear was sewn back on with big uneven red stitches.

I held him close and let images of each of my boys holding him, sharing him, loving him flood over me. I remembered my oldest, JJ, sitting on the sofa using that red thread on Cody's ear, so determined to sew it back without my help.

I carried Cody into the living room and put him down next to Kalayla. "This is Cody," I said, "He belonged to my four boys."

Kalayla reached out, pulled Cody close, and buried her face in his fur just like my boys had done when they needed comfort. That was more than I could take. I marched myself into the kitchen and set about cleaning things that didn't need cleaning. I could hear Kalayla crying, and there wasn't any part of me that wasn't crying along with her.

I was glad it got dark early. Kalayla had been fading long before the shadows came, which was no surprise since she just lived through the worst 24 hours of her life.

I thought I'd try one more thing, so I said, "Going to sleep angry interferes with digestion, and given all you ate, you could develop a gigantic stomach ache. You might prevent that if you went home and talked to your mama."

"She'd be the only one talking, and all she does is lie!" Her words were angry, but her face was forlorn enough to make a stone heart weep. She held onto Cody like she was never planning to let go.

I sat down in the chair near her and waited a minute. Then I took a deep breath and said, "I'll take that as a 'no.' So exactly where did you have in mind to spend the night?"

Her voice cracked when she said, "I was hoping you'd let me stay here."

I knew that was as close to pleading as she would ever in her life come. Sweet Jesus, how I struggled to keep myself from wrapping my arms around her, pulling her close, and crooning to her the way I had with my boys when they were little and hurting. Even Mark, who picked fights with anybody in sight, and JJ, who wanted to be cool and tough like his dad, even those two would let me pull them close when they were her age.

But right then, it seemed like what Kalayla needed was time and space to work her way through the mess her mama and daddy handed her. And that was something I could give her. I said, "And what did you plan on doing if I said 'no'."

She squared her shoulders and pulled herself upright. "I'd go find another dumpster."

"HA! Then I'll have some cop dragging me out in the cold in the middle of the night so I can identify your frozen body. At least if you stay here, my old bones will be warm, and I might even get some sleep."

She almost—not quite, but almost—smiled. "Can I sleep in the white room and keep Cody with me?"

All of a sudden, my boys were shoving at each other, all of them wanting to claim Cody for the night. JJ turned to me, asserting his privilege as oldest. Mark grabbed Cody and ran for his life. The twins used their secret sign language to divide up the night, equal shares of Cody. Then they tore after Mark.

Mark, furious and knowing the two of them would overpower him, hurled Cody by the ear, shouting how they were unfair assholes, too chicken to face him one on one. All four boys froze in mid-step, stunned, and focused on the ear that was in Mark's hand. JJ screamed, "You're the asshole for hurting Cody," and launched into Mark.

A voice broke through the memory, calling me back.

"Can I, Lena?" Kalayla was staring at me, waiting for my answer, not realizing I was listening to my boys' voices fade away.

"Of course you can," I said, taking a deep breath, holding back exhaustion a few more minutes. "Cody has to sleep someplace, and he likes kids. If you want to, you can sleep on that sofa you've been hogging. The only bed in the spare room is the floor."

"I don't care," she said, sticking her chin out, stubborn as always. "It's quiet there. And it's empty. I like it."

***

Quiet. Empty. Reminding me of the big house that had been Joey's showpiece, where bit by bit, the sounds had faded into silence and all the life was gone.

JJ was the first to leave, moving to an apartment with friends after high school graduation. Joey wanted him in the business full time right away, so he went nights to Lowell Tech.

Mark was the next to leave. To Boston, to New York City, and then out West. At the beginning, he sent occasional postcards, but the last one was years and years ago. I wondered if his broken body was buried in an anonymous grave. JJ gave me an odd look when I asked if he knew where Mark was, but then he shrugged and didn't answer. I gave up asking.

When Joey died, his absence didn't leave a hole in my life, but I was a lost soul when the twins were killed. In spite of all the protests against the Vietnam War, they were determined to enlist. JJ encouraged them, saying they would make their father proud by enlisting. I didn't know if they believed him. When I asked why they insisted on going they said, "Look, Ma, those guys going to Canada are a bunch of shit-faced cowards. The Marines need guys like us, guys who'll stand up and fight for our country."

I didn't tell them that JJ was wrong, that serving in the military was the last thing Joey would have done, the last thing he would have encouraged any of them to do. He told me war was for ignorant schmucks too stupid to figure a way out of going. His happiest day was when World War II ended before he was old enough to go.

Whatever the reason, the twins enlisted and were shipped home in body bags. At first, I wandered around Joey's house, poking in the boys' rooms and straightening this or that. Or I'd go down the basement to their game room, staring at the pool table, or up to the attic, picking through toys, pulling out drawings, or report cards, or prized possessions like the twins' first stripe on their karate belts, or the first dollar JJ earned shoveling snow, or the dog-eared playing cards Mark bragged taught him how to cheat and not get caught.

Carlotta said I was a fool, acting like my boys would be home for dinner, keeping their rooms and all their things just like they left them. "Face the facts, Lena," she told me, "Mikie and Jimmy are dead. Mark jumped into a black hole, and JJ is making his own life. He'll never come home."

She meant well. I knew that. But she had no idea how I felt. What happened to my boys was my doing. If I had gotten them away from Joey, they all might have had a chance. I couldn't stay in that house by myself, so I left and slipped into the gutter, drinking my way from one dive to another. That's where Dom found me.

"Clean yourself up," Dom ordered. "Mother asked to see you and you're not fit to see anybody, especially not her!" He drove me back to Joey's house to shower and change out of clothes that reeked. I longed to drown myself in scotch, but Dom followed me up to the bedroom and then waited outside the bathroom door. I swear he would have come in with me if he thought I'd hidden a bottle underneath the sink. Right then, I wished I had.

My mother, the family matriarch and my mentor, was on her death bed. The shades on her bedroom windows blocked out the sun and the room felt sick to me, in need of airing. She could barely lift her hand to shoo the nurse away and motion me close, so she could whisper in my ear. Her bony fingers pressed into my arm. "Don't you dare let those vultures get you, Lena! We bury them. They don't bury us. You're a survivor, just like me. Don't you ever forget that!"

I nodded. I understood what she was telling me. The family would accept a skillful woman in a high position, but a drunk would hurt the business, and that would never be tolerated. She was telling me to get out of the gutter and follow in her footsteps the way she had taught me.

I dried out, threw myself into work, and stripped the house where I'd raised my boys to bare bones. I gave away or threw away almost everything connected to life with Joey. Then I sold the house and moved into the apartment building. I gave up the showy life and bought only what I needed. I could imagine someone walking in my door and wondering if I hadn't finished moving in or wasn't finished moving out. Almost thirty years of living here, and I still wouldn't know what to tell them.

Nothing except the photos and Cody carried memories, and Cody had been buried in the back of that closet until Kalayla gave me a reason to open the box and take him out.

Maybe the white room would be a haven where Kalayla could begin to heal. She was young and innocent, so different from me. I had spent days exposed and defenseless in that room, staring out the windows seeing nothing, enduring a self-styled flagellation without a whip. Maybe she'd find something in there I hadn't.

I pulled out some blankets and sheets. I'd buy a blow-up mattress if the girl complained about the floor, and if, Sweet Jesus help me, it looked like she'd be a long-term guest.

The next morning came way too soon for me, but Kalayla was probably glad enough to get off that floor. Not that she said a word about it being too hard or uncomfortable. Once her stomach got filled, I marched her out the door, and reminded her there were laws requiring kids her age to attend school.

She resembled a zombie, but that didn't stop her mouth from going full tilt as she took the stairs two at a time and yelled back at me, "What'd somebody old as you know about school? It wasn't invented when you were a kid."

The minute she was gone, I plopped down on the sofa. My old bones and muscles might have been aching for a lullaby, but my thoughts were jumping beans. IF Kalayla actually got to school, and IF she stayed until the end of the day, what was I going to do when she got home?

Was it foolish self-deception that persuaded me to offer a child—a hurting child—shelter in my house? I had no answer. All I could do was hope that what I did now would be better than anything I'd done before.

MAUREEN

DINNER AT LENA'S

Every day when I came home from work, I stood in the apartment doorway and held my breath. Please let my girl be at home. Every time I called her name, speakers blared the silence that filled every room. I covered my ears, but there wasn't any way to shut it out.

Every day after I came home from work and stood in the apartment doorway and heard the silence, I knocked on Lena's door. Every day Lena opened the door, and shook her head. I went home to an empty apartment.

On the eighth day, Lena opened the door and then opened her arms. I walked into her hug. "Oh, Lena, she just has to talk to me tonight. She just has to."

"She doesn't have to, sweet girl, but I sure do hope she will. Whether she does or not, you have to keep on trying. She's holed up in the room right now doing homework. Leastways that's what she said she was going to be doing. For all I know she could be standing on her head."

I couldn't help being terrified. Losing Kalayla would be worse than losing my family, worse than losing Jamal. It would be the very worst that could ever happen to me. "What will I do if she won't ever come home?"

"Now, Maureen, don't you go making it worse by exaggerating. You stay here and eat with us tonight. I'll make coffee and finish getting dinner together. If anything can get that girl out of that room, it's food. But don't get your hopes up. Nothing is going to make her be civil."

I didn't care if she was silent or scowling or obnoxiously insulting. At least I'd be sitting at the same table with her. At least I could see for myself that she was all right. Really, anything would be better than hearing her shout through the door, "Go away, I hate you."

"But what if she won't come out?"

"Well, then, the two of us are going to have a good meal without her. Don't you be worrying. She won't be wasting away from any lack of food if she decides to be stubborn—more stubborn. It's high time we gave her a little shove. Waiting for the perfect circumstance is beginning to look like we might be waiting forever."

I sat on the sofa wringing my hands and fidgeting. I hadn't changed from my work clothes, and I hoped I didn't have a spill on my slacks that could stain her sofa. Whatever possessed her to buy white? I guess if you lived alone, you could buy whatever you wanted.

I hated waiting so much, and I could have made a whole meal in a quarter of the time Lena was taking to brew coffee. My life was a mess, and I was waiting for coffee. I bet a songwriter could have turned that line into a solid gold recording. Too bad I wasn't a songwriter, or a singer, or a musician.

FINALLY! The smell of coffee and Lena calling from the kitchen, "Dinner is ready. Come carry the food to the table while I go prod that girl of yours."

Lena went to the spare room door, knocked once and said, "Kalayla, come on out here to eat. And put a brush through that hair of yours. We've got a guest for dinner."

I heard some shuffling behind the spare room door, and then Kalayla said, "Maybe I'll come out, and maybe I won't. Who's the guest?"

"If you don't come out, maybe I'll be tossing your share of fried chicken, green beans, mashed potatoes and gravy, and Lotta's lemon meringue pie in the garbage. And for your edification, a more polite response would have been: 'Thank you, Miss Lena, for going to all the trouble of cooking my favorite dinner."

"I don't need any vocabulary lessons, Miss Lena, and you already gave me enough polite lectures to last me forever. If I'd known what the menu was, I would've said thank you on my own. Who's the guest?"

"It's your mama."

"Eating with her would make the food taste like cow turds. I'll bring my plate in here or else I'll eat after she leaves."

"You will eat with us now, at the table, or your next meal will be a long time coming. This is not a fast-food establishment where you order what you want when it pleases you."

Silence from the room.

I prayed the smell of Lena's cooking, especially the fried chicken, would make Kalayla's mouth water and her stomach growl and lead her to the table. More than anything, I prayed she'd open the door.

"Fine!" she said, "but I'm not talking to her and don't think you can make me."

"Suit yourself. It's a free country."

I truly hoped Lena didn't hear her answer, "Fat chance with you around, you old crab!"

A few minutes later, Kalayla stomped to the table and sat down facing Lena, as far from me as she could get. We hadn't bothered waiting to serve ourselves. Lena had motioned me to the table, probably so I wouldn't be the first thing Kalayla saw when she opened the door.

I hadn't seen my girl in over a week, and that's not long compared to six months or a year, but she looked different and older. Well, maybe not older exactly, but more grown-up and serious. Her 'in your face' attitude still seemed on the verge of bubbling out, and I had trouble imagining her sitting at the kitchen table singing under her breath and giggling while she stuck Red Hots all over Clarence's gingerbread devil cookie.

Kalayla helped herself to a chicken breast, poured gravy on top of it and the mashed potatoes, while she muttered, "Least she left me some food." I didn't know if she meant Lena or me, but either way, she made certain she got her share plus some.

My appetite drained away. When I asked how school was going, and what she had been doing, and if she needed anything, she acted as if I was invisible. I ended up pushing beans around my plate, wishing I knew what to say or do. Lena was absolutely no help. When I asked how her day had been, the only thing she said was, "Just fine, thanks."

Staying for dinner had turned out to be another terrible mistake, and that seemed to be the only thing I was good at—making terrible mistakes. And then, right out of the blue, Lena said, "So, I haven't seen that Clarence fellow poking around lately. He must be busy working or something. More likely, it's 'or something' than working."

Kalayla's head snapped up, and she stared at Lena.

"Clarence?" I said. "Funny you ask because he called to say he might be stopping by this weekend. And he does work, Lena. He calls himself a free-lance car location expert. I'm not quite sure what that means. And Layla, he was very curious about when you'd be at home, so I know he wants to see you, but I told him you might not be around this weekend."

Kalayla kept staring at Lena. "Clarence never wanted to see me before! Ask her why all of a sudden, he'd wanna know when I'm gonna be home! Ask her that, Lena!"

I thought Lena would yell at Kalayla for being so rude, but other than give her a deadly stare, she didn't say one word. And for once, I didn't care. Even if Kalayla hadn't talked directly to me, at least she acknowledged I was actually in the room.

And really, I wondered the same thing. Why would Clarence want to know when Kalayla would be home? I would have said that, but I didn't want to sound like I didn't think Clarence was trustworthy. Even though he wasn't. He did find the car for us, and he did give Kalayla those cookies so she could earn money and I was grateful to him for that.

Then Lena said something even more surprising. "Yes, I've been thinking about how decent it was of him to share those cookies he happened to acquire. I've been thinking I'd like to meet him so I can get myself added to his cookie list."

Really, I couldn't imagine what was on her mind, but I didn't get a chance to figure it out because then she said, "My oh, my. I didn't realize Clarence had a car location business. I'm aware of the skills that line of work requires. My son Mark tried his hand at it for a short time. When I meet Clarence, I'll inquire if he's light-fingered enough to relocate one of those cute little Mercedes convertibles into my garage. Just think, Kalayla, we could ride with the top down all summer."

I was totally flabbergasted. I opened my mouth, but the words jumbled together and all that came out was, "Agg."

Kalayla was not the least bit tongue-tied. She slammed her fork down on the table and said, "Don't you dare say anything like that to him, Lena! He didn't steal our car. He told me he got it from a friend. He won't like it if you say stuff like that!"

I was shocked when Kalayla looked directly at me and said, "Mama, you tell her! Tell her she better not be messing with Uncle Clarence! Tell her she better keep away from him!"

I was so happy I almost jumped out of my chair. My daughter talked to me! Directly to me! Lena sat there smirking, clearly pleased with herself.

Before I could gather my wits and answer, she turned to Kalayla and said, "Don't talk with your mouth full, Kalayla. I'm not taking any trip to the emergency room on account of you choking on food. And I will thank you not to be telling me what I should or should not dare to do. You'd be surprised what I'm willing to do at my age that I wouldn't have dared do when I was your mama's age. Back then, I was just as chicken shit scared as she is now."

I gasped, and Kalayla sat bolt upright and pointed her finger at Lena, "My Mama is not chicken shit scared! You don't know anything!"

"Well, girl, my eyes may be old, but they see better than yours do. Your mama IS chicken shit scared. She's scared she's going to lose you!" Her gaze narrowed as if she was gauging Kalayla's reaction. Which was to scowl and glance sideways at me.

"If she wants a kid so bad, let her give some street kid a home the way Grandma LeeRoyce does. She can tell them big fat lies!"

My heart was pounding, and sauna heat would have felt cooler than I did at that moment. Coming here was a terrible mistake.

Lena threw her napkin on the table. "You don't understand your mama at all, Miss Smarty Pants! Your mama is just like me and you and everybody else! She does stupid things, just like the rest of us. You're the one who put her on the Perfect Mama Pedestal. She never belonged there. Nobody does."

Kalayla stared down at her plate, her face screwed up like she was about to spew out rotten food.

Lena took a quick breath and said, "And it's about time you gave your mama a chance to explain WHY she lied to you."

I held my breath. Kalayla blinked a few times. Lena helped herself to potatoes and gravy. Of all the totally ridiculous things, words from that old gamblers' song popped into my head: Know when to hold them; know when to fold them; know when to walk away, and know when to run.

Lena had laid her cards face up on the table, and I prayed my daughter wouldn't jump up and bolt for the door.

Time passed in slow motion. Kalayla stared at her plate. Lena spread gravy around the top and sides of her mashed potatoes. I watched.

Finally, Kalayla looked up, speared a drumstick with her fork and said, "At least I was smart enough not to put YOU on a pedestal!"

Lena shoveled potato onto her fork and into her mouth, and gave a good chew before saying, "Well, Miss Smarty Pants, that remark just earned you your walking papers! Once you get finished stuffing your face, you get in there and clean up the room where you've been squatting.

Then you get on home and practice acting decent!"

Mustering her dirtiest of dirty looks, Kalayla said, "Fine!" And then under her breath, "Turdy old crab!"

Lena twirled her fork around in the potato pile before picking up another glob. She turned to me. "And I'm expecting you to let me know when I should come over and meet the famous Clarence and his white horse."

I nodded. I was afraid anything I said might change Kalayla's mind. Might take away my chance to make things right. I held tight to my hope, cleared the table and wiped the dishes, while Kalayla was in the spare room straightening up and gathering her things. My baby girl was coming home!

When Kalayla came out dragging her canvas bag, Lena handed her a hunk of Carlotta's lemon meringue pie on a paper plate. After Kalayla left, Lena hugged me and whispered in my ear, "Telling her you love her is enough for now. That and this."

She handed me another plate of pie.

MARCH 2000

KALAYLA

CLARENCE

The second the Old Lady brought Uncle Clarence up at dinner and Mama said he'd be coming this weekend, I knew I had to get back home even though it meant declaring a temporary truce with Mama. I couldn't take a chance of not being there when he did us the big favor of showing up, so I was gonna be chained to the apartment. What a pisser!

The problem with Lena was she thought she knew everything, and she didn't know a thing about Clarence. If I told her what he was like, she would've flipped into one of her tirades, and who knows what she would've done after that.

Like if I told her about the time he showed up with a whole pile of gold bracelets and necklaces a friend gave him. He told Mama to take whatever she liked, and he'd come by for payment sometime when I wasn't home. I guess he thought I didn't have ears attached to my head. He got pissed when Mama said she didn't like any of the stuff.

Another time he offered to take care of me for a couple hours while Mama ran errands. He dragged me to one of his favorite bars and said I could order any kind of drink I wanted and it'd be our secret. He laughed like anything when he saw how good I was at playing pool. He said I had a natural talent, and my innocent face would be a fine enticement for fools if I wanted to make a little side money for myself.

Mama said Daddy was a good, honest man while Clarence was quick, shifty, and not to be relied on, but I should be nice to him anyway 'cause Daddy said Clarence had a hard time when he was a kid. So what? I was a kid and I wasn't having a great old time, but I didn't see people falling out of the sky being nice to me. Except maybe the Old Lady, sometimes. And the people at Eddie's, all the time.

I didn't care what Mama and Daddy said. Anybody could see Clarence was sniffing around Mama, and I wasn't gonna give him a chance to do anything more than sniff. The Old Lady would've said I didn't know a thing about sniffing around, but she would've been wrong. I watched Mama and Daddy plenty of times. He used to slap her on the butt and ask how his honey pot was. She'd snuggle up close to him and laugh and tease him about being in heat.

Well, Clarence was in heat. When the Old Lady saw Clarence with Mama, she was gonna notice that right off, and then she'd be sticking her nose in full time. I didn't know what Uncle Clarence might do if she started shooting off her mouth, and I didn't want to find out.

The fact that Mama wasn't interested in Clarence wasn't gonna cool him down. Which was why I was stuck standing guard. He ruined my Saturday by not showing up, and Mama insisted on telling Lena that he called Saturday afternoon to say he'd definitely be stopping by on Sunday morning.

Wouldn't you know the Old Lady knocks on our door at 9 a.m. with a bunch of magazines and tells us she's gonna stay "for the duration." We were lucky she didn't come the night before! Mama was just thrilled as she could be having Lena over. She made it a big deal, putting on a tablecloth and putting out dumb teacups and saucers and little plates. The only good thing was she made caramel covered brownies.

While we were waiting, Mama dragged out the photo album to show Lena. They sat next to each other on the sofa turning the pages, yakking it up. About eight million photos were of me, plus three million were of Mama and Daddy and me. There were a few of Grandma and Grandpa with the three of us and a couple with them and me.

There wasn't a single photo of anyone from Mama's family and the more I thought about it, the madder I got. By the time Uncle Clarence banged on the door, I was pissed enough to slam it in his face. The only reason I didn't was seeing the way his face dropped when he saw me standing there. That was the best thing that happened to me in about six months! He was probably hoping I fell in a sewer and was drowned.

"Kalayla!" he practically shouted, "I didn't think you'd be here! Your Mama said you might be staying with a friend for a couple days."

As usual, he must've found a parking space right out front 'cause there was hardly any snow on his leather jacket. He swiped a hand over his shiny bald head and wiped the moisture on his jeans. His loafers looked new, and with any luck, they'd get ruined.

I gave him my sweetest smile and said, "Hey Uncle, aren't you happy nobody kidnapped me?"

Before he got a chance to answer, the old lady pushed herself off the sofa, grabbed his hand and shook it the way you would a bottle of salad dressing.

"I'm Lena Barzetti from across the hall," she told him. "Maureen and I were making plans for our next Neighborhood Watch meeting. I'm certain you're happy to know that we all keep a real close eye on each other around here."

Neighborhood Watch?

I don't know who was more shocked, Uncle Clarence or Mama or me. I knew the old lady was going to pull something but, cow turds, a neighborhood watch?

Anyway, Clarence got over being stunned and said hi, but I noticed he didn't put down the oversize shopping bag he was carrying. So, by way of encouraging him to open it, I pointed at it and said, "Oh, Uncle, did you bring some goodies for us like you always do?"

He looked daggers at me, so I gave him another big smile. This was turning into the best day ever.

"This is … ah, ah, I went clothes shopping and bought some things I didn't want to leave in the car," he said, shifting from one foot to the other.

Before I could say anything, Lena said, "Oh, I know just what you mean. It's best to be careful. If some thief decided to relocate your car, I imagine he'd be happy to get new clothes thrown into the deal!"

My smile kept getting bigger. "Oh, goody gumdrops! Uncle Clarence please, please try on your new clothes and give us a fashion show! I love fashion shows, don't I, Miss Lena?"

I knew when I had a good thing going and was about to load on more, but the old lady butted in AGAIN.

"Clarence—you don't mind me calling you Clarence, do you Clarence? I notice every time you come to visit Maureen and Kalayla, and I told Maureen it was high time I met this kind-hearted brother-in-law of hers. Why, everyone in our Neighborhood Watch keeps track of the way you check on Kalayla and her mama. Just recently, one of our Watch members said, 'What a fine man that uncle is.' Now while we're eating, I want you to tell old Miss Lena all about yourself and all about your business deals. It's so good of you to bring gifts like the cookies your sweet little niece sold me!"

I almost wet my pants! That Old Lady's mouth must've tasted like sour lemons and vinegar from calling me sweet. Her nose was gonna wrap around the world twice for that one, but I had to admire the way she rocked Uncle Clarence back on his heels. You can bet I was not gonna let her forget those words! Sweet little niece!

Mama hadn't said a word, and just when I thought she was gonna smile, she turned her back on us to inspect the table. Then she said, "Why don't we all sit down for coffee and a sweet? Uncle Clarence's fashion show can wait until after we eat. Isn't that right, Clarence?"

Once Daddy said something that made me laugh, but I never got a chance to say it myself—'til now. Uncle Clarence looked like he was about to shit a brick. Which would've been a real pisser with him all dressed up in his silk shirt and tight blue jeans! Bet he wouldn't've dressed that way if he knew I was gonna be there or if he knew the Old Lady was too.

One thing about Uncle Clarence, he did know when it was time to retreat. He took a couple steps back and opened the door, hanging on real tight to that big shopping bag.

"Ahhh, sorry, Maureen," he said, "I guess I forgot to tell you I can't stay today. I just stopped by, ah, to see that you were okay. I'll catch you another time when there's less, ah, when there's less going on." He turned and went bounding down the stairs.

Lena called after him, "I'll look forward to chatting with you next time you come, Clarence, dear." Mama closed the door and all three of us burst out laughing. I laughed 'til my stomach ached.

I decided my truce with Mama could keep going long enough to celebrate with a few of her caramel brownies.

After that morning, being home was about as much fun as playing in cement. Mama tip-toed around like she was scared I was gonna explode if she breathed too loud. And I didn't feel like my good old cheerful self.

Don't get the idea I wanted to go back to the Old Lady's. Her mouth going all the time was a pisser. Like one day I was maybe seven minutes late getting home from school, she said, "That smart mouth get you detention AGAIN?"

Just showed she didn't know a thing about school. No teacher kept you a measly seven minutes! They tortured you a lot longer. If I was still staying over at the Old Lady's, I would've bought myself a pair of ear-plugs.

Once I got home, I started thinking about how I could help her out by redecorating her apartment. I'd start by giving her walls a fresh coat of paint and maybe adding a mural to the living room with flowers and trees, and maybe a pond or lake. If she ever got in a good mood, I might mention it to her.

And another thing. Lena's place was too quiet, but there was no way I could fix that. She had a radio and TV, but she said they were off-limits to me. I never saw her turn 'em on either, so why'd she waste her money buying stuff she never used?

All that white and quiet must've got my brain charged up, and it wouldn't shut off once I got home. I couldn't stop thinking about my O'Rourke family. Now that I knew they were alive, I kept wondering when Mama was gonna take me to meet them. And how was I supposed to act when she did? Like, would my grandma and grandpa expect me to run up and hug them? I didn't just go around hugging any old person, even if they were my grandparents. I didn't want 'em to think I wasn't friendly, so maybe I should shake their hands. And what about my cousins? They might be assholes like the kids at school. Or what if they were nerds?

I was wondering a bunch of other stuff, too. Like, why didn't any of Mama's family come to Daddy's funeral? The crash was in the newspapers and on TV. Maybe they didn't watch TV or read newspapers. But they must've 'cause their picture was in that sports article. I kept thinking maybe they didn't know Daddy was dead, but I couldn't come up with a good reason for why.

I was stopping by the Old Lady's every day after school to make sure she hadn't dropped dead without me there taking care of her. When I told her what I'd been thinking 'bout my grandparents and cousins, she said, "Now you listen to me, Kalayla. Don't you be thinking the O'Rourkes are going to be your new best friends. When you meet them. If you meet them."

Why'd she have to go and say something like that? Like maybe I oughta be nervous about meeting 'em, or scared of what they might be like. It made me feel all weird inside.

Well, I wasn't scared of meeting them, if that's what she thought. I wasn't scared of anything, and I had scars to prove it. When I was about five, a neighbor kid said I was too scared to jump out a window on the second floor of his house.

"Am not," I said.

"Are, too."

"Am not."

"Are, too."

I jumped just to shut him up. The pisser was I landed on broken glass, and my hands and knees got all cut up, but I didn't care. He never called me chicken again.

Even though I wasn't scared, the whole thing kept aggravating at me. Anybody would get aggravated thinking about meeting relatives that were supposed to be dead.

And besides all that, being home was a real pisser. Mama and I got into a regular routine competing for first place in a politeness contest. I'd be polite saying goodbye when I left the apartment, and polite saying hello when I came back. I'd be polite eating dinner even if I had to cook it myself, and polite telling her goodnight when I went to bed.

There was only so much being polite a person could take. By the fourth day, I was sick of being civil and didn't think I could stand doing it much longer. At least when I was at the Old Lady's house, I could act like my regular self.

A couple days later I was sitting on the sofa at home munching an apple, surfing channels when Mama came home from work. She was all hyped up about how wonderful it was we were spending more time together.

Yeah, but as usual, it didn't occur to her to ask me if I thought it was jolly wonderful, so I got pissed and said, "Yeah, right! And now there's plenty of time for you to take me over and introduce me to my O'Rourke family, right?"

Mama turned white as the Old Lady's walls. She acted like she wanted to say something, but was having trouble getting the words out. It was kind of funny watching her, and I was thinking about what I should do to help. Like maybe I should call a dentist so he could come pull the words out, one by one. Or maybe I should get a pliers and do it myself—except my clothes might get all bloodied up.

Anyway, she finally swallowed, and clenched her fists. Then she started pulling out words one at a time, real slow like getting out every word was wicked painful. "I … will … call … my … mother … and … she … will … hang … up … on … me … again."

Now that really pissed me! I was almost feeling sorry for her until she said that. "Yeah, right," I said. "She did that 'cause you never let her meet me, right? I don't blame her. I would've hung up on you, too!"

Mama sucked in her breath, and her face twisted like I'd cut her open and was watching her guts spill out. And then even if my ears had been stuffed full of cotton, I would've heard what she whispered. "That's not the way it happened, Kalayla. My mother … my mother never wanted to meet you. She never wanted to meet your daddy, either. She didn't want me to marry him … because he wasn't … because he wasn't … because he was black. When I married him, they kicked me out of the family."

She stopped whispering, but what she said kept echoing in my ears: "They kicked me out of the family."

Families couldn't do that, could they? I was sure they couldn't do that. But maybe they could. Maybe they did.

Maybe that's why Mama's name wasn't listed as one of Kevin and Colleen's children. Colin, Leah, Kate were, but Maureen wasn't.

Mama started talking again in that same whisper. "When I found out I was pregnant with you, I was so, so happy, Kalayla. I wanted to tell my mother. I thought for sure she'd forgive me. You were her first granddaughter and she'd been waiting for a granddaughter. Your daddy warned me not to call, but I wouldn't listen.

"When my mother answered the phone, she said, 'I used to have a daughter named Maureen, but she's dead.' And then she hung up.

"But even though she said that, I thought if I ever really needed her help, she'd be there for me. When I was so shaky and was having such a hard time figuring things out when you and I moved back home after Daddy died, I tried again. I went to the house, but she slammed the door in my face. I knew then that we were on our own."

Mama didn't say anything else. She stood there looking at me. I sat looking back at her. Neither of us saying anything.

I wanted to know the truth. Now I did. I didn't feel mad or glad or sad or upset. I didn't feel anything at all. My brain had gone numb.

A remote-control operator made me stand up. Made me walk to the apartment door. Open the door. Walk across the hallway to Lena's. Knock on her door. When she answered, it made me walk past her into the spare room. Close the door. Sit in the chair. Stare out the window.

LENA

FACING THE ELEPHANT

That girl walked right on past me like I didn't exist. She went into the spare room and closed the door while I stood there watching her, acting like I was Lena the Dunce. I turned and saw Maureen standing in her doorway. Sometimes when I saw her, I got the feeling she was hovering about a foot off the ground and was about to float into outer space. But right at that moment, she looked oak solid with roots planted deep in the earth. My, oh my! Something big caused that. Probably the same something big that drove my squatter back into the spare room.

Maureen crossed the hallway, looked me straight in the eye, and in a matter of fact tone said, "I told her, Lena. I told her the whole truth. And you know what? It felt like I was clearing out rancid garbage and throwing it in the trash. It felt really good."

Maureen smiled the most peaceful smile I'd ever seen on that beautiful face, and I do admit I heaved a huge sigh of relief. I put my arms around her and gave her a big hug. "I imagine it made you feel clean all over, the way a good soaking in a hot tub does for me."

She nodded. "But what should I do now? Kalayla walked out without saying anything, and you know that isn't like her, Lena. She always says what she thinks. You know she does. Should I have stopped her from leaving? Do you think I did the wrong thing?"

"First off, I sincerely doubt you or anybody else could stop that girl when she got something in her mind to do or to say. Her saying nothing means she's got nothing to say. Yet. This has been a real shock to her, probably felt like a bolt of lightning out of nowhere hit her square on. That girl has been imagining all kinds of reasons why you didn't tell her, but nothing she imagined could have prepared her for the truth. You have to let what you told her sink in. She needs time to wrap her brain around it the way we all do when something gives us such a shock."

"Do you think I should come over and wait to see if she wants to talk?"

"Now, Maureen, there is no way of telling how long she'll need. I think you should leave her be. And don't you be worrying. At least she didn't take off for that damn dumpster again. That counts for a lot. And now she knows the truth. You finally did what had to be done."

Maureen smiled, turned, and went back to their apartment. I brewed a cup of the lemon ginger tea Carlotta gave me for Christmas, and settled down on the living room sofa. The confident face I had put on for Maureen was a long way from what I was actually feeling. I didn't think Kalayla would be coming out of that room anytime soon. And when she did, I doubted her mama would be on the list of people she'd be talking to.

What worried me was I didn't know how Kalayla would react to being blindsided again. What worried me was this could turn her good-natured feistiness into hatred and anger because of the way the O'Rourke's had treated her mama and her daddy. And because of the way they had treated her, acting like she didn't exist. There was no way of knowing who might end up on Kalayla's hate list, but I sure hoped one of those names wouldn't be her mama's.

I spent a couple hours turning the whole thing over in my mind, asking myself what I could do, what I should do. Wondering if doing anything was better than doing nothing.

I finally got disgusted. All my thinking wasn't going to prevent that girl from walking out of that room and out of this apartment just as fast as she walked into it. And she wouldn't bother to stop and ask my permission first. I went over and knocked softly on the door.

Silence. I waited a couple of minutes, and then I knocked again. Silence.

"Well," I said to myself, "Lena, old woman, you can't be waiting for that child to get herself ready. You need to do something right now." I went to the closet and pulled out one of my folding chairs. I knocked on the door one more time, and then I opened it and went in.

Kalayla was slumped over in the chair, her elbows resting on her knees, her face hidden in her hands. She didn't move when I put my chair down right next to her. We sat side by side for a long time, with neither of us moving. Until I couldn't take it any longer. Until I reached over and rested my hand on her back.

And then that girl did something that broke open my heart. She leaned over, put her head on my shoulder, and came as close to curling up in my lap as she could. It took me back to the times when one of my boys was little and hurting and curled in my lap for comfort.

Her crying started out soft and muffled, building to a crescendo, with every bit of her skinny body sobbing out grief.

"It's okay, girl," I whispered through my own tears. "Your mama loves you. I love you. We'll find a way out of this. We'll find a way."

It took a long, long time, but her tears finally dried up.

She stayed so quiet after she stopped crying, I started worrying about what might be going on in that head of hers.

Then all of a sudden she blurted out, "Is there anything to eat in this house?"

I burst out laughing, a geyser of relief flooding me. "You know very well there is always something to eat in this house. Let's go out and see what I've got."

I grilled her two tuna and cheese sandwiches and got out the bag of sea salt and vinegar potato chips. After she'd eaten every bit, she turned and looked at me and said, "Families can't kick you out, can they Lena? Even if you're a real jerk, they have to keep you, right?"

Sweet Jesus, help me. That innocent child didn't know a thing about parents who sold their kids like chattel. She didn't know a thing about a husband disfiguring a wife while her family stood by and watched. She didn't know a thing about a family that said you had to stay married for the sake of the business, no matter what your husband did to you.

I prayed she'd never learn all the things families were capable of doing. But she did need to face what her Mama's family had done.

"Some families do take care of you and love you no matter what. Other families don't. Your mama's family is one of those that don't. What they did to your mama and to your daddy and to you is beyond my ability to explain or understand. What they did caused horrible hurt, and that's just plain wrong."

I shut my mouth then, but sometimes after you think you're done talking, you find out you aren't because your old mouth opens itself up and keeps on going. "And that's their loss, Kalayla. It's their loss. If they were willing to get to know you, they'd love you, just like I do. They'd be proud to have you as their grandchild, same as I'd be if you were mine."

She stared at me, those beautiful green eyes wide, her head cocked to the side like she wasn't quite sure she understood what I said.

"You said if they got to know me, they'd love me like you do, right?"

I nodded.

"You said they'd be proud I was their granddaughter, just like you're proud I'm your granddaughter, right?"

If this didn't beat all! My ears might be old, but I was sure I heard what she said, and I did believe that girl just granted me grandmother status! I nodded and when Kalayla smiled, my old heart bloomed spring flowers.

My own son JJ hoarded his gold-plated kids, my flesh and blood granddaughters. When his girls were little, the only time he would bring them to my apartment was on Halloween and I don't doubt Joey reached out from Hell and whispered that idea into his ear. I can hear Joey chortling: "Halloween is the perfect time for the girls to visit that old bitchy witch." Juliana would come dressed as a princess or a kidnapped damsel in distress. Ronnie would come as a cowgirl or Wonder Woman or an astronaut.

I was well aware that JJ disapproved of where I lived and the way I dressed. When the girls were small he told me, "Look Ma, I don't want you giving my girls the idea that the way you live is normal. Because it isn't. If Dad was alive, you guys would be living in Weston near us, and you could see the girls all the time—like a real grandmother." He did invite me out there for Thanksgiving and Easter, and every few months I'd invite them to dinner at a restaurant JJ suggested. Joey would have been proud that JJ was living a life of luxury in the manner to which he was accustomed. Of course, JJ never let his distaste for my lifestyle interfere with our business relationship. Our goal and purpose at work was to ensure the success of Manzetti Properties, and both of us knew it.

I was well aware the occasionally lovable pain-in-the-ass girl sitting next to me had just given me a most precious gift. She'd chosen me as her honest to goodness grandmother! If life was a fairy tale, we'd all live happily ever after. Kalayla would make lots of friends, Maureen would marry a prince. And I would, well, I would be a grandmother in more than name.

"Miss Lena," Kalayla said, interrupting my daydreams. "I was wondering. Would it be okay for me to stay here? Just for tonight?"

Sweet Jesus. I hoped calling me Miss Lena wasn't her lead up to selling me more of those damn cookies. Letting her stay the night might be swinging wide the door and letting in all kinds of trouble, but I sure wasn't saying no.

"OK, but first you get on home and show that mama of yours that you are among the living. Cody will be waiting when you come back."

"I'll go, but I'm not talking to her. She could've told me a long time ago that her parents are assholes."

"Did I say a word about sitting down and having a chat? I said show her you're breathing, and let her know you'll be staying the night here. And since I imagine you're planning on hogging the shower, don't forget clean clothes."

"Fine!" she said, in her oppressed martyr tone, so I'd be sure to know it was about as fine as being chased by a swarm of yellow jackets.

So much for "Miss Lena" and fairy tale endings!

MAUREEN

WHAT'S NEXT?

I twirled around the apartment singing tee hee hee, ha, ha, ha, laughing, and almost stumbling, and catching my balance and twirling again. I knew I was being silly and childish, but I couldn't stop. In fact, I might never stop. It was over. At long last, it was OVER!

I told Kalayla the truth. I'd never again have to worry about how to do it, or when to do it, or where to do it, or if I should do it. It was done, finished, fini, finito, terminado!

How silly to be laughing and crying at the same time. How wonderful to be free of wanting to barricade myself in a closet and never come out.

The hurt wasn't gone, and maybe it never would be. But I have finally accepted the fact that Mummie might never change her mind. Jamal tried to help me understand what awful things people can do because of what they believe, but I couldn't face the thought that I'd lost my family forever. I was so sure Mummie's love for me would be greater than her hatred of . . . than her hate. Mummie never gave me any reason to believe that, but I truly couldn't believe Jamal was right and I was wrong.

Kalayla was so upset she wasn't talking to me, but I knew she would get over that. She did before. And when she does, I'd explain that I knew what I did was unfair to her, and I was sorry. I think she'll understand that. At least I hope she will. But I'm not sure she'll ever understand why my mother turned against me. How could she?

Mummie said the luckiest day of her life was the day she met Daddy at a St. Paddy's celebration in Boston. She'd grown up in Southie, and Kalayla wouldn't understand how hard that was and what a huge step up marrying Daddy and moving to Brighton where his family had lived for generations was for her.

I knew that was always in the back of Mummie's mind when she told me about her plans for me. "We're moving up, Maureen, moving up. I took the first step. Now no one can ever call your children or Kate's or Leah's or Colin's children poor white Irish trash. You'll build on what I did. Kate and Leah are lovely, but they aren't smart like you are."

The truth was, I was never what Mummie hoped I'd be. She didn't understand my passion for art. She didn't see a world as colors and textures and shapes that were malleable, outside the confines of a prescribed structure. A world that opened my imagination to what could be.

Mummie's world didn't leave room for nuance or shading. She expected me to marry the lawyer's son. She expected me to be a nurse. She expected me to live in the same white world she did.

Before I met Jamal, I used to tease her, "No, Mummie, I'll marry a doctor, not a lawyer."

"No, no, Maureen, not a doctor," she said. "Lawyers go into politics, doctors don't. With a lawyer, you could end up a governor's wife or a senator's wife. Set your sights high the way I do."

I didn't set my sights the way she wanted. I fell in love instead. I still turn around and expect Jamal to be smiling at me from across the room. If I ever did fall in love again, he'd still be there, smiling, encouraging me to live my life fully.

Kalayla is so quick at seeing everything, so clear about how she feels and what she thinks. She faces life with the same clarity Jamal did and she adjusted more quickly than I did when he died. And afterward, I hated living with Lucinda and Harmon, but she did fine with them, and she did fine at the school near them. When we moved here, she went to another new school and settled right into the apartment and didn't mind me working two jobs. And when she found out I lied to her, she adjusted to that, too.

She has so much potential, and she'll be her own person, I'm sure of that. She won't ever have a closed mind like Mummie. She'll be able to see possibilities and imagine what might be, and I'll help her as much as I can. As soon as she starts speaking to me again.

Jamal and I used to talk so much, and that's what I miss most. Being single is lonely, at least for me. I wish I had someone to talk to, someone who hasn't followed all the rules and done everything the way his family expected. The only one I can think of who's like that is Rico. He definitely didn't do everything the way his family wanted. The afternoon we had coffee he gave me his cell number, and said I could call him anytime.

So, I guess I could. After all, he was the one who found Layla, and he knows what it's like to be in your thirties—which is nothing like being in your twenties. I could talk to him. Not that I couldn't talk to Lena because I could and I did all the time, but, well, she was so old. She probably doesn't remember what it was like to be my age, and besides that, she had been married then, and raising four boys.

I found Rico's number and punched it in so quickly I wasn't certain I'd gotten the right numbers, but he answered on the second ring. "Maureen?" he said in such a friendly way before I even said hello and he sounded really pleased to hear from me. I was so startled I almost hung up. But I couldn't do that, not after I'd been the one to call.

I managed to say, "Rico, hi, yes, it's me, Maureen. I'm calling because, well, I think you might like to know, I mean, since you found Kalayla and all. It was such a big thing for me and took me such a long time, but I wanted you to know I finally did it."

Oh gods, I sounded like a total airhead! But he must have thought I was funny, because he laughed. And when he answered, his voice was soft and low key and still friendly, and he didn't sound the least bit annoyed or upset that I called.

"You did 'it'? Well, the only thing I can imagine that would make you so happy is that you told Kalayla about your family. Am I right?"

"You are! Can you believe it? I actually did it. And I'm so glad, and I wanted you to know. Because you helped us, and because, well, I wanted you to know."

"That is news worth celebrating! I'm glad you called. How about meeting me for a bite to eat?"

Which was exactly what I hoped he'd say, but I didn't think he'd say it so quickly, and I certainly couldn't tell him I needed to think about it, and anyway I didn't need to think about it because I knew what I wanted to do. "Oh, I'd love to. I can meet you right now because after I told Kalayla, she went over to Lena's, and that's where she is now so I know she's safe, and Lena would call me if something was wrong."

"All right, then. Let's do a twofer. There's a pub right across the street from Matty's Way called The Connemara. We can meet there, have a bite, and then I'll show you the gym."

It was so funny, really, because he was waiting for me in front of the gym, and I think he was guarding the parking space because parking in

Cambridge is so awful in winter, and sometimes people get in fights if somebody steals the space they shoveled out.

I'd thrown on some black wool slacks and an orange long sleeve sweater, the lovely soft wool I'd been lucky to find at the Thrift Store, and as an accent, I added two gold chains and my dangle earrings. Even though it was so cold, I didn't pull on my jacket hood because it always messed up my hair.

"Hey," he said, a gallant knight opening the car door and holding out his hand to me. Even though he'd been standing in the cold, he looked warm in a dark blue pea coat, turtleneck and cords, and I bet anything his boots were genuine L.L. Bean, not the knock-offs I had to buy.

"So," he said, pointing toward the entrance to Matty's Way, "this is the gym. We'll go in after. There's more parking around back."

I looked up and down the block and saw the walks were clear, with periodic spaces open so people could get into the street without walking all the way to the nearest driveway.

"We put on an addition almost five years ago and that gave us nearly three times as much space. Dad had to admit it made sense for us to buy the two lots next to us when his old friend Larry was ready to retire and sell the appliance store."

Rico was so proud of what they'd done and really, it was tasteful and attractive. I said, "It's really great, like you gave an old neighborhood a facelift. I mean, like somebody really thought things through instead of, you know, tearing things down and building bigger and higher."

"Well, we worked with reps from every business both sides of the street. The process was slow, but when they saw models with the new look, they all got on board. Business has improved for everyone, and that's been a huge bonus. I'll tell you more inside if you want to hear about it. But let's get moving before we freeze in place or I die of hunger," he laughed.

He took my arm as we crossed to The Connemara. Customers were going in and out of Pete's, the convenience store adjacent to it, mostly men picking up Friday night beer and snacks, the way Jamal and Clarence used to.

The lighting inside was dim, and people seemed relaxed, standing around the bar talking, maybe hooking up or just chatting with friends. We worked our way through the crowd to the hostess who got menus and took us to a back booth. I realized I was totally famished and wolfed down popcorn, then a cheeseburger and homemade coleslaw, the house specialty. Everything was good, and the Merlot added a little glow while we talked about little things, and I was really, really glad Rico didn't ask if there was a reason I decided to tell Kalayla that particular afternoon.

The waitress was clearing our dinner dishes when he smiled and said, "I'm glad you told Kalayla. That sort of cleared away a hurdle. The thing is, I have thought about calling you, but, ah, it seemed like you had a lot to work out. If you know what I mean. And frankly, I got out of a messy relationship a while back, and I wasn't real hot to jump into another."

Oh! My jittery stomach was back. He waited for me to say something, but I didn't know what to say, so I nodded. And he went on.

"The thing is, I was dating a divorced woman, and she had two terrific little boys. I really liked those kids. Actually, I guess I ended up liking them better than I did their mother. When we stopped dating, I missed seeing them. What I'm saying is, dating somebody with kids adds complications. You get that, right?"

I nodded again and almost laughed because it was like I was in a business negotiation. I could just imagine him presenting the facts about the renovation to the other owners on the block. No fuss or frills—just a straightforward presentation.

"I have to tell you the truth. I got off to the worst possible start with Kalayla. You see, when we take on a new martial arts student at Matty's Way, we push them a little to find out if they've got trigger points that could come back at us later on. If it seems like their motive is to learn to hurt people, I won't take them as a student. That's what I did with Kalayla, and she exploded. It was not pretty.

"But I saw a different side of her at your birthday party. My aunt Carlotta said Kalayla planned most of it, and everybody did pretty much what she told them to. The kid did that out of love for you. And then when I found her at the dumpster in spite of the way her mouth was going, it was obvious that she was scared and hurting. I don't mean to put bad on you, Maureen, but that was my take on it."

He was right. What could I say except, "I know it was all my fault for not telling her, Rico. She was scared, but she was brave, too, because running that way meant she really did hear what I told her. She wasn't acting like it never happened or avoiding it. She's always been brave, and I guess I take that for granted."

Rico nodded. "Well, I was thinking, if you and I decide to date, I need to make peace with her. And the way she wanted music and dancing at your party gave me an idea. *Riverdance* is coming to town—you know, the Irish step dancers, and I thought maybe I could get tickets, and the three of us would go. That's not until the end of May, so Kalayla would have plenty of time to get used to the idea. But obviously before I get any tickets, I need to know if you'd like to go."

I took a deep breath. An actual date, well sort of like a date with my daughter as the chaperone. I could handle that. "Oh! I would like that, but I'm not sure how Kalayla would react."

"Good! As far as Kalayla goes, you don't need to mention it. I'd actually rather ask her myself. Assuming that's all right with you. What do you think? Does this sound like a plan?"

My heart was racing and I wasn't positive I wanted to say yes, but I knew I didn't want to say no. And anyway, it was almost two months away, so I really didn't need to panic. Yet. So I said, "I think that would be okay. I mean, I think it would be okay if you asked her about *Riverdance*."

Rico waited, probably expecting me to keep babbling and explain what I meant by 'I think' and 'I mean,' but that was all I could say right then. So that was all I said.

"Okay then. I'll get tickets, and I'll come over and invite Kalayla. Now, how about dessert? They make great bread pudding!"

SPRING 2000

LENA

WHAT'S NEW?

The bath temperature and bubble bath were just the way I liked. I eased into the tub, slid down to my neck and sighed. My old bones settled in for a good long soak. This beat a pounding shower any day. Thank the lord Kalayla was back where she belonged again, and I was back to having some peace and quiet. Sweet Jesus, please let her stay home this time. I always figured raising girls would be easier than boys, but I could see how wrong I was.

Anyway, after I saw what Joey was like, I stopped praying for girls. There was no way of knowing what he'd take it in his mind to teach them. Still, if my four boys had run off the way that girl was prone to do, Joey would have installed revolving doors, and the men wearing white coats would have carted me off to the nuthouse. Not that my boys were any models of good behavior, but they all stayed at home until they left for good. There it was, happening again—Kalayla reminding me of my boys.

I slid down until the bubbles were tickling my nose. Shifting my butt from side to side felt so good, I added hot water. No need to hurry this pleasure. I leaned my head against the back of the tub, letting my mind wander from this to that. The expression on Clarence's face when Kalayla opened the door that Sunday popped into my mind and got me to giggling. But not for long. We might have let the air out of his tires that day, but now that I'd seen him up close, I knew slowing him down like we did sure wouldn't be enough to bring him to a dead stop. What with his brash manner of staring at Maureen, and the fact he showed up in that flashy silk shirt and tight jeans made it clear he was on the hunt. And the fact he high-tailed it out of there showed he wasn't stupid enough to try and go through me and Kalayla to get to her. He'd wait until he got her alone to get pushy.

If Maureen was still cleaning houses, I wouldn't have put it past him to follow her to a job and try something dicey there. Eddie gets thanks for giving her enough hours to get that possibility squashed. And I considered that a real hoot, like I played a big fat joke on Joey. When it came to women, Joey held the belief that a man could and should do whatever he wanted in whatever way he wanted. I had no doubt his ghost was coaching Clarence on how to get Maureen cornered. Well, Joey, I'm glad to say I learned enough since you've been gone to make sure Clarence isn't going to have an easy time of it. I just wish I had learned how to flush your ghost down the drain with the bathwater.

After leaving Helping Hands Shelter the next day, I stopped by to see Carlotta at work. She was at the front desk in the middle of doing several things at once as usual, and she showed no inclination to take a break.

"Now don't go putting on that aggravated look, Lotta. I can see you're busy, but you're always busy. I've got important things to tell you that can't wait any longer—like how I put the skids on a jackass who was planning to take advantage of Maureen. You'll be downright proud of me, and Kalayla too."

Carlotta flipped through the index cards and made a couple notes before she looked up and said, "Humpf! Why am I not surprised that Kalayla would be mixed up in whatever you're doing? If you've got saving on your mind, why don't you help me save some animals and change the No Pets Rule in your apartment buildings?"

"Lotta, there you go again, launching right into your crabby old woman routine. I have been thinking about the No Pets Rule."

"Right! You've been thinking about it since you and Joey bought your first building, and that was before JJ was even born!"

"Oh, come on, you really have got to hear this. You're the one who's always telling me prevention is easier than mopping up after the damage is done. Anyway, I'll spring for take-out dinner."

"Well," she said, "seeing that you're willing to open those deep pockets . . .!"

An hour later we were sprawled on the sofa in Carlotta's living room, munching on chips and roast beef sandwiches with horseradish. Carlotta slapped her sides laughing over Clarence's visit. "God, I wish I'd been a spider on the wall and seen you outsmart that man! Really, such a victory deserves a prize. Why don't we go shopping?"

"Well, now that you mention it, I have been thinking I could use a few new things."

"Yeah, way more than a few. I'm sick of that black party dress you've been wearing for the last thirty years. Those green flowers didn't hide the fact the material is getting so thin pretty soon you'll be wearing next to nothing at all. That might have been fine when you were in your twenties and thirties, but trust me, nobody would get hot and bothered looking at you now! Well, maybe nobody except my brother."

"Oh, stop that, Lotta! I was thinking I could use a few new blouses, maybe one light blue and one that deep red I always liked. And while I'm at it, I might look for a dress and maybe a skirt or two."

Carlotta narrowed her eyes and gave me a good long stare. "Well, damn! It is about time!"

And I had to agree. I looked in the mirror that morning and did an assessment of things as they really are and what I saw was the extreme to which I had let myself go. Wearing those green flowers must have done something to my brain because I said to myself, "Lena! It is time you made some changes!" Whatever had cracked open inside of me might have started in one tiny place, but I could feel that opening growing bigger and bigger all the time. Letting in light. Letting in life. Letting in almost anything.

The funny thing was, letting in color shocked me the most. When Mark and JJ left and then the twins died, the color leached out of my life and turned me into one of those old black cast iron pots with a whole lot of dings and scratches. I felt like I was clawing my way out of a tomb and was seeing sunlight for the first time in years. The problem with that was I had no way of knowing what might use the tunnel I made and come slithering out after me. No matter. I wasn't scared, and I wasn't crawling back.

Lotta loved making outrageous predictions, but she didn't know what else I might take it into my head or my heart to do. Neither did I. Sweet Jesus. Thinking such things was as unsettling as the thought of going to hell and seeing Joey again. Well, maybe not quite.

KALAYLA

LENA'S FAMILY

What if I never felt like my old self again?

I kept thinking about people lying to me. Daddy was dead, so I could cross him off my list of liars. He always used to tell me, "The more you practice, Kalayla, the better you'll get at doing anything." Mama had so much practice lying, I bet there wasn't anybody who could lie better than she could. She'd be on it forever.

I knew never to believe Clarence 'cause he was always shading the truth. And I never had to worry about Carlotta, 'cause she told everybody way more of the truth than they wanted to hear.

The Old Lady was the one really bugging me. She didn't lie, but there was plenty of stuff she wouldn't tell me. Like why her kids and grandkids never came to visit her. There had to be a reason. What if she was like my asshole grandparents and kicked her kids out of her family 'cause they did something she didn't like?

I tried telling myself she wouldn't do that, but I wasn't sure of anything anymore. I decided to find out. Only this time I wasn't gonna go to the library or computer or newspapers. I was going over there and ask her and maybe get a snack while I was there. She always wanted to pass her stale old food off on me, and the least I could do was take it.

She opened the door right away when I knocked, and she said, "I figured it must be time for your afternoon snack. Oatmeal raisin cookies and milk. Take it or leave it."

"I'll take it," I said, walking past her and sitting down at the table. I was planning on eating as many cookies as I could while I had the chance. The cookie plate and milk were already on the table, so I didn't waste any time digging in.

"Sweet Jesus, Kalayla! You're going to choke! Stop gulping that milk.

And exactly why would you be stuffing your pockets with cookies? Have you taken up hoarding food as a hobby? That'll give your mama something else to worry about!"

That Old Lady was always trying to sidetrack me, but this time I wasn't going to let her. The quicker I found out what I came to find out, the sooner my stomach would get a chance to settle down. "I came to ask you a question."

She shrugged her shoulders and her hands like that was no big deal and I should get on with it.

So I did. "You know that photo on your bookcase, the one with you and those little boys? Did you kick them out of your family the way my asshole grandma kicked out my mama? Is that why they never come see you?"

The Old Lady didn't yell or throw me out like I thought maybe she might. She sat across the table looking down at her bony old fingers, rubbing one after another. Then she stood up, and held on to the table like it was the only thing that was gonna stop her from falling over. She moved one hand from the table to the back of her chair and stood there for a minute. Then she let go and walked to the bookcase slower than I ever saw her walk before. She reached over and took down the photo. If my life depended on how quick she came back and sat down next to me, Mama would've been picking out my coffin.

"It's not some secret I didn't want you to know, Kalayla. It's that telling it ... well it's just that telling brings it back all over again." She held the photo so I could see it and pointed to the tallest boy. "These are my four sons. This one here is JJ, my oldest. He lives in Weston, which is maybe half an hour from here. He has two daughters. When they were little, he used to bring them over on Halloween. Now one of them is a senior in high school and the other is in college. They're ... too busy to come over, but they'd be welcome if they did. I go to their house on Thanksgiving and Easter."

She pointed to the next boy. "This here is Mark, my second born. He moved to Boston after high school and then to New York City, and after that he went West. The last postcard I got from him was about 15 years ago from Chicago.

"These two are my twins, Mikie and Jimmy. Maybe you saw their photos and trophies at Matty's Way. They joined the Marines after high school, and they were killed in Vietnam. I wish I had kids and grandkids coming over,

Kalayla, I sorely do wish I did. They'd be welcome anytime they came, no matter what they did or said or how much trouble they got into."

The old lady looked so sad, my stomach turned real sour. I shoved the milk and cookies away. If I'd known she was gonna tell me stuff like that, I'd have passed on eating anything. If I'd known she was gonna tell me something like that, maybe I wouldn't've asked. I felt like a jerk.

I took the photo and stared at it a long time. Her kids were like any regular kid you see on the street. My mama had pictures of me standing next to her just like that when I was their age.

"If I ever got a chance to know 'em, I might've liked 'em," I said. "Leastways, if they were like you, I might've."

Tears were rolling down the Old Lady's face, and I sat there, wishing I knew what to do.

After a long time, she wiped the tears off with her hands and said, "You better get home so your mama doesn't start worrying."

I didn't think my mama would be worrying, but I wasn't gonna say that. "Okay, but if you don't feel like pigging out on those cookies, could you save a few for tomorrow when I come?"

I got up and pushed my chair under the table. And then I did something pretty dumb. I reached over and patted the Old Lady on the head.

I never expected Lena to tell me anything like that, and I kept thinking about her sad old face, her real old and real sad face. Later on, Mama asked why I was so quiet, and I said, "I don't know. I must've caught pneumonia or the flu. There's lots of that at school, and plenty of AIDS and hepatitis, plus some other stuff. Maybe I oughta stay home for a few days and figure out what kind of disease I have."

I should've known better. Right away she went running to the medicine cabinet to get a thermometer.

"I'll call Lena," she said. "She knows what all the symptoms mean."

I grabbed the thermometer out of her hand. I knew that wasn't polite, but sometimes she was so aggravating I couldn't help myself. "Mama! I was joking! I'm not sick. And I'm not talking because I don't feel like talking. Stop bugging me all the time!"

'Course then she acted like I hit her in the stomach, which made me feel like a piece of dumpster garbage.

"Oh," she said. "I was just trying to take care of you."

I wanted to say, yeah, right, just like you always took care of me! But then she'd start crying, and I'd get pissed and leave again. I was getting tired of doing that. "Just stop saying you wanna take care of me! Will ya just leave me alone, PLEASE?"

"Okay," she said, but I knew she wouldn't.

My brain was jammed with asshole grandparents, an uncle in heat, a lying Mama and a sad Old Lady. That didn't leave room for updates on the weather, which was about the only subject Mama and I could discuss without me getting pissed.

For once, I was glad I had to go to school and learn useless stuff about ancient Egypt even though I was never gonna live in a pyramid. If Cambridge was near some mountains, I might've found a big old cave and moved in there but bears or mountain lions probably already claimed all the good caves. And I wasn't gonna mess with them.

Anyway, I kept doing my neighborly duty, stopping in to see the Old Lady every day, 'cause I knew somebody had to check on her. About a week after she told me about her kids, she opened her door, and she was wearing a red blouse. I closed my eyes for a minute. When I opened 'em, the blouse was still red. I squinted. Still red.

Cow turds!

"Well," she said, "once you get finished making faces, I guess you're planning to come in and take up space on my sofa."

Then I got pissed. I admit she had a reason to wear green to Mama's party, but what the heck reason did she have for wearing red?

I got even more pissed when she said, "I hope some poor fool of a fly doesn't come along and mistake that open mouth of yours for a new home."

I clamped my mouth shut. "The flies you knew back in the Stone Age must've been dumb. Now they're smart enough to know a mouth when they see one!"

"Is something wrong with you, Kalayla? I should think you'd want to tell me how much you admire my new blouse!"

"Only reason you're wearing red is you're so old you forgot you only wear black!"

"You can stop worrying. I haven't gone 'round the bend yet. I went shopping with Carlotta, and I bought some new blouses and skirts in colors I'm partial to. Like red. Pardon me if I forgot to ask your permission! Now, I suppose you're dying of hunger as usual."

She walked into the kitchen and came back with cookies and milk.

I started wondering how many cookies I could eat before my stomach exploded. Math teachers oughta tell you how to calculate important stuff like that. A lot more kids would stay awake in class.

I was thinking that after I ate a few cookies, I might call 911 and tell 'em they better come get the Old Lady 'cause she went whacko. That'd show her!

LENA

KALAYLA'S QUESTION

I'd seen Kalayla shoveling in cookies plenty of times, but never like this. She gobbled one after another, with a gulp of milk in between. You'd have thought she was one of Carlotta's starving strays that wouldn't stop eating until you took the food away. If I didn't put the brakes on her quick, she'd be vomiting all over my floor.

"Kalayla! Stop hogging those cookies. I'd like one, you know!" I would have gotten more reaction from a wall. Another gulp of milk, another cookie. I got out of my chair, reached over and grabbed the plate. Not that there was much of anything left on it. No point asking her what was wrong. The list stretched halfway around the world, and there was nothing to be done about one single item on it.

Kalayla looked up at me and asked that same question again. "How come you're not wearing black?"

I shook my head and sat down next to her, "Well, first off, my slacks are black in case you didn't notice. The truth is I'm wearing a red blouse because that's what I feel like doing. Hard as it might be for you to believe, that fact probably shocked me more than it shocked you.

"I can hardly remember back to the time when I wasn't wearing black. I started after my twins died, and it never occurred to me to do anything else. Up until now. All I can tell you is something inside of me changed. I don't understand what, and I don't understand why. I just know it happened. So now I'm wearing red."

Kalayla looked disgusted, "If I said I was gonna do something forever, I wouldn't stop just 'cause one day I felt like doing something else!"

"Now Kalayla, I never did say I was going to wear black forever, but it went on for so many years, it felt like I'd be doing it forever. Sometimes things change even if we don't expect them to."

That shut her up for a long time. I was used to her sudden silences, but I knew better than to think nothing was going on inside that head of hers. Something was gnawing at her, and I wanted to find out what it was. Which meant I needed to give her time to tell me. I got up and took the plate with the last cookie and her empty glass to the kitchen.

When I came back in and sat down, she said, "Do you think that means my asshole grandparents might wake up some morning and decide they should let Mama back in their family?"

Oh, Sweet Jesus, I should have known! I should have guessed what she'd be thinking and headed her off. Her world got blown to bits when she found out about her grandparents. If they changed their minds, she thought she might be able to put a few of the pieces back together.

"Now listen here, Kalayla, me being old doesn't mean I can answer impossible questions. And that is an impossible question."

"Yeah, I know, but you're older than anybody and you changed your mind about something big, and you didn't have any reason to, well, not a real reason that makes sense. Anyway, who cares what an old lady wears? But Mama's parents could change something big that matters a lot, to Mama anyway. If somebody told 'em what stupid assholes they were, they might listen and change. Right?"

Oh, child, child. You sit there with those huge green eyes looking so earnest, and hanging on to that small hope like a lifeline. Sweet Jesus, what am I supposed to tell her?

"Well. I suppose that's not impossible. BUT. Even if you think I'm living proof old people can change, being able to change and wanting to change are two entirely different things. I wouldn't have the least idea how to predict what your mama's parents might do today or tomorrow or next year. I can't predict that for myself."

"But that's what they oughta do, right? They oughta let her back in."

Now what could I say to that? Things were simple for Kalayla the same way they were simple for Carlotta. But that sure wasn't true for me. As far as I could tell, life was a lot of things, but simple was absolutely, definitely not one of them. If Kalayla's grandparents cut off Maureen because they didn't want her black husband in the family, my prediction was they wouldn't welcome a half-black grandchild either. And I was willing to bet Kalayla's real question was about that as much as it was whether they'd take her mama back.

I did agree with the girl about one thing. If Maureen's parents ever did care to, they could work at making amends for all the pain they caused. As long as they were alive and breathing, there might yet be a chance for that.

That still left the other question she asked. Was there somebody who could deliver that message to people who likely wouldn't want to listen? If the answer to that was yes, I sure as hell didn't know who that would be.

MAUREEN

A CALL FROM THE SCHOOL

Eddie's was quiet after the morning breakfast rush, giving me time to do a more proper wipe of the tables, set out napkins and silverware, check that salt, pepper, and sweetener containers were full. Carolyn was taking care of the counter and Eddie was out back doing his usual. He was a match for my mother when it came to kitchen cleanliness. Nothing less than gleaming surfaces was acceptable.

I glanced up at the apartment window, not that I expected any sign of Kalayla on a school morning. I wasn't looking forward to seeing her later because I'd have to talk with her about the call from her teacher.

I was just starting my shift, and that call threw me into such a tizzy I gave Dave the hot chocolate with double whipped cream his wife Ellie always has, and gave her his black coffee.

Thank goodness she laughed, "You must be distracted today, Maureen. Raising a girl on your own can't be easy." They gave me the usual tip, which some people wouldn't have, and I was really grateful because I count on tips. Well, all of us do.

So much happened with Kalayla during the winter, I can understand how I might get a call from the school. I mean, because she was distracted or something and probably lots of parents got calls from the school all the time, but this was an absolutely awful first for me. Not that what the teacher said was totally awful. It's not like Kalayla swore at a teacher or hit another kid. But it was so … unexpected.

Mrs. Spencer started by asking if there was a reason Kalayla hadn't turned in roommate choices for the mountain trip at the end of May.

Duh! How could I be expected to answer that when I'd never heard a thing about any mountain trip or permission slip or roommate list? All I could say was, "The mountain trip?"

"Oh, yes, you remember, we sent the information home with students almost a month ago. The trip is always at the end of May, and there's so much to organize with these overnights we start way ahead of time. We always allow students to make three buddy choices so they'll be with at least one of their friends. Most kids turn in their choices about five minutes after we explain our system to them.

"I was double-checking yesterday morning, and that was when I realized Kalayla hadn't turned in a permission slip or bunkmate choices. I'm sorry I didn't pick that up sooner. I was certain we had accounted for everyone. Yesterday when I asked her who she wanted on her buddy list, she just shrugged, so I thought I better call and ask you about it. It's such a wonderful opportunity for the kids to bond, and we do encourage all of them to participate."

"Oh. I understand how that would happen. I mean, spending three nights together, definitely lots of time for bonding. Well, I'll certainly ask Kalayla about it tonight and encourage her to go."

I thought that was the end of it, but it wasn't. Mrs. Spencer kept talking. "Actually, there's another reason for my call. At team meeting—you recall we have weekly team meetings—the team teachers mentioned that they'd seen a change in Kalayla. She's been a solid B/B+ student all year, and she always does homework and we've never had to chase her for assignments.

"Recently her grades have dropped—not that she's failing, but C's are so unlike her, and sometimes her homework is half done or late. I might not have mentioned it, but it isn't only happening in one class. It's all the major subjects, and as you know, third term is ending shortly."

I gulped. Third term? I had no idea when third term began or ended. Or when first or second term did. Maybe there was a fourth term, and I didn't know about that either. Jamal was the one who kept track of everything at the school, and he always showed me Kalayla's progress and report cards. But I certainly couldn't tell the teacher that, so instead I said, "Oh, Mrs. Spencer, thank you so much for calling. I'll have a good talk with Kalayla tonight."

I wanted to cry when I hung up, but I couldn't, not at work. If I did, everyone who'd been so kind and helped find Kalayla would think I was totally hopeless and helpless. I'd talk to Lena after work. She knew so much about raising kids, and she gave me such good advice.

At least I could count on some things not changing, and going to Lena's was one of them. She always brewed coffee and offered me something sinfully sweet or a full meal if it was dinner time. I was lucky I didn't gain weight the way some people do. Customers at Eddie's were always moaning and groaning about putting on pounds and that was funny because it was usually while they were shoveling down pie with ice cream. I could walk by cookies or cake and not even notice them, and I guess that was unfair.

Lena came out of the kitchen with coffee and brownies. "Carlotta's best," she said, but I was too upset to eat anything. "Oh Lena, the most awful thing happened today. I got a call from Kalayla's teacher and her grades have fallen."

Lena didn't look the least bit surprised. "Well, I'm guessing all this winter's turmoil is coming home to roost."

"I guess it had to at some point, really, but it's not just that her grades have fallen. All the kids in her grade are supposed to go on this mountain trip, and Kalayla didn't even bother to tell the teacher who she wanted to be with in the hut."

"Hut? You mean they'll be staying overnight in the motel?"

"No, no, not a motel. It's a real hut in the mountains, and it has bunk beds and outhouses and kids have to cook their own meals and carry everything they need in backpacks."

Lena laughed. "Really? That sounds like just the type of thing Kalayla would hate. Did the teacher say she had to go? Is that why you're worried?"

"Oh no. But she didn't put down any buddy choices, and that got me to thinking. She never mentions any friends, and I'm honestly not sure she has any. So maybe that's why she doesn't want to go. I mean, she's never been to a sleepover or wanted us to have one, and I used to go to them all the time when I was her age. But I don't know, maybe kids don't do that anymore.

"But she must have friends, don't you think, Lena? I mean, all girls have friends even if they gossip and say mean things to each other. I used to have lots of friends, or at least I did until I met Jamal. After I started dating him, I dropped my old friends, or really the truth is, they dropped me. So I guess I haven't been a very good model for her."

Lena shook her head. "No point in blaming yourself for her not having friends. Some people are loners and don't care about being part of a group. It might be that she's one of them. Anyway, I wouldn't be pushing this trip. Pressuring her to go could backfire in a way that would make us all sorry. That's separate from the grades, and I sure wouldn't let her off the hook in that regard. She ought to be keeping up on her schoolwork."

"Yes, that's really the most important thing, isn't it? Because then she can go to college and do what she wants. Lena, you are so smart about kids, and you've been so helpful, and I've learned so much from you."

KALAYLA

THAT JERK RICO

One good thing was the snow piles were gone, and I could finally go outside without wearing about five layers. Another good thing was the last few nights I didn't have any freaky dreams where my O'Rourke non-grandparents turned into monster flies, and I killed 'em with a giant fly swatter and threw them in the trash.

Those good things fooled me into thinking it was gonna be a good weekend. It turned out to be a real pisser. The minute I walked through the door on Friday, Mama started in about school. Was something wrong that I wasn't doing my homework? Was I having trouble with the kids? Was there a problem with a teacher? Was I feeling depressed?

Double cow turds! What really aggravated me was that pissy old Mrs. Spencer would've never had a reason to call if I'd have followed my RULES! I had the whole school thing figured out my first day in kindergarten. Most of the kids were a bunch of babies hanging onto their mama's legs and screaming when they tried to leave. Not me. I could hardly wait for Daddy to get out the door and leave me on my own.

I could see how the teacher was talking real sweet to the kids, taking their hands, herding them into the storytelling corner. I decided right then the best thing I could do was stay as far away from teachers as I could. So while I was waiting for the crying to stop and the class to start, I started making rules.

Rule #1: Never give the teacher any reason to pay attention to you.

When I saw what jerks the kids were, I decided I needed another rule. Like for when I was walking down the hall, or waiting in line, and some kid said something that pissed me off, and I wanted to punch 'em in the face or kick 'em in the balls. Rule #2: Don't ever do anything that would make the teacher call your house.

I guess finding out all that stuff about Mama being a liar and her parents being assholes made me forget about the Rules. And now I was stuck with Mama freaking out. I didn't see why Mrs. Spencer would call Mama anyway. If they wanted to know about me, they should've asked me!

And why'd she have to go and tell Mama about that dumb mountain trip? Those teachers were whackos if they thought I was gonna stay in some crummy old cabin with no heat, no electricity, so I could use a hole in the ground to pee and poop along with a bunch of jerks. No way was I gonna ask Mama to buy me a sleeping bag. No way was I gonna carry a backpack stuffed with toilet paper and bug spray and snacks and extra socks, and all the other junk on their required list. No way was I going.

I told Mama that, and she said, "But Kalayla, honey, you might make some good friends. It could be a real bonding experience."

Yeah, right! Our shit might bond in the outhouse, but that was all. I told her she could go on talking forever, but no matter what she said and no matter what Lena said, I wasn't gonna go. But, IF she stopped bugging me, I'd get my grades back up. She said she would, but that was probably another lie.

I went over Saturday morning and told the Old Lady what I thought of the mountain trip, and she burst out laughing.

When I asked what was so funny, she said, "I had a fine image in my mind of you sitting on the hole in the outhouse being dive-bombed by flies!"

I don't tell lies—anyway not real right-out lies—and I said I'd get my grades up so I spent the rest of Saturday in the library working on homework and doing assignments I never bothered to finish. I even looked over notes for two tests I had on Monday.

I could've aced 'em both, but I wrote a giant reminder in my notebook: Do NOT get an 'A' on any test. I wasn't gonna screw up again and have the teachers telling me how wonderful it was that I studied so hard, and didn't I understand that if I kept that up, I could get 'A's all the time and that would make my mama so proud. And then pissy Mrs. Spencer would call Mama and tell her how I'd improved and how wonderful I was! I wasn't gonna put up with any of that. My usual B would get them off me and onto somebody who'd probably be thrilled to get the attention.

I showed every assignment to Mama when she got home from work. She seemed so relieved and happy I thought I was gonna get a break, and the rest of my weekend would be good. It was, 'til around noon on Sunday. We weren't expecting anybody, so when the buzzer rang, I thought it was gonna be good old Uncle Clarence dropping by to see if I got hit by a truck.

It wasn't. It was that jerk Rico from the gym. I had to buzz him in 'cause Mama came rushing out of the kitchen the second she heard his voice on the intercom. When I opened the door, he said, "Hey Kalayla. How ya doing?" all friendly and smiling.

Cow turds!

Mama was standing beside me and she grabbed the doorknob like she thought I might be planning to slam the door in his face. She didn't need to worry. I wouldn't've done that. I have manners. I would've politely explained to him that turds weren't allowed in my apartment. THEN I would've slammed the door in his face.

Naturally, Mama had to invite him in and offer him a cup of coffee. I was sure he was gonna say yes, and I'd be stuck there all afternoon because I wasn't leaving him alone with Mama. I thought if I glared at him long enough, he might take the hint and leave. He ruined that idea by saying, "Thanks, Maureen, but actually I came over to talk to Kalayla. If you don't mind."

Triple cow turds! Why the heck would he want to talk to me! I didn't want to talk to him.

"Oh, I don't mind at all," Mama told him. "I'll be in the kitchen."

I tried glaring at her, but she walked away and left me alone with him. He turned toward me and said, "So, would you be willing to talk with me for a few minutes, Kalayla?"

What a pisser! A lot of kids would've told him to stuff it up his ass, but they weren't properly trained in how to treat a guest. Which I was because Mama and Daddy lectured me about manners nearly as much as the Old Lady did. Naturally I said, "I guess so," like he offered me a worm and caterpillar sandwich, but I was too polite to refuse it.

He sat on the sofa, and I sat in the chair opposite him with the coffee table between us. I wished it was a twelve-foot high concrete wall. He leaned toward me with his elbows resting on his knees. I leaned as far back in the chair as I could without falling over backward.

He said, "I came over to apologize to you, Kalayla. I like kids and I work with them all the time. And I get along with them. I've been thinking and thinking about what happened the day Miss Lena brought you over to the gym. I said a lot to you, and I guess what I said upset you. And I'm sorry about that, and I'd like to make up for it. The only way I can do that is if you give me another chance. Would you be willing to do that?"

What a pisser! Any normal adult would sit a kid down and lecture them about how whatever the adult did was right and whatever the kid did was wrong because the kid was immature or smart-ass, or impatient or dumb. Unless they were an adult like Mama. She took the blame for everything and hit the sorry replay button 'til I thought I'd go crazy if she repeated it one more time.

But 'stead of acting like a normal adult, Rico was sitting there waiting for me to answer. Double pisser! I could just hear that Old Lady lecturing me, "Don't spend your life being mad, Kalayla. Don't turn your back when a person is trying to reach out to you." Just like always! Sticking her nose where it didn't belong.

I didn't want to give him another chance, but I wasn't jerk enough to say that. So I said, "Maybe."

"Okay, then." Rico reached into his pocket and took out an envelope. "I have a peace offering. I'd like to take you and your mama to see *Riverdance*. They're Irish step dancers, and everybody says it's a great show. Do you think that's something you'd like to do?"

There were a lot of things I'd like to do. I'd like to go see what was happening at Clean Duds. I'd like to hit Eddie up for a free root beer. I'd like to go over to Lena's and visit Cody. Instead, I was stuck talking to him.

"I have a lot of stuff to do. I'm probably busy that day."

"Well, you can check your schedule. I brought a flyer for you. Why don't you look at it when you have time and you can let me know. It's on Saturday afternoon, the last weekend in May. That sound okay to you?"

Oh sure, I thought that sounded as peachy keen as the outhouse did. But I said, "Okay."

He got up, and I was sure he was gonna go into the kitchen to hang around with Mama. But he didn't. He stood where he was. "Thanks for talking with me, Kalayla. Hey Maureen," he called, "I'm going to take off now. I'll talk to you soon."

And he left. Mama came out of the kitchen looking kind of puzzled. She said, "That was a short visit."

I snorted, "Yeah, just long enough to mess up my whole weekend!"

LENA

BEING A GRANDMOTHER

I just put on my slippers and settled onto the sofa when Kalayla came pounding on the door. When I opened it, she said, "I've been over here three times and you weren't home," as if I'd gone out just to spite her.

"Well, if it's any of your business, I was shopping with Carlotta. What put you in such a fine mood?"

"I hope you didn't buy another blouse. You already bought every color there is. What have you got to eat?"

"I should have known your stomach was the reason you were so charming! I have mint chocolate chip ice cream."

"With chocolate syrup? And almonds?"

"Sweet Jesus! Yes! Chocolate AND caramel syrup and almonds."

"Okay."

It was beginning to sink in that a grandmother—biological, step, adopted or would be—was considered the equivalent of a quartermaster in charge of supplies while a granddaughter—biological, step, adopted or would be—considered herself Chief of Staff.

Kalayla was settled at the table by the time I brought in two dishes of ice cream. "It's about time you learned to get your own food and stopped acting like I'm your personal maid," I told her as I set the bowls down.

"If I went into your kitchen and got food, you'd throw a fit and yell at Mama for not teaching me manners."

"I would not. As long as you put things back where you found them and cleaned up after yourself and told me when supplies were low."

"That's too many 'ands' to remember."

I shook my head. There was no dealing with that girl. Too bad she wasn't Carlotta's daughter. It would serve both of them right.

Kalayla spooned a huge mixture of ice cream, nuts and chocolate syrup and shoved it in her mouth. “Yum, that’s good. What do you know about Irish step dancers?”

Ah! Now I knew why she came over in such a state. Rico must have talked to her. As a matter of fact, I saw *Riverdance* with my brother Dominic and his family a couple of years ago, but I knew good and well Kalayla didn’t come pounding on my door to ask my opinion as a dance critic. She waved a flyer in my face, and my guess was she’d looked them up on the internet and knew more about them than I did.

“Why? Some tickets come floating down from the sky and land on Clarence’s doorstep, so he asked you to peddle them? Am I your first mark?”

Kalayla scowled. “No! HE invited me to go.” She handed me the flyer. “I haven’t decided if I will.”

“HE? I guess that would be Santa Claus? No? Maybe the Easter Bunny? No? Hummm.”

Kalayla was getting more agitated by the second, and I could see this was not the time for teasing her, but I wasn’t about to let her off scot free. “No? Well then, I’m guessing HE must be Rico who is Carlotta’s nephew, the very same one you attacked at Matty’s Way. Would I be right about that?”

She scowled.

“Yes, I have seen the Irish Step Dancers. They were wonderful and I’d go again in a minute if HE happens to have any extra tickets. And I’m sure you told HIM how nice HE was to ask you in spite of all the names you called him.” Let her stuff that in her mouth along with the ice cream!

That earned me a combination of scowl and glare, but no smart remark. I guess she was done talking, because when she finished her ice cream, she actually said “Thank you” and went home.

KALAYLA

MAGIC ONSTAGE

One time the Old Lady told me I put her between a rock and a hard place. That's where I was stuck now, and it was a real pisser. All because of Mama's wannabe boyfriend. How dumb did he think I was? He was sucking up to me 'cause he was afraid if he asked Mama to go alone, she would've said no. He figured if he invited me that would help convince her. I could've asked him if he was using me as bait, but he'd probably looked confused and said, "Bait? I didn't say anything about going fishing."

If I told him no, he'd take Mama, and they'd sit next to each other, and I'd be sitting at home with no way of keeping him from doing whatever he wanted to do. If I said yes, I could sit between them, but that meant sitting next to him which meant I'd have to talk to him. Anybody with good manners knows if somebody buys you an ice cream, you can't ignore them while you're eating it. Cow turds if I went and cow turds if I didn't.

When Mama asked what Rico wanted and I told her, she said, "Now, wasn't that nice of him!" Yeah right!

Mama didn't mention the step dancers again, and that was way weird, 'cause Mama never left things alone. I decided the Old Lady must've told her to keep quiet. Which was just like her, butting in. Anyway, I finally told Rico I wasn't dumb enough to pass up a free ticket.

Our seats were in the first row of the balcony. He said a dancer friend of his told him we'd be able to see the dance patterns better from there, but I knew he was too cheap to get the good seats closer to the stage.

'Course Mama had to tell him this was my first time in a real theatre. Which, as usual, wasn't exactly the truth. When Daddy was alive we went to tons of movies and they were all in theatres. I kept waiting for Rico to brag about how cool he was to be taking me someplace I never been, but he didn't.

Our seats were actually pretty cool 'cause I could see the whole stage and the theatre had all these old decorations and a high fancy ceiling that was way different from the movie theatres. I was getting kind of excited, and then the lights started blinking out one by one, and little by little, people stopped talking 'til it was dark and silent and a little scary.

The curtain opened into another world, another time, another place … a place of enchantment … and magic.

The music, wailing and eerie,
Like nothing I'd ever heard.
Rolling over me and then passing away,
A voice on the wind called to me:
Come, Kalayla, come with us.
And I did. I was following, joining in.
Surrounded by fog.
Standing straight as a flagpole,
Arms tight at my sides,
My feet moving, slowly, slowly
Then faster and faster
Mimicking the sound of the drum, following.
Deep inside me something stirred,
Stretched upward,
Like a flower sheltered from winter cold and wind
Reaching out for the sun's caress.
Yearning for spring.
I felt like crying.

***

The next day everything was back to normal. Mama was bugging me about being so quiet, saying dumb stuff like, "Layla, you're not sad you didn't go on the mountain trip, are you?"

Where'd she come up with such a double dumb idea? When she was my age, she probably did all that stuff and loved, loved, loved it. If she listened to anything I ever told her, she should've known I would've hated, hated, hated it.

The teacher told Mama I had to stay in the Guidance Office and do assignments while the other kids were in the mountains so the guidance counselors could keep an eye on me. Yeah, right, like I needed a babysitter. I could've been earning money at Clean Duds, but when I told Mama I was gonna skip school, she took a fit and said I had to go. One other kid didn't go, but he stayed home 'cause he was sick. I bet! I could've played sick, too, but the secretary in Guidance kept a stash of candy in her drawer and let me help myself to Snicker's bars.

Anyway, I was okay sitting around there because I needed a lot of time to plan. Which was why I was quiet at home, too. Naturally the Old Lady noticed and asked if I was okay, and I told her even a genius needed time to think. She kept giving me her hawkeye, but she didn't pester me about being quiet the way Mama did.

Mama and I got in kind of a routine going to Lena's for dinner a couple times a week. Mama asked her back when I said I'd help, which meant I did most of the cooking while Mama spent her time deciding how she should set the table. Like always.

The weather was good again, and the trees and flowers stopped looking like skeletons. That was kind of funny. I was stripping down on clothes while the trees were layering up with leaves. I was free again, out on my own, seeing the world.

I picked a sunny day for walking to Matty's Way. On the way there I tried not to think of all the things Rico did to piss me off, like calling Mama, or dropping by Eddie's, or asking me how I was doing whenever he saw me. I figured I'd use the same approach with him that I did with the Old Lady when I was gonna ask her for something.

I had to wait at the desk while a couple of hot babes in workout clothes chatted with the receptionist. I was glad Mama wasn't the exercise type. When I told the receptionist that I wanted to talk to Rico, she pointed toward his office as if having a kid ask for him was no big deal.

When I got there, he was stuffing his face with a sandwich and shuffling through papers. I wondered if seeing me was gonna make him choke. "Mr. Rico," I said in my best Miss Lena voice, "Is it okay if I talk to you?"

He looked up from the paper he was reading, and his eyes took a minute to focus in on me. He didn't say anything right away. I bet he was calculating the odds of me dumping all his papers on the floor or throwing the desk lamp at him. No point scaring him, so I repeated, "Mr. Rico. Is it okay if I talk to you?"

"The only Mr. around here is my dad, Mr. Matty, and he's not in today."

"I thought kids might call you 'Mr.' You know, out of respect." His eyes narrowed, and I was afraid I was laying it on too thick. The Old Lady would've told me to cut the crap, but he wasn't as smart as she was.

"Nope. They call me Rico. So, what brings you here?"

I stood up straight as I could, wishing I was six inches taller and had a booming voice he couldn't ignore. "I want to take lessons."

He frowned and looked sort of puzzled. I was getting tired of repeating myself, so I just stood there 'til he said, "What kind of lessons did you have in mind?"

"I want to learn to dance like the Irish step dancers."

And what does he say to that? Nothing. He was way worse than the Old Lady. I thought maybe he was too dumb to remember who the Irish step dancers were, so I gave him a clue. "You know, like they did in *Riverdance*?"

"Yeah, yeah, I know what you mean. The thing is, we don't teach step dancing here. But I know the owner of a dance studio in the next block who does. She's the one who gave me the *Riverdance* flyers and told me to get balcony tickets. I can give her a call and find out what the deal is if you're interested."

If I was interested? Did he think I walked all the way over here just to talk to him? I told myself not to get pissed 'cause I remembered how the Old Lady lectured me about cutting off my nose to spite my face. I wasn't gonna do that.

"Thank you, Mr. Rico. That'd be great. There's some stuff I have to figure out before I can start. Like, lessons cost money, right?"

"Right."

"That means I need a job so I can pay for them. Clean Duds doesn't get me enough, and working for the Old Lady is like working for free. Well, not exactly for free, but I never know when I'm getting paid or how much I'm getting from her. I need, like, a regular job. Can I work for you?"

I was getting tired of waiting around for him to get his brain going and answer my questions. This time he picked up a pencil and started tapping it on the desk. A bunch of people walked by his office laughing and talking, and he looked at them and waved.

"Aerobics class just finished," he said, as if I cared what class the hot babes were in. "Huh. So, the thing is, you're too late for shoveling and too early for raking."

As if I didn't know that. "I didn't mean doing stuff outside. I meant in here, in the gym."

"Oh." He sat there thinking for about an hour. Then he said, "Well, now that I think of it, there might be a few things you could do, but I doubt that you'd like doing them."

I squared my shoulders, "I don't care what they are. I need a job."

He smiled and nodded. "I could use somebody to check the women's locker room. That means picking up stray towels or coffee cups, checking for toilet paper supplies and making sure none of the toilets are plugged. Women leave in a hurry and forget to tell us that stuff. The cleaning crew comes in every night, but sometimes we could use a pick up during the day."

"The girls at school are slobs, too."

"So you know what I mean."

"Yeah. When can I start?" I wasn't gonna give him time to change his mind.

I didn't know what he thought was so funny, but he laughed and said, "You can start today, right now, if you like. First let me call the dance studio and see what we can set up for you."

He showed me where the ladies' locker room was, and I started thinking about other stuff I could do there. If I was getting paid by the hour, I had to find other stuff to do 'cause picking up cups and towels would take me about five minutes, and the lessons weren't gonna be cheap.

I checked out the whole gym, while he was yakking on the phone. Classrooms, exercise equipment room, storage rooms, lobby trophy case. While I was at the trophy case, I stared at the photo of Lena's twins, trying to imagine them with her. Trying to imagine what she was like back then. When I finished looking around, I went back to see Rico and he told me I could have my first lesson on Monday after school.

"Monday? They too lazy to work tomorrow?"

He laughed, "Tomorrow is Sunday, Kalayla. The Dance studio is closed."

Well, that was a pisser!

SUMMER 2000

LENA

FUR AND FAVORS

Monday night around 8:00 Kalayla came banging on my door. You wouldn't think I'd be glad about that, but I was. Banging on my door was normal for her, and she hadn't been acting normal since the night she went to *Riverdance* with her mama and Rico. What I mean is, she'd been so quiet sometimes I almost forgot she was on my sofa or sitting across from me at the table. Maybe she got in a snit because I told Maureen to hush up and give the girl a chance to decide about going to *Riverdance* on her own, although I would think Kalayla would be thanking me for that. Her mother's nervous chitchat and constant questions could sorely try a person's patience. If somebody invented a technique for putting the brain on temporary pause, Maureen would have benefited greatly from using it.

Another reason the girl was being quiet might be that Rico was coming around to see her mama, but it seemed to me that'd be more reason for her to shoot her mouth off than to muzzle it. Recently, I got the feeling that Kalayla's body might be in front of me, but her brain was busy someplace else, and my attempts at conversation were nothing but a bothersome interruption. I was getting fed up with that.

She was fairly jumping up and down with excitement, and whirled past me into the living room, twirling around like she was on stage dancing. If that didn't beat all!

"Well now! Something sure turned your light bulb bright! Did that shifty uncle teach you a guaranteed way of fleecing people out of their hard-earned money?" Now that was the type of comment that would get her smart mouth going, but she went blathering on like I hadn't said a word.

"Oh Lena, I LOVE it! I had my first lesson today! And I have a job! I didn't tell you 'cause I wasn't sure it would work out. But it did!"

The girl was brimming over with joy! Sweet Jesus, thank you for gifts large and small!

"Now you just settle on down here and explain exactly what job and what lessons you're talking about. If you've been doing something shady on that computer that might get you arrested, you better think twice because I am telling you right now, I am not using my good money to get you bailed out of jail!"

She didn't bother to answer. She poured out the whole story in one long breath with no periods or commas, only exclamation marks. It turned out Rico worked a deal for her. For every two hours she logged working at the gym, she got a lesson in step dancing free.

"Well, not really free," she explained. "Rico said it was bartering. I work at the gym, but he doesn't pay me in money. I get paid in dance lessons. Awesome, huh?"

Now I did know a bit about bartering because on rare occasions, I agreed to a barter arrangement for Manzetti Properties. That never, ever involved anybody getting anything from us for free. In fact, it would be more than safe to bet the balance sheet tilted in our favor.

What Kalayla described was the strangest barter arrangement I ever heard of. Rico must have worked out a deal with a dance teacher who didn't work at the gym. And obviously somebody had to be paying cash money for the lessons. The only person I could see that being was Rico. My guess was those lessons would be costing him a sight more than the hourly wage he would have paid Kalayla. My guess also was that he was financing this little transaction himself and keeping it off the books at Matty's Way.

I wasn't about to point that out to Kalayla. I was quite certain Rico would get his money's worth out of her. I knew for a fact the girl wasn't shy when it came to work. Besides, the fact that Kalayla was happy was all that mattered to me.

"So, Miss Lena," she said, and then paused a minute.

Oh boy, here it comes. The fact she was calling me Miss Lena meant she had in mind to suck me in, too.

"So, Miss Lena," she repeated, "you know I'm good at carrying laundry, and picking up coffee at Eddie's, and running to the drugstore, and …"

"Yeah, you are good at all that, Kalayla. Now, why don't you skip to the reason you're falling all over yourself to be polite and tell me how this self-praise is connected to something you're going to ask me to do."

She didn't like that, but she swallowed her smart-ass answer and instead said, "I'm going to need money to buy two different kinds of dancing shoes. First you use soft ones like ballet slippers, and then later you get some that are like tap shoes. So I was thinking about all the stuff I could do for you, like maybe clean your apartment. You know Mama is an expert at that and she taught me everything she knows. And I could do stuff like order the taxi for you so you wouldn't have to bother. I'd be real good at that, too."

Sweet Jesus! I had wracked my brain to find anything at all that would interest that girl, and she'd gone and found something for herself! Now she was figuring out how to pay for it! Good thing I gave up because I could have spent the rest of my life and never come up with the idea of Irish step dancing. Of course, if I had, she'd have probably said, "No way I'm jumping around a stage in dumb shoes with my arms glued to my sides!"

Relief went swishing down from my white hair to my gnarly toes. Summer vacation wasn't too far off, and I was already having nightmares about her hanging around on the streets, a year older and getting closer to looking like a real girl. The way she was setting things up, her schedule would be packed full, and she wouldn't have time for any of that nonsense.

I had to admit I was proud of her. I knew she'd never ask her mama for money, and she didn't come to me until she'd worked out a plan for herself. Best of all, she didn't come asking for money. She came asking for work!

I could definitely add on to her workload with me, but I suddenly got a MUCH better idea, one that gave me a great big chuckle. I was sure I could work it out if Kalayla was willing to be a little patient. "I just thought of a way you could be making money doing something I bet you'd like a lot more than cleaning my apartment or calling taxis for me. Give me a couple of days to work on it, okay?"

"Okay."

My, oh my. She said, "Okay" without even asking me what I'd be working out. Now how do you like that?

The next day I taxied over to the Animal Friends. Whenever I interrupted Carlotta at work—which I rarely did—it generally got her attention, and I counted on early morning being a quiet time.

Greg was at the front desk sipping coffee brewed with the big, gleaming espresso machine sitting on the counter. Lotta researched all such purchases before making them. She said reviews online warned that you could clog or ruin the machine completely if you didn't use and clean it properly. Naturally, Lotta gave all her staff lessons on proper use and maintenance. They had to pass a proficiency test before they were allowed to brew coffee!

"Hey Lena," Greg said and motioned me toward Carlotta's office.

I walked in without knocking. "Hi dear, isn't this a beautiful day?"

She scowled. "Crap, Lena. If you think it's beautiful, something must be going on that I'm not going to like!"

"Don't be a silly old grouch! I just wanted to hear your cheerful voice and see your beautiful face. I was thinking earlier this morning about how hard you work, and as your dearest friend with your best interests at heart, I taxied all the way over here so you could take a little coffee break."

"What flavor of bull are you peddling today, Lena Manero? I know a scam when I hear one. What do you want besides coffee?"

"It's not a question of what I want, Lotta. It's what you need."

"I have everything I need. In case you haven't noticed all these years, I take care of myself, which is a hell of a lot more than you have sometimes done. Now, cut the crap. What do you want?"

Why did I think dealing with Lotta on this particular day would be any different from any other day?

"Well, I was thinking what a good idea it would be if you ran a pilot program—a work-study opportunity here at the Animal Friends." I paused a couple of seconds to give that time to sink in. "You know, kids could find out what's involved in running a business at the ground level. They could clean cages and stock the supply room, and you know, help around in general. And of course, they'd also get to see what a fine service you provide the community."

Carlotta's eyes narrowed. Why was she always so suspicious of my good intentions?

"You know, you could start small and test it out with one kid. Naturally you'd only pay minimum wage and ..."

"Will you stop saying 'you know' as if the point of your rambling was obvious. And exactly why would I be paying anything at all? You're the one with bags of money, even though you refuse to spend it on necessities like a house or car. If this is such a fine project, why don't you finance it with your own money?"

"I can't just outright hand her money, Lotta. It has to be a legitimate job. If the Shelter is hard-pressed for cash, I'll cover it, but you'll have to be the one to write her paycheck."

"Ah, so now you've gone from 'the kids' to 'her'? And why do you suppose I'm certain I know exactly who the particular 'her' is that you have in mind? I must be turning into a psychic."

"Well, really, Lotta! Think of it as a family project. Kalayla IS practically part of your family. At least she might be if Maureen and Rico got together. She could end up Rico's stepdaughter, and then she'd be something like your niece once removed. Or whatever. Anyway, you'd be doing a really good deed and earning points toward heaven, which you know you sorely need."

"I earned enough points to get me and three other big-time sinners into heaven by putting up with you all these years!" Carlotta looked daggers at me, but she didn't say no. I took that as a good sign.

By the time I finished explaining why Kalayla needed money and the independent way she'd gone about getting it, Carlotta was laughing.

"I might enjoy helping a young woman who knows her own mind and who has enough sense to go after what she wants. So, I might be willing to take her on. But don't you start gloating, Lena. You're not getting my cooperation for free. IF I do you a favor, you will owe me one in return."

I could tell from her smug expression that the minute I started my sales pitch, she had in mind what the return favor would be. The truth was Carlotta helped me plenty over the years, and she had never asked for anything in return. I got the feeling my I.O.U. just came due, and I'd be paying back the principal with hefty interest.

"I know that," I snapped. "I can take out a full-page ad about the Shelter in the Chronicle and all the other local papers and I can …"

"I can do that stuff myself and better than you could. I operate in the electronic age, whereas you haven't figured out how to text on your cell. Unless someone like my brother has given you a crash course. And you'll be relieved to know, I don't need your cash.

"However, there IS something you can do that I can't do for myself. You can institute a Pets Permitted policy in your building. Oh crap, Lena, don't look at me like you're in life-threatening pain. I didn't say

ALL of your buildings. Just the one where you live, so you could monitor it yourself.

"And as a bonus for your good deed, I'd be happy to screen any tenant who wants to get a pet and eliminate anything like, oh, you know, boa constrictors or tarantulas. That would include checking out anybody who wants to move in and already has a pet. You have to admit that is both fair and doable."

I knew someday her determination would make me cave in. Once she got on a crusade, she never let go. I nodded, glad to be off the hook until the time when she got around to pushing for the policy in all our rental properties.

"Now," she went on, "You understand I will be doing two things for you, creating an internship for Kalayla and paying her. You certainly wouldn't want to be indebted to me, so the second thing you can do for me is to adopt two adorable kittens."

Sweet Jesus! Kittens! Not that I didn't like cats and dogs. I loved them. I never let the boys have animals because I could imagine Joey hurling a cat across the room or kicking a dog down the stairs. And how could I have a Pets Allowed policy in the rental units if I told the boys they couldn't have one at home? They'd have steamrolled right over me on that one.

The smirk on Carlotta's face made very clear she knew she had me. The only way not to get crushed was to give in, but I didn't have to go down easily. "Lotta, you know very well I don't have the time to litter train kittens and scratch-proof the furniture and ..."

"Oh, stop making a fuss. I said two kittens to aggravate you. The cats you're going to adopt are actually two older Siamese, a chocolate point and a blue point—gorgeous animals. I promised Becky Foster I'd find a good home for them. You remember Becky, don't you? Well, she has end-stage cancer, and her daughter can't take the cats.

"They're named Napoleon and Petunia, a brother and sister. They're four years old, and perfectly trained indoor cats. I'll bring them over right after work along with everything you need, including scratch posts, beds, litter boxes, well, everything you need."

A Pets Permitted policy. Two cats. So, this is what happened in old age. Life as you knew it disappeared. First I had acquired a granddaughter, and now I was getting two cats. The next thing I knew, I'd be getting a boyfriend. Now that was something I might really enjoy!

"Fine! But you call before you come. I want to make sure I'm there so you don't accidentally drop off a snake and a guinea pig along with the cats."

"Now Lena, don't be a spoilsport. You do know I'd never dream of doing such a thing. Don't you, dear?"

MAUREEN AND RICO

EVERYTHING COMING UP …

I just knew everything would be better once the snow was gone, the trees had leaves, the flowers were blooming, and daylight didn't disappear in a blink. Everybody's spirits would perk up, especially mine. This winter had been SO long and awful and traumatic. I was afraid spring might never come but it finally did and June was such a beautiful month.

Best of all, Kalayla seemed so much happier! She was taking dance lessons—of all things, dance lessons. I mean, really, Jamal was always trying to get her interested in sports but she turned her nose up at anything even vaguely athletic, especially organized sports. Not that dance was really a sport. It was more of an art like painting, or sculpture, or drama, and she was totally captivated by it, in such a good mood, bubbling over with energy.

The most amazing thing was she worked it all out herself! She had two jobs and hadn't asked me for any money for her lessons or shoes or anything at all. She was truly the most independent and resourceful child, nothing like me. Well, I admit, I was independent and stubborn, and she did take after me in that, but she didn't blow up the world around her the way I did. At least not yet.

Up until this morning, everything really was coming up like lovely roses, but then Rico called and asked if we could meet for coffee, and he didn't sound like his upbeat self. My very first thought was that I wished the song said tulips instead of roses because tulips were just as lovely, but they didn't have thorns. What if Kalayla had done something at the gym and now everything had turned prickly? Rico hadn't said that or even implied it, but I knew I had to prepare myself just in case, well, just in case.

I knocked on Lena's door when I got home from work because she was so level headed and always helped me calm down. She wasn't home, and I couldn't wait because I really didn't want to be late.

Anyone who ever tried to park in Harvard Square knew it was useless unless you could afford a parking garage, which I couldn't. I decided to walk, but really I practically ran, hoping I wouldn't be sweaty and smelly by the time I got to Starbucks. Rico was near the front of the line inside, and he smiled that big smile and waved me over and I felt a little better.

"Hey, Maureen, how ya doing? You want a latte? I was thinking we'd take the coffee and walk to the Common. How does that sound?"

That was absolutely perfect. We walked slowly until we found a bench that was partly in the sun. Rico told me what had happened at the gym that morning, and I sat there wishing that we weren't really sitting on the bench in the Common and what he was telling me was part of a dream, and I'd wake up and it would be morning, and I could start the day all over again.

RICO

It started out when I got this text from Jennifer at the front desk that said, HELP!

That made me laugh because Jen could force a full-grown grizzly to beg for mercy. She wouldn't squeal for back up unless she was desperate. She must have known what I was thinking because her second text said: ABOVE MY PAY GRADE. Whew, so it probably was just something like a client asking for a discount on something or other.

The guy standing in front of her at the desk didn't look ferocious or impatient or demanding. He was on the small side, maybe five feet eight and carried himself like he was, or at least had been, fast on his feet. I could tell his nose had been broken once or twice, so he wasn't a guy who'd knuckle under without a fight. Despite the paunch, bald head, and age, which I put somewhere in his 60's, this was a guy who knew his way around and was willing to push for what he wanted.

Jen was good at reading people, and she was right, pushing back with a client was above her pay grade.

"Hi," I said, "I'm Rico. What can I do for you?"

"I'm Kevin. Nothing for me. For my grandson."

I looked around. No stray kid in sight.

"I left him in the car. This is private."

Private. Just the type of meeting I hated. Parents/grandparents who came in without the kid always had an agenda. Most of the time they wanted me to do a make-over. Fix the kid up. Turn the kid into something he wasn't.

I could have saved them time and money if I wrote a book explaining why that wasn't going to work, but I wasn't a writer. I was willing to give their way a shot even if it meant they would find out the hard way that no gym was going to turn the kid into their idea of what he should be.

"Okay, let's go talk in my office." I led the way. If the guy was looking for real privacy as in not visible to anybody walking by, he wouldn't find that in my office. The corridor wall was solid on the bottom, but the top half was glass. Open and public, just the way I liked it. I sat behind my desk and gestured him to a chair. "So, tell me what's on your mind."

"I want you to teach my grandson to defend himself. I asked around, and they tell me this place is the best. We don't live in Cambridge, but I'll see he gets here."

"And you think your grandson needs to defend himself because …?"

"He gets picked on at school and in the neighborhood, you know, teased. You'll see why when you meet him. He doesn't fight back."

"Some kids don't."

"My grandsons do. And he will. That's why I'm bringing him here. I don't want anybody saying he's a sissy. He needs to toughen up, prove he can handle himself. You know what I mean?"

Yep, fix them up. Make them over. Try and turn them into something they weren't and probably never would be.

"Yeah, I do know what you mean. I need to talk with him alone first. Let me do that, and we'll go from there. Is that okay with you?"

"Yeah, I guess. I'll send him in. I'll be waiting for him outside in the car."

Five minutes later I heard a soft knock. The boy standing in the open door could have been the model for a 'Fair Game for Bullies' poster. Red hair with cowlicks, pale white skin, freckles covering his face, and arms so skinny you could wonder if there was any muscle attached to his bones. I didn't think any of that was what made his grandpa drag him to Matty's Way. What had done that was the hint of softness—his mother might have called it sweetness—in the boy's demeanor. His grandfather had sniffed it out, interpreted it negatively, and was determined to annihilate it.

"Hi. I'm Rico."

"I'm Kieran."

At least he wasn't shy. His gaze wandered from the floor to the ceiling before finally turning back to me. "Grandpa wants you to teach me to defend myself. He thinks I'm a wuss because I won't fight. He owns three garages and wants me to learn about cars, and I won't do that, either. And I don't like ice cream."

I've got to tell you, Maureen, I stifled a laugh. The kid might have the demeanor of a pushover, but no way was that the case. He'd use his brain to defend himself, not his fists, and he wasn't going to be pushed into anything. I bet he talked his way out of situations a fair percentage of the time. A kid like that in a family of street brawlers? He must be driving them crazy. Anyway, I said:

"Humm. No ice cream? I suppose you don't like cake or pie, either?"

"Sure I do. And brownies with walnuts—they're the best."

"That sounds normal enough to me. Why don't you hang around a while and watch some classes? That would give you a feel for what we offer, and you can decide what you'd be willing to take. Some of our hard-core martial arts might not be for you, but Tai Chi might appeal to you."

"Would I have to hit anybody?"

"Not in the Tai Chi classes, but yeah, there'll be sparring in forms like karate."

"Okay, I'll watch one of those classes."

A little later, Kieran found me in the hallway. "Grandpa would think Tai Chi was for sissies, but I liked it."

"Tai Chi is a lot of things, but sissy isn't one of them. I'll go talk with your grandfather. Why don't you wait in my office? If he gives the okay, we'll get you signed up."

The kid told me he'd fill out the registration form, and then go get his grandfather to sign the permission form. I looked over the form while he went out to the car, and I have to tell you, I did a double-take when I looked at what he had written. The kid's name was Kieran O'Rourke. I stared at the form, and all I could think was, damn! His name was O'Rourke. You told me that was your maiden name, and then the grandfather signed the form as Kevin O'Rourke. Didn't you tell me that's your father's name? Was he your father, Maureen?"

Rico paused and waited for me to answer, but my heart was pounding in my ear, and I was holding my breath. Kevin O'Rourke.

My father. Yes, Kevin O'Rourke was my father.

Kieran had to be my brother Colin's son. Colin always said he was going to name his second son Kieran. He was the nephew I'd never met. A cousin Kalayla didn't know existed.

Rico kept talking, but all I could hear was my brain repeating over and over: my father, my nephew, my daughter—the three of them at Matty's Way. Together in the same place. Rico stopped talking and was staring at me, and I finally nodded. Yes, Kevin O'Rourke was my father.

"I thought so, and you know what it reminded me of? That movie Casablanca when Lauren Bacall comes into Rick's and Humphrey Bogart says something like 'Out of all the gin joints in the world, she walks into mine.' That's how I felt. Out of all the gyms in the world, Kevin O'Rourke walked into mine and brought along his grandson. Unbelievable!

"When the grandfather came in to sign, I explained that Tai Chi could be used for defense once a student learned the forms. What I didn't tell him was that we don't offer that level of training. He probably pictures Kieran turning into the Karate Kid by next week.

Anyway, I knew you'd want to know what happened and that's, well, that's the whole story."

Daddy. Kalayla. What if he saw her? I had no idea what Daddy would do. She looked so much like me. He'd know right away who she was. And then what?

"Do you think he might run into Kalayla, you know, by accident?" I managed to ask. "That could be just awful, I mean, if he made a scene. Or if Kalayla did. And she could. You know she could. She calls them her asshole non-grandparents, and she might scream at him the way she did at you and ..."

"Whoa, Maureen. Let's not go jumping right to the worst-case scenario. The thing is, we don't have Tai Chi competitions the way we do for Karate. So, there's not really anything parents or grandparents would come to watch except a class and your dad wasn't interested in doing that when I mentioned it. I think getting the kid enrolled was the extent of his obligation. He said he'd make sure the kid got dropped off for classes, but I didn't get the impression he was going to be the taxi service.

"I think we have to hang tight and let this play itself out. Kieran and Kalayla might never bump into each other. She's got a tight schedule what with the gym and dance lessons and working at Animal Friends. Right?"

What Rico said was true, but how could I not worry? It wasn't like I could count on bad things not happening. They did happen, and they happened to me. My life had fallen apart two times for two completely different reasons, and I bet the law of averages said that is really, totally unusual. Rico might not have to worry because he didn't have a target on his back the way I did.

I was going to ask Lena if she thought lightning could strike three times in the same place. I mean, if it could, that meant I did have to worry, no matter what Rico thought. And all the way home, I kept stopping, and looking around to make sure—I didn't know what I was making sure of. Maybe that no monsters were following me. There wasn't any rain or thunder or lightning, so I didn't have to worry about that. But you never could tell what might be hiding in plain sight. Something might leap out from behind a tree or a car, with no warning.

I kept thinking about my parents. I didn't know why I used to believe they knew everything and whatever they said was practically the word of God. No parent could possibly know everything. I mean really, all you had to do was use me as an example. I was a parent, and I didn't know anything at all.

I understood why Mummie was furious at me. I wrecked her dream, but she wrecked a lot of my dreams, too. Why did she designate me as the only one who could move the family up in the world? Kate and Leah were only interested in getting married, and setting up house and having families. Mummie acted thrilled that Kate married a plumber, and Leah married a carpenter. And she was thrilled that Colin was going to take over Daddy's business. She didn't complain that his wife was a salesgirl at Filene's, or moan because mechanics were considered blue-collar even if they did own three garages.

But she cared about what I did, and she cared about who I married. She was outraged when I told her I was going to be an artist until she talked to Carol O'Brien at one of the church coffees, and that changed her mind. "Carol's son Paul is perfect for you, dear. He's starting law school this fall and he's going to take over his father's law practice, and he's thinking maybe he'll become a judge. Carol said it would be just fine for him to have a wife who dabbled in the arts. So, you see, it's all going to work out perfectly!"

Except that it didn't.

And my father—I always counted on his support, but when I really needed it, he turned away from me. Both of them always said they loved me so, so much, but I found out that was true only as long as I did what they wanted.

Kalayla was right—not that she should be calling them assholes, but she was right in saying what they did was wrong. Lena said the same thing without calling them crude names.

When Jamal said my parents were racists, I covered my ears, but he was right. It's too late to tell him, and I am so sorry.

I couldn't bear to admit I didn't admire and respect my parents the way I used to, the way I was raised to, the way they expected me to. Not that it mattered now. I was just glad I wasn't like them. I was glad I married Jamal. I was glad I had Kalayla. And I really did hope that someday, someday I might be able to go back to art.

KALAYLA

A FRIEND

The last few days of school were always filled with field trips and parties and junk like that. Usually I didn't care, but this year it was a pisser to have dumb stuff taking up my time. I was thinking about dropping out. I didn't mention the idea to Mama because she would've freaked out. When I told the Old Lady, she said, "Good. The world needs more ignorant, unemployable people. You could live with your Mama forever and take care of her in her old age. You could take care of me, too. You never know, I might be getting old pretty soon."

She might be getting old? Cow turds! If she had her way, I'd be stuck taking care of her and Mama and Carlotta, too! I wasn't gonna take care of anybody but me, same as I always did.

Anyway, I might stay in school. I heard about some girl who competed in gymnastics in the Olympics. She got a tutor and didn't have to go to school for classes. Step dancing wasn't in the Olympics, but it might be by the time I got good enough to try out.

I loaded up on hours with Rico and Carlotta so I could buy a cheap bike to get places faster. Most of the time Carlotta was a wicked witch boss, so it flipped me out when she showed up the next day with a bike she said was mine—for free.

I must've acted like I didn't believe her 'cause she said, "Don't fall all over yourself thanking me. In case you didn't notice, it's a boy's bike and needs greasing and new bearings. There's a bike shop that will let you use their tools and show you how to do your own tune-up."

It was an awesome old bike, with fat tires and no gears and scratched blue fenders. The guy at the bike shop gave me a special rate on parts when he saw that I had good hands for fixing things and didn't need much help. I was going to ask Eddie if I could park it in back of the Eatery so

I didn't have to drag it up and down four flights every day.

I told Carlotta to pay me for four hours that week instead of the seven, and she said, "Well, it's a pleasure doing business with you," and she stuck out her hand to shake mine. She was weird and strict and hard to get along with, but sometimes I liked her.

Once school was out, I was riding from Matty's Way to Animal Friends to the dance studio all the time so I had to cut way back on supervising at Clean Duds. I kind of missed hanging out with the Old Lady.

I wasn't around home much either, so I had to keep asking Mama if she'd heard from Uncle Clarence. Seemed like everybody but me forgot all about him. I could tell Mama thought it was weird I was asking, so I told her I wanted to make sure I got to see my favorite uncle. I never could've gotten away with that kind of bull with the Old Lady, but Mama smiled and said, "That's so sweet, Kalayla. I never thought you liked him that much."

Yeah, right!

I was gonna be really pissed if heading off Clarence meant skipping a class or changing my work schedule. The only good thing about Rico liking Mama was that Clarence wouldn't be stupid enough to mess with him.

Being at the gym was a blast, especially after Rico said, "Let me know if you hear any complaints we need to act on, okay?" I figured I was supposed to be like an undercover spy, and that was kind of cool. I'd hang around the locker room being my usual invisible self while some hot babe told anybody who'd listen every single detail about all her sex life. I might look into doing snoop work for the police or being a private detective instead of being a dancer. All you had to do was slouch next to a wall and look like you were a piece of the furniture.

Sometimes I had time to kill between jobs, so I'd watch classes if I was at the gym. You could sit in the hallway and look through the glass without the teacher taking a fit. I started noticing this funny looking red-headed kid hanging around, too. Sometimes we'd watch the same class, so we started saying, "Hey." I wasn't looking to have any conversations with a nerdy kid, but one day he said, "What classes are you taking?"

Staff like me was supposed to be friendly to the members all the time, even when they were acting like jerks. Which he wasn't, so I said, "I don't do any of the stuff they teach here. I take step dancing. I work here to pay for my lessons."

"That sounds neat!" he said. "I'm here because my grandfather says

I need to learn to fight. He's paying for my lessons."

"Awesome! I'd like to learn how to beat the shit out of assholes. Maybe you can teach me."

He started laughing, and looking at him, I could see why. He was skinny as a green bean and a little shorter than me. His face was one big freckle and his hair stuck out in every which way. He could impersonate a scarecrow easier than he could a fighter. I was pretty sure I could deck him with my little finger.

That got me to laughing with him, and the two of us were practically rolling on the floor hysterical. We were just about over it and gasping for breath when he puffed out his chest like some show-off weightlifter who had more muscles than brains, "Beware of Monster Man II in disguise!" he said.

That set us off again. After we calmed down, I said, "How about if we team up to beat the shit out of assholes? I'll kick them in the balls, and you break their bones with one of those fancy karate moves, okay?"

"Okay!"

I flopped down on the floor next to him. He told me the kids' summer program let you try different classes and decide what you really liked. He thought everything but Tai Chi was vicious. That was the only class he was willing to take.

"I didn't tell my Grandpa that. I told him the gym had lots of great classes. He gave me a pat on the head and said, 'Good boy.' Sometimes adults are really dumb."

I knew right then I was gonna like this kid. I bet he could get away with anything just by looking innocent and harmless. He might be able to teach me how to fake out the Old Lady.

His name was Kieran, and we started hanging together and fooling around. We called ourselves the Two K's.

After I watched one of his Tai Chi classes, I said, "I didn't get how you're supposed to beat the shit out of anybody doing that. It looks kinda like some type of complicated dance routine."

"I know, but Rico told my grandpa eventually you could use it for self-defense, and that's why he's paying for my lessons. I don't care, I'd way rather be here than stuck at home."

I wanted to take Kieran over to the Animal Friends, so I told him to ride his bike to the gym sometime so I could show him stuff in Cambridge. I wasn't sure where Brighton was, but if it was close enough for me to ride, he could show me around there, too.

"That'd be neat, but I don't have a bike," he said. "I used to, but it got trashed."

"Why'd you trash it?"

"I didn't. My brother Col did."

"So, isn't he gonna get you another one?"

Kieran laughed, "Sure, he said he would after I beat him in a fight."

"So why don't you?"

"No way I'd be stupid enough to try. He'd kill me, and then he'd steal a bike and tell the kid he stole it from that I was the one who took it, and that kid would double kill me."

"Assholes! Well, we probably couldn't figure out how to ride to Brighton anyway."

"Yeah, I could. I know a lot of ways to get there."

"You do?"

"Sure. I'm always looking around to see where I am. You know, kind of like the way an escape artist imagines all the ways he could get out of a locked box. I figure how to get back home, like it's a game I play."

"That's a weird kind of game."

"Not if you're me, it isn't. One time one of Col's friends thought it would be funny to blindfold me and drop me off in Newton. He said he'd give me twenty-five dollars if I could get home without calling anybody for help."

"Did you?"

"Sure, but the jerk never paid me. But now I, like, always pay attention to how I'm getting to where I'm going. So I could find my way back, you know, just in case."

"Don't you have a phone so you could just call somebody?"

"Sure, but I'd never do that. The kids would make fun of me and tell everybody I was too chicken to find my own way home."

"What a bunch of jerks. Somebody oughta kick their ass."

"Well, Col's not really so bad. He just tries to act tough when he's with his friends."

Watching karate classes together was cool. We'd each pick the kid we thought was gonna win a sparring match. Kieran was good at spotting the ones who looked like losers but would win, and I was good at picking the flashy show-offs that were gonna lose.

When Rico was teaching the class, sometimes he'd go over and put his hand on the shoulder of some kid without saying anything. It was weird 'cause if it was a kid I picked as a flashy loser, he'd win that day.

"What do ya think Rico's doing?" Kieran said.

"Don't know. Maybe they're nerve cases and he's like giving 'em a blast of The Force."

When I asked Kieran why his Grandpa was so hot to have him fight, he said, "He thinks I'm hopeless. Col is really strong and a good athlete, and Grandpa wants me to be like him. The only time I make a team is when they don't have enough kids or if the rule says they have to let everybody play, no matter how bad the kid is. Grandpa says anybody as weak as me better learn to defend himself."

"No offense, but your grandpa sounds like a jerk. But at least you know him. I never met mine."

"Really? Why not?"

"My Mama told me he was dead, but she lied. She didn't wanna tell me what an asshole he is. He hates me because my dad was black."

"How is that your fault? Anyway, what difference does it make?"

"A lot to him, I guess. At least your grandpa cares about you enough to try and keep you from getting the crap beat out of you."

When I told the Old Lady I was hanging out at the gym with this kid I met, she said, "Is this a living breathing kid, or somebody you made up?"

That Old Lady was a real pisser!

"I didn't make him up! Rico knows him, too. His name is Kieran."

She got a funny look on her face when I said that, so I added, "When he gets a bike we're gonna ride over here, and you can cough up one of Carlotta's desserts for us. I'm gonna take him to Eddie's so he can meet Mama, too."

LENA

WHEN WILL OLD AGE GET BORING?

Sweet Jesus! The girl never once said a good thing about another kid, and never ever talked about wanting to make a friend. She finally did, and who was it? Her cousin! And she didn't know it!

Just when I was thinking everything was going along fine. Just when Kalayla had stopped ranting about Maureen being a liar and hadn't mentioned her grandparents for a few weeks. Just when her Mama seemed to be doing better, too, finally getting some perspective on that nasty business with her family. And now this.

Maureen told me how her father showed up at Matty's Way with his grandson, and right then I got the feeling trouble was coming. Wasn't I right! I didn't tell Maureen that. I told her it was unlikely Kalayla would run into her cousin, and it was closer to impossible that Kalayla would ever meet her grandfather.

The damnedest things do happen! The world was moving too fast for a person my age to keep up. It felt like one night when I was sleeping, my apartment got moved to an earthquake zone, and the ground under my feet kept on shifting and trying to dump me on my butt. Somebody somewhere must be getting a big guffaw by joking at an old woman's expense. I didn't know who was laughing, but it sure as heck wasn't me.

As if all the stuff going on with Kalayla wasn't enough, the darn cats settled in like they owned me and the apartment, jumping up and sprawling out, taking over a bed I used to call my own. Napoleon and Petunia snuggled their way into my life, but I admit I liked having their furry bodies purring, stretched out next to me.

I have to tell you, being responsible for two cats was a whole lot easier than taking care of four boys, even though the litter box was a permanent fixture and diapers were not. Instead of picking up jackets or sneakers,

I'd be cleaning fur off my clothes and furniture. Be that as it may, the cats were no way the kind of worry my boys had been. I worried about what those boys were doing at school and what they were doing out on the streets. I worried about how they got along with each other. I worried because the twins were together so much. I worried that Mark was alone so much. I worried because JJ admired his dad so much. And I worried about what Joey might be teaching all four of them. I spent my days and my nights worrying. Cats were no kind of trouble in comparison.

When I mentioned to Carlotta that the cats were constantly meowing, she said, "Well, what did you think you were getting with two Siamese? Talking is a characteristic of the breed!" As if I knew anything about cats before she tricked me into getting not one but two of them!

Naturally that was not the end of her commentary. "Now you have somebody to talk to besides Kalayla." I knew she was just hinting for information. She was dying to know if her brother had called me, and finally I told her the truth: he hadn't.

And what do you think she said? "Well then, you should call him. You're the one who rejected him, in case you forgot that little fact. Men can be totally dense, and my brother is not the mind-reading type. You'll both be dead before he figures out you gave up wearing black because you're ready to go out with him."

"That's not why I ..."

"Oh, pooh-bah! It was, too. Your motives are perfectly transparent to anyone who knows you like I do."

Well. I guess I could ask Mattwo to have coffee, but doing that out of the blue with no reason didn't feel right. Men did that all the time, but that's what they were supposed to do. At least that's what a man of my generation was supposed to do. Things were a lot different in 2000 than they had been in 1950. Nowadays Lotta probably called a man without thinking twice about it. Women would NEVER have done that when I was young, or at least I wouldn't have. And I honestly didn't think Lotta would have, either.

But that was then ...

Lotta would tell me I didn't need to bother with deception, and maybe she'd be right. Sweet Jesus, don't tell me I was going to turn into a modern woman at age 72!

MAUREEN AND RICO

TRYING TO STAY CALM

I stretched my arms way up toward the ceiling and then bent over the way you do in yoga class. You were supposed to warm up before you exercised, not that cleaning the apartment would be considered exercise to anyone except me. I mean, really, Matty's Way wouldn't offer a class in Pre-Cleaning Stretches, but cleaning the proper way included moving end tables and chairs instead of cleaning around them. Which meant you should stretch first. And I did.

Every time I cleaned the apartment, I thought about giving a few things away or maybe selling some. But Jamal and I picked out everything together and giving anything away felt like I was severing a connection to him. No one sat in his recliner except Clarence, and the only reason I'd give it away would be to stop him from doing that.

Kalayla was sure Rico and I were having a big romance, but we weren't and I didn't know if it could ever turn into that. I mean, I wouldn't say it couldn't because I did really like him, but loving someone is different. It means giving a part of yourself to someone else—and right now I had to hold on to every bit of me so I could focus on taking care of my sweet girl.

Anyway, look at Lena. Her husband died years and years and years ago and she didn't remarry. It must have been a wonderful marriage and she must still love him, or she would have moved on, wouldn't she? And she would have stopped wearing black a long time ago. I guess I could have asked her about it, but I worried it might be painful for her to think back on those happy times.

Lena was different from me in so many ways. Take our apartments, for example. Hers was a white canvas that drew your eye to simplicity of shape rather than color. Your eye could settle in one place and rest there. Our apartment was a kluge of color and design that moved you along in the perpetual motion of shifting visual enticements. Actually, the apartments were mirrors of our lives, unfinished works of art.

It's such a relief that I had time for silly thoughts and didn't need to run from one job to the next. I could relax and maybe have a third cup of coffee and sit back and appreciate the patterns the sun created as it poured in our windows. Such wonderful light, so different from the cloudy grayness of winter.

Kalayla came charging out of her bedroom directly to the coffee pot, from which she poured her usual half cup and then added half a cup of milk, her express version of café au lait.

"Layla, honey, slow down."

"Can't. Places to go, things to do, people to see," she said, slapping together two pieces of toast with chunky peanut butter and strawberry jam. "Gym, Shelter, class. Later," she called, a whirlwind slamming the door before I could ask if the sandwich was breakfast or lunch. Or both.

Really, I had to make sure she ate more. I mean, with dancing and two jobs and biking everywhere, she needed more energy than one sandwich could provide, even though globs of peanut butter and jelly ran out the sides. I might buy some of those energy bars, the ones with lots of protein. Or maybe the ones with lots of carbs. I'll ask Lena what she thinks.

I saw Kalayla darting across the street, running down the side alley next to Eddie's. She rode out of the alley, pedaling at full speed. I had no idea how far away a planet or a star was from earth, but Kalayla had traveled at least that far since winter. Really, she changed from being a sassy mouthed and angry almost teenager to being a dependable employee working two jobs, and a serious dance student. And maybe most amazing, she was actually being civil to Rico. What an astonishing transformation!

Except for one thing. One weird thing. She kept asking if I'd heard from Clarence. Now why would she do that? I mean, in the past if Clarence stopped by when she wasn't home, she wasn't the least bit interested. But now she was. And what did she give as a reason? She wanted to be sure she was here when her favorite uncle came to visit. I might have believed her if she said her only uncle, but really, her favorite? She's never liked Clarence, and she went out of her way to prove it by being rude, sarcastic, and generally unpleasant every time she saw him.

I put my mug on a wooden coaster and flopped down on the sofa. Maybe it would be better if Kalayla was here when Clarence came over.

Normally I wouldn't have thought that, but last week I ran into him so unexpectedly, and I wasn't alone. Which would have been perfectly fine except the way Clarence acted made it feel awkward and awful.

Rico and I were planning to take a walk before Kalayla got home from dance, and I was going to change out of my uniform, when I saw Clarence's car parked right in front of the apartment building.

I got this terrible feeling in my stomach, and I wanted to turn and walk in the other direction, as far away from him as I could get. Which was really silly. It wasn't as if Rico and I were holding hands, or doing anything we shouldn't. All we were doing was crossing the street.

I turned to go in the opposite direction, but Rico said, "Maureen? What's up? I thought you wanted to change first." I didn't know what to say, so I turned back and we crossed the street and met Clarence just as he was coming out of the apartment house.

He looked us over in a really insulting way, and said—in the rudest tone—"So this is what you've been up to, Maureen." He made it sound like I was doing something terrible. Even if I had been, which I wasn't, it was none of Clarence's business!

Rico didn't seem the least bit offended or defensive or annoyed by Clarence's sneering tone. He stuck out his hand to Clarence. "You're Jamal's brother Clarence, right? I'm Rico Eccli, a friend of Maureen's."

Clarence did the only thing he could and not look like a total jerk. He shook Rico's hand. But then he gave me a nasty look and said, "I'll stop by when you're not so … so busy, Maureen." And without another word, he got into his car and drove away.

"That went well, don't you think?" Rico said, laughing.

Rico could joke about it, but I couldn't. It hadn't gone well at all, and who knew what stories Clarence would make up and carry back to Lucinda? Who knew how Lucinda might react? I'd come so far, worked so hard to show her I was capable of taking care of Kalayla, but Clarence could ruin everything if he wanted to.

Rico didn't ask me anything about Clarence, but he must have been wondering. What was I supposed to tell him? Clarence acted like he had a claim on me, but he didn't, not at all. He was a connection to my life with Jamal, and that was all he would ever be.

I remember when Jamal and I went to see "Chicago," and the lawyer for all the lady murderers sang this song about all the dicey techniques he used to win a case. "That's the perfect description of Clarence. He's a razzle, dazzle, flim-flam man!"

Jamal said it in such a sad way. He had tried so hard to encourage Clarence by giving him ideas about how to get a normal job instead of, well, instead of whatever it was Clarence actually did. Clarence had a standing invitation for dinner every Friday night, and I couldn't very well tell Jamal I wished he'd take it back.

Clarence could make up anything about seeing Rico and me, and Lucinda might believe him. And what would happen then? My life was fragile and all the pieces could collide and explode if I wasn't really careful. I just couldn't let that happen. Again.

I jumped up and got busy cleaning the apartment. By the time it was spotless, I felt much better. Then I went to the grocery store and talked to one of the clerks who told me she ran around Fresh Pond every day and always took GORP as a snack. That reminded me that Jamal used to make GORP with raisins, almonds, peanuts and dried cranberries, and chocolate bits. He ate it all the time because he was so physically active. I bought everything and had just finished making a batch for my girl when Rico called. He said we needed to talk about something that happened at the gym that afternoon.

Oh God, not again! I didn't ask him what it was about because he said he'd come right over, and we could walk to the Common and talk. I just hoped nothing awful happened with Daddy and Kalayla. I managed to hold it together until Rico came. Sitting on the Common with him on such a gorgeous afternoon and feeling the warm breeze helped to calm me down. Especially because Rico seemed so relaxed, I thought maybe it wasn't so bad. But then I found out that it was.

RICO

Don't look so worried, Maureen. Really. Look, first let me tell you how impressed I've been with the way Kalayla has conducted herself at the gym. She's been respectful and helpful, and nobody has bitched about having her around. If she annoyed anybody, trust me, they'd let me know in a second. It turns out she has been keeping an hour by hour log of what she does. The kid is something else, Maureen. You can be really proud of her. She told me her goal is to go to the dance camp for two weeks in August—and I'll do everything I can to help her with that.

So that's all good.

Here it comes, I thought, but it can't be a total disaster. Rico would have told me the bad news first, wouldn't he? I mean, if something was the worst of the worst, you didn't wait to tell that. Did you? "That's good," I said. "BUT?"

He hesitated for a minute and then told me the rest of it.

Well, the thing is, I need to explain how it went, sort of step by step, so you get the whole picture. I already told you how Kalayla likes hanging out with Kieran. I see them all the time, huddling together laughing at some kid joke. I wondered if I should discourage that, but both of them need a friend and what they're doing is harmless, so I let it go.

Then today I was on the way to my office when I get a text from Jen at the front desk: COME NOW!!! I jogged past the classrooms and rounded the corner to the front desk. And I knew immediately why she called me. I had asked her to alert me if Kieran's grandfather came by when Kieran and Kalayla were both in the building, and today they were.

Your dad was leaning against the front counter, relaxed and casual, chatting with Jen. Which was good. I figured with luck, I'd be able to snag Kieran and steer him and his grandpa out of the building without any problems.

I gave him the old glad hand greeting, "Hey, Kevin. How's it going?"

He glanced down the hallway like he was expecting Kieran to be tagging along behind me.

"Better for me than it is for you if you have to jog everywhere. I gave that up when I retired. Now I go at my own pace."

I laughed, "Yup, my dad says the same thing. Look, if you hang out here a minute, I'll find Kieran, and you two can take off."

Instead of saying okay the way I hoped he would, he moved closer and lowered his voice. "So, how's that grandson of mine doing?"

Whew! I knew I had to be very careful about the way I answered. I'd seen the two kids watching karate classes, but Kieran was adamant that Tai Chi was the limit of his tolerance for the martial arts. So, I said, "Well, I think he likes being here, and I've watched him in class, and he's learning the moves and improving. You know, Rome wasn't built in a day."

The thing is, Maureen, no matter how clumsy a kid was—and Kieran was remarkably agile—you could usually steer things away from the touchy stuff by saying the kid was improving. In Kieran's case, that absolutely was the truth. I was surprised when I observed him in class. He seemed to understand how the Tai Chi moves flowed and connected like it came naturally to him.

I wasn't about to tell the grandfather that quite aside from that Kieran didn't seem to have one ounce of fighter instinct. Of course, the fact he wasn't showing it didn't mean it wasn't there, under the surface. Sometimes that kind of thing comes out suddenly, like when somebody unexpectedly hits the trigger point. Then, wham, there it was!

Anyway, I didn't give him a chance to get into a big discussion. I turned and went down the hall where I figured I'd find Kieran and Kalayla watching a karate class. I was halfway there when I met them walking toward me slowly and talking.

"Kieran," I called, "your ride's here. Hey Kalayla, why don't we go over your hours now?"

Kieran looked at Kalayla, "That's my grandpa. So, you want to meet him?"

"Oh, yeah! Can we do the hours later, Rico? I gotta meet this old guy."

Before I got a chance to head them off, the two of them zipped past me, and I went jogging after them. They stopped in front of the grandpa, and Kieran launched into a few gestures that somebody who didn't know a thing about karate might interpret as fighting moves.

"Better watch out, Grandpa! I might knock you over!" Both kids giggled, and Kalayla mimicked Kieran, exaggerating like crazy.

The old man shifted his attention to her, and I watched his expression change from curious to puzzled. He squinted and put a hand up, you know, the way you do when you're trying to block sunlight from your eyes. "You look familiar," he told Kalayla, "but I can't place why …"

Kieran's and Kalayla's laughter petered out. They looked sideways at each other, like they were silently agreeing this wasn't the best time to fool around. Kieran said proudly, "This is Kalayla, Grandpa. She's my friend."

I have to tell you, Maureen, watching the old guy was heart-wrenching. I know you might not want to hear it given how they treated you, but that's the only way I know to describe it.

He just stood there looking uncertain and confused, the way an old guy might when he was walking down the street where he lived, but he didn't have a clue which house was his. Frankly, I was afraid he might have a stroke or a heart attack.

But the thing is, at that point there was nothing I could do but face the situation head-on. Free-floating shit was bound to hit the fan sometime, somewhere, and it just landed in the gym.

So I plunged in, "Well, you might actually have an idea who Kalayla is, Mr. O'Rourke. Her last name is LeeRoyce."

The old man staggered and turned white. He put his hand on the counter to steady himself, and I could see he was trying to pull himself together. To be honest, I heaved a sigh of relief. He stood there looking at Kalayla, and she turned and looked at me and then back at him—all without saying a word.

I kept going. "That's right, Kalayla. His name is O'Rourke. He's your mom's father."

I hadn't been paying attention to Kieran, but right then, he cleared his throat and started talking—going step by step, trying to figure out what that meant. "So … if my grandpa is Kalayla's mom's dad … and he's also my dad's dad, that means my dad and her mom are brother and sister. And that means Kalayla has the same grandpa I do. I think. And that means—K! I think you're my cousin!"

I heard what Kieran was saying, but I'll tell you, Kalayla was the one I was watching. Her silence was a booming crash of thunder in comparison to his soft voice. Her green eyes were dark and wide and glued to Mr. O'Rourke, and her body was stone still.

Then she backed away from your dad real slow and whispered, so I had to strain to hear her, "That means your grandpa is the exact same asshole as my grandpa."

I'll tell you the truth, Maureen, if I was predicting, I would have predicted she'd explode, and I was ready to stop her from charging the old guy the way she charged into me. She had a lot more reason to react like that with him. Right?

But she didn't. She stayed where she was with her hands clenched into fists at her sides, and I could see her body was trembling. Maureen, the thing is, she was crying. I kid you not. Tears were rolling down her face.

I felt so, so bad for her. I stepped over to her, put my arm around her shoulder and pulled her close. There wasn't much else I could do.

And Kieran … No question it was traumatic for both the kids. I was having trouble taking it in myself, and neither of them acted the way I would have predicted they would.

Kieran watched his grandpa and Kalayla without saying a word.

Then the kid straightened himself up, pulled his shoulders back, and grew about two inches right in front of me. And then he started talking. His voice was quiet and composed and absolutely clear. "So, are you going to do the same thing to me you did to Kalayla's mom, Grandpa? Are you going to kick me out of the family because I won't fight back when kids tease me?"

The old man's face crumbled, and no question he would have fallen over if he hadn't been holding on to the counter. "You don't understand, boy. You can't understand what this was like for me and for your grandma. Grandma couldn't … she couldn't … "

He couldn't find the words, maybe because there weren't any to find. He didn't know how to explain it. He turned and shuffled toward the door looking—looking so defeated, Maureen. And I was sure of one thing—that old guy was crying the same as Kalayla was, even if his tears weren't showing.

When he got to the door, he stopped and looked back at Kieran. "You coming with me now, boy, or you want me to send somebody?"'

Kieran looked at Kalayla for a minute, and then he gave her a little wave and said, "See you tomorrow, K." He went over and took his grandfather's hand and led him through the door like you'd lead somebody you knew wouldn't be able to make it on their own.

"Those two kids … it was enough to break your heart. I took Kalayla into my office, and we stayed not saying anything until she looked up at the clock, and said, 'I gotta go, Mr. Rico. I gotta work at the Shelter. Thanks for … thanks.'

You know, Maureen, I read a book once where a prisoner was forced to choose between losing an arm and losing a leg. I thought that was an impossible choice, but honestly, I think that's the way your dad felt. He was forced to choose between two people he loved. I'm not making excuses for him or trying to defend him, but it seems to me that he had to decide what held his life together. You know, what the load-bearing wall in his life was. And he decided that was your mother, not you.

Kieran let him know he wasn't willing to make that kind of choice. Kieran was keeping his grandfather, and he was keeping his friend. That was good for Kalayla to see and frankly, it was a damn inspiring thing for me to see, too.

I think when you turn away from someone you love the way your mom and dad did, your life had to be diminished. Part of the brightness and joy had to be gone and you'd always know you were the one responsible. I don't know what else to tell you, Maureen. That's what happened."

LENA

SOMETHING ELSE?

Well, the first clue that something had sent her off kilter was her pounding on my door about fifteen times. I was in the bathroom, and sprinting was not on my agenda, or in my mobility range. My patience was getting to the tipping point, and I could see the only way to keep her from disturbing the cats' peace would be if I gave her a key.

When I opened the door, she came strolling in like she owned the place, chanting at the top of her lungs. "Piss, dung. Piss, dung. Dungy, pissy, dung, dung. Piss, dung. Piss, dung. Dungy, pissy, dung, dung. Piss, dung. Piss, dung. Dungy, pissy, dung, dung."

I put my hands on my hips and gave her a look that would have scared the monsters in any horror film. "What do you think you're doing coming in here shouting garbage like you just crawled out of a cesspool? Stop that this minute or I will get out my bar of lye soap, and we will see how much you love the taste of that!"

Well, of course she didn't answer, so I pointed to the kitchen and she went in and sat down at the table. She mumbled something like, "Old Crab oughta be put in jail for the way she tortures poor, harmless kids."

Which I chose to ignore. That girl would benefit from an application of a good old-fashioned hairbrush to her butt. Not that it would do a lick of good! I got out the peanut butter cookies.

"Is it okay if I help myself to some milk?" she croaked in a stilted voice. I nodded, and she took her time about getting a glass and pouring herself some milk. At least staying here taught her a few things. Like to ask before she emptied my refrigerator and cupboards.

"So," I said, "Did some nine-headed serpent bite you, and you came over here so I could suck out the poison?"

Her face fell about down to her feet, and she said, in the most dejected, sorrowful voice, "Only one head … one crappy old head."

She paused, and I could tell she was working her way up to telling me the rest of it. I kept my mouth shut and waited.

While I was waiting, I got busy making a cup of the coffee that drove Carlotta wild. She called it lazy man's coffee. All you had to do was insert a little cup and push a couple buttons. There are probably a hundred flavors, but three or four did me fine.

Miss Petunia came sauntering in. You could always trust a cat to soothe trouble spots or hurting kids. She went right to work, brushing against Kalayla's leg.

Which caused this smart-assed comment: "Why'd you pick such an ugly cat? Old people have crappy eyesight." As usual, that girl was just blowing off steam. She bent down and picked Petunia up. The cat circled her lap one way and then the other before settling with her butt against Kalayla's stomach, her purr volume cranked high.

I didn't bother to answer that either. Petunia was about as gorgeous a Blue Point as you'd find anywhere and sweet-tempered, too, to put up with that girl's nonsense. Whatever was going on, I figured Kalayla couldn't keep quiet for long, and I was right.

"It's not fair. It's wicked not fair."

"Okay, and that would cover more than 85% of what happens in this world. Would you like to tell me if you were referring to any particular unfair thing?"

"It's not fair when you hate an asshole jerk, and then you meet him face to face and find out he's nothing but a pathetic old man."

"Hummm. Well, I guess maybe you could end up pitying him instead of hating him. Would you be willing to tell me who this poor, pathetic, former asshole is?"

"Kieran's grandpa."

Now I understood. I bet the old man came to the gym when she was there, and the shock of her seeing him was what caused the pounding on my door. Kieran's grandpa evidently hadn't come across as the mean, hateful, vicious old man she'd conjured him up to be. Well, I thought, add another chalk mark to the 'Things are not always what we think' column.

"So," I said, "Kieran's grandpa—and just so we're clear here, that would also be your grandpa—isn't what you thought he'd be. You don't think he's worth hating, and you don't feel sorry for him. Which leaves the big question. How do you feel about him?"

"Don't know … maybe nothing … probably nothing … don't know."

Now that surprised me. It didn't seem likely she could go from full tilt hating to feeling nothing. She was always willing to blurt out her gut reaction, whether you asked for it or not. Even in her sad times, the spark was there, maybe beneath the surface, but still there. If it was there right now, it was sure buried deep because I wasn't seeing any sign of it.

That girl's life was one big complication piled on another. It had gone from high gear to overload. And none of it her doing. These last few months, she had more thrown at her than most folks have in a lifetime. When I thought of it that way, it was no surprise she didn't know how she felt. All I could do was hope things would be getting easier for her at some point soon.

I looked out the window. Nearly 7:30 and not dark yet, a gift of summer that'd be gone soon enough. Past Kalayla's dinner time, but Maureen hadn't called or come by. Maybe she thought Kalayla was still in dance class, or just as likely, she probably thought she was eating over here.

"I suppose you told your mama you were coming here for dinner. Will a turkey melt suit you?"

"Haven't seen Mama. Turkey's okay."

"All right then. Put that neglected, ugly cat down and go see if your mama is home and knows where you are. Then get back here and help."

SUMMER
INTO EARLY FALL
2000

KALAYLA

BEING NUMB

I opened the door, and right off Mama said, "Are you okay? You must have been at Lena's. It must have been awful for you. I mean, a shock seeing him … and … are you okay?"

What a pisser! She couldn't say, "Hi," like a normal person. She had to ask a question and then give me her answer to the question, same as always. Like I couldn't figure out my own answer.

"Yeah. Eating at Lena's. Back later." I didn't have anything else to say, so I went back to Lena's. If I stayed at home, Mama would've kept up the questions 'til I got mad and said something that would've made the Old Lady wanna wash my mouth out with lye soap. AGAIN. If she would've done that all the times she said I needed it, she would've been buying cases of the stuff!

At least the Old Lady could be quiet sometimes. Not all the time and not always when I wanted her to. But way quieter than Mama ever was. When I got there, she was at the stove flipping the turkey melts and she started right in ordering me around.

"Get a plate. You know where the pickles are. Get out the chips. Cape Cod or Lay's sea salt and vinegar, your choice."

When I felt like talking I was gonna ask her when she was gonna give out promotions. I was sick of being a private.

"How come only one plate?" I said. "Aren't you eating?"

"You think my old stomach can wait until the middle of the night to get fed? I might munch on a few chips as my nighttime snack."

Middle of the night? Her kitchen clock said 8:13—normal dinner time for Mama. I did what she said and soon as we sat at the table Petunia jumped onto the Old Lady's lap. As if I cared. Anyway, then the ugly brown cat came in and sat next to my chair.

I was starting on my second sandwich when Lena said, "You're eating so fast you're giving me indigestion."

"Yeah, well, you don't have a cat sitting next to you like a vulture that's waiting to swoop down and steal your turkey!"

"Oh, for goodness sake! Napoleon is keeping you company. Now Napoleon, you be a good boy and I'll give you a treat when she's finished eating."

It was gonna be a real pisser if the cat answered, "Okay, I'll take the minnows."

Carlotta said dogs were sensitive and could smell danger, like if the house was on fire or if a person had cancer, the dog might know before a doctor did. If dogs could do that, maybe there were cats that could talk the way parrots do. Well, too bad if Napoleon was in the mood for a conversation. I wasn't.

I didn't feel like talking to him. I didn't feel like talking at all. My brain was blank as Lena's walls. Nothing going out. Nothing coming in. My body felt heavy, and slow, and moving was too much effort. Maybe I'd go home and sleep for the rest of my life. I finished eating, dragged my way through rinsing my plate, and put the Cape Cod chips and pickles away.

Lena said, "Want to take a few cookies for the road?"

"Naah. Thanks for dinner." I went home. Mama was talking non-stop as I walked past her into my room, flopped on the bed, and went to sleep.

I must've slept all night 'cause Mama barged in and woke me up before she went to work at eight the next morning. She was all nerved up. As usual.

"Oh, my goodness, Kalayla! You're not up yet? Won't you be late for … for something? I'll pick out something for you to wear and fix a sandwich for you …"

Cow turds! "Lemme sleep."

"But you must have work or class or …"

"Lemme sleep."

"Well, maybe I should call Rico or Carlotta or …"

"Lemme sleep." If I wanted to talk to her, I would've turned over and looked at her, instead of staring at the wall with my back to her.

She gave a loud sigh, and I heard her close the door.

I went back to sleep. I was still sleeping when she came home and barged in again.

"Kalayla, honey, you slept all day. You must be coming down with something. Let me feel your forehead."

I buried my head under my pillow.

"Oh dear, I better get Lena."

I stuck my head out. "NO! NO! NO! Lemme alone. Lemme sleep!"

The next time she woke me up, the clock said 7:50 a.m., and she was going off to work.

"Kalayla, you've been sleeping 36 hours. Really, you must be sick. Lena said to let you sleep, but I think we should go to the doctor."

"MAMA! Lemme alone! I'm not sick. I'm TIRED!"

She kept on sputtering, but I turned my back, and she finally left.

Next thing I knew the Old Lady was shaking my shoulder.

"What!" I said, trying to focus on the clock by my bed. 11:30 a.m.

"I got lunch," she said, all cheery like it was a big treat. Probably a dumb tuna sandwich.

Cow turds. First Mama and now her. You couldn't get any sleep around here with them making such a big deal out of it.

"Lemme sleep." At least she didn't keep bugging me. I heard her go out and close the door.

Next thing I heard was the phone ringing and ringing. I ignored it 'til Lena came in, pulled the covers off me, and took me by the arm.

"Get your butt up NOW!" she said. "Carlotta needs to speak to you."

Carlotta! What'd she want me for? I dragged myself out of bed and into the living room to the phone. "Yeah?"

"Well, if it isn't sleeping beauty! I suppose you remember the dog with two broken legs that you convinced me to take to the vet? She's back at the Shelter with her hind legs in casts. Should I send her out to play in traffic, or do you think you might possibly be able to take time out of your busy schedule and come over here and help me with her?"

That funny looking reddish-brown dog that was found by the side of the road. The one with the floppy ears and big sad eyes. Cow turds! I had to get over there fast! Carlotta probably wouldn't put her outside on her own, but I wasn't gonna take any chances!

"I'm coming! Don't you let anybody mess with her! She knows me, and she'll wanna see me."

"Well! Yes, of course, Your Majesty. Whatever you say, Your Majesty."

The old bag hung up on me. I charged back to my room, splashed water from the shower over me, grabbed clean clothes and pulled 'em on.

When I went out to the living room, the Old Lady said, "I called a taxi. You can eat on the way. I made two peanut butter and jelly and two chicken salad sandwiches which ought to hold you until later. Plus, chips and cookies and root beer. The bag is on the kitchen table. Call me when you're ready to come home."

The taxi was waiting downstairs, and when I got to the Shelter and saw the dog, I almost cried. You wouldn't believe how sweet she was. She put her head in my lap and let me pat her like she'd been waiting for me to come. If I ever found out who abandoned her, I'd break their legs and their arms and see how they liked it.

Carlotta explained all the things we'd need to do for the dog, and she showed me how to be careful and not hurt her when I put diapers on her. "I can stop by to see her about three times a day," I told Carlotta. "And I can sleep here in case she needs something at night and …"

"NO, you absolutely are not sleeping here. The dog will be fine. I'll be checking on her. That is, IF I have your permission to do that?" She was standing with her hands on her hips, daring me to say no. She was the one who paid the vet, and she and the other Old Crab had helped me a lot. I felt kind of like a jerk, so I nodded and muttered, "Thanks."

The next day I told Carlotta we had to get a real name for the dog. It wasn't right to keep calling her 'the dog'. Carlotta said animals already had names, and I'd have to figure out what hers was. When I asked how I was supposed to do that, she said, "Go ask her and see what she says."

Cow turds! First talking cats and now talking dogs! I opened her cage door and sat down in front of it so I could reach in and pet her. I tried saying lots of different names like Lassie and Red and Tammy and Fido and Cookie. She watched me with her big eyes like she understood what I was doing and was wishing I'd hurry up and find the right name.

When I looked at her leg casts I thought of a dumb name, but nothing else worked, so I figured I had nothing to lose. I said, "Hi, Hopalong."

I couldn't believe it! Her tail started thumping on the floor and she looked real happy! When I told Carlotta, she smiled and nodded instead of acting like her usual sour puss self.

The next day I went back to my regular routine. I told Rico I'd make up the time I missed, but he said he'd count it as vacation days, and not to worry. I was getting to like him better, but I didn't know if Mama was. She needed a chill pill.

I went back to practicing dance steps so Miss Megan wouldn't go ballistic 'cause I'd missed some classes. Anybody who thought dancing was for wimps was dumber than dumb. You got blisters and bruises, and your muscles ached, and the teacher yelled at you and made you do the same steps over and over and over, until your legs felt so weak you were afraid they were gonna buckle and dump you flat on your butt.

I might've ditched the whole dance thing 'cept for Miss Megan. She could tap fast as a machine gun shot or slow and steady as a sink drip that made you crazy. "Class!" she'd yell at us, "the dancer controls the feet. The feet do not control the dancer!" She was a real pisser, but she was a good teacher, and I wasn't gonna give up just 'cause it was hard.

Rico posted the class schedule at the front desk, so I always knew when the back hallway would be empty. I'd take a break from working and go back there to slap out the rhythm or practice the steps. When we were hanging out, Kieran used to help by banging out the rhythm on the floor.

The first time I saw him after the thing with his grandpa, I was back there practicing steps. He saw me and waved and came over acting kind of shy. He said, "Could ya use a drummer?"

"Sure. Why wouldn't I?"

"Well, you know, I went home with Grandpa instead of telling him he was an asshole."

"Oh. Yeah. Well, if I told the Old Lady what you did, she'd give you a gold star for admirable behavior."

He kind of smiled. "How come I didn't see you the last few days?" he said.

"I was sort of on vacation."

"I thought maybe you were avoiding me and didn't want to hang out with me anymore."

I grinned at him. "Hanging out with you is better than eating worms cooked in hot sauce."

We both laughed.

"I've been spending a lot of time at the shelter with this one dog. Her back legs were broken, and Carlotta had the vet fix her up. Her name is Hopalong. She's kind of funny looking, but she's really, really sweet. When Carlotta says she can leave the shelter, I'm gonna see if Mama'll let me keep her. I might be able to get the Old Lady to take care of her during the day when I'm at school."

"Hopalong? I never heard of a dog named Hopalong."

"So what? Did you ever hear of a girl named Kalayla before you met me?"

"Naah, but Kalayla kind of sounds like a girl's name. Hopalong sounds like a boy's name."

"I don't care and neither does she. That's her name, and she likes it. You can come to the shelter and meet her if you want."

"Do you think you'll be able to keep her?"

"Don't know. Mama might say okay 'cause she's trying to make up for being such a liar. And the Old Lady used to be a real crab about pets, but she's gone whacko since she got the two cats, so she might be willing to take care of Hopalong. When you get a bike, you can ride over and help me convince her."

He raised both arms and yelled, "The two K's will strike again!" We laughed, and he slid down on the floor and started banging out the rhythm. That day instead of practicing steps, I started banging with him. He'd go soft and I'd go loud and then we'd switch. We sounded pretty good. He was a weird kid, but I liked him.

Things at home were aggravating, as usual. Mama kept wanting to discuss what happened at the gym. I kept telling her there wasn't anything to discuss.

On Sunday a couple weeks later, I wanted to get to the shelter early 'cause it was gonna be a pisser of a hot day and I didn't wanna be dripping sweat when I got there. Naturally, Mama wouldn't let me out the door 'til after we had one of our fabulous Sunday morning talks.

"Fine!" I told her. "Say what you wanna say quick. I gotta go!"

Mama gave me that exasperated sigh and put down her coffee cup. "It's not what I want to say. It's what I think we need to discuss."

"Yeah, okay. So discuss."

Another big sigh from her. She didn't get how annoying that was.

"I just wanted to know how you felt when you saw my father. Will you tell me that? Please."

Why'd she have to say please and make me feel like a jerk?

"Yeah, okay. When I found out who he was, I wanted to punch him in the face and tell him he was an asshole. But I didn't. I didn't … 'cause … I don't know why I didn't. So, are we done now?"

If she sighed one more time, I was definitely gonna walk out the door.

"No, we're not. Please tell me how he looked and how he seemed."

"Mama! He looked like an OLD MAN. He looked upset. He looked like if I yelled at him, he was gonna fall on the floor and Rico'd be calling 911, and it'd be my fault."

Mama frowned like maybe she didn't understand what I told her. "Oh," she said. "Well. Did he ask anything about me? Did he ask how we were doing?"

I almost left then. Did she think we were just sat there having a friendly chat? Like all of a sudden, he turned into the good old friendly neighborhood grandfather and cared how his daughter and granddaughter were doing? Mama was just plain dumb.

"No. And no. He didn't ask anything about you. He didn't ask anything about us. He acted like he was gonna fall over and Kieran took his hand and led him out the door. Can I go now, PLEASE?"

Even though I knew she didn't want to, she said, "Okay."

MAUREEN

TIME ON MY HANDS

A superficial glance would lead you to believe nothing had changed. Eddie's was still Eddie's: same sign, same tables, same staff. Mass. Ave. was still Mass. Ave.: same limited parking, same specialty shops, same motley pedestrians. Our apartment was still our apartment: same furniture, same color walls, same tension.

Everything depended on how deeply you chose to delve. For example, if you only explored one painting rather than the artist's entire portfolio, you might miss the subtle changes. You might not see how the technique had deepened and expanded. You might not see how relationships between brush and oils and artist had shifted and realigned.

What a lot of bull! My brain was drying up in this SLOW summer season, and I was staring out Eddie's window desperately trying to entertain myself with ridiculous observations about everything in general and nothing in particular. Because standing around waiting for customers was so unbearably BORING.

I suppose I could do something practical and plan Kalayla's 13th birthday party, even though it was months away. But that would be totally absurd given the fact that last March 15th, her communication with me was limited to monosyllables. She not only refused to have a party, she refused to have a birthday. She might do that again.

She might agree to a party if I suggested an Ides of March celebration, but she'd probably take that as permission to assassinate anyone she wished, Julius Caesar style and joyfully start making an assassination list, and I'd be at the top of it.

I could always count on Lena for an idea, and maybe she had a suggestion for living with temporary boredom at work. That afternoon I cut a hunk of zucchini bread and went over for a cup of coffee. She opened the door, and when I went in, the funniest thing happened. All that white lifted my spirits. Lena laughed when I told her work was so slow I could hardly wait for the time when I could run frantically from table to table again and Kalayla was too busy to do anything with me (not that she'd want to even if she had absolutely nothing else to do) when I got home.

Lena looked a little puzzled. She was always busy, so maybe she didn't understand how awful it was to twiddle diddle your life away.

"Ahh," she said. "Aren't you doing your artwork? I thought you loved that."

"Oh Lena, I do, and I wish I could. But I can't and I know it would really help and make me feel better and ..."

"All right, so let me ask again. Why aren't you doing it?"

"Because I don't have a workspace. I had to rent a storage unit for my art supplies when we moved here. Even if I did have a little space, everything is there. I mean, in storage. When Jamal was alive our apartment was big enough that I had a studio all my own. No matter what medium you work in, you really do need that. There's so much equipment and so many different materials. I don't have that space now. Unless I shared a bedroom with Kalayla and then I'd have a room for my art, but you know that would be a total disaster."

"Humm, yes. I wouldn't want to be the one to tell Kalayla she'd be sharing a room with you. Let me think about this and talk with Dom. We might be able to come up with a little space somewhere in the apartment building."

"Oh Lena, that would be SO wonderful! I mean, I'd be so grateful and happy and ..."

"Hold on. Hold on. I can't promise anything except that I'll do some exploring."

I felt SO much better when I went home, and I really wished I could tell Jamal how much better I felt. Which maybe sounds crazy, but I did talk to him sometimes, and I really do think he heard me, or at least I imagined he did and I could imagine what he would answer.

At least I could talk to Rico and in a way, that was better than talking to Jamal because Rico really did talk back. And what he said about my father was really important and made me think. Maybe Daddy did side with Mummie instead of me because she was his load-bearing wall.

And when Rico said that, I realized that Jamal had been my load bearing wall. When he died, everything fell apart. Maybe that was what my dad was afraid would happen to him. His world would fall apart without Mummie.

I could imagine Jamal shaking his head and telling me that we were both part of the wall, that it took two of us to build it. Telling me that I did it once, and I could do it again if I chose to. That made so much sense. You build the wall with love and with integrity and with your true beliefs, and that's what Jamal and I did. I could do that again. If I wanted to, I knew I could.

I decided right then I was going to do a painting for Lena. As a present. As a thank you. Because she was my friend and Kalayla's …

The phone rang and when I picked it up and said hello, I almost hung up because nobody answered. But then, I heard a man's voice say, "Maureen … Maureen, it's your dad."

I almost dropped the phone.

"Maureen? Are you there?"

Was I … there? I wasn't sure where 'there' was. I took a deep breath and could almost feel Jamal's arm around me, his voice low and strong, "Steady now, Sweet Babe." The phone in my hand seemed real enough. But I'd been hoping to hear my father's voice for so long, maybe I was imagining the way I did Jamal's.

The man's voice went on. "I called to ask you if … I called to ask if it would be okay for me to take your daughter for ice cream. With her friend Kieran. Ah, with her cousin Kieran. With Colin's son Kieran."

My father. On the phone, asking if he could take Kalayla for ice cream. My impossible dream coming true. My throat was tight, and my voice must have sounded weird—if he remembered how my voice used to sound. "Yes," I said. "I guess, that would be okay with me."

"All right then. I'll, ah, I'll ask her if she wants to. Thanks." He hung up.

I stood holding the phone, the magic wand in my hand that had conjured up my heart's desire. My father, who never added dressing to his salad, or sauce or gravy or relish to anything he ate. Plain. Straight. To the point, without embellishment. Asking if he could take Kalayla for ice cream.

For the first time since Jamal died, I sat in his recliner. I could feel his love surrounding me. And I cried with joy. My father was taking our daughter for ice cream.

LENA

FINALLY DOING SOMETHING

Well, it was about time! I had something specific I could do instead of spending my time watching and waiting and hoping I'd find a way to help that girl and her mama.

I decided to meet Dominic at my office in Home Base and bring up a space for Maureen at our weekly check-in. I'd act like it was just another agenda item, and maybe he wouldn't suspect it wasn't.

When I asked if there happened to be an empty room in the apartment house that she could use, he squinted his eyes and cocked his head. A smile tugged at his lips when he said, "A space for Maureen? Humm, if I hunted around, maybe I could find one. And if I did … how much are you willing to invest in this project, Lena?"

Damn! He knew me too well. "Dominic! Don't you make it sound like I'm buying a new building! All I'm doing is looking for a small space in the building where I live!"

"Yeah, I understood what you asked for. And you know I have a specific use for every space in every building. Did you think I could pull an extra room out of my hat along with a magic bunny? So, I ask again, what are you willing to invest?"

"Sweet Jesus, Dom, sometimes you are such a pill! What do you mean?"

"I mean, three weeks ago, I found old man Spencer near the flower shop, and he didn't know where he was. I walked him home and called his daughter. She's taking him to live with her. Good luck to her on that one."

"Ahh! I didn't know it was that bad … I should have …"

"You shouldn't have done a damn thing, Lena! It's up to his family to pick it up and that's what they're doing. The point is, his apartment will be vacant at the end of the month, but don't think you'd be getting it for free. I got a bottom line to think about."

Dom and his bottom line! He sounded more rigid than he actually was. His financial wizardry kept the business successful for fifty years, and he wasn't about to let me or JJ or anyone else change that. Not that the rent on one of our bed-sitting room apartments would make or break the business, but it was just like him to act as if it would. He kept track of every penny like a squirrel with his hoard of winter nuts.

"Well, damn it all, Dom! Don't I at least get a family discount?"

He actually did smile at that. "I'll think on it. I suppose you'd want it painted and cleaned up?"

I gave him such a look he smiled again. His smile got broader when I said, "Maureen will paint it herself and save you some money! Now, I have two other things."

His smile faded fast. "Oh God Lena, you never stop, do you? When are you going to retire and give up this office and …"

"Don't you dare lecture me about retirement, Dominic! Who has the office next to me and who is two years older? You're the one who should retire! Why have we been grooming Marita and Marco to fill those gigantic shoes of yours if they're going to be ready for their own retirement before you step down?"

"Oh, bug off. So, what are the two other things?"

"First off, I think it's time we looked around for an internet package deal and picked up internet service for all the buildings instead of having the apartment or office tenants do that individually."

He screwed up his face like the Grinch he wasn't.

"Don't you go apoplectic on me! We can raise the rent to cover it, and it will enhance our public image. IF we do it before everybody else in the entire world does. Honestly, Dom, we got through Y2K without the great computer in the sky crashing. Have a little faith."

"Okay, okay. I'll do the figures."

I almost laughed at how quickly he caved in.

Then he noticed my frown. "All right. I'll have Marco do it! What else?"

I raised my eyebrows.

"Damn it, Lena! I do not favor the boys! But just to keep you quiet I'll have Marita do it."

I smiled sweetly. He knew good and well Marita was better than her brother at anything to do with business projections. She always took unintended consequences into consideration and in addition to long term costs/benefits, she suggested creative solutions for potential stumbling blocks.

"Good! On to the next item. I've been thinking about those stackable washer and dryer units for the apartments. We can try two sets as an experiment. I'll ask Maureen to take one and I'll take the other. IF they pass muster, we'll put them in more units and go from there. And yes, we can add that into the rent hike."

"Well, about time! Dad and I bet on how long it would take you to move out of a fourth-floor walk-up that didn't have a washer and dryer. He bet a month. I know how stubborn you are, so I said six months. Turns out it's been, what? Almost thirty years! Unbelievable how stubborn you are.

"I'll have a proposal ready for our next board meeting. I assume you'll do the presentation, and I'll supply the back-up as usual. On another note, I don't suppose you know which day you'll be in next week?"

"Dom, really you are a riot. You know I specialize in surprise visits. That's it for now? Good. May I say, it has been a pleasure doing business with you, as usual."

"Yeah, right." Despite the grumpy tone, he gave me a hug on his way out.

Thank you, Sweet Jesus, for that good man!

That evening when I told Maureen about the new space, at first she was off-the-wall excited. Then she gulped and said, "But Lena, a whole apartment? I can't afford that."

"Oh, don't worry. I've got it covered, but you won't get it for free. You'll have to help out with this and that. You can ask Kalayla. She earns what I pay her. You can start by buying the paint and painting it yourself. How's that?"

"Oh, really, that would be wonderful."

"Same rules as the apartment. No colors that will be too hard to cover."

"I know. The funny thing is, I think I might paint it white. Your apartment always makes me feel peaceful. And Kalayla mentioned she might want her room white, too, so I could do that at the same time."

Sweet Jesus, Maureen wanted to paint the studio white and Kalayla wanted her bedroom white? What was the world coming to? Maybe I wasn't the only one changing.

Maureen went on babbling about moving her stuff out of storage, and just for the fun of aggravating Dom, I assured her that he'd be glad to arrange that for her. Which would remind him not to push me too far!

And I thought of another way to aggravate him. We had four of the small apartments on the first floor. We could advertise them as artists' studios. The ceilings were six inches higher than the other apartments and lighting was good. A fine place for a community of artists! Now that I thought about it, I could turn the whole building into an experimental nightmare for Dom. Now that gave me a good chuckle.

On the way home, I got to thinking about other things. When Maureen told me that her dad asked to take Kalayla for ice cream, I have to admit I could have kissed that old jackass! I told her to let him handle it with Kalayla. In his own way, in his own time. She might actually do that now that she'd be busy setting up her studio.

Kalayla said her mama needed to take a chill pill, and although I'm not a believer in pills, there were moments when I thought the idea might be worth trying. Funny thing was, I could understand why somebody with such a good heart was so jumpy about life. Her mother's treatment of her was an extreme example of the same bigotry shown by the young men who'd spit on Maureen and Jamal, and the landlords who'd refused to rent to them. In return, Maureen and Jamal had shown more grit, perseverance, and willingness to take punishment than I ever did.

And damn it all, if that didn't make me think back to Joey and my boys. When I first got married, I thought Joey would be the perfect husband and the boys would be the perfect sons, and I could help to shape them like pieces of clay. Maybe that's what Maureen's mother thought, too. When she found out she couldn't, she turned away. She never saw the beauty and the strength and the kindness in her daughter.

It made me wonder if in my own way, I'd done the same thing.

JJ had worshipped his father. I always thought that was because he couldn't or wouldn't see his father the way I did. Maybe the truth was that he saw something in Joey I didn't because I was so focused on all the rotten things he did to me. Joey's construction crews felt the same way JJ did. Maybe they saw that other side, too.

One night when I went to pick Joey up from work, the foreman made it a point to come over to me. He said, "Come for the Boss, Mrs. Barzetti? You know he's a good boss, don't you? The guys are glad to work here, because he respects them. That's why you got such low turnover."

That was a couple days after Joey had taught me a lesson, and I remember thinking the man was a suck-up and a liar.

And my boys. I wonder if I did the same thing with them. Was I so busy agonizing over their callous actions that I minimized their caring ones?

I thought about the gentleness JJ showed sewing on Cody's ear. I thought about the first time Jimmy raced his bike and fell. Mark led him into the bathroom and washed off the bleeding scrapes and said, "Come on. I'll show ya a couple things about turning when you're going fast." I thought about the night Mark was all dressed up for a date, and Mikie punched him in the arm and said, "Looking sharp, Bro." And Mark's face lit up with pleasure.

And then I thought about my granddaughters, JJ's two girls. I barely knew them. Why hadn't I reached out and asked JJ about their activities so I could be there, at whatever sports or drama or music recitals they might have had? I knew the answer. I was so determined to solidify my place in the business and show them all what I could accomplish that I was willing to skimp on everything else.

And Mark. No word from him for fifteen years. Why had I waited for him to get in touch with me instead of reaching out to him? Sadness came at me from every direction, but then I thought about Kieran's grandfather. After all these years, he had called Maureen, and asked to see his granddaughter. That was an act of bravery.

And if that old man could be brave, maybe this old woman could, too. I could call my granddaughters. I could search for Mark. Mattwo would help me with that if I asked him. He knew how to search dark alleys and avoid trouble spots.

I suddenly felt shy and nervous and scared. Asking Mattwo for help meant I would have to face reality. I would have to face the possibility that if I did find Mark, my boy might not want to see me. So be it. It was time I stopped fretting about what other people were and weren't doing and did something about myself. Late was better than never.

KALAYLA

ICE CREAM

I was back in my normal routine taking care of Hopalong, dancing, and working. When I mentioned getting a dog to Mama she got real quiet, but she didn't say no or freak out. I told her not to worry about the money. She wouldn't have to pay for anything 'cause I had that covered.

When I talked to the Old Lady about it, all she said was, "And I suppose I'll be stuck walking her when you're busy." I wasn't gonna lie and say I wouldn't ever ask her to because I probably would if I got desperate.

Carlotta said, "I'll do what I can to help." She had already helped me a lot. I could ask her stuff about animals. Like, when I asked her what kind of dog she thought Hopalong was, she said, "That girl is a genuine, 100% mutt! I don't know how many breeds are in her, but I'd guess at least three or four."

"That's really awesome! She's like me—a mix of stuff!"

Carlotta looked startled, which I thought was kinda funny. Did she think I didn't know I wasn't a 100% purebred? Anyway, she said, "I imagine she's more mixed than you are—and from her sweet disposition, I'd say she got the best of whatever she is."

I told her I was gonna ask Mama who I got my sweet disposition from. Carlotta laughed, and I decided maybe I really would ask Mama. She could use a good laugh.

Carlotta said we had to put a chip in Hopalong so if she ever got lost again, a vet or shelter could call us. I bought a real nice collar, too—about an inch wide and bright chartreuse, so it wouldn't get hidden by her fur. The tag on it had her name and our home phone number and the name of the Shelter, too.

One of the techs at the Animal Friends rigged up a cart with wheels so Hopalong could rest her back legs on a bed while she moved the cart with her front legs. It looked real weird and took a while for her to get used to it, but at least she wasn't stuck in the crate all the time. The vet said it would be another three weeks or so before the casts could come off.

Hopalong seemed to understand we were trying hard to help her same way she understood when I was trying to find her name. I could hardly wait to walk her down Mass. Ave., and I already decided if I saw that guy Ray Ray and his dog, we were gonna go in another direction. Thor must've weighed 120 pounds, and Hopalong only weighed 35. No way that hulk was getting near my sweet little girl.

I started calling her Hoppy for short, but I got worried something was wrong with her. She didn't thump her tail or look my way when I did that.

Carlotta said, "Nothing's wrong with her except she doesn't like that nickname and I don't blame her. Really, Kalayla, would you like it if people called you Hoppy?"

She was such a know-it-all old crab! Anyway, I sat down in front of Hopalong and wrote her name on a piece of paper. HOPALONG. I stared at it. And I stared at her.

I tried out a few nicknames: Pal, Longie, Alo, Hopa. Her tail didn't move one inch. I kept thinking and thinking, but I wasn't coming up with anything decent. Finally I tried Opa, and when she heard that, she looked me straight in the eye and slapped her tail on the floor. I found it!

When I told the Old Lady I found a nickname for Hopalong, she said there was a movie called Zorba the Greek where they shouted "Opa!" when they were doing Greek dances. That was awesome. I bet Hopalong liked dancing same as I did.

I was hoping I could go to the dance camp for a week in August, but that took up seven hours a day, and by then Opa'd be out of her casts and home with me. Even if the Old Lady took her out once while I was at camp, I didn't wanna leave her alone while she was adjusting to the apartment. And while Mama was adjusting to her.

Once I got back to school, I decided maybe I'd throw a fit in the front office, and tell the principal I needed to bring my service dog to school to prevent my attacks. I might try the idea out on the Old Lady. If it worked with her, I could definitely pull it off at school.

On Labor Day we were going to Grandma and Grandpa LeeRoyce's for the usual cookout, and I was gonna ask Grandma if I could bring Opa. She liked kids, so she probably liked dogs. If she said, "No," I could tell her Opa was less trouble than some of the kids she took in, but then she'd lecture Mama about teaching me to be polite. As if Mama could stop me from saying what I wanted to! Grandma couldn't stop me either. The only reason I shut my mouth around her was I wasn't gonna get Mama in trouble.

I was still practicing dance a lot and taking two classes a week, so I was at the gym working almost every day. One day Rico drove me and Kieran to the shelter so they could meet Opa. Carlotta smiled when she saw us, and Rico rolled his eyes at me and Kieran and said, "Nosy Aunts!"

Things were always busy with people looking for pets to adopt and the techs doing in-take assessments and stuff like that. I led Rico and Kieran into the back where Opa's crate was and when she saw me, she slapped her tail and barked twice.

"She always says hello to me that way," I said. I opened her cage door.

Kieran got down on the floor and was petting her with me. "You could bring her to my house," he said, "but she might get scared 'cause there's always so many kids around all the time."

"Yeah," I said, "and some of 'em are jerks."

Rico said, "She'll be out of the casts by the time you go to dance camp, right? I have a big fenced in back yard. She can come to my house while you're in class, and she'll have plenty of room to run around."

"Yeah, that'd be awesome, but I was thinking I might not go, 'cause, you know, if she needed me."

Rico had squatted down to pet her, too, and he sat back on the floor and said, "Whoa, now, wait a minute here, Kalayla. You've been working and saving and practicing so you could go to that camp."

"Yeah, I know, but I told Mama if she let me keep Opa, I'd be responsible for her. So I have to be around to take care of her."

"Enough with the 'yeah, buts.' The thing is, kid, dancing and the dog are both important to you. Sometime you might have to choose which one of two things is most important to you. But this isn't one of those times. Don't give up something you've worked so hard for when you don't have to. Between me and your mom and Lena and my aunt, this dog will get plenty of attention while you're at camp."

I would've kissed him 'cept I don't go around kissing people. I held out my hand to shake his hand, and he and Kieran started laughing. Rico reached over to grab me and I twisted away, and he fell over.

We were all on the floor rolling around laughing when Carlotta came in and said, "Oh my God! Three beasts that nobody checked in yet. I'm not sure I have a crate big enough for that one!" She pointed at Rico. "And I'm positive I don't have a big enough muzzle! He'll definitely need to be quarantined!"

It was pretty funny.

I kept thinking about Rico saying that I oughta go to dance camp. If he was gonna pick Opa up and bring her home, and Lena and Carlotta went over and played with her, it might work out okay.

I was gonna be making a lot of extra angel cookies for Christmas, and maybe I'd tell Mama we had to make 'em for Halloween. I'd make Casper the friendly ghost for Lena and Carlotta and Rico, and a big, ugly vampire for Clarence with extra special frosting. I'd get Carlotta to tell me what the worst tasting one she ever heard of was, and I'd add hot sauce to it for my favorite uncle.

About a week after that, I was working at the gym when I saw Kieran coming down the hall with his grandpa. My stomach turned yucky and I thought I might puke.

Kieran waved, and even though I didn't wave back, they kept walking toward me. When they got to me, his grandpa said, "Hi Kalayla. Kieran and I are going for ice cream. We'd like you to come with us. Your mom said it was okay to ask you."

Cow turds! Why'd he think he could come here and ask me to go for ice cream? Like it was a normal everyday thing and not a reason for me to drop dead from shock. Did he think I was gonna jump up and down and yell, "whoopie!" Did he think I was gonna tell him it was a swell idea, and thank him for asking me? Did he think I was gonna go all mushy, and hug him? Did he think …

What the heck DID he think I was gonna do? He was an asshole non-grandpa, and he had a lotta nerve asking me anything. He had a lotta nerve thinking it was okay to talk to me, or stand next to me.

But I kinda wanted to go.

When you weren't sure if you should do something, the Old Lady told me flipping a coin was a good way to figure it out. If you hated the way the coin landed, you'd know you oughta do the opposite of what it said.

I didn't have a coin. I still had a weird feeling in my stomach, but it didn't seem like I was gonna puke.

I looked at Kieran and he smiled and said, "Come on, K. Go with us. We go to a place where you can get mix-ins like M&M's and nuts and chocolate bits. It's neat."

I kinda wanted to go. I mean, it wasn't like I got a free ice cream every day. But he was a real turd if he thought I was gonna call him Grandpa.

I said, "Okay, so say I do go with you—what am I supposed to call you?"

Kieran's grandpa frowned. Then he looked down at his feet and then back at me, like maybe I was talking some foreign language and he wasn't sure what I said. Well, tough turds to him if he couldn't figure it out.

"A lot of kids call me Mr. O. I guess you could, too."

Mr. O. like I barely knew him, like he was just any old guy I met at the gym. I probably could do that. Yeah, I could do that. Maybe.

"Why's Kieran going? He doesn't like ice cream. Did you tell him he had to?" I looked at Kieran. "Is he making you go?"

"Naah! It's a neat place and I like the mix-ins. I usually get M&M's and gumdrops and peanuts without the ice cream."

The kid was weird. But I kinda wanted to go. Finally I said, "Okay. I guess I'll go."

"Okay then. Come on." Mr. O. turned and walked back down the hall. Kieran put his hand up for a high five, and after a minute, I did, too.

The car was parked out front like he might've been planning to make a quick getaway.

Mr. O. said, "You kids can get in back. Seat belts on."

We got in and it was funny 'cause his car was about twice as big as ours. A bunch more kids could've piled in back with us. Kieran smiled at me like he read my mind and said, "So how many kids do ya think we could fit in here? I say five."

"We could get way more than that if we only take kids that didn't have big butts and some sat on the floor. I say nine."

Mr. O. said, "Naaah. You two are way underestimating. You've got to think layers. You put four little ones on the floor. You put three hulks on the seats. Then you have a layer of four medium size on top of the hulks. Then you'd squeeze as many little ones as you can on top of them. I say fifteen, and that's not counting how many you could put in the front seat."

"Fifteen!" Kieran and I said together.

And Kieran added, "You're smoking something, Grandpa!"

"And what would you know about smoking, young man?"

"Nothing, but you do. Or did. Daddy told me you quit smoking when you were my age."

"That's your Uncle Colin, Kalayla. Everybody knows he lies all the time!"

"Grandpa. He does not!"

"Oh, well. Maybe just some of the time."

We were all laughing, and it was kinda fun. We parked about a block from the ice cream store, and there was a line once we got inside. Mr. O. saved our place so Kieran and I went to the counter to check out what they had. When our turn came, I decided I'd do the same thing as Kieran. I got gummy bears and heath bar bits and almonds heaped in a medium cup.

Mr. O. shook his head. "Kids nowadays! Next you're gonna tell me you don't like chocolate cake!"

Kieran looked at me and I looked at him and we giggled, and Kieran said, "I don't like chocolate cake."

And I said, "I don't like chocolate cake."

And together we said, "We don't like chocolate cake." And I added, "But we're kidding!" And we all laughed.

Mr. O asked if I wanted him to drop me off at home, but I had to get my bike at the gym and then go see Opa.

Before I got out of the car, I said, "How'd you know it was okay for me to go for an ice cream with you?"

"I called and asked your mama."

"You called my mama?"

"Yeah. I called her."

"It's about time," I said as I got out of the car.

He nodded. K gave his little wave, and they drove off.

I biked to the shelter as fast as I could, strapped Opa onto her cart to go out so she could sniff around in the grass area out back. She was sniffing, and I was thinking. Mama was gonna ask me about going with Mr. O. and Kieran and I had to tell her something. I decided I was gonna tell her the truth. I had fun.

MAUREEN
TULIPS IN THE FALL?

Up and down the stairs, fourth floor to first floor, from the apartment to the studio and back again with supplies like paper towels and toilet paper and glasses, plates, and some silverware for me and Kalayla in case we decided to have a meal there.

Lena scrounged around for a spare refrigerator—at least she said it was a spare even though the Sears' sticker was still on it. When I saw that, I said, "But Lena, this is brand new."

She pursed her lips, and said, "Oh, is it? Well, my brother assured me it was a discard he found in somebody's trash, so I don't see how it could be new. What else do you need?"

Her brother Dominic, that sweet grumpy old man, had everything in my storage unit moved to the studio, and I was so glad I didn't have to pay for storage anymore. Not that it was a lot, but every penny made a difference.

When I told that to Dominic he grunted and said, "Tell that to my sister!"

The studio was basically one big room with a separate small kitchen. Dominic found a small table just right for two people, and Lena had two extra folding chairs.

Layla and I were practically best friends with the clerk in the paint section of Sears because she helped us when we moved in and painted the apartment. This time we discussed the pluses and minuses of every possible shade of white. I decided to add the tiniest tinge of orange so every time I came into the studio I'd be reminded of a sunrise.

Layla decided on the same color, and she moved everything into the center of the floor and took everything off her walls to make my job easier. I painted her room on Sunday while she was at Matty's Way and the shelter. When she saw it, the smile on her face lit up my whole world. If only Jamal could have seen it. It was the first genuine smile she'd given me since—since I told her the truth about my family. And then she actually gave me a hug. A hug!

As a "Studio Warming Present," Lena gave me a clock with GIGANTIC numbers—the kind you get for people with limited vision. "You keep track of the time!" she scolded me. "Don't you be getting lost in your art and forget about your daughter! Eight o'clock is no proper dinner time for a girl who keeps the type of active schedule she does." I put the clock where I could see it from anyplace in my workspace. I promised her and myself that I would pay attention to it.

One day soon after that, Kalayla came home and said, "Mr. O took me and Kieran for ice cream."

Mr. O.? Mr. O. took her and Kieran for ice cream? Did she mean the Mr. O. who was my father? That was what all the neighborhood kids always called him.

I took a deep breath. So he actually did it. My father took my daughter for ice cream. I wasn't sure he would even though he asked if he could. I thought he might change his mind. But he didn't, and he'd taken her with my brother Colin's son.

I wanted to know EVERYHING about it, but I could hear Lena saying, "You've got to give the girl room to breathe, Maureen. Stop crowding in on her." So all I said was, "How did it go?"

"It was fun. We went to this ice cream place that had mix-ins and that's all Kieran and I got. Kieran doesn't like ice cream and I decided to try his way. Mr. O. asked if I wanted to go again, and I said sure."

My father asked her if she wanted to go again and she said sure. I guess I didn't really need to ask her anything else.

He called me the next week, and the week after that. Would it be okay if he asked Kalayla to go for ice cream? The third time he called, I told him he didn't need to ask permission every time because she was the one who decided if she wanted to go. I didn't tell him that was what she always did.

He said, "Yeah, well, I'm going to call so everything's on the up and up." My father always stuck to the rules, but I hoped maybe he wanted to talk to me, too, and that was why he called. Not that we said more than a few words, but at least I got to hear his voice.

And then last week he didn't just ask and hang up when I said okay. He said, "You and the kid doing all right? You need anything?"

Did we need anything? Dear God, if I told him all the things I had needed, all the things we had needed … all the things I'd managed without … all the things Kalayla didn't know she'd missed …

"No. We're all set. Thanks."

I stewed over his question for the next two days. Tuesday was my day off, and as soon as Kalayla left, I took some coffee cake over to Lena's, hoping she'd be up. Or at least hoping she wouldn't mind having company at 7:30 in the morning.

She was up, dressed in a blue blouse and black skirt, her hair up and neat as usual. "Well now," she said when she opened the door, "is the Welcome Wagon paying early morning visits to longtime residents or did they send you around to take the pulse of old people?"

Despite my glum mood, I had to smile. "No. I just need … I need advice … or something."

"Well, you lucked out. 'Or something' is my specialty. Come on in."

We settled at the kitchen table, and I breathed a sigh of relief. Lena got two cups, brewed Hazelnut Keurig coffee and we sat quietly for a few minutes. One thing about her, she didn't push you unless you gave her a good reason to.

"It's about my father."

She waited.

I built up so much steam I just spewed it all out at once. "When I really needed my father, he wasn't there and he didn't care how we were doing, and now he has the nerve to ask if Kalayla and I are all right and if I, if we need anything! Why didn't he ask that when I married Jamal? Why didn't he ask that when Jamal died and I went to Mummie for help, and she shut the door in my face? Why would I want his help now after I managed to … Oh, I'm just so mad at him and …"

I ran out of breath. And really, there was nothing else to say except how hurt I was and how sad. If I kept talking I'd just keep repeating the same thing over and over and over again.

Lena took a sip of coffee and small bite of coffee cake. "Ymmm. Good … Well, the first thing I'd say is that I think the hardest job anybody ever had was being a parent."

"Oh, Lena really, I know that. I'm just awful at it, and you were so much better, and you've helped me so much …"

"Oh my God, child! If I tried walking on water the way you think I can, I'd be at the bottom of one of those Great Lakes with a thousand-pound weight of mistakes holding me down.

"But that's not the point here. The point is, your father did call you, and his calling shows he has more courage than I ever did. Now, don't you be looking so shocked and aggravated. Give me a chance to say my piece, and then you can yell, and tell me I'm wrong all you want.

"I truly do not know where you got the idea I was some kind of ideal mother. I wasn't. For one thing, I made a terrible mistake with my boy Mark, and if I ever find out where he is, I'll tell him I know what an ass I was. I hope he'll listen when I tell him how sorry I am.

"The fact is your dad knows what he did was wrong, and he's trying to fix that as best he can. I admire that even though it took him so long to do it. It takes courage to admit you were wrong no matter how long it takes you to do it. No doubt seeing Kalayla pushed him over the edge. But no matter how he got there, the fact is, he did.

"You could thumb your nose and say, 'Turn-about is fair play.' Maybe it is. But I don't see what you'd gain by that. I hope you'll give him some leeway, same as I hope my boy Mark would do. When your dad asks what you need, he means what you need now. He knows damn well he can't give you what you needed five or ten years ago. You can punish him for that, but you won't have much of a relationship with him if that's what you decide to do. Maybe the most important thing you can do is show him that you came out the other end okay, and so did Kalayla. To your credit. He has to admire you for that. Just like I do."

Lena stopped talking, and I thought about how jumbled my feelings were. One minute I wanted to throw my arms around my father and tell him how glad I was he called. How glad I was he wanted to spend time with my—with Jamal's and my beautiful daughter. The next minute I wanted to scream at him and tell him how much I hated him. How much he'd let me down, and disappointed me, and hurt me.

I took a few sips of coffee, and when I looked at my watch, it was 9:30. "I don't mean to be rude or anything, but I have to get the studio set up," I said.

Lena nodded. "You've got a lot to think about. I'll tell you the same thing I told Kalayla: I hope you won't cut off your nose to spite your face."

Lena was right. I had a lot to think about. I did know this for sure:

I really did want Kalayla to know her O'Rourke family. Even if they didn't want me to be in the family. I really did hope they would accept her. Even if they never accepted me. What I didn't know was if I wanted my father to be my Daddy anymore.

I dropped the plate off at the apartment and bounced down the stairs. I had a studio again! I loved the first-floor location so convenient and close to the front door. It would be so easy for me to drop off art supplies. The building actually had two front doors. The first was the building entrance and it was never locked. The second, the glass security door, was up three steps on a landing and it was always locked. A panel on the wall beside the door had a buzzer and intercom system along with a list of apartment numbers and names of occupants.

I spent a couple hours emptying boxes, setting up my easel and getting organized. I had just come out of the studio carrying a bag of garbage when I heard a knock on the glass door. I turned, and saw Clarence on the landing. Oh dear! Clarence with his sneering smile, almost daring me to turn away.

On such a beautiful sunny day he appeared out of nowhere like a menacing cloud, but keeping him behind a locked door wouldn't make him go away. I managed a smile and opened the door and said, "Hi. This is an odd time for a visit."

"I stopped by Eddie's and he said it was your day off. I wanted to make sure that you were coming for the Labor Day cookout. What's the deal? Are you cleaning apartments in this building now?" He pointed to the trash bag.

"Oh, no. I'm … I'm getting my studio set up. Let me go dump this." I walked to the end of the hall, put the bag in the garbage chute, and walked back toward him.

"What'd you do, move down here to a bigger apartment?"

I had no idea how to explain Lena's incredible generosity. Especially to him, because he always saw a dark side, like the time he said, "You married my brother because he'll work while you play at being an artist—clever girl!"

No matter what he thought, I had to say something. "No, we haven't moved. A friend is doing me a favor and letting me use this apartment for a studio, and I'll be working to pay the rent."

"A friend? You mean the guy I saw you with? Yeah, I'd say that was a very friendly gesture, and I bet I know just how you're paying for it."

"Clarence, stop! Rico has nothing to do with this. It's my friend Lena. You met her. She owns the apartment house and she …"

"Yeah, sure she does. That old lady owns the building, and she lives in a fourth-floor walk-up just for the fun of it. Give me a break, Maureen!"

He moved closer to me and I didn't know what he might do. Jamal always said I shouldn't take Clarence seriously, but Jamal wasn't here and my back was against the wall, and Clarence didn't sound like he was joking.

I heard the landing door open and saw Mrs. Meade come in with a bag of groceries. "Oh, Mrs. Meade," I called out. "How nice to see you! Let me carry up your groceries for you."

"Maureen, dear, that's so kind of you. Here, if you take this bag. Lena told me you had an uncle. It's nice he came to check on you."

Lena must have told everyone in the building about Clarence. I took the bag she held out to me and said, "No, no, he's not my uncle, Mrs. Meade. He's Kalayla's uncle."

"Oh, yes, of course, the girl's uncle. I remember that now. Hurry up, dear. I have ice cream in the bag."

Clarence scowled, no doubt wishing Mrs. Meade would fall down the garbage chute.

"I'll tell Kalayla you stopped by. We'll see you next week at the cookout," I said as I turned and followed Mrs. Meade up the stairs.

He stood there for a minute. "You can bet on that," he said as he went out the door.

Oh dear!

KALAYLA

LABOR DAY PARTY

Mama was her usual nervous self 'cause we were going to Grandma and Grandpa's, but I was excited. Grandma said I could bring Opa, but she'd have to stay in the backyard. I didn't care, 'cause that's where Grandpa had the grill and I bet I could sneak a hot dog for Opa.

Opa was out of her casts, so we could've walked, but Mama said we had to drive. She was bringing her four-bean salad, and she always made it in her biggest casserole dish. I brought plenty of treats for Opa and her tennis ball. Mama said I had to keep her on leash 'til we saw how she did in a crowd. Grandma and Grandpa knew a ton of people, so there always was a crowd.

We had to park about halfway down the block, and all the way walking there, I was telling Opa about who she was gonna meet and what we'd be doing. We went around the back and through the gate, and what a pisser. The first person we saw was Uncle Clarence. He strolled over like he was a big shot movie star and we oughta be thrilled he was talking to us. He ignored me and said, "Huh, Maureen, you really are something. First a studio, and now a dog. You're settling into some kind of life, I'd say."

I pushed in front of Mama and said, "The dog's mine, and you better be nice to her. She'll bite you if I tell her to." Which was a big fat lie, and nobody who saw Opa's friendly face and wagging tail would believe it. But I didn't care.

"Well, aren't you the grouchy one! Bet your mama's new boyfriend got the dog for you because he was sucking up to your mama!"

Mama turned all flustered and said, "He's not my boyfriend. And the dog was a stray Kalayla got from a shelter."

She got me so pissed when she let Clarence say stuff like that and acted like she had to explain everything to him! She might've been scared of talking back to him, but I wasn't! "I got the dog myself and Rico is my friend. A good friend. He's an expert in karate, so you better watch how you act with Mama."

"Layla!" Mama said, "You're being rude. Clarence didn't mean anything by that."

Yeah, right! He was a jerk and Mama should stop defending him!

"Chill out, Kalayla. I was only joking around. You should know that by now."

Cow turds! What I knew was Clarence never joked when it came to Mama. I tugged on Mama's arm, "Let's go find Grandma and introduce her and Grandpa to Opa."

We left Clarence standing there and walked toward the grill. Everybody wanted to pet Opa, so Mama finally went ahead to put the salad down. When I finally got over there and Grandma saw Opa, she said, "Oh, my, isn't she sweet looking! And she seems to be walking just fine now. Go in the kitchen and get her a bowl for water, Kalayla. Put it over by the fence." Grandma rubbed Opa's head, and Opa licked her hand.

Grandpa said, "Well, she can't just exist on water, Lucinda. I bet she'd like one of these hot dogs. What do you think, Kalayla?" Opa really liked him.

There wasn't room to throw the tennis ball 'cause the yard was getting so crowded. Grandpa kept putting on more hamburgers and hot dogs. A lot of the kids went down the basement to play ping pong, and Keesha came over and said she'd beat my ass, but I wanted to stay outside with Opa. Anyway, I could beat all of 'em, including her, and she knew it.

I filled my plate and took Opa around to the front porch. We sat on one of the steps, and she and I ate. A lot. Grandma always said nobody would ever go hungry at her house and she was right, but her desserts weren't as good as Carlotta's.

When I went around to the backyard again, Mama was talking to Clarence over by the fence. I saw him grab Mama's arm and she should've punched him, but Mama never wanted to cause a scene, 'specially not at Grandma's house. I got over there fast, and I said, "Mama! Opa just threw up and we better go home quick before she does it again. We gotta say goodbye to Grandma and Grandpa. See you around, Uncle Clarence." Under my breath, I said, "I hope not." He probably heard me, but I didn't care.

While we were driving home, I asked Mama how come she let Clarence grab her arm, but she shrugged it off like always. That got me so aggravated. School was starting on Wednesday and between school and working and dancing, I wouldn't be home much to watch out for Clarence. What a pisser! I was gonna tell the Old Lady she better be on the super lookout so he'd never be alone with Mama.

LENA

THE PERFECT STORM

Maybe if I had let my boys have a dog or a cat ... I couldn't believe I was thinking such a thing. Seeing the difference Opa made in that girl's attitude, it did get me to wondering. As long as I was being honest, I could add that having those foolish cats made a difference to me, too.

Hindsight, and silly thinking. I was the one telling Maureen to stick to the present, and I should be telling myself the same thing. I have to admit when Kalayla was at dance camp in August, I found out playing with a dog, at least that dog, was a real pleasure. Lotta and I couldn't agree on how to divide the time, so we both went over there every day for a couple of hours.

Rico took Opa home around five, and Kalayla would come dragging in a little after that. The first day she said, "They're trying to kill us! All we do is stretch and strengthen, stretch and strengthen and go over the same routines about a hundred million times! Then we have lunch and do the same thing all afternoon."

"Too bad it's such waste of money," I said. "Will they give you a refund?"

"I never said it was a waste of money! Aren't you always telling me working hard never hurt anybody? Anyway, it's not so bad 'cause at lunch everybody sits around and talks."

Maybe my hope that Kalayla would make some friends—any friend beside Kieran—would come about. "Huh!" I said. "Anybody there you want to bring over to meet Opa?"

"Naah. None of 'em like dogs."

Now, for that, I gave her a LOOK. She came up with the damnedest excuses for not doing something that would be good for her!

I wasn't the one to lecture about making excuses. I made up plenty of my own for not calling Mattwo. I spent about two weeks trying to decide if I should suggest coffee, or lunch, or dinner. I imagined Carlotta rolling her eyes.

It didn't matter because when I finally did call him, he said, "How about lunch day after tomorrow? You know that little Greek place just down the street from you? I think it's called Dimitri's? How about that?"

Which gave me a bunch of other things to worry about. Like what I should wear. And if I should get my hair cut the way Lotta had been nagging me to do. I'd worn my hair in a bun so long it felt like part of my skin. But I'd gone this far, so what the hell. In for a penny, in for a pound.

On Thursday at 12:30, I was nearly at the restaurant when Mattwo pulled up and parked across the street. It was ridiculous for an old woman to feel like she was seventeen again, but that's how I felt. He walked across Mass. Ave. and smiled that warm smile, and I smiled right back.

The restaurant was long and narrow, with tables for two or four on either side with an aisle. Not the place for real intimacy, but about right for two old people getting reacquainted.

We sat down and ordered, and Mattwo said, "I don't know what you did to your hair, Lena, but I like it! Now, tell me, to what do I owe the pleasure of your company?"

The fact he went right to the point sure hadn't changed! The flush creeping to my hairline told me that the seventeen-year-old was blushing, but she wasn't the one about to make a fool of herself.

I could have beat around the bush stalling, but before I walked over here, I sat down and had a talk with myself. And I said, 'Lena, if you die tomorrow, when they're putting you in your grave, what are you going to be wishing you told Mattwo that you didn't?'

I said it right out, "I guess one thing I'd like to tell you is that I've been thinking about you for a long time."

Sweet Jesus, the smile on that man's face was so true and open and warm, it would have convinced the Grinch not to steal Christmas! And it convinced me to keep on talking. "I've been wanting to call you, but I felt too shy and like too much of a dunce. So, I didn't. Except when I needed help with Kalayla. And now I need help again, but not with her. But I want you to know I would have called even if I didn't need your help."

I hung my head down and squinted up my face and said, "So. What do you think of that?"

Mattwo laughed! Then he reached over, and took my hand and said, "My Lady, I am at your service! What is it that you need?"

"I need to find Mark, and I don't know how. The last I heard he was in Chicago, but that was fifteen years ago, and he could be long gone from there. I thought you might know how to find him."

Mattwo nodded and blew out his breath. He waited a little, and then he said, "I can try. Do you think JJ knows anything?"

"All JJ told me was that Mark was gone for good, and I wouldn't be hearing from him again. Now, if Mark was dead, that was a funny way of saying it, don't you think?"

"Well, so maybe I'll start with JJ. Or maybe not. Let me think about it. Now, on another subject, seeing that you've been wanting to see me, how about a movie on Saturday? We can sit in the back row and hold hands."

Now I was the one laughing.

Thursday afternoon the week after that, Opa and I went out to do a couple errands despite the forecast of rain. It was Maureen's day off, and I told her I'd keep Opa with me while she spent time in the studio. When I got home, I knocked on the studio door. No answer.

Opa and I went up the stairs and when I got to the third floor, Mrs. Meade opened her door and stuck her head out. She must have been looking out the window for me because as soon as she saw us, she said, "Thank goodness you're here! I didn't know if I should call the police or not."

Sweet Jesus! "What's the matter? Did something happen?"

"I don't know. Maybe nothing's wrong, but I'm not sure. I heard noise from upstairs. You know, from that young woman's apartment. I think she's there alone because I saw the daughter go off to school. A little while ago, I saw that uncle park across the street and heard him going up the stairs. Pretty soon after that, I heard arguing and the woman yelled something like, 'Leave me alone,' and it sounded like something fell on the floor."

"When was that?"

"Just before you got home. Do you think I should call the police?"

"No, no, you don't need to do that, Mrs. Meade. You did the right thing telling me. Now you go on and enjoy a nice cup of tea."

She smiled and closed her door, and I got up those stairs faster than I had in twenty years. I listened at Maureen's door, but I couldn't hear any sounds. I unlocked my door, put down my packages, unleashed Opa, and told her to stay put. I didn't know what I'd have to do, but whatever it was, I didn't want a dog underfoot.

All the while I did that, I was thinking about Joey, and what he told me and the boys. When the twins asked if they could bring friends over to see the guns, he said, "NO! Guns aren't show and tell time for a group of yahoos. You use them to get food, you compete with them, or you can use them to defend yourself. If it ever comes to defending yourself, you shoot to kill. You hear me? You shoot to kill!"

I didn't know what was going on in Maureen's apartment, but I wasn't going in there unless I could defend her and me if it came to that. I went into my bedroom, into my closet, into the locked drawer where I kept my pistol. I took it out, loaded it, got my master key out, and went to Maureen's door.

I opened and then closed the door as quiet as I could. I listened and heard crying coming from the bedroom. Then Clarence said, "Come on, Maureen. I know you want it. I got more than that jerk-off you been seeing!"

I marched right into the bedroom. Maureen was on the bed with Clarence holding her arms down, trying to get on top of her. She was crying and trying to twist away.

It was like I was laying there. It was like Joey taunting me. No, not again. Not this time. I felt the weight of the pistol in my hand, and I took a deep breath, walked over to the bed, and yelled, "Get off of her, you bastard or I will blow your head off."

Clarence half-turned to look at me as he let go of Maureen and said, "What the fuck?"

Maureen said, "Lena ... thank God" as she rolled away from Clarence, pushed herself up and off the bed, and leaned over, hugging herself.

Clarence stared up at me. I remembered every single thing Joey taught me. I pressed the pistol hard against his cheek and said, "You are wrong if you think I won't pull this trigger."

And then.

What happened to Clarence was so shocking I stood frozen in time and place watching a heart-wrenching transformation in slow motion.

His expression was dazed and confused, as if he couldn't understand what was happening. Then slowly, almost gracefully, like a building imploding, one floor after another giving way until all that was left was a pile of debris on the ground, the grown man curled himself into a ball, wrapped his arms around his legs, held himself tight and small.

He began rocking back and forth, moaning and calling out so faintly I wasn't sure what he was saying. And then I realized.

He was calling for his mama.

I lowered the pistol and stood watching the man intending rape turn into … turn into … a terrified child calling for his mama.

I felt Maureen grab my arm for support. Her voice sliced through my trance, forced my focus away from Clarence, but she wasn't talking to me.

"Oh my God. Jamal, I am so sorry. I am so sorry I didn't understand when you said it was traumatic for Clarence. I never imagined . . . what it was like for him, and for you, then and after."

It was too much to take in.

"I have to call Lucinda," she said, pulling on my arm. "We have to tell her what happened. She has to come and get him."

Maureen, the panicky, uncertain woman, telling me what needed to be done. She picked the phone up from the cradle on her nightstand, dialed and waited. "Lucinda. It's Maureen. You need to come. It's Clarence. It's awful. You need to come right now."

Sweet Jesus! Her words might be enough to scare Lucinda to death! "Give me that phone!" I said and grabbed it out of her hand.

"Mrs. LeeRoyce. This is Lena Barzetti. I live across the hall from Maureen. Your son Clarence is here. We're with him. I think he had some kind of breakdown. He's curled up in a ball and crying for you. You'll need help getting him home."

"Oh no, oh no, no, no," she said. "What … What happened?"

"He was trying to rape Maureen. I stuck a gun in his face and told him to stop."

"Oh, my poor boy. My poor sweet boy." I could hear her calling to her husband. "We're coming," she said. "Tell my boy we're coming."

I hung up the phone and realized that I was still holding the pistol. I put it down on the nightstand. Maureen and I stood looking at each other, and all the while Clarence was rocking back and forth, crying for his mama.

Her poor boy. Her poor sweet boy. Lucinda's words made no sense. He was a man aiming to commit rape who had to be stopped, and I stopped him.

I looked at the figure on the bed. I had no idea where that man had gone, but what I saw now was a little boy curled into a ball calling for his mama. Like any one of my boys would have done. Much as I might despise the man, the little boy needed help.

I did what any mother would have done. I sat down next to him, put my hand on his back, and rubbed gently while I whispered, "She's coming, Clarence, don't you worry. Your mama is on her way. Shhhhhh, now … You'll be okay. Your mama and daddy are coming." I kept on saying that and saying that and saying that.

I had no idea where Maureen had gone, or what she was doing until she came into the room with Clarence's parents and a neighbor friend of theirs.

I got up, and Lucinda took my place on the bed with her boy. She put her arms around him, pulled him close, hugging him, crooning like any mother would to her hurting child. "I'm here now. Daddy's here now. We'll take care of you."

All I could do was cry for her and with her. Whatever happened to her boy that had caused his breakdown—no matter what he had done, if he was my child, I'd be holding him the same way Lucinda was.

When the boy's crying stopped, I heard her say, "Now Clarence, honey, we're going on home. Daddy and Raymond are going to help you, okay now? We'll just go down to the car and drive home. Everything's all right now. We're all taking care of you. Okay now?"

Mr. LeeRoyce and Raymond stood beside the bed, and helped Clarence slowly to his feet. "You put your arms around us now, boy," Mr. LeeRoyce said. "We're taking you home."

Clarence put an arm around each of them, and they helped him walk out, one shuffling step at a time.

Lucinda came over to me and took my arm, "Thank you for staying with my boy. He had a bad time when he was a little one and we …we lost him back then."

She turned to Maureen. "You were good to call. We thank you. Jamal would thank you if he were here with us. I'm sorry for what Clarence did and for what he tried to do."

Maureen surprised me for the second time that day. She wrapped her arms around her mother-in-law. "I know," she said, "I know, and I'm so sorry too. And I'm sorry that I pushed you away. I didn't understand when Jamal died, all you meant to do was take care of us."

"That's what family does, take care of each other," Lucinda said. "You're part of our family. Since the day Jamal married you, you've been part of our family."

The two of them stayed wrapped together, and finally I said, "They probably got Clarence to the car by now."

Lucinda and Maureen walked arm in arm out of the apartment and I followed them down the stairs and waited on the landing. Lucinda got into the back with Clarence. Maureen waited at the curb until they pulled away. Then she turned and came back inside, into my arms, and said, "I'm so glad Kalayla wasn't here, and I'm so grateful that you were."

I went back with her to her apartment, got my pistol and went home to put it away.

Opa greeted me at the door, side by side with Petunia and Napoleon. As if they knew what I had witnessed. As if they could see how it had shaken me. As if they understood the only remedy for some kinds of pain was love.

Afterward, Maureen told me the story of Jamal and Clarence, the story of two little boys on a summer day out exploring on their bikes, caught in the wrong place at the wrong time, treated viciously. One of them less harmed and more resilient, the other forever changed, a shattered child living inside a man's body.

None of us knew what kind of man Clarence might have become. If only he and his brother had stayed at home that day or ridden their bikes someplace else. If only the young men in that car had chosen to drive by or gone to see the movie instead of choosing to terrorize, instead of choosing to harm. If only we could turn back time, rewrite the script, change the ending. None of us knew what kind of man Clarence might have been. We only knew the kind of man he had become.

It was enough to break any mother's heart.

KALAYLA

THE RED SOX

Something was wrong with Mama. She was acting weird, and I mean like, way more weird than usual. A month ago, if somebody told her she had to call Grandma every day, she would've cut out her tongue instead. Now she was on the phone with her like every other minute. She told me Uncle Clarence was sick, but I didn't see why she cared about that. I didn't.

Mama said he wouldn't be coming around for a while and I was glad. I was taking two dance classes a week and working at Matty's Way on Saturdays, and at the shelter every Sunday. I didn't have time to worry about being home when that jerk showed up.

Mr. O. said he was gonna give Kieran and me a Back to School present and take us to a Red Sox home game on Saturday, Sept. 23rd. The game was at 1:00, and Rico said I could make up the time I'd miss at the gym.

Kieran told me his grandpa loved, loved, loved the Red Sox no matter how bad they did. Even if they were doing great in July, Kieran said by September they could be in the toilet. This year they were in around second or third, which wasn't awful unless you were panting for 'em to be in the World Series, which I guess Mr. O. was.

Mama was like a non-sports person even though Daddy said she was agile and athletic, and would be good at most any sport if she wanted to. He said I had real good hand-eye co-ordination and could run as fast as he could, but I wasn't gonna spend time running around some dumb track. Daddy loved every sport there was except baseball, which in his opinion, was boring with more standing around than actual playing.

Kieran rolled his eyes when I told him what Daddy thought. He said, "Do NOT, I mean do NOT say that to Grandpa! We'll get a two-hour lecture on why baseball is the most challenging, most difficult, most interesting game ever invented. He completely, totally, seriously believes that."

I thought that was completely, totally, seriously funny, but I kept Daddy's opinion to myself. I met Kieran downstairs the day of the game, and it turned out his brother, Colin, and their father, Colin, were going with us. When Mr. O introduced me to Colin, the kid, I said, "So how do you know when someone's talking to you if you're both Colin?"

The kid said, "I'm Col. My dad's Colin."

I screwed up my nose and looked at Mr. O. and pointed at Kieran's father. "Yeah, and what am I supposed to call him?"

Mr. O said, "You could call him Uncle Colin if you wanted to. Or you could call him Mr. C. That all right with you, son?"

Mr. C. nodded.

Mama was always telling me to show people my real self, so I figured that's what I'd do that day. When we were driving to Fenway Park, I said, "Col, so, when are you gonna get Kieran a new bike?"

Kieran was sitting between me and Col, and he gave me an elbow, made a face and shook his head.

"I never said I'd do that!" Col said.

"Yeah, but, you know, since you wrecked it." I let that dangle a minute, then I added on, "Kieran's always saying what a great brother you are. So I just, like, you know, figured since you didn't get his old bike fixed, you were probably gonna get him a new one."

Kieran gave me another elbow. What he actually told me was, "Col will say anything to get out of trouble. He's the biggest liar in the family."

Mr. O. said, "You wrecked his bike, Col? I didn't hear anything about that."

"Yeah, well ..." Col said.

Mr. C. turned toward the back seat and said, "You told me Kieran wrecked his own bike, Col. Kieran! Who wrecked your bike?"

"I didn't," Kieran said.

"Col!" Mr. C said.

"Yeah, so maybe I did sort of wreck it, but it's not like I did it on purpose, and I was planning to get it fixed when I got the money. I didn't tell Kieran that 'cause he'd be bugging me all the time about when I was doing it."

"Well, I have a simple solution to that," Mr. C. said. "I'll pay to get the bike fixed, and you will pay me back. Seems fair to me. Seem fair to you, Col?"

Col gave me a dirty look. "Yeah, I guess."

Awesome! No point stopping when I was scoring so many points! "That's cool," I said. "then Kieran'll be able to ride over to my house and meet my mom, right?"

Mr. O. started laughing. "I told you, Colin. I told you, she's my girl Maureen's daughter all right."

"I can see," Mr. C. said. "So, Kalayla, did your mom tell you the nickname us kids gave her?"

"Naah. She told me you were dead."

"Jesus, Mary, and Joseph! Dead! Only Maureen would come up with something like that! That's exactly why we called her Miss Sharp Tooth."

Sharp Tooth? Mama? As in MY Mama? He must've got his sisters mixed up. If I was gonna give Mama a nickname—which I wasn't—it would've been something like Miss Toothless. "Yeah? Mama calls me Miss Smart Mouth. You can call me that, too, if you want."

Col said, "I will!" And then muttered, "And a few other things, too!"

Kieran said, "Me, too." He gave me a double-quick elbow and his big-eyed, "What, who? Me?" look so I knew he wasn't really mad.

Everybody was laughing. Just one big jolly old family, right? The rest of the way Kieran and I had to listen to the three of them discuss baseball stuff. Like that the Orioles couldn't possibly beat the Sox 'cause even though Hector wasn't great, he was better than Kohlmeier.

Then Col asked me if I knew the words to "Sweet Caroline," which I didn't. They all booed and said I couldn't get into Fenway if I didn't learn them because there was some dumb tradition that when the crowd sang "Sweet Caroline," EVERYBODY had to sing along. They taught me the words, and we spent the rest of the ride practicing and mostly yelling whenever we got to, "So good, so good, so good."

It was funny.

They could hardly wait to show me the Green Monster. I figured that'd be some real scary thing, but it turned out to be a fence. Yeah, right, a high fence, but still, a dumb old fence. I could see why Mama was whacko being in a family that thought a fence was the coolest thing anybody had ever seen.

Anyway, we ate Fenway Franks and yelled 'Sweet Caroline' in the eighth inning and the game went into overtime and the Sox won in the tenth, 8-7, so everybody was jacked up on the drive home. Mr. O. dropped Mr. C. and Col and Kieran off and then took me home.

Usually he dropped me off, but today he said, "What do you think if I come up and say 'Hi' to your mom?"

Cow turds! What if Mama freaked out? But I wanted him to meet Opa, and if Mama didn't wanna see him, she could stay in her bedroom. Or go for a walk. Or go down to her studio.

"I don't know how Mama'll feel, but Opa'll be happy."

"No time like the present to find out," he said as he parked down the block from the apartment house. I knocked on the studio door as we went by, but Mama must've been upstairs. I told Mr. O. Mama might show him the studio. I didn't tell him she might go off on one of her crying binges and make it a super duper pleasant visit.

Opa jumped all over me when I opened the door, but I made her sit and shake hands with Mr. O. so he'd see how well trained she was. I didn't see Mama, so I called, "Mama, we got company."

Mama came out of her bedroom saying, "Oh good, is Lena …" She stopped walking. Stopped talking. Her eyes got so wide they filled her whole face. She put her hand over her open mouth. Probably to stop herself from saying something rude.

"Mr. O. wanted to say 'hi' so I invited him for one of Carlotta's desserts. You know, just showing off what good manners you taught me. I'm going to Lena's to see what she's got in her dessert stash. Mr. O. can stay here and tell you all about the game. The Sox won and Kieran and Colin and their dad went with us. You stay here, Opa. You're on guard duty." She wagged her tail and licked my leg.

It was kinda funny 'cause Mama was standing there like a statue in a museum. It didn't seem like she was gonna say anything, so I beat it out the door quick. I heard Mr. O. saying, "I wanted to see for myself you're all right." He must've looked around then, 'cause he said, "Look at these colors! You've made a beautiful home here, Maureen."

I banged on Lena's door, and when she came I said, "Get some desserts and bring 'em over quick! I left Mama alone with Mr. O. and Opa."

"Sweet Jesus! Watch you don't let those cats out! Get in here and help me carry the stuff." She kept taking lemon squares and cookies out of her bread box 'til I said, "That's enough, Lena! Let's get back over there!"

We rushed in the door, but it was like nothing happened while I was gone. Mama was standing in the exact same place, and Mr. O. was looking around. Opa was on duty watching Mr. O. She didn't know Mama needed protection from her own whacko self, not from Mr. O.

Lena took charge like I knew she would. "Well, hello, Mr. O'Rourke. I hear you know the best place for ice cream mix-ins. So, how did Carrasco do today? Any strikeouts?"

Strike outs? Cow turds! That Old Lady knew less about baseball than I did, which was zero until today. How the heck did she know who was pitching today?

Naturally Mr. O. was thrilled to fill her in. Mama stared at the two of 'em like she was sure they were gonna disappear in a puff of smoke if she blinked or turned away.

Lena hustled to the table and I was scarfing down a few lemon squares when Mr. O. turned to Mama, and said, "You were the one who kept track of the stats for us. You still doing that?"

Up 'til then, Mama hadn't said one single word. She eye-balled Mr. O., blinked about 30 times, and then said, "Counting today they're 81-74 and ranked third. Carrasco has zero starts, 18 finishes, including today."

"See, what'd I tell you?" Mr. O. said.

I stared at Mama.

Then Lena said, "Don't look so surprised, Kalayla. Your mama and I talk baseball all the time."

COW TURDS! LIAR, LIAR, PANTS ON FIRE! "Oh, yeah," I said. "I must've forgot!"

Lena smirked. I ground my teeth. Opa wagged her tail. Mr. O. and Mama talked stats.

OCTOBER 2000

MAUREEN

DADDY

When my father said he had to shove off, Lena jumped up from the table and said, "I forgot I have to feed the cats. You come with me, Kalayla, so you can learn to do something useful." Kalayla looked at Lena like she had three heads, but she followed her to the door.

"Come on Opa. You better learn, too. See ya, Mr. O. Thanks for an awesome day."

I couldn't stop myself from staring at my father. He looked older and tired, like maybe he needed sleep. His belt fit under his belly now, instead of on top of it the way it used to.

After Kalayla closed the door, he waited a minute and said, "I'm glad to see you, Maureen. Your daughter is just like you. And I'm … grateful you were willing …"

"She's like me and Jamal," I said. "She got his good traits and a lot of my bad ones. But she's her own person."

He laughed. "Colin thought she was a lot like you."

Colin. I wondered what made him go to the game. He must have known our father was taking Kalayla. He and I used to fight all the time. But once, he punched Jimmy McDonald for saying I was a know-it-all. That was funny because Colin always said that's exactly what I was.

"Does Mummie know what you're doing?"

"That's my girl. No beating around the bush. She knows. If you want to know if she approves, she doesn't. But I don't think she has the energy to fight me anymore."

Mummie, always the fighter, not having the energy. What did that mean? Did I care? Should I care? I guess I did even though I wasn't sure if I should. I didn't know who Mummie was anymore. She wasn't the person I depended on. She wasn't the person I went to for advice. She wasn't the person whose opinion I valued.

But my father was here, trying, driving a wedge through a closed door and forcing it open. Taking his granddaughter for ice cream and to a ball game. Inviting my brother to go with them. Coming to visit me. Taking that chance even though I could have closed the door in his face the way Mummie did to me. Lena said what we did here and now counted for a lot, no matter what happened before. She said people could change. If we let them.

It felt so odd, so disconcerting to have him here, in my living room after so much anguish. For years and years, I had longed to see him, to feel his solid presence, to have his understanding. My father always said we had to face facts, but I—back then, I couldn't.

Once Kalayla told me I was a scaredy-cat because I was nervous and edgy about everything. My father would have been shocked by that. He would have said, "Since when is my daughter Maureen afraid of anything?" But I was. After they kicked me out, and after I saw how Jamal and I were treated, it seemed like I was nervous and afraid of anything new.

Until now, with my father. I mean, after all, no matter what I said, what was the worst he could do? Tell me I was expunged from the family records? I felt free, like I could say or do whatever I wanted. I realized then that I wasn't going to treat him the way he and Mummie had treated me. I wasn't going to turn away from him.

"I'm glad you're seeing Kalayla," I said.

"I did the wrong thing back then," he said slowly. "There's no point making excuses or giving reasons. The fact is the fact."

"Would you feel that way if Jamal was still alive? Would you have come here if he lived here, too?"

He sighed deep and long. "Back then I wasn't willing to get to know him and find out if he was a jackass or a good guy. You can't buy back time, but I wish I'd at least have tried to find out. I hope I'd have enough sense to do that now, if he was here with you."

My father. Always honest. Wishing that he'd done things differently. I think he would have liked Jamal. I think Jamal would have liked him once he got used to his gruffness.

"I can live with that," I said.

"Could you live with your old dad giving you a hug?"

"Yes. Yes, Daddy. I could."

LENA

FALL SURPRISES

When I told Lotta I'd be throwing a little party for Maureen's thirty-first birthday, she said, "And I suppose you'll want to borrow my china and linens, seeing that you gave all yours away when you joined the nunnery."

"I never did any such thing, Lotta! You know good and well no self-respecting nunnery would take me!"

"Well, you're not in one now, that's for sure. I know you've been seeing my brother. And I bet I know what you've been doing with him, too."

I scowled. "I wasn't planning on a formal dinner. I was thinking more along the lines of a nice buffet."

"There you go, changing the subject! An obvious sign of guilt, probably because you are an unmarried woman having SEX!"

"Damn it, Lotta, will you get your mind off sex and onto the party? I'm going to invite the in-laws and the father. And you. Unless you make me so mad I change my mind!"

"You can't borrow my china and linens if you don't invite me!"

"Oh, pooh-bah! What do you want to make? I thought I'd do the three-cheese lasagna with hamburger. You could do fish or chicken."

I decided not to tell Maureen the guest list. I said it would be just the three of us unless she wanted to invite Rico, which naturally she did. Little did she know it would be a fine chance for her in-laws to check him out. Of course, if I dared mention any such thing, Maureen would have sputtered gibberish in protest. As if she was fooling anybody but herself. It seemed like that girl was the last one to figure out a lot of important things.

And speaking of naturally, just to irritate Lotta, I did invite my own date. Well, maybe not just to irritate her.

I have to say, my place looked pretty good. Lotta lugged over "accent" pillows and throws in orange, brown, yellow and gold, along with flowers from her glorious all-season garden for what she now was referring to as a late fall soiree. She wanted to send invitations, but I told her that was over the top.

It all came together seamlessly. When Kalayla saw Maureen hug Lucinda and Harmon, she made a face and gave me "What the heck?" hand signals, which I ignored. In this particular case, what that girl didn't know would not hurt her.

Everyone except Maureen's father had arrived. I was in the kitchen chatting with Lucinda while Harmon, Lotta, Mattwo, and Rico were watching Kalayla show off Opa's proficiency at Sit, Down, Shake, Stay.

I gave Kalayla strict instructions to call me when she heard the door buzzer and NOT to answer it herself. The instant I heard her call, I went out to the living room and without asking who was there, I pressed the security door buzzer. As I turned back to the kitchen, I called to Maureen, "Will you get the door? We're busy in here."

Soon as I got back to the kitchen, I grabbed Lucinda's arm and escorted her into the living room. In time for me to see Maureen standing near the open door with her hands on her cheeks like she was trying to hold her face together. I sure did hope she wasn't about to faint from shock. Her father came in the door carrying a big cake box. He was followed by a lovely woman and good-looking young man, both of whom resembled Maureen.

"Look what the cat dragged in," her father said.

Some cat in the O'Rourke family must have been a real hunter because all of them, even Maureen, burst out laughing like that was the funniest thing they ever heard.

The young man said, "Yeah, remember when our cat caught the rat, and put it in Maureen's bed, and Maureen put it in my bed, and I put it in Kate's bed, and Kate put it in your bed, Leah? You were so mad you put it in the refrigerator and Mummie freaked out."

Maureen had recovered herself enough to say, "And we all told Mummie Leah was the one who did it, and Mummie told Daddy, and Daddy said Leah had to make a casket for the rat. We all picked flowers and buried Leah's rat with honor in the backyard."

They were all laughing, and how could we not join in?

"And this is for you—a little late, but freshly made." Maureen frowned and looked at the box her father had put down on the coffee table. When she opened it, one hand covered her mouth as she took a huge, audible breath and said, "Oh my God. An orange crunch cake!"

"Katie's home with your mum. The two of them made it this morning. It was as much as she could do, Maureen."

Maureen's tears were flowing, joy and sadness mingled together. I sighed. Sadness and joy. If that wasn't the definitive recipe for life, I sure didn't know what was.

Her mother had done as much as she could do, reaching out as best she could, letting Maureen and everyone else know she wasn't as rigid and unforgiving as she once was. Even if she never took another step toward her daughter, the one she had taken meant a lot. The writing on top of the orange crunch cake read, "For all the missed birthdays, Mummie."

Before Mattwo left the party, we made a date for Tuesday. I didn't hear from him until he called that afternoon. He said he had news about Mark. I couldn't tell from his tone how good or bad the news was. If Mark was dead, he wouldn't have called at all. He would have come as soon as he found out.

I pulled together a light supper of left-overs. It wasn't until we'd eaten and were settled in the living room that he told me about Mark. He sat on the sofa, and I took the overstuffed armchair facing him. I needed to see his face. The cats must have sensed my nervousness and were snuggled against me like two bookends.

"He's in Denver," Mattwo said.

"Denver. Oh, my. I didn't know he liked mountains. I wonder if he learned to ski."

"He's been out there for fourteen years. He and his partner started an industrial cleaning business. They've expanded, and are well respected. He settled down, Lena."

My Mark. Alive. Settled. A businessman. "That's wonderful news! Is he married? I wonder if he has kids? JJ must not know."

"He knows Lena."

"Oh, I don't think so, Mattwo. JJ and I might not be that close, but I'm sure he knows how much I've wanted to hear from Mark, to hear about him. Well, I haven't actually told him that, but I'm sure he knows."

"I don't know why JJ didn't tell you, but Mark called him after he got to Denver. JJ told him to stay out there, to stay away from the family and the family business."

Sweet Jesus! That sounded like what Maureen's family would do, nothing like the way my family operated.

"That can't be right. You know what our families are like, Mattwo. When you're in, you stay in. Six feet under is the only way out. Whoever told you that story is wrong."

"They're not wrong, Lena. Do you think I would come to you with a story like this and not check it out first? I went out there. To Denver. I flew out Sunday morning right after I left here. I took the red-eye back this morning."

So that was where he had been. Why had he gone without telling me beforehand? None of this made any sense. If this kept up, my old brain was going on strike. "Well, I don't believe JJ would do that. I remember when Joey put JJ in charge of Mark. The two of them might not have been best buddies, but they were definitely connected to each other."

"I think that's true. I think JJ didn't know what else to do because he knew that Mark was … well, he knew that Mark is gay."

Right then my brain did go on strike. I was certain Mattwo said Mark was gay, but that couldn't be right. Mark was the brawler. Mark was the one who never let anything go. He always got even, and he was never willing to make peace.

Mattwo moved to the edge of the sofa, close enough to reach over and take my hand.

"Lena, sweetheart, he really is settled—-and he seems happy. He found a partner, a guy named Frankie Gonzales. Mark met him when he first went to Denver and they've been together ever since."

Mark. Settled. And … gay. Joey would have called him a queer. Joey would have said we couldn't allow a queer in the family. Joey wouldn't have stood for it. Joey would have killed Mark.

If what Mattwo said was true, Joey never knew. He couldn't have known. But that wasn't possible either. Nothing got by Joey. Unless. Unless somebody had been on Mark's side. Unless somebody had been protecting Mark from Joey and from the family.

There was no other answer. Somebody had been watching out for Mark. Could that have been JJ? Was that why he was so hard on Mark? Why he tried to toughen him up? And when that didn't work, did he tell Mark he should move to Boston, to get out of Joey's sight? But Boston was too close, so he told Mark to go New York and then to Chicago? Farther and farther away from Manzetti Properties. Farther and farther away from their father and his influence.

I remembered how Mark was always introducing me to new friends, boys he'd just met, not friends he kept for years. Nothing like my other boys—even now at Thanksgiving, JJ would have friends stop by he'd known since first grade. Once a friend, always a friend. But not with Mark. He went through friends like they were tea light candles that flared, burned out, and were discarded. It was the same when Mark started dating. There was never a steady girl. Joey once bragged that Mark had a different girl for every day of the week.

When I asked Mark why he fought so much, he said, "I didn't like the way the kid looked at me, so I rearranged his face." I thought he'd outgrow the violence, meet the right woman and raise a family. That's what the Manero family did. That's what the Barzetti family did. But that wasn't what Mark did. He didn't meet the right woman. He met the right man. Sweet Jesus. I finally understood.

All that anger, all that fighting. Mark had been trying to prove to himself and everyone else how tough he was. That's why he never cared if he got hurt. That's why he never cared how many he took on in a fight or how big they were. He was proving he was a man. The kind of man the family would accept.

JJ was the one who carried Mark home when he'd been beaten so badly he could barely walk. JJ would be bruised and bloody, too, and when I asked him why he'd gotten into the fight, he shrugged it off, "I couldn't let them kill him, Ma." JJ was always there, protecting his little brother.

JJ must have told Mark to stay away because he knew what would happen if he came back. The family would look weak if it tolerated him, or if it turned a blind eye. In our world, weak meant vulnerable, vulnerable meant easy prey. That would never be allowed.

All the years I worried that JJ's attachment to Joey had turned him into a clone of his father. All the years I hoped and prayed JJ's marriage to Amelia wasn't what mine had been. All the years I told myself I'd help Amelia get free if she ever came to me. All those years, I assumed JJ was just like Joey. Maybe I was wrong.

Maybe JJ was my boy after all. My boy and Joey's.

I took some time to think, and a week later, I asked Mattwo if he wanted to take a trip.

"Sure," he said. "I have the plane schedules and I found a good B&B near Mark's house. We can do a little sightseeing, maybe drive into the mountains, depending on the weather. How long do you want to stay?"

I smiled into the phone. He knew I'd have to see my son.

The trip was something of a blur, the drive to the airport, then four and a half hours in the air. Mattwo quietly pointed out the mountains, the airport shaped like a string of desert tents, the wide-open space between the airport and the outskirts of Denver.

I was on automatic pilot, barely aware of the shuttle ride to pick up the rental car. When Mattwo told me we were almost there, I focused in on passing street signs: Washington and Grant and Lincoln. Just like the East Coast: no women, unless Logan or Corona were named for women whose names I'd never heard.

Our B&B, Molly's Nest, was named for a woman. Mattwo told me likely after Molly Brown, the face on the barroom floor in Central City. He said it was close enough to Denver that we might go and see it. He said we could walk from the B&B to the gold-domed capitol near downtown Denver. He knew I was half listening. He knew I only wanted to see my son.

"I let Mark know our arrival time, so he—so they'll be expecting us. Their house is a couple blocks from here," Mattwo said. "An easy walk. Do you want me to take our bags up and drop them off, or do you want to freshen up before we go?"

I cocked my head but didn't answer. He nodded, already pulling our suitcases from the back seat. "I'll be right back."

The day was cool and dry. I wondered if this was typical early November weather in Denver as I pulled my sweater on. During the drive from the airport, all I saw was sky. It was closed off by the density of houses now, and seemed smaller and less ... expansive.

Mark's house was older, a dignified two-story brick with wrought iron fence around the yard. Well maintained. They must be water conscious. The lawn area on the street side was filled with succulents and carefully placed rocks of various shapes and sizes. Inside the gate was much the same, although the succulents were larger and the rocks were small boulder size. I would never have imagined my Mark living in such a quiet, lovely, ordered neighborhood.

Mattwo took my arm, and we walked up the concrete stairs onto the concrete porch. A well-used swing, garden tools in a large woven band wood basket, a pair of rubber boots beside the front door. I rang the bell and waited.

The man who answered the door was my Mark—older but still with an athlete's body. His brown eyes looked directly at me. "Ma," he said, holding the door wide open with one hand, reaching out with the other to take my hand.

"First let me look at you," I said holding off his hug. I could see so many differences.

The boy was always moving, ready to slip away the instant I stopped talking. The man standing next to me was rock solid, comfortable in one place. The boy's eyes constantly roamed and I could hear myself repeating, "Look at me. Mark! I'm talking to you." The man was looking at me now with unwavering clear eyes. My son had found peace.

I let him pull me close. I had my boy back.

Frankie had steered Mattwo past us into the living room, and I could hear Mattwo asking about their yard and Frankie explaining that Mark was head of the Neighborhood Conservation Association, which was fighting an uphill battle.

I kept my arm around Mark as we went in to join them. "This is Frankie," he said.

Frankie was shorter than Mark, darker-skinned with penetrating black eyes, wavy black hair, wiry and narrow-shouldered, like a gymnast. His face was that of a mature man, and I guessed he might be close to Mark's age. He put out his hand, and I took it.

"Welcome to our home," he said, and they did welcome us.

Dinner that night was chicken on the grill with vegetables and a salad. Delicious and all Frankie's doing, according to Mark. "He sees that we eat healthy," he said.

The next day we walked downtown Denver as far as Larimer Square. "They took most of the old buildings," Frankie told us. "I remember Gano Downs and Neusteder's—not that we could ever afford to shop there. Woolworth's was our haunt." We had dinner at The Brown Palace, also a part of Denver history. The next day we drove into the mountains.

"Please stay with us the next time you come," Mark said. "I'd come there, but ..."

I shook my head. "JJ tracks the undercurrents more than I do. If he's told you, 'Not yet,' it would be best to wait. There's no point in taking unnecessary chances."

On the return drive to Denver International Airport we passed a huge sculpture of a blue mustang with fierce red eyes and front legs rearing toward the sky. Like he was issuing a challenge, saying to anyone who passed by, "I'm proud of what I am. Are you?"

I smiled and imagined my Mark standing beside the mustang. At long last, he was able to live openly, without apology, without allowing fear to drive him away.

I sighed. If Mark could do it …

Maybe it was time for this old woman to do the same. Maybe it was time for me to stand beside them. At long last.

I went to see JJ the day after we got back. I knew I'd find him at Home Base, working as usual, even on Sunday. I walked past my own office and turned into his. He kept the small CEO sign, the same one Joey had. "No need to brag," Joey used to say. I always thought that strange because he bragged about so many other things.

"Hi," I said.

JJ looked up from his papers. "Ma. Something going on to get you here on Sunday?"

He was always friendly whenever there was work to do. Maybe that was normal with a business family, cordial at work despite distance in the personal relationships.

"I went to see Mark. Mattwo and I went."

"I thought you would," he said. "When Mattwo asked me about Mark, I knew he'd find him, and you'd go. How is he?"

"He's good. He's better than he's ever been. But I guess you know that."

JJ nodded.

"I didn't realize that you … that all these years, that you … Thank you for looking after him."

JJ nodded again. "He's my brother."

We stared into each other's eyes, and for that brief few seconds, I felt as if I could see into his heart. For the first time. "So," I said after a bit. "There's something else. I've been thinking about your two girls. About spending time with them, getting to know them. I thought at some point, I might take them to Denver to meet Mark."

I could see him weighing the costs and benefits. Finally, he said, "That's a surprise—that you'd want to spend time with them. They're old enough I'll leave that up to them. As for going to see Mark, that's okay with me. Their world is different from the one I grew up in, and I doubt finding out he's gay would be a problem for either of them. But you'll find out with Juliana, you won't get off cheap. The only way that one will go is if you fly first class. Then she'll go anywhere you want. It's only her sophomore year in college, and she's already on the lookout for some guy who'll make her more of a princess than she already is. If that's possible."

I laughed. No wonder he didn't bring them to my place for dinner. She probably thought my apartment was the steerage section.

"And Ronnie—would she come?"

"Oh, she's different from her sister. You wait. She's looking at colleges now and whatever she does, you can bet it'll be on her own terms. I actually was going to talk to you about her. About whether you'd be willing to take her on, train her, you know, sort of an internship thing. The kid has ideas.

"One day out of the blue, she said to me, 'You should start putting up parking garages, Dad. Design them to go with the surrounding area. You could make them beautiful, instead of functional and ugly.'"

Now that almost took my breath away! JJ was asking me to mentor his daughter! "I'd be happy to do that. If she's willing. Let's set up a meeting with the three of us and talk it over."

On Friday night Mattwo came in carrying a shopping bag and a huge bouquet of white and yellow roses. "Special order from Magneson's," he said with a big smile followed by a kiss. "Let's talk."

Well now! Did that man have it in his mind to propose to me tonight? If he did, there was no doubt in my mind or heart how I'd answer him!

"About what?" I said.

"About taking a trip. I'm getting sick of all these smirks and sideways looks we get when people see us holding hands. It's like being one of the animals in a zoo. Let's get out of here for a while. Let's go to Italy."

Well, that wasn't exactly the proposal I hoped for, more like a step along the way. "Italy?"

"Yeah, you know, the old homeland. Neither of us has been and we can roam around, go wherever we want, the cities, sure, but the countryside too. So, what do you say?"

I hesitated. "I say yes ..."

Suddenly wary, he said, "There's a 'but' coming, isn't there, Lena?"

"Yes, but not about going. Not about being with you. More than anything I'd love to go. To have time on our own. To be together."

His sigh of relief made me smile. "Okay, so, what's the but?"

I'd been thinking about telling Mattwo for a long time, and I guess going to see Mark made up my mind. I couldn't go to Italy with him unless I did. He had to know what really happened that night Joey died. "There's something I've been wanting to tell you. I was waiting for the right time. I'm not sure anytime would ever be the right time, but if we're going globe-trotting, I better tell you now."

He frowned, waiting for me to go on.

"It's about the night that Joey died."

"Damn, Lena, that's ancient history. Gone and buried long ago, same as Joey."

I took a deep breath. "It's ancient history that I lied about, Mattwo. Ancient history I never told anyone. If you and I are going on together, I don't want to carry this kind of secret along as baggage."

"OK," he said. "So, tell me."

I gave myself a minute, collecting my thoughts, tracing the guilt seed back through time, back to June, 1969. I kept the secret so long, you'd think it would be hard to open it to the light. But it came like a story with a beginning and middle. Only I wasn't sure what the ending would be.

"Part of it did happen the way I said back then. Joey started drinking early. I never did understand that. He always waited until later to be sure the twins were gone. It was the weekend after their high school graduation, and I guess he knew there was no way they'd be hanging around the house. Both had steady girls.

"He and I were in the kitchen, and booze always put him in a mood for sex. I told him we should wait because I bought a special outfit to model before we went to bed. I knew he would get whatever he wanted at UG's. When he came home from there, the only thing he'd do was pass out.

"But he grabbed me and twisted my arm around my back and pressed me against the counter. He'd hurt me so many times before, I barely felt it. But he kept it up until I thought my arm would break, and by then I was crying.

"Right then the twins walked in the kitchen door. Friends had dropped them off so they could pick up Miss Clementine. I never said anything to any of the boys about Joey. What he did to me was my problem. I wasn't going to make it theirs. I don't know what they thought when they first saw us, but I couldn't hide the fact that he was hurting me. Maybe they knew Joey had a vicious side, but they'd never seen him turn it on me.

"The twins stared at us, and it was obvious they were shocked and outraged by what they saw. Mikie glared at Joey, and said, 'Jesus Christ, Dad! What the fuck are you doing?'

"Joey turned to face them, letting me slide down to the kitchen floor. I remember how cool the ceramic tiles felt. I remember closing my eyes and thinking, 'Oh no, they've done it now. They crossed the line.'

"Joey lost it. 'What do you mean, what the fuck am I doing? I'm teaching my wife a lesson!' He kicked me in the butt to show them that he meant it.

"The twins looked at each other in that private way they had, sorting through the options, deciding what to do without saying a word. They were almost eighteen then, strong as oxen. Not even Joey would have stood a chance against them.

"They lunged at him. Each of them grabbed one of his arms. They slammed him against the counter and pinned him there. 'You're a fucking coward,' Jimmy screamed.

"And then Mikie said, 'You ever touch Ma again and it'll be the last thing you do. You get that? You ever touch her again and we will kill you!'

"They let Joey go, and he stumbled out the kitchen door. I heard the tires screech as he pulled out of the driveway.

"My boys helped me up. I told them I was fine, and they should go see their girls. I told them the truth. I was better than I'd been after a lot of Joey's lessons.

"I was afraid to go to bed that night, afraid I might fall asleep, and then he'd find me in bed and I'd be helpless no matter how drunk he was. I stayed in the den watching videos and was halfway through *Butch Cassidy and The Sundance Kid* when I heard him come in and slam the front door.

"He screamed, 'Lena, you bitch. Get out here!'

"I knew right then he was going to kill me. He'd been shamed by his sons, and he'd make me pay for that.

"I had to get away. I ran into the kitchen. Maybe I could get out the back door and run before he caught me.

"He knew what I would do. Even as drunk as he was, Joey was fast, ever the athlete. He caught me and lunged for me just as I reached the kitchen door. He grabbed at my blouse and it ripped as I twisted away. He was off-balance and he spun around and tried to catch himself. But he slipped, 190 pounds tumbling in free fall. He cracked his head on the counter and landed with a thud on the ceramic tile. He laid there. Not moving.

"I could see a blood puddle pooling near his head. All I could think was: What if he's dead? And then, please, please let him be dead. Because if he wasn't, I knew I would be.

"What I did next still wakes me up in the middle of the night.

"I ran to the den and grabbed one of the throw pillows that lined the back of the sofa. I ran back to the kitchen, and I put the pillow over Joey's face and I held it down. He wasn't moving, but I knew Joey. He could be faking, and if he had the chance, he'd grab me.

"I pressed as hard as I could. The kitchen clock read 2:45 a.m. and I held the pillow on his face for almost fifteen minutes. That had to be long enough, but I had to be sure. I had to be absolutely certain. Ten minutes later I decided it was enough. Not even Joey could hold his breath that long. He had to be dead.

"The pool of blood on the side of his head was larger, but I didn't see any on the pillow. I left everything the way it was: lights on, the half-empty bottle of Glenfeddich 18 and his glass on the counter, his body where he had fallen.

I went back to the den, turned off the video player, and rearranged the pillows on the sofa so the one I had used was half-buried. I turned out all the lights and went upstairs. I took a shower and then two Advil to stave off the pain that was sure to come. Then I went to bed.

"The next morning when JJ came at 7:30 to pick Joey up for work, he found his father's body. He rushed upstairs to get me and woke me up from what had been a dead sleep. I stumbled down the stairs after him, and when I saw Joey's body, it was as if I'd never seen it before. JJ called the police and then a doctor because by then, I was hysterical."

Mattwo slowly shook his head. "The police said it was a tragic accident. He'd been drinking and must have fallen and hit his head."

"Yes, that's what they said. It did look like a tragic accident. The twins were broken up and felt guilty because they'd threatened him. I didn't tell them what really happened, and then they went to Vietnam, and it was too late.

"Joey was JJ's mentor and tutor and model, and he took Joey's death harder than the other boys. Mark was living in Boston by then, but he came home for a while. I think now that was to help JJ through it. JJ threw himself into the business, and I rarely saw him. And I guess you heard from Lotta the direction I went. After I straightened myself out, I saw JJ all the time because of the business. But we were never close the way we had been when he was little."

Mattwo sat quietly and so did I. Maureen said she felt relieved when she finally told Kalayla the truth. But mine had been a different kind of lie, because the truth was murky. Joey had been dead for thirty years, and I still didn't know if I was the one who killed him.

I told Mattwo the truth because I hoped we'd have a life together for whatever time we had left. And that life had to be built on openness and trust.

"Well then," Mattwo finally said. "You kept that buried for a long, long time."

"That I did." I let out my breath wondering what would come next.

"I don't see there'd be any point in digging it up now," he said. "There's been enough bleeding."

I nodded. There was nothing to gain, and there was no way we'd ever know the truth for sure. "But I've never stopped wondering," I said. "If he was already dead. Or if I killed him."

"I think it's time for you to stop that, Lena. You've done your best to lead a decent life for years. That's enough for me."

"Are you sure you want to travel with a woman who might be a murderer? You know that was my intention, even if it might not be the fact."

Mattwo reached over and gently ran his fingers over my face. Then he smiled and said:

"I'm sure I'd like to travel with the woman I've loved all my life. And I say let's get on with that."

DECEMBER 2000

KALAYLA

CAT SITTING DUTY

So the day the Old Lady and the Old Guy were going off to Italy, she gave me a list of all the stuff I was supposed to do while she was gone. As if I didn't know what to do!

Feed the cats two times per day.

Clean the cat litter two times per day.

Change their water once per day.

Water the plants.

Check on Mrs. Meade. If her sink is full of dishes, wash them.

While you're at it, ask if she wants you to vacuum.

Check on the other neighbors and do the same for them.

I knew she put in that last stuff just to piss me off! If she thought I was gonna wash dishes for all the neighbors, she was wrong. And I knew enough to check on Mrs. Meade without her telling me!

When I told her so, she said, "Well, I did forget one thing. If Petunia throws up a furball, you have to clean it up."

Cow turds!

She stacked about twenty-five cans of cat food and two gigantic bags of dry food on her kitchen counter. Along with their cat brush and about ten bags of treats. She put two gigantic bags of litter next to the litter boxes.

No chance I'd run out of anything except my normal good humor.

She left a copy of that dumb list with Mama and another one with Carlotta! I bet anything Carlotta was gonna come check on me every other minute, too.

The Old Lady said they'd be home for Christmas, and I told Mama she better quit hanging around with Rico so much and finish the painting she was giving Lena as a present.

Then I told Mama maybe she oughta teach me to knit so I could make the Old Guy a neck scarf.

And you know what she said? "Why would I waste my time doing that? You told me the only thing knitting needles were good for was to stick up the butt of kids you hate."

Cow turds! What happened to her being Miss Toothless?

So I said, "Oh yeah. I must've forgot! I guess I'll ask Rico to help me make a coffin. Grandma LeeRoyce might know what size would fit Uncle Clarence. Giving him a coffin might encourage him to croak!"

"Layla! Shame on you! Don't you dare say anything about Clarence and coffins to your grandmother! He is not going to die and don't you suggest he might!" When Mama launched into her kindness lecture, I knew she was talking to that Old Lady too much. Her lecture was the same as the one Lena gave me again and again and again.

I was counting up all the cookies I had to make for Christmas, like maybe a thousand so far. I was gonna give a bunch to Grandma and Grandpa LeeRoyce, one to Clarence, a bunch to Kieran, maybe one to Mr. O. I'd need a whole lot for the Old Lady and her Old Guy, and a few for Carlotta, and Dominic, and Rico. Plus, some for everyone at Eddie's, and a couple for Old Mrs. Meade, who kept asking me to bring my sweet dog to see her. Maybe one for Miss Megan, and one for Jen at Matty's Way.

Carlotta gave me a special recipe for dog biscuits and I already made a double batch for Opa. I was thinking about asking Carlotta if she knew of a recipe for cat treats that had arsenic. It'd save me a lot of time if the cats croaked while the Old Lady was gone, but Lena would probably have a heart attack when she got home. Then for sure the Old Guy would have a heart attack, and I'd be stuck taking care of both of them.

I better just take care of the cats. Or maybe Opa and I oughta take a trip, too. Like to New Zealand. Or the North Pole.

But then I couldn't go biking with Kieran.

And I couldn't go to dance class.

Or to Matty's Way.

Or Animal Friends.

I'd miss out on Carlotta's Christmas desserts.

And what if Opa threw up on the airplane?

That'd be a real pisser!

If you enjoyed reading KALAYLA, please leave a review to recommend it to other readers. Thanks a lot for your time.

Made in the USA
Columbia, SC
30 November 2020